PAINTING
SKY

PAINTING SKY

RITA BRANCHES

Published by Rita Branches

ISBN: 978-989-99562-1-6

Front cover by Rui Oliveira
Editing by Mikaela Pederson, A-step-up-editing
Interior Design and Formatting by E.M. Tippetts Book Designs

www.ritabranches.com
rita.branches.author@gmail.com

To my family, especially my mother, who saw me as a writer when I was just a baby.
To my grandfather, who was great story-teller.
To my brother for the amazing cover art.
And to my boyfriend, who kept asking when I was going to, finally, publish anything.

CHAPTER ONE

There is something soothing about watching the trees blurring through a car's window. At the same time, there is also something dramatic about it, like life is passing too fast and you're missing something. I felt like that right then, sitting in my boyfriend's car, moving away from the only home I knew.

Growing up is exactly that: feeling like life is going at full speed without being able to grasp the essentiality of it as you leave pieces of yourself scattered along the way.

Cody smiled at me and held my hand while we crossed state borders, but I couldn't prevent the melancholy at the sight of the welcoming sign announcing a new state. Nothing dramatic happened in my life, which was actually pretty boring. I am quite boring. Maybe that's why leaving for college was hard.

"Are you excited?" Cody asked, turning the radio down.

I wasn't exactly excited; I was more worried, sad, and missing my parents and my sister. I wasn't going to tell my giddy boyfriend I wasn't eager to live in the same house as him, though. My answer was a noncommittal shrug. I should have felt happy and I should have been looking forward to spending more time with my boyfriend of four years.

The first time I'd met Cody Hale, I'd thought he was the most beautiful boy I'd ever seen, with his sparkling blue eyes, bright blond hair, and wide smile. He'd approached me through our backyard's fence and had offered me a daisy. We'd become friends instantly. He had been my first friend in the new town my family had just moved to, and I had been terrified of going to first grade in a place where I didn't know anyone.

I had always been shy and hadn't made friends easily. My brother, Ryan, on the other hand, had been as sociable as it got. He'd made me spend ninety percent of my childhood blushing.

Ryan was three years older than me, and, as much as we hated each other like siblings do, we also loved and cared for each other. He wasn't very pleased with my future living arrangements, even though I was going to be living with him, too. Maybe that was the reason he wasn't pleased.

Cody and I had grown closer during that summer. Matilda, my sister, had been too young to play with me and Ryan had been too old, so Cody had become my best friend. During the first day of school, he'd introduced me to some of his friends, not caring when some of them had made fun of him for speaking to a girl a year younger than him. He hadn't minded and, for that, he had been my hero.

Ryan, on the other hand, had treated me as if I had been invisible. In fact, we'd gone to the same school for almost a year before his friends had realized we were related, as we were very different in appearance. I also have to point out that I was never in detention, nor grounded.

To my brother's friends, it didn't matter that we shared the same surname—it wasn't something that crossed a nine year old's mind. Only one of his friends had known about me; he had been our neighbor and Ryan's best friend for all these years.

He was also Cody's older brother.

I had met Keith Hale three days before Cody. My opinion of him was the exact opposite of that of his brother: he'd been annoying, obnoxious, and full of himself. He'd pushed me to the ground that first day, and, even when he'd claimed it had been an accident, I hadn't believed him. Knowing him now, I know it had been a lie. Even my six year old brain had told me to stay far away from him.

That was my concern: living in a house with a person who hated me.

After we reached the midway mark on our nine hour drive, I finally relaxed and felt stupid for my earlier reaction. I found myself asking the same question for what felt like the millionth time. "Is Keith okay with me going to live in his house?" I fidgeted in my seat while twirling my light brown, wavy hair, with a finger.

"I already answered that question a dozen times. Yes, he is. It's not like he spends a lot of time at home, and, when he does, it's usually in his attic creating art, or so he claims." Cody rolled his eyes, as if to say that art was nonsense. He forgot the subject I'm going to study is art, as well. He's just like my parents: pragmatic. I tried to see past that, though.

"It's his house too. Actually, he's been there for over three years; I don't want to intrude." I glanced away, trying to loosen the knot in my stomach, which had been created at the reminder of living with Keith.

On the other hand, I was going to live with Ryan too. I missed spending time with my brother. I would be living with Cody, of course, as well. It had been so hard this past year, with him away in college. He'd tried to come every time he could, but I knew he spent too much money on gas, not to mention time on the road.

When the sign welcoming us to Corvallis appeared on the horizon, I sat straighter in the seat and tried to take everything in. It was similar to my hometown, but it had a more cosmopolitan center. Cody took a detour, so I could see the commercial roads and then the center, where the campus was situated. It was almost as a town of its own. It was similar to some colleges I had visited the previous year, courtesy of my father's insistency, with its brick buildings and vast lawns.

The house was a twenty minute walk from everything, which worried me. I would depend on Cody or my brother to take me to classes and every other place when the weather wasn't cooperative enough to walk in.

Cody had prepared me for the house, but my breath caught in my throat when I spotted it.

My boyfriend had described it as a spooky, almost horror movie-style, old, big house. He'd advised me that I wouldn't like it, but that the interior was quite okay. His description hadn't been far from the truth. The only difference was that I wasn't horrified—I was amazed. It was beautiful.

The long dirt road stood within the forest, with trees overshadowing it. Pebbles hit the car here and there as we drove. It opened to a large driveway in which ten or twelve cars could park. The house was in need of a fresh layer of paint, as the dirty dark gray was peeling. Some parts of the roof needed to be replaced and the windows were so dirty that you could write on them.

The garden was completely abandoned: weeds were growing everywhere and the bushes had no particular form or place. The nearest trees were in need of a good pruning and one of them was actually dead.

The oak in front of the house was huge and surpassed the height of the house at three stories. The attic seemed to occupy as much area as the floors under it, and it had huge windows incorporated in the roof.

Near the house, the forest undergrowth was cut short to the ground. As we went farther, however, it seemed to abruptly grow. It also smelled as if it had been freshly cut. How someone could worry about cutting the forest undergrowth and not the garden grass exceeded my comprehension.

"They changed this place. Someone cut the plants," Cody murmured as he looked around at nothing in particular. "So, what do you think?" He placed one hand on the hood of his car and the other on his waist, which made me smile. I leaned in to meet his lips before answering.

"I love it. I just hope I won't be eaten by a werewolf on a full moon," I joked as I looked into the vast forest around the long road I would have to walk, if I wanted to go to town by myself.

He laughed and held my hand, pulling me to the front door. My bags had been forgotten in the car.

The smell hit me as soon as Cody opened the door: tobacco and food, mixed with sweat or dirty laundry. I was suddenly glad my parents hadn't been able to come with me: they would have regretted their decision as soon as they saw the forest. If that hadn't been enough, this smell and mess would have done it.

There were dirty dishes and plastic cups on every surface available: tables, sofas, and even on the floor. The hardwood was so beautiful that it pained me to see it dull and dirty. How could someone live like this? The television was on, but it didn't look like anyone was home. I could hear music blustering from upstairs, though.

"I swear to God, I'll kill them," Cody swore under his breath. "I promise we don't live like this." He waved around us, disgusted. "We don't actually live in a dumpster. Of course, we're guys, but come on—they went beyond inhabitable."

I wasn't pleased, but it was funny to see Cody so upset about my opinion.

"I'll kill you, you son of—" Cody stopped his yelling and looked at me sheepishly. I raised one eyebrow; Cody didn't use to swear. I guess he'd changed. "Son of our mother," he continued. "Come down, Jane's here!"

He showed me my room, which was lovely. Maybe I would think every detail was beautiful, but this room was my favorite, so far. It had two windows, which let in the last sunrays over the hardwood floor. The double bed was bigger than the one at my parents' house and had green covers—my favorite color. I guess Cody had remembered when he'd bought them for me. A desk was in front of the bed and the wardrobe was next to it. They both looked old, but very well-preserved. The bedroom almost seemed out of place from every other room I'd seen, so far. It was so unlived in and clean that it almost felt sacred.

My light gray eyes were reflected on the mirror on the wall and they were as big as a child's on Christmas Eve.

"My room is down the hall." Cody pointed to two doors on the right. Between our rooms were my brother's bedroom and a bathroom, which I had to share with Ryan—the morning nightmare would start over again.

Cody said I could use his, but, for now, it was too personal.

Keith's room was the closest to mine, but his was on the left and he had his own bathroom. Apparently he hasn't used it lately, though, by what Cody told me.

"Where does he sleep?" I asked, curious.

"Upstairs." He nodded at the ceiling before rolling his eyes. "It's very artistic of him. He only comes down for food, drinks," he seemed to be looking for the right words, "and girls. Well, sometimes he comes down to talk to us and play some games, but it's rare." I had seen at least three different video game consoles downstairs, which would make anyone believe they were gamers.

"Wasn't he at school?" I'd thought he was attending college, at least. I couldn't envision his father letting him live like this.

"Yeah, he goes to college, but he only has a couple classes a week. I don't really understand him. Your brother does the mediation, because, if we were alone, we would have killed each other, already."

I remember Cody and Keith always fighting, and not like Ryan and me, but really fighting: always competing to be better than the other. They should have been over that by now.

It was already getting dark, so I didn't have the urge to go outside. Cody brought our bags in and I spent the rest of the afternoon unpacking in my room. I hadn't realized I was hungry until Cody poked his head in to announce that the pizza guy was at the door. It wasn't a good idea to start my time here by eating take out, but my mood to cook was nonexistent.

"Does your brother come down to eat with us?" I sat on a chair in the kitchen, careful to not touch any dirty surface.

"You don't need to worry about him. Like I said before, he doesn't show himself much." I heard the finality of his statement. I wouldn't ask about Keith, anymore.

"Tomorrow, I need to go to campus, but just for a couple of hours, to pick book lists and stuff. In the afternoon, I can take you to town to buy groceries. Is that okay with you?" I nodded while Cody threw the empty pizza box on the already-overflowing trash can and kissed me. "Now what do you want do?" he murmured against my neck.

"I'm tired. Maybe I'll just go to bed?" I didn't mean for it to sound like a question, but it turned out that way, anyway.

"Alone?" His mouth found mine before I had time to answer. He pulled me to my feet and hugged my waist.

"Not today, Cody; I'm really tired." I excused myself, kissed him, and pushed him gently away. I then went upstairs, leaving him frowning in the kitchen.

I'd have to gather the courage to just sleep with him. For goodness' sake, he'd been my boyfriend for four years. What was I waiting for? Marriage? That was plain ancient! I just didn't feel it, though. Whenever he got closer, I would freeze. I didn't feel that spark like I read about in my books or watched in the movies.

He didn't come to my room and I didn't go to his. After I took a shower, I crashed on my comfy bed.

CHAPTER TWO

The next day, I woke up at nine and my stomach was rumbling with hunger. I skipped down the stairs, remembering the clutter in the living room as I reached the first floor. My day would be splendid, cleaning everything—not. At least the sun was shining. I opened the kitchen door absentmindedly and hit someone so hard that I fell backward and screeched when my butt hit the floor.

"Fuck! What the hell?" Someone screamed and I opened my eyes to my worst nightmare. I had forgotten I wasn't alone, so I hadn't bothered to change. My short pajama shorts and tank-top were now drenched with milk and cereal, which made me look even more ridiculous.

"Oh, it's you." His voice was so full of animosity that I quickly stuttered an apology.

"Sorry. I didn't mean… I thought I was alone." I pulled myself up, trying to keep my shirt away from my skin.

"Obviously you're not. This is still my house—never forget that. And please put some clothes on; you seem ridiculously childish." Keith walked away, leaving the cereal bowl on the kitchen counter for me to wash.

He was different from the last time I'd seen him, which was almost two years ago. Keith always had a dark, mysterious, and dangerous appearance, which matched his personality perfectly. His hair looked darker—three years ago, it had been cut as short as possible, but now it was mussed and over his forehead.

Keith was a bad boy; my friends would have called him "dangerously hot." He was neither nice, nor popular—at least, not in the common sense of the word. He had his group of friends and that was it: he wasn't nice to anyone else. Keith was a one night stand, heart-breaking type of guy.

He now had a piercing on his right eyebrow and a tattoo on his left arm. I didn't think his father had seen him like this.

I tried to push away my thoughts about Keith and started my long cleaning day. After taking a quick shower and putting on proper clothes, I started with the dining room and took the plates and glasses to the kitchen sink. I then did the same with the living room.

I cleaned and washed until my hands were red and everything was spotless and smelled like lemon. I was lucky they even had cleaning products.

The kitchen took me until three in the afternoon to clean: the fridge had to be cleaned twice before its strange smell dissipated. Two of the shelves were full of beer and the freezer was packed with frozen dinners; the shelves in the kitchen were empty.

Cody arrived the moment I stopped to admire my masterpiece.

"Wow, you hired a fairy crew? Maybe some birds and squirrels, too?" He kissed me, fell on the couch, and put his feet up on the small center table.

"No, dummy, it was all me." I shoved his feet off the table I had just cleaned a couple hours ago. "And I expect you and Ryan to keep this place clean. I'll ask my brother to tell yours, as he wouldn't listen to either of us."

After Cody ate something, we left to buy groceries.

Cody helped me put everything in its place when we got home and then left me to cook dinner. My brother showed up when I was setting the table.

He rushed to my side and pulled me into his arms, cutting off my circulation. "I missed you, little sister," he said, our difference in height clearly, as he towered over me. I hugged him back while he stole a slice of tomato from the cutting board.

He put me down and leaned over the counter. I said, pouting, "I didn't know if you were coming to dinner. You didn't get back yesterday."

He averted my eyes. "I was... with a girl. I didn't want to bring her here on your first day."

"A girlfriend or just a girl?" As if I had to ask: a smile spread on his face while his light brown eyes shone with mischief.

"Do you have to ask? If it does matter, we've been hooking up for a month," he said, as if it was a great feat for him to be with a girl for more than a couple of days.

"Where's Keith?" Ryan asked as he helped with the pasta bowl, making me doubt that he was really my brother, who never helps around the house.

"Where do you think?" Cody answered sarcastically as he hugged my waist and placed a kiss on my temple.

"Yo, I agreed that Jane could live with us, but I'm not tolerating that." He waved at us, disgusted.

When Cody and I had started dating, we had kept it secret for three months, until my brother found out and punched him. He had actually gone three weeks without speaking to either of us. After that, he'd started accepting it, but I decided I shouldn't push it. Maybe it would be good to use Ryan as an excuse to delay sleeping with Cody.

Surprisingly, Keith joined us when we sat down on the dining room. "Wow, you cleaned up nice, Sky," he said before sitting down. I knew he was talking about the house, but, for a second, I wondered if he was starting to accept me living here. His next words killed that immediately, though. "Maybe it'll be good to have a woman in the house." He took the seat in front of me. I tried to keep my boiling temper down, but I just couldn't. It wasn't that I didn't like my middle name, but the way he'd shortened Skylar to Sky with a sarcastic tone only he could produce, just to get on my nerves, had me all worked up.

"My name is Jane and I'm not your maid. I would appreciate it if you and my brother could keep the house clean." I served myself and took a deep breath.

"Always so polite," he leaned back on the chair, crossed his arms and smirked at me, looking smug. "Isn't my baby brother included on that list? Or will you be cleaning up after him?"

My politeness would be ending very soon. "No, your brother already knows I won't be playing housemaid. If we make a group effort, this place will always be like this." I smiled and looked around.

The rest of the meal was civilized and the three boys talked about mutual friends. My brother and Cody made an effort to keep the cursing to a light level, but Keith was as crass as a sailor. He made sure to look at me every time a curse left his mouth while smiling mockingly.

After Ryan and Cody helped me with the kitchen, Cody took me to his room. I hadn't been in it before and I tried not to think about why I hadn't had the curiosity.

"It's… messy. I said downstairs that I wouldn't clean up after you, but, if you want, I can clean your room tomorrow—just this once." His face said that he wasn't very pleased, but he covered it quickly. "No, that's not necessary. I'll do it myself. You need to use your time wisely: next week, you'll start school, too." He pushed me to his bed, taking my mind away from the concern about the why he didn't want me in his room.

Ryan banged on the door a few minutes later. "I meant what I said earlier! Stop whatever you're doing." I heard laugher farther away. Was Keith laughing? That would be a first.

Cody sighed and rolled onto his back. "Come on in." I sat up on the bed and rearranged my hair.

"Are you sure? I don't want to see my baby sister—" Ryan was cut off by Cody groaning that he was sure. "Good, because, if you're messing with her—" Ryan opened the door, one hand covering his eyes.

"Come on, Ry, like she's that innocent. She's almost eighteen and they've been dating for years." Keith leaned against the door, smirking. One of these days, that smirk would get stuck on his face.

"Argh—I don't want to know. Just don't want that kind of," he waved at us, making me roll my eyes, before continuing, "Behavior with me in the house. Got it, little Hale?"

Keith laughed out loud again, vibrating something inside me: hate.

"He's also not that little anymore," Cody's brother said, which made me blush. I didn't even want to know what he was talking about.

Cody frowned. "Shut up, Keith. You're not helping."

Keith turned around and disappeared from our sight, but I still heard when he said, "Like I would make it easier." It was followed by a chuckle.

After kissing Cody on the lips and getting a groan from Ryan, I left for my room. I was so tired of cleaning and shopping that I just wanted to go to sleep. I had been honest when I'd said I wouldn't be this house's maid, but I at least wanted to start my life here with a clean house.

I spent the next day in the laundry room, which wasn't big enough to accommodate all of the dirty clothes. After washing each set of clothes, I hung them in the garden on a line that I supposed was for just that. I loaded the machine again and again; after five rounds, everything was drying in the garden and the sun was setting. Great: tomorrow I would be folding clothes all day.

I sat on the couch and turned the television on.

I must've have fallen asleep, because, when I woke up, the sun was long past setting. Dark gray eyes gazed at me, turning my stomach. Keith was curious, not angry, but, as soon as I really opened mine, his changed.

"I was starting to worry," he said, and then his head fell back and he laughed. "No, not really. Do you usually sleep like the dead? And drool?"

My hand went to the corner of my mouth instinctively at the same time my brain caught up with the joke. I wasn't interested in keeping a conversation with Keith, but, after looking at the clock on the wall and realizing it was already eight, I had to ask, "Where's your brother? And mine?"

"Out. You should get used to it—they're never here." He sat on the couch, placed his feet on the table, picked up the remote, and changed the TV to a sports channel.

"What do you mean? They have to study, eat, and…" Sleep, right? I was here, now, so at least Cody should come home.

Keith laughed again. "Are you worrying that little head of yours?" He leaned toward me from the other side of the couch. I shook my 'little head' no and he laughed again. Maybe I should join a circus: I seemed to make Keith laugh a lot.

"No? You should. Your boyfriend has a lot of study dates. The key word here is 'dates.'" His pierced eyebrow shot up suggestively.

I couldn't let him get to me. "You're just saying that to make me doubt Cody. I trust him. He's not like you." I crossed my arms defensively.

"I've never cheated on a girlfriend." He grew a small wrinkle on his forehead, as if I had offended him somehow.

I laughed. "That's because you've never had one," I answered, knowing I had won the argument.

"How do you know?" It was Keith's turn to cross his arms. "Were you paying attention to the girls I dated?" He seemed amused.

"Only when they cried in the school's bathroom." I didn't want my voice to sound as venomous as it did, but Keith brought out the worst in me every time.

His face changed and I saw something like regret there. "I never promised them anything. They knew exactly what I wanted."

"You're disgusting." I got up, tired of this conversation, and went to the kitchen. He followed me.

"They know I don't date, but they still stay. Maybe girls are just as

14

disgusting as I am." He leaned against the door with his arms still crossed. He wasn't as amused as before. Maybe I had hit a nerve with Keith. Who knew that would have been possible?

"That's where you're wrong. I don't know them all, but usually they stay to see if they are the one who can change you." How naïve of them.

He stepped forward, resting his elbows on the kitchen island, irritated. "No one can change me, but me, and I'm not interested in changing." He stepped back and sat on a stool. I shrugged my shoulders to say it had nothing to do with me. It didn't.

"One day, one girl will change that. You'll see." Maybe not, though. Maybe he was hopeless.

I made an omelet and shared the meal with Keith. Both of us ate silently.

At midnight, Cody came home. I had been sitting on the couch, watching TV and counting the minutes, like an angry wife. I took a deep breath before asking him where he had been.

"I'm sorry, baby," he slurred. "I was with a group of friends. We were kind of celebrating the start of school, like a goodbye party to the summer, you know what I mean?" He hovered over me and the smell of alcohol hit. I regretted waiting for him. He had been to a party and he'd forgotten I was here, waiting for him and enduring his brother's presence.

"You're drunk. We'll talk in the morning." I shoved him away to get up and didn't accept the kiss he was trying to give me.

I thrashed all night with Keith's words repeating in my head. Should I have doubted Cody's fidelity? After all, he was almost twenty and we hadn't even slept together. He'd always said he would wait as long as I needed, but, should I have been worried? Damn Keith and his stupid, puzzled words.

The next day, I slept in and woke up with a killer headache and a matching mood. I dressed, went to the kitchen to eat my cereal, and bumped into Keith again.

"Not you," I groaned.

"Had a bad night, Sky? Dreamed about the big, bad wolf? Or was it what I told you yesterday?" He sat next to me.

"It's Jane. Please, don't call me Sky. And no, I didn't have nightmares and your words were forgotten the moment they left your mouth." I finished my cereal and placed my head on my arms.

"I heard Cody last night. My words were playing in your head, weren't they?" He wasn't being sarcastic, now. Maybe he was trying to warn me. I couldn't let him get in my head.

"Shut up. Cody is the best boyfriend in the world. You just wish you were anything like him." I left for my room, not before seeing the hurt in Keith's eyes.

Ryan came home with Cody at seven that night. I hadn't cooked dinner for them, after having eaten a late lunch. My encounter with Cody was tense and I was already tired.

"Hi, baby," Cody kissed me when I stepped into the living room. I didn't kiss him back. "I'm sorry about yesterday. We were just gathering in one of the frat houses but the party lasted more than I had anticipated. I should've called."

I wanted to tell him that he should have taken me to meet his friends. We were just starting out, living in the same house, though, and I decided that maybe I should give him time.

Keith was watching us, and I kissed Cody with a little more passion than normal. Before stepping back, I looked at his brother again: he had turned around and was fidgeting with an apple. He hadn't even made a snarky comment—strange.

I didn't see Cody much for the rest of that week, nor Keith, who stayed in the attic all day. My brother was the one to keep me company in the afternoons, and the way things had changed between us was strange. Ryan was actually being a friend.

"Have you called Mom and Dad this week? You know they worry about you." I said, while sitting on the couch one night.

Ryan shrugged and picked the remote to change channels. "Yeah, but whenever I call is for them to grill me about school or to behave, it's exhausting, you know?"

Yeah, didn't I know.

"And how is school going?" I asked, turning away from the horror movie playing on TV.

He shrugged one shoulder, nonchalant. "Not you, too. It's good. Everything's under control."

I wanted to know more about my brother's life. "And girls? Have you found anyone special?"

"You sound like Mom, or Grandma. Special, what's that?" He shook his head and continued, "I have a girl-friend, does that count?"

"Friends with benefits don't count, Ry." I rolled my eyes.

"Well, that's exactly what we are and it's fine." He finally changed channels. We kept talking about his life for a couple of hours. I never had this relationship with Ryan, as close friends.

On Friday night, my house—or the house I was living in—turned into a nightclub. I would have been okay with it if anyone had told me, but I guess they'd all forgotten.

"Hi, sunshine." A guy approached me in the kitchen, holding a paper cup in one hand and resting the other on the counter. "Name's Teo. What's yours?" He leaned closer and I stepped back, wondering if I wanted to engage in conversation with this stranger.

"It's none of your business." Keith's angry voice sounded from the kitchen door. Teo backed off and went back to the living room.

"This is my house, too, now. You could've at least warned me about this party." I crossed my arms, trying not to flinch when Keith brushed against my arm when he stepped forward to get a bottle from the shelf.

"It wasn't my idea," he said, shrugging. "But you should get used to it: this happens every Friday." He turned with a smirk on his face. "And Saturday, and every other damn day we want. And no, this is not your house. You might be playing house with my brother, but this is not your house." He leaned forward until we were almost touching.

"Why do you hate me so much? What did I ever do to you?" I had to scream over the music when someone opened the kitchen door.

Keith opened his mouth to answer, but he glanced over my shoulder and closed his mouth. He stepped back and replaced his angry face with his usual smirk. "You should take care of your girlfriend, little brother, or someone might steal her from you." He disappeared through the crowd. Was he talking about Teo, or was there some other meaning?

"It was just a guy introducing himself." I shrugged. Cody smiled, took my hand, and pulled me to the living room to introduce me to some people.

I felt so disconnected. This wasn't the Cody I knew: it was a new Cody, who was thrilled with all of this college social life. Maybe it was me—maybe I hadn't grown up, yet. I missed my parents, my sister, and my friends from high school.

Was this empty feeling that something had changed and would never be the same what growing up was supposed to feel like? I supposed the next time I'd feel like this would be when I graduated from college. I just hoped it wouldn't be sooner.

CHAPTER THREE

The next day, the house was almost as it had been the day I arrived, and I felt anger boiling inside me. I had asked them to respect me, but what I wanted and what I'd gotten were two very different things. I had to clean the kitchen counter just so I could look at something clean while I ate my cereal. I gave up when I realized I couldn't avoid the smell of alcohol, so I went to the garden to sit on the back porch.

I could work on the garden today, after convincing my brother and Cody to clean up the house. I didn't even bother thinking about Keith: he would be pleased to just cross his arms and smirk at me. I was getting angrier by the second. It was noon and no one else had woken up, yet.

I picked up Cody's car keys and left a note in the kitchen: the first place they would go the minute they woke up.

"Went to town. Clean up the house, please. Jane."

I got lost a couple of times before arriving at the supermarket. I bought some groceries, which didn't include frozen meals or drinks—the fridge was still full of those. After that, I wandered around town, trying to find the best places to buy new clothes, of which I was in need.

I ended up not getting much of anything. My parents had given me some money for school supplies and rent for the first couple of months, which I was supposed to give to Keith.

I didn't understand why I had to pay Keith and not Cody, the house had been inherited, supposedly, by the both of them, but I never asked. Maybe it was because Keith had stayed here with his grandfather for almost a year before he passed away three years ago.

I had finished my shopping spree when a beautiful green dress in a shop window caught my eye. It was very simple, strapless, with no embellishments, and it came down to the knee. The price was a little over what I had planned on spending, but the dress would be perfect for my eighteenth birthday, which was in a month.

When I arrived home, the house was still a mess. I refused to clean and they didn't bother to do so. The next day, I cleaned the kitchen, because it was starting to get impossible to eat there. I was actually glad that my classes would be starting, because I would have gone crazy if I stayed in this house all day.

Cody took me to my first class on Monday morning. Before I entered the room, he gave me a sweet kiss that left me lighter and more prepared to face my first day of college.

My first class was Representational Drawing and Painting. This was one of the most important classes I would be taking and it upset me that almost all stools were taken. I hated to draw on easels, but I guess I had to get used to it.

I sat in the only stool available, by the window. It was farthest away from the professor's desk and I hoped she wouldn't assume I had sat there because I was lazy.

The professor introduced herself and explained that we would be painting human form throughout the semester. "We will start with simple

objects, so I can see the extent of your… talent. Today, we'll start with this."
She pulled some boxes from a closet and placed them on the table in front of us and I almost laughed. A college professor wanted us to draw boxes? She then threw a cloth over them. Okay, this would be more difficult.

The rest of the class went by quickly. I kept correcting my drawing and I didn't get it right until the end of the class.

Professor Collins stopped next to me and I waited for her to speak. She just shook her head and made a disapproving clicking with her tongue. I blushed bright red when two of the closest students looked at me and leaned back to peek at my drawing. It wasn't that bad, was it? The texture of the cloth was quite right and the color was fairly accurate. I didn't understand why she was so displeased.

I packed my things, still dumbfounded, and headed to the door, when a second clicking froze me midway.

"What's your name?" Professor Collins asked without looking up.

I swallowed before answering, "Jane. Jane Keaton." I fidgeted with the straps of my backpack and waited for another question. She never glanced up. After a few seconds, I coughed and she looked up, seeming surprised.

"Do you need something, Miss Keaton?" It was as if I had been the one who had come to her.

"Did you need anything else, Professor?"

"No, I just wanted to know your name." She went back to her papers, so I left. She was a strange woman. I knew she wanted to know my name for the wrong reasons.

I arrived home, tired, due to the distance from the bus stop and the house. I had never discussed my transportation with Cody or Ryan. It would be really annoying to have to rely on them to drive me around.

The house was messy, of course. I let myself fall on the gray couch and closed my eyes for a couple of minutes. My first day hadn't been what I was expecting, but hopefully tomorrow would be different. I was, actually, looking forward to a couple of the classes I had, but the one I struggled with the most—and the one that I had needed to be good—had been an utter disaster.

CHAPTER FOUR

That night at dinner, Cody finally remembered that this had been my first day of college and asked me how my classes had gone.

"Fine." I shrugged, not wanting to voice my uncertainty. I think I did a poor job at it, but neither Cody, nor Ryan said anything. They started talking about the football game that would start on TV in a few minutes. Both of them looked at me apologetically, so I sighed and nodded. They shot out of their seats and ran to the living room to get the best place on the couch—as if it wasn't big enough for the four of us.

I got up, tired both physically and emotionally from this first day, and started gathering the plates when I realized Keith hadn't gotten up with the other two. I raised an eyebrow at him when he picked up his own plate.

"I'm not as much of a pig as you want to believe, Sky." He brushed my arm as he went into the kitchen ahead of me.

"I don't think you're a pig—just rude." A smirk plastered onto his face and I almost smiled.

"'Rude,'" he rolled the word on his tongue. "Why are you so polite and polished? You can cuss at me. I'm not going to tell Daddy." He rinsed his plate and glass and reached for the ones I was holding.

"I just don't feel like cussing. Why can't you accept that?" I would have liked to throw some ugly words at him every now and then, though.

"It just pisses me off that you seem to control yourself for the benefit of the people around you. You don't even yell at me and I must piss you off often." He looked over his shoulder to where I was standing with my mouth hanging open. I couldn't believe he was being real with me, even if it was just to see how I was going to react.

He set the rinsed dishes on the counter and dried his hands on the towel before turning to me. I was coming up with an answer when he spoke again.

"How was your day?"

I was puzzled. Was this a trick question? Was it meant to set me off? "I already answered Cody that it was fine." He threw the towel on the kitchen island beside me, making me flinch.

"Don't say 'fine.' I know that's bullshit. Tell me the truth."

My frown couldn't get deeper. He was kind of mad, but reasons opposite of usual. He had caught my fake reassurance in the dining room. Keith barely knew me, but, beyond all reason, he'd understood me better than my own brother and boyfriend.

I didn't know what to say; I certainly wasn't going to confide with him. He was Keith and I would never forget the hell he, along with my brother, had put me through in school.

He sighed. "I know we aren't friends. I don't want that, either." His smirk came on, full-force. "But I want to know if something bothered you—you know, for our brothers' sake, who are too busy to notice when something is wrong with you." He nodded at the closed kitchen door and I looked back, still puzzled, and heard the boys cheering for their team.

"It's just the novelty of all of this." I stared at the floor between us, feeling childish with my confession. "I'm really fine. It's just... different."

"Yeah, I know what you mean." He nodded and went into the living room to join our brothers.

It didn't go unnoticed that his eyes left the TV when I walked behind the couch to go to my room. If Keith hated me, why was he being nosy about my life? The only answer I could come up with was that he thought I was going to break and run to my parents. He was just waiting to gloat and have his house Jane-free—no, Sky-free.

The next few days went by without much happening.

Cody officially started school, with study dates and group projects. I had a paper to write and some studying to do, but I wasn't doing any better in Representational Drawing. On the contrary, the professor was starting to think I had no business being in her class. Every time she went by my easel and made that irritating clicking with her tongue, I had the stupid urge to cry. I missed my friends—people I could talk to. Text messages weren't as comforting as speaking in person when they tried to help me cope with this.

Keith's attitude didn't help. After our little talk in the kitchen, when he'd actually sounded like a human being, he had gone back to ignoring me when he was upset or bickering with me when he was bored. My brother never defended me from him. In fact, he actually incited most of the verbal aggression between us. Cody had given up defending me long ago and would just shrug and place his arm around me, possessively, which only gave Keith ammunition. Sometimes, he even tried to turn Cody and Ryan against each other, which bothered me more than when the conversation was focused only on me.

After a long and agonizing day, during which my professor had displayed my drawing as an example of what not to do, and I received a C on my first essay, which was worth 20% of the grade in Composition and Rhetoric, I came home to a house full of strangers playing on one of the consoles in the living room.

I was so tired of coming home to surprises like those. Fridays were partying days; Saturdays were calmer, but had parties, as well. One time, I had gone into my room to find a couple going at it in my bed—it had disgusted the hell out of me. I'd screamed at them to leave and I've been locking the door ever since.

With these guys, I never could know. One day, they'd have to study or go somewhere to study, and the next, they'd drink beer like they were on vacation with all the free time in the world.

I closed the front door with a little more violence than was needed, which made the guys raise their heads to look at me.

One of them had piercings all over his face. He appraised me from head to toe, lingering at my shorts and cleavage, which left me uncomfortable. His friends were eyeing me, too, but not as intensely. I was about to ask for the guys who actually lived in this house, when Keith came from the kitchen, holding a tray full of beer bottles—and a bag of chips I had bought with my own money. I would never be cheap enough to point that out, though.

"Do you know when Cody will be home?"

"Oh, this is the girlfriend, would never have guessed," the overly-pierced one sneered. He raised his eyebrows and looked over my body once again, as if he couldn't believe someone like Cody could be with someone like me. I hated when people made me feel like that, and I hugged my body to somehow shield myself from them.

"Yeah," Keith answered, gulping his beer and eyeing me, amused. I should've known he wouldn't defend me from his friends.

"You're an asshole!" That had come out of nowhere and surprised the hell out of me. I had been thinking that for days, but today it just slipped. Keith was surprised, as well: his eyebrows shot up. It was time for me to flee before I made an even bigger fool of myself. So, I did something I was good at: I ran upstairs, leaving his friends chuckling behind me.

I knew my cheeks were red with embarrassment. I shouldn't have given Keith this power; I really needed to start standing up for myself. How difficult could it be?

I changed clothes and lay on my bed, looking at the perfect, white ceiling. I sucked at this college thing. I hadn't made a single friend, hadn't enjoyed a single party, and hadn't had a single drop of alcohol. Wasn't that the spirit of college? I was a good girl, but I didn't even get the good grades that would make an acceptable package.

Groaning against my pillow, my thoughts trailed to my relationship with Cody. We weren't as close as we had been in high school, but at least now I could see him every day and not every other month, like last year.

My birthday was a week away and I was seriously considering losing my virginity on it. I couldn't shake the feeling that I would be giving Cody a present, instead, and it felt very wrong. I couldn't do it just for him. I was messed up.

I groaned against the pillow once again and almost missed the light knock on my door. I wasn't interested in anyone, but Cody—or, perhaps, my brother—and neither of them would have waited as long to open the door. When I thought the person had given up, another knock came—a little louder, this time.

"Yeah?" I was tired and wanted to get it over with.

Keith entered and closed the door behind him. I guess his friends were still downstairs and he didn't want them to hear what he had to say.

"I'm sorry." His voice came as a whisper and I almost thought it had been my imagination. Keith Hale apologizing? I snorted then, incapable of holding it in, anymore.

He frowned and sat at the end of my bed without an invitation, which made me cross my arms protectively. "I'm not joking. I am sorry. I was a jerk just then, letting Vince make fun of you." He nodded at the door and my eyebrows shot up. Was he kidding me?

"'Just then?'" I spoke my mind, not minding the hurtful words that would come at any second.

"I don't regret the other teasing when we're alone, or with the guys, but I understand that I was letting a stranger disrespect you in front of me. Vince won't bother you again." He stood up and didn't seem to be troubled about whether I forgave him. I guess the apology was to make him feel better.

Cody came home just before dinner. He had texted me, though, to let me know, so I couldn't actually feel bad. He had to put his classes before me, of course, but it hurt, anyway.

He wrapped his arms around me pulling me against his warm body. I felt safe, then—finally, after the crappy day I'd had.

"I missed you," I mumbled against his shirt. He chuckled against my cheek.

"We saw each other this morning, remember? I remember very well. I was just thinking about it when I was supposed to be listening about politics." I blushed. We hadn't done anything memorable—just made out in the car before leaving the driveway. I was being irrational with this sex thing. We were living together: I might as well get the best of it, right?

Most of my friends were no longer virgins, which was just one more thing that wasn't right with me. I was dating the hottest boy from school and delaying something that was supposed to be good. I just felt that something was missing. Not knowing what it was bothered me more than it should have.

"My birthday is coming up," I said, before losing the courage. "We could do something different." I looked up to Cody's face and saw surprise there. Had he lost all hope of having a normal relationship with me? Was he tired of waiting?

"What do you have in mind?" His voice dropped from the lighter teasing tone and got rougher. I had to get it out before my courage went through the door.

"I was thinking… uhm." I played with a strand of hair, trying to sound sexy and not freaked out. "We could go have dinner—or stay. I don't know." The confidence was turning the doorknob, now, but he understood my meaning. We had talked about this before, but now it wasn't the "I'm not ready" and the "I'll wait as long as you need;" it was the real thing.

"Are you sure?" He knew me well enough to discern exactly what I was talking about. I nodded and he looked relieved, as if he had already given up.

"Sure about what?" Ryan came barging into the kitchen, trying to get to the food before anyone else, as always. I blushed deeply and Cody stood between me and Ryan, pretending that we were just making out. He didn't like to see us like this, but it was better than having my older brother know about our plans.

"She's sure that she loves me. What else?" Cody said. I smiled at my brother's disgusted face, but the smile went away when I noticed Keith waiting by the door.

Since his friends had gone home, he had locked himself in that damned attic, doing God-knows-what. His face was unreadable, but I knew he was still thinking about the way he'd treated me earlier. Maybe he was afraid I would tell on him. I smirked then, maybe for the first time. His posture went more rigid.

"I met Keith's friends today. They are very... interesting." I kept the playful tone, but Cody looked down at me, scowling. Maybe I shouldn't have gotten between them. Their relationship was already not good.

"Did they say anything to you?" Cody's eyes darted from me to his brother.

Dislike was something I was used to, but this look was bordering on hate. I never wanted Cody and Keith to hate each other. "No, they just commented on the fact that I was your girlfriend." It was the truth.

"That's all? I have a hard time believing that." He scanned his brother's face for some kind of confirmation, but, if he saw what I saw, he wouldn't get anything.

I swear Keith was made of plastic. He set his face on the expression he chose, even when he was thinking the opposite. Even when he teased me, I could feel something else there—some unspoken advise. It was as if he didn't want me to like him. Maybe that was his plan to send me away, screaming "bloody murder."

I wouldn't give him that satisfaction, though. Not even if he was actually murdering me—no, I'd suffer in silence. The thought made me snicker, which made both Hale boys frown at me. This made me laugh even harder.

"Let's eat. I've waited long enough for both of you." I had made a point of looking at only Ryan and Cody and forgetting the fourth person in the room.

I made Ryan carry our dinner to the table while Cody carried the plates. I once again ignored Keith, who chuckled when it was just the two of us in the kitchen. I had my head inside the fridge, deciding on what I wanted to drink, when that smooth laugh behind me made me turn to glare at him.

"What?"

"You're ignoring me, which just prevented me from carrying anything. I don't know if you're punishing me or not. You're confusing." The last sentence was said right into my ear as he pushed by me to get a beer. I was so stunned by the shiver running through my body that I forgot to answer.

I was boiling with rage all through dinner, which interfered with my meal.

"Are you okay, sis?" Ryan looked at me, expecting an answer I didn't have. "You're flustered and Cody isn't even touching you." His face scrunched up at the thought of his friend touching his little sister.

"I'm… just not hungry."

"You were just complaining about waiting." Keith had to make a point— he just had to. I closed my eyes and breathed in deeply. He knew I was worked up because he was a jerk.

"Just go find a hole to hide in." I was so surprised by my outburst that I'd almost put my hand over my mouth. The small regret I felt, however, dissipated the moment Keith's laugh hit my ears. Of course he would find this amusing.

Having endured enough, I got up, leaving my plate exactly where it was, and went to my room. Before I could close the door, the argument downstairs had already started. I didn't care if Cody scolded his brother, anymore: he was just unbelievable. I set my head on the pillow, thinking about how Keith, at least, had served a purpose: I had forgotten about my shitty day, and of the anticipation of my upcoming birthday.

CHAPTER FIVE

The day I feared snuck upon me without notice. I remember, when I was a kid, anticipating the day and counting down, screeching with happiness when it came along.

Today, I had the opposite feeling: I had a huge knot in my stomach and the wrinkles on my forehead wouldn't go away. I headed downstairs in a somber mood.

When I pulled the door open, the last person I wanted to see was sitting on a stool, sipping his morning coffee. He didn't acknowledge me.

I poured some coffee in a random mug, since Keith was using my favorite one, and tried to reach the last package of cookies on the top shelf. I really didn't want to use the stool in front of Keith.

What was the least humiliating decision? Trying to reach it by jumping on the counter or getting the stupid stool? I almost decided on just eating something at school when a throat being cleared sounded just behind me. I knew that, if I turned around, he would be invading my personal space. I had no intention of letting him ruin my birthday, so I stayed put with my arms crossed over my chest.

"Were you deciding between the cookies, the canned peas, or the rice? Because I can help with either one of them, just not sure which one you get in the morning." Keith snickered. I could smell him, and the fact that such a pleasant smell could come from such an unpleasant person puzzled me.

I had the strong urge to turn and flip him the finger. I had never done that in my life, but could now understand why people did it. Instead, I turned slowly, thinking about how to have the upper hand this time.

I was right about the personal space: I leaned back and rested my hands behind me on the counter. He was standing so close to me that I had to look up to see his eyes. For a second, I saw the indecision there, as if he knew he should step back.

I had to think of a witty response fast, but then I noticed he had shaved— that was where the amazing smell was coming from. He had a small cut on his throat.

Keith wasn't smirking now; he was genuinely waiting for me to do something. I wished I could read his thoughts so I could do the exact opposite of what he was hoping for.

I quickly took the wish back. It was my birthday, after all, and we never did know when a wish would be granted. This was one I really didn't want to come true. Hearing his words hurt enough without having to hear his thoughts, as well.

"Next time you shave, try standing an inch or two closer to the blade," I whispered, leaning closer to his shoulder.

I was so pleased with my joke that I pondered going upstairs and writing it down. I smiled triumphantly at my quick response and did a little happy dance inside.

"Did you have to think on that one this whole time, or were you just checking me out?"

My smile faltered and then completely disappeared. That had been a good one. Okay, I must have thought about it a little longer than I realized. Maybe I had been kind of checking him out—not in a "you're so hot" way, but more of a "if you could just be a statue and never speak or move, I would thank the powers that be" way.

I stuck my chin out to try to appear taller. "That was a good one and you know it." I crossed my arms again and brushed against his chest in the process. Maybe I needed a little more space to think clearly, but never in my lifetime would I be the first to move—not even if I had to miss class to win this staring contest.

He laughed this time; it wasn't just a chuckle, but a resounding laugh. I felt like he wasn't laughing at me, but with me, and that was major progress. "Yeah, that was somehow fitting." He scratched his neck near his cut, and I had the urge to move his hand away so he wouldn't scratch the already forming scab. I didn't, though.

"You need to take care of that cut. Don't touch it."

His face changed: the playful look was gone and his eyebrow piercing lifted. How he could move one eyebrow without the other was beyond me, but I thought it was extremely... cute. My friends had classified that expression as sexy, but I couldn't use that word with Keith. He shifted his feet and reached for the cookie package. He then ripped the plastic and set it on the table after taking the first cookie.

"I won," I whispered, more to myself than to him. He looked at me and stopped chewing. "You moved first: I won." I was beaming now, seeing how upset he was about it.

"Yeah, you did," he mumbled to the table, while scrolling on his phone. He was probably checking texts or e-mails, but I was curious, so I leaned over the table. He immediately covered his phone.

"I'm not interested in your social life. You can relax." I sat straighter on the stool, trying to look indifferent.

"Cody told me he wanted the house to himself tonight." He said it so out of context that I had to think for a few seconds before I could come up with why this had anything to do with me.

I suddenly choked on the cookie I was chewing, which attracted Keith's full attention. "I, it's just..." I stuttered, looking everywhere but at Keith's face.

"I don't care," he said, more rudely than necessary, "I was just wondering how long it's going to take. I want to sleep in my bed."

He was back at his phone, maybe making plans for his night, while I thought about how to answer him. I had no idea how long it would take to… finish things.

The knot in my stomach intensified. Since I had gotten to the kitchen, tonight had been the last thing on my mind. Now, however, my resolution was flying out the window.

I was going to lose my mind by stressing. I had convinced myself that, with some settled date, it would be easier. How wrong I was. I should have just jumped on Cody as soon as I realized I was—kind of—ready.

"It's just a romantic dinner. He'll text you, or something." I shrugged, trying to look composed.

Keith jumped off his stool and glared at me as if I had said Cody was going to shoot him. "Really tacky, Skylar. That's exactly what Cody will be thinking about: texting his brother," he spit the words, shoved the phone in his back pocket, and turned to leave, only to turn back when he'd gotten to the door. I waited a few seconds, my cookie forgotten.

"Happy birthday," Keith spat.

He turned and left.

The first person wishing me a happy day was the one I thought hated me the most. This was one promising day, no doubt.

Of course, my professor had to pick on me—she wouldn't have been happy without the usual pick-Jane's-drawing-and-show-the-class-how-wrong-it-is. It was starting to get on my nerves. I would have to do something quickly. Next week, we would start with the human form; she had told me, quite explicitly, that I would fail if I kept going on like this.

I looked at the complex scene in front of me and then at my drawing and saw nothing short of accurate. Everything was there: the proportions of the drawing were correct, the colors were pretty much the same, and the shading was the only thing left for me to do. The human form would be terrifying. Not only had I never seen a man naked in person, which would change tonight, but I had also never been good enough with human features. The only thing I thought I was good at were hands.

I loved to draw hands. I had done dozens of drawings of Cody's hands, but I would never ask him to pose for me naked—not in the near future, anyway.

"You're dismissed. Don't forget the supplies I told you to buy."

The supplies were going to hurt my wallet. The set required was expensive, and the money my parents had given me was running low. I could always wait for their present, though, which would be money. I had visited a couple of stores in the past week looking for those damned pencils, but they were out of stock. I had just one option: asking Cody to drive me to the next town to get them. The other students already had everything required for this class; I had just thought that buying them as needed would be less painful.

I dragged my feet over the sidewalk until it changed to gravel. I was almost shivering with anticipation—it was starting to feel ridiculous. I inhaled and opened the door. No one was home, I hoped: I wanted to get ready alone. Cody would be home in two hours and then we would be headed to town. I had found a cute Indian restaurant and was hoping the spicy food would get me a little more in the mood.

I took my time in the shower, shaving and washing every part of my body. I put on makeup and pulled my hair into a sophisticated bun. The dress was a little shorter than I had intended, but maybe that would please Cody. My only nice shoes were a pair of gray heels, which I put on. Sneakers would have ruined the outfit, even though they would have been my first choice.

My mother called when I was almost finished getting ready. "Hello sweetie. Happy birthday honey!" I heard my Dad next to her wishing me a happy day, as well.

"It's going well. I had class and now Cody's going to take me out to dinner." I answered, as I opened my jewelry box.

"Oh, I'm so glad." My Mom beamed with delight. "I sent a care package through the mail, you know, just a few things so you won't starve there." I knew my mother well, a 'few things' would end up being boxes of homemade food, as if I didn't know how to cook.

"Did Matilda call you?" After reassuring Mom that my sister had texted me this morning, as well as Ryan, my Mom gave the phone to my Dad so he could wish me a happy day and to be careful tonight. I resisted the urge to roll my eyes.

Cody barged into my room as I put on a necklace and picked me up.

"I missed you. So sorry I had to leave so early in the morning. I wanted to wake you up to wish you a happy birthday, but my brother was right."

"Keith? About what?" I stepped out of his embrace.

"He was coming down the stairs and said you would be happier if I let you sleep. He was right, but I still felt like I was forgetting about you."

"Don't worry. Next time, wake me up." And don't listen to anything your brother says, I wanted to add, but I bit my lip, instead.

"Keith was up that early?" I joked.

"Yeah, he had an early class. Must've left shortly after me," Cody pulled me against him again and his lips met mine, hungrier than earlier. I couldn't shake what he'd said from my head.

If Keith had a class at eight and woke up that early to go, why had he been at the kitchen table at nine thirty, as if he had just woken up? I knew I shouldn't tell Cody anything. I kissed him back, at last, and he sighed against my lips.

"I was starting to think you were sleeping," he joked. He gave my body an appraisal and murmured, "That's all for me?"

"No, the restaurant employees were my first thought, actually." I smiled back at him. This was easy, this carefree teasing. Kissing and holding hands—that was natural to me.

"This is for you." He handled me a small gift and I couldn't unwrap it quickly enough. It was a simple, but beautiful bracelet with my name on it: Jane. I lifted on my toes and kissed his lips, softly, while whispering a thank you.

"I'm going to take a shower and then we should head out, okay?" He kissed my forehead and my heart squeezed.

It was little things like this that made me love him. I put on the bracelet and went downstairs. I sat on the couch, trying to relax and enjoy a TV show, but my racing heart was in the way.

"Let's go!" Cody stepped in front of me, doing a little dance. He had dressed up, too, in dark blue jeans and a button-down white shirt with a black jacket on. What disturbed me the most was the fact that my second thought—after how attractive he looked—was that he was wearing Keith's favorite jacket.

I almost slapped myself. Instead, I pretended that the little episode had never happened and I put my hand on Cody's extended arm.

The late afternoon air was cold and my bare legs instantly got goose bumps. Once I was inside the car with the hot air turned on, I relaxed a bit. I decided that I should take this night minute by minute and not wonder about my first time. When Cody put his hand on my knee, I jumped and bumped my head on the window.

"Relax, baby. We're celebrating your birthday, not your funeral."

I tried to smile and failed miserably; he just shook his head. This was a celebration that had nothing to do with the day I was born, but I refrained from saying so. Cody was so sweet and he had waited all this time for me. I should have been grateful.

The dish I ordered was too spicy for me. The waitress had advised me against it, but, lost in the wrong thoughts, I had dismissed her warning. I ordered a second pitcher of water when I decided I couldn't take anymore. I already had tears in my eyes, which were going to smear my makeup. My lips felt swollen and my cheeks were red.

"Do you want to order something else, Jane?" Cody was starting to notice that I wasn't into this at all. I had been trying to talk about anything but our plans for later.

"No. I can't eat any more food." I wasn't exactly full, but the thought of throwing up and wasting more money was clouding my head.

We asked for the bill after our main course, uninterested in desert. I didn't want to go home just yet, but I couldn't find a way to postpone, and Cody was more than eager to get back.

The night had gotten even colder, so my perfect boyfriend placed his jacket over my shoulders. I was openly sniffing it when I realized the smell was of Keith. Cody didn't notice, though, and opened the car door for me.

My cheeks couldn't have turned redder. Now, beside the thoughts of getting home, I was mesmerized by Keith's smell. Fate was doing a great job of getting me in the mood.

I had pulled the coat off my shoulders during the ride but had to get the jacket again when we arrived home. I would be willing to go into the cold without it, but Cody would find that odd, surely. So, I pulled the jacket tighter against me and placed my hands in its pockets to keep them warm, too. I felt a small, crumpled paper and squeezed my hand around it. My curiosity was strong. It was probably some girl's phone number, or some message from one of them.

Cody opened the door, already frowning. Leaving the music and lights on when no one was home wasn't that rare, but tonight it was, at the least, strange.

Of course the disastrous night wasn't over—why we had bothered talking to Keith was beyond my comprehension. We could have asked him to be home tonight and I'm sure he would have found something amusing to do on the street.

He was sitting on the couch with a blond all over him. Music blasted through the TV and several beer bottles were on the table. His eyes wandered to Cody; his usual smirk was in place, while his right hand rested on the girl's butt his left was holding a beer bottle.

Cody tensed and started complaining about his brother necessity to piss everyone off. I was almost hidden by Cody, but then he moved to pace in front of the TV and left me standing at the door. Keith's eyes never followed his rambling brother: he stared right at me. His smirk was long gone, a wrinkle set on his forehead, and he pushed the girl off of him. I realized what had caused the change: he'd noticed his jacket on my shoulders. I was waiting for him to tell me to take it off, but he never did.

Cody had to pull my arm for me to follow him up the stairs, as I hadn't listened to a word he'd said to Keith, nor had his brother, by the way he was looking at me. Of course he would be mad at me for taking his jacket without asking. Not even Cody was allowed to take it, so it was a miracle that the jacket hadn't been ripped from my cold, dead body tonight.

"He's unbelievable. I can't—I don't even know how we could've been raised by the same parents. It's like he's an alien. Yeah, that's it. Maybe he's adopted."

I pictured Keith with a green complexion and antennae and a giggle escaped my throat. The comment about being adopted bothered me, though.

"Don't say stuff like that. He has a right to be different from you. Yeah, he can be an ass, sometimes, but he's still your family. I know how much I would enjoy strangling Ry and Matilda, every now and then, but I love them."

"It's different and you know it. Ry messes with you, but he shows he loves you. Keith, on the other hand, enjoys making me feel bad."

"Maybe he forgot we wanted the house to ourselves." I shrugged. Maybe this slip of his was something I could use in my favor. I would never have my first time with Keith downstairs with his tongue down some chick's throat, so that's exactly what I told Cody.

"Oh, come on, baby. He has his own company tonight." Cody advanced and I stepped back, falling on the bed. He took the opportunity to lie down over me, kissing my cheek and lowering to my neck.

"Cody, no. I know I said… but I can't focus now. Please." My hands fumbled on his shoulders.

He groaned and sat on the bed's edge, resting his head in his hands. "Come on, Jane. I'm starting to believe I'm the problem. Don't you love me?"

That was low, but I could understand him, somehow. I did love him—that wasn't the problem—but the sparks were missing. I was praying they would come any time now. Every time he kissed me, I searched for that feeling I heard my friends talk about. The love was there, but the passion wasn't. I was starting to fear that there was something wrong with me.

"Of course I love you." I hugged his back and rested my face on his shoulder.

"I think you're anticipating too much. There's just too much expectation." He looked at me, kissed me softly, and pushed the jacket I was still wearing off my shoulders.

"Yeah, maybe." I leaned back. "But not when someone's home."

"Fine. I'm going to my room. If I see my brother again, I can't promise that I won't break his neck." He got up and left my room, shutting the door with hostility that made me shiver.

I pulled the jacket up to my shoulders and lay down, hugging it against my chest.

Cody was hurt, but he had a point. We'd been dating for so long that it shouldn't have been this complicated. I silently thanked Keith for the first time in my life while I fished the crumpled paper from his pocket. I opened it over my knee, and, there, in writing so messy that it was difficult to decipher—writing that could only have been Keith's—it said: "Happy birthday, Sky. K." It wasn't that weird, really, but it made me think. Keith must've written this before I came down the stairs this morning. He had to have planned on leaving the note on the counter, or something. Why had he waited for me if he'd had classes?

I closed my eyes and crumpled the paper in my closed fist.

CHAPTER SIX

The next day I woke up to the beeping of the alarm I hadn't turned off last night. Seven was too early to be awake on a Saturday. I stretched my arm to turn it off and noticed several things. First, I had never taken off the dress from last night—I had fallen asleep on the bed, but I was now under the covers.

Second, my dress's zipper was undone to the middle of my back. Third, the jacket and crumpled paper were nowhere to be found. Cody must have come back to what? Apologize? Was he supposed to apologize about something? Maybe.

I went to the bathroom to take a shower and clean the makeup off my face. I thought about what I would say to Cody today. At last, I settled on pretending that nothing wrong had happened last night.

The house was quiet until ten, when Cody came down the stairs. My stomach turned at the sight of him, but it settled when he lowered his body over the couch, where I was sitting, to kiss me good morning.

"Did you sleep well? Sorry I was so grumpy last night. You know Keith has that effect on me."

I smiled and almost sighed silently. "I know. It's okay." I followed him into the kitchen and sat on the stool while he got his cereal ready. "I'm sorry, too, for—you know—the change of plans. Did you come back to say something, or was it just for a goodnight kiss?"

"When?" He sat on the other stool with confusion on his face.

"Last night. Didn't you come back? I fell asleep in that dress." I didn't continue with the explanation. I was already feeling that I'd been mistaken about who had been in my room.

"No, baby, sorry. I should've said goodnight, but I fell asleep right away, too." He looked remorseful. "Classes are killing me, already. I have an exam Tuesday, so this will be a weekend of studying. By the way, I'm going to Ty's house this afternoon. You know we camp there when we have too much to study. It's closer to the dorms and most of the guys live there. I'll try to be home as much as I can, though." He kissed me and stood up to wash his bowl.

I had noticed he spent a lot of time out, and so did Ryan. I wished Keith and I could be friends. I would be lonely for a while.

"Can I borrow your car today? I'll take you to your friend's house and then drive to town. I need to search for some supplies for drawing class."

"Sure, baby. We can have a little time just for us until lunch." He grabbed me by my hand and took me to my room. We rarely went to his—I didn't understand why, but I never asked. Maybe it was because of all the clutter.

Keith was leaving his room when we reached mine. The door was open and he stretched his arms over his head, making his shirt rise up over his stomach and arms. He had another tattoo on his lower abdomen but I couldn't see what it was.

"'Morning, love birds." His smirk was almost a smile today. Cody mumbled something behind me and shoved me to my room before I could answer his brother, who seemed to be in a good mood.

"I'm not gonna talk to him for a long time. I just want to rip that smile off his face whenever I see him."

I nodded, knowing the feeling.

We spent the morning and part of the afternoon talking about school. I showed him my drawings and knew he would praise them, saying they couldn't possibly receive less than an A for a grade. He knew nothing about art and wouldn't be any help. There was only one person in this house who could help me.

Neither my brother, nor Keith showed themselves during lunch; I was glad to have some alone time with Cody.

When we were ready to leave, I put my coat on and followed Cody outside. The weather was getting colder: autumn was coming quickly.

I spent the next hours running through our town and the next one, searching for the damned material without any luck. Every salesperson said the same thing: "At this time of the year, the art students have already bought them all." I would thank them for their help and go to the next store.

At six o'clock, the sky had darkened considerably and I decided it was time to give up. The art store at school had said they would receive the material during the next week, so I would have to make do with my old ones and hope my professor wouldn't notice.

The house was quiet when I arrived. Some soft, depressing music was coming from the attic. Go figure: Keith and depressing music. I would have bet my allowance that he only listened to rock.

I tiptoed to the bottom of the stairs, thinking about how I could sneak up on him. When we were kids, scaring the hell out of me had been one of his favorite hobbies. One day, I almost fell off the balcony. I think he stopped shortly after that.

I remembered Cody saying that Keith didn't even let Ryan go upstairs. I didn't need any more drama in my life right now. Keith had never hurt me physically, but I didn't know how far I could push him.

The music stopped while I was cooking dinner for myself. I regretted not having thrown more noodles in the pan and was contemplating asking Keith if he wanted to share mine when he stepped into the kitchen.

"I didn't know anyone was home," he grumbled. I'd done the right thing by not pushing him today—but I could still tease him.

"I've been home since six. I heard your music and almost went upstairs to see if you'd taken your own life, yet. A person can dream," I mumbled loud enough for him to hear.

His head shot up. "Never ever go upstairs. Do you hear me?" He took a couple of steps forward and I backed away.

"Yeah, yeah, Cody advised me on that. I'm not looking for a broken neck, so you're safe with me." I turned to stir the food.

I felt him behind me and gripped the wooden spoon, waiting for his reply.

"I would never hurt you, Sky. I hope you know that." He soaked the piece of bread he was holding in the soy sauce and shoved it in his mouth. "That doesn't mean I wouldn't throw you out if you ever went into the attic, though."

With that, he left to the living room. I dished up and followed him. I was waiting for a TV show to start, so he could not spoil my evening.

"Don't even think about it," I warned. I sat on the couch as far away from him as possible, set the plate on the table, and lunged for the remote.

"I don't think so. Like I said, this is my house."

"It's Cody's, too, and you already had the house for yourself today and yesterday."

"Are you sure about that?" he asked, holding the remote away from me.

I jumped to try to reach it. "Yeah, I am. I was out all afternoon. Yesterday, you ruined something for your brother."

"I wasn't talking about that—I was talking about this house. We can talk about last night, if you want. I ruined something for my brother? What about you?" He smirked and I gave up on the remote. I sat back on the couch and pulled my legs under me. I would make him believe he was winning and then steal the remote.

"That's none of your business. What about this house?"

"It's none of your business," he mimicked in an annoying voice. He smiled that lopsided smile that made all the girls drop their panties—the smile I hated so much.

"You started the conversation—you end it. My relationship with Cody is none of your business, but this house is kind of mine, since I'm living here." I eyed the food, which was getting cold.

"If you're not going to eat, I'll take your food, too." He added in a whisper, "This house isn't Cody's. But he asked me not to tell you, so, here I am, ruining something else for my brother."

"What do you mean it isn't Cody's? Wasn't this house your grandfather's?"

"Yes, but he left the house to me and the money to Cody. I took care of him during my senior year, when I lived here. Taking care of someone dying from cancer isn't easy."

He was trying to sound nonchalant, but I could see the heavy feeling settling upon him as he averted his eyes. Keith was trying to sound like he'd had no choice but to be here, but I knew well enough that wasn't the case. His mother had cried for weeks when he'd begged her to let him live here. I had also known how much Keith had cared about his grandfather when we were little and he'd visited our hometown.

"It must've been difficult, seeing someone you love like that." He turned to me, frowning, like it was me who was rude all the time and not him. I could be nice—we could even be friends, if he would let that stupid guard of his down.

"It was. He was the father I didn't—never mind."

"Your father is incredible. You can't blame your inability to connect only on him. You were always jealous of Cody and that was what strained your relationship with your father."

His frown deepened. We were doing so great and I had ruined it. Of course, I had to defend Carl: he was amazing with his sons. Keith had pushed him away because Cody seemed to be their father's favorite. He was the sociable one, the jock, and he accompanied his father to games.

"It's always my fault. I'm the one who is always wrong. I'm used to it." He shrugged, threw the remote into my lap, and stood to go upstairs and sulk.

By that time, the TV show had almost ended, my food was cold, and I couldn't appreciate either of them. I had hurt Keith this time, and, as much as I wanted to gloat, I couldn't. I didn't like to hurt people.

He was in the attic for the next few hours and I didn't want to even knock, so I did the same as he'd done yesterday: I wrote a note.

'Sorry. Cody isn't better than you. You're just different. S.'

Before I lost the courage, I snuck it under the door. Just then I realized I had signed as Skylar. I had never in my life referred to myself as Skylar. I groaned to the almost empty house and went to my room.

Of course, he couldn't let it go. The next morning, he entered the kitchen, smiling like it was Christmas Eve.

"Morning, Sky." He made a point in rolling my name off his tongue.

"Morning, Keith." I tried the same tone, but I came out sounding like a spoiled child, which made him laugh. "You're happy this morning. Did some chick come over while I was sleeping?"

His smile faltered, but he quickly composed himself. "Nope, no chick. It's Sunday. What's there not to be happy about, Sky?" I rolled my eyes at him, but a smile was tugging at my lips. "What are you going to do today?"

"I was thinking about going to another town to get those damn supplies, but I don't want to. I need to work on my drawings."

"What supplies?" he asked, before biting into a piece of toast.

"Art." I groaned involuntarily.

"You have Elizabeth, right?" He laughed at my face. "Of course you do." He shook his head.

"Elizabeth? Really? Are you that intimate?"

He faked indignation and disgust, but smiled again. "Sure—rolled in the hay," he said, rolling his eyes at the same time. The woman was not old or ugly enough for him to be surprised at my question. There had been rumors at our high school that he had slept with a teacher. "She's a friend. I was her best student, so, what's not to like?" Keith stretched his arms out.

"Best student? Does she have one? She critiques everyone—no one's ever good enough. I'm at the bottom, of course."

"You? Really?" He did sound surprised and my ego inflated a bit, until I remembered he'd never seen my work.

"Yeah, me. I suck completely at her class. She makes a point to show everyone how bad I am."

"I do believe that: she likes to pretend to be mean. You are good, though. Maybe you just need something pointed out. Elizabeth likes to make the students she thinks have potential suffer."

"Did she make you suffer?"

"Nah," he answered, laughing. I was starting to think he was kind of cute when he laughed. "She tried a couple of times, but gave up. I don't let people bully me around. You, on the other hand…"

"I was never bullied by anyone, but you and my brother." I crossed my arms stubbornly.

"You let us affect you. You have to grow some calluses, or life will destroy you, like now, with Elizabeth."

"You could talk to her. She's your friend, and all." I flirted, playing with my spoon, and eying him like I saw girls do all the time. This time, his laugh surprised me and made me jump. This was not the reaction other girls received.

"Are you trying to flirt with me?" He threw his head back and laughed again. Maybe his laugh was not cute.

Feeling stupid, I leaned forward, resting my weight on my hands. "Well, I'm sorry I'm not very good at convincing you I want to jump in bed with you to make you do something nice for me. I am not blonde, nor do I have fake boobs."

I got up and threw the bowl in the sink, not bothering to wash it. I just wanted to run the hell away and hide my hurt pride.

He leaned on the stool when I went past him and grabbed my arm, pulling me so strongly that I crashed into his chest. I had to steady myself with one hand on his chest and the other on his knee. His mouth was near my ear while the hand that wasn't holding my arm grabbed the back of my neck.

"I never said you weren't good at convincing me to jump in bed with you." His rough voice startled me and I couldn't move. Something like dread mixed with excitement ran over my spine. He wasn't hurting me, but he had a firm hold. "But I'm not talking to Elizabeth. You are going to learn how to stand up for yourself. I can, however, help with your work." He let me go and stormed out of the kitchen. I was so dumbfounded that I sat on his stool for some time, gathering my breath and trying to understand what the hell had just happened.

I avoided Keith the rest of the day by locking myself in my room. I worked on a couple of sketches and started to dread the next day. I was going to be drawing naked people for the first time. In fact, I was going to be seeing naked guys for the first time in my life. How much more pathetic could I have been?

Cody got home sometime around five and we talked for what seemed like five minutes before he said he was so tired that he needed to crash. For the time he spent studying, he should have been getting As in every class.

The next day started as badly as it could have. I missed the alarm and dropped toothpaste on my shirt, which forced me to change and be late. Cody had already left, so I had to run to the bus stop. I arrived to class sweaty and tired.

The other students were already in their places and I hurried to mine. Before I could set the sketchpad on the easel, Keith strolled into the room, wearing only a robe.

CHAPTER SEVEN

My world came to a stop right there. Keith looked at me, not surprised at all to see me. He smiled that hundred volt smile, which made the other girls in the room sigh.

I gulped and tried to take my old pencils out from the wrong side; they went rolling to the ground and every head turned in my direction. If my face wasn't red enough by then, it became so hot that I knew I was sweating again. I couldn't even come up with an apology, as my throat had closed up.

While I was on the floor, focusing on the pencils, I saw a pair of bare feet approach me. Not here. Please, not now.

"You forgot these at home," he said, loud enough for everyone to hear, and dropped a plastic bag on my lap. Some girls even groaned. At this rate, I wouldn't make any friends. He went back to the middle of the room, leaving me speechless and more embarrassed than I've ever been.

"You can sit on that table, Keith. Maybe we can start from a sitting position—and cross your legs, for now. I don't want them to be distracted." Professor Collins rolled her eyes at him, before she settled on my still-red face. This was making her day, I was sure.

Of course, he wouldn't make this easy on me. He did sit, and he did cross his legs, but he turned to face me. I had no doubt he would be staring at me the entire time. If I thought seeing and drawing naked people for the first time would be difficult, this surpassed all my expectations.

"So, I assume you all have the required supplies for today?" The professor's tone was clear: if you didn't, you could leave. I was going to open my mouth when I saw Keith's subtle nod toward my lap.

I opened the bag and there it was: all the material required, and more. It wasn't new, but it was all in decent condition. I lifted my head to Keith and he gave me a small smile—one that didn't make me want to kill him on the spot.

I mouthed "thanks" before remembering that he would be posing naked for the next three hours and had never bothered to tell me yesterday. Of course he'd already known—maybe this was exactly why he'd teased me.

One of the boys in class didn't have the required supplies and Professor Collins did exactly what I'd feared: invited him to leave. I thanked God that Keith wasn't that cruel.

I focused my drawing on Keith's face for almost an hour. It was completely wrong of me to start detailing a part and neglect even the basic lines of the rest of his body. Professor Collins couldn't go by my stool without embarrassing me. This time, what bothered me the most was Keith's presence. He would see my humiliation firsthand.

"What do we have here? What are you, a nun? Why are you shading his face when you haven't completed the rest of the body? Are you that shy? Don't you live with the guy?"

My fading blush rushed back. I couldn't even lift my eyes from the drawing.

"It's time to change positions," she said to the class. "This time, stand up, Keith. Stay facing this direction. If you don't draw everything, you will leave this class and I'll have to think about letting you come back." The last part was meant for me. I could hear some girls giggling.

I felt tears threatening to spill and it took me almost two minutes to lift my gaze to Keith. I could do this. I wouldn't give anyone the satisfaction of watching me give up on this class.

Keith was still looking at me, but, instead of the smirk I expected, he was frowning—almost pitying me. I didn't need his pity any more than I needed his rudeness, so I focused on the rest of his body. Professor Collins said to ignore the tattoos, but I hadn't even lowered my eyes to finally see what they were.

His body looked exactly as I'd expected: every muscle in his stomach ripped through his skin. The tattoo formed a dragon, which wrapped all over his upper body. The head came around his shoulder with its mouth open to sink its teeth into his skin. The body draped down his torso to his lower abdomen. It was expertly done and the scales of the dragon were so realistic that they almost shone under the room's light. I took that time to look at the rest of his body. I'd never seen a guy naked, but, according to the occasional sighs that broke the silence, he was gifted. His legs were pretty toned, as well, but not as much as his upper body.

I started outlining and kept thinking that, if I didn't look at his face, I could pretend I was drawing a statue. It was just the color that was off.

After another long hour, the professor came back to my stool, stating that Keith could change positions before she saw my work. I took a second to realize I had drawn his face from memory and that it wasn't as perfect as my first drawing.

"Now that you took your time appreciating his body, you forgot his face. How predictable you girls are." She went to her table without further comment, which I thought was, somehow, positive. Other students laughed at me, but this time I didn't even get flustered. I'd done it and was pleased with myself. I changed the page, not wanting to see his body again, and started the third and last drawing of the day.

I didn't acknowledge him on my way out and he didn't try to stop me. I was still mad as hell. He had deceived me again, and this time it had messed me up in a class he had offered to help me with.

I stopped at a vending machine to buy a bottle of water and studied the inside of the classroom through its windowed door. Keith was frowning at Professor Collins and she shook her head at him. Trouble in paradise? I hurried down the hall to my next class before he could come out.

After class, I texted Ryan to know if he could drive me home. Cody would be in one of his study dates and I didn't want to face Keith so soon after this morning. The sky was threatening rain any second, and I didn't want to arrive home drenched. Ryan texted back that he would take ten minutes to get me. I decided to walk to the main road so he wouldn't take as long to get me. I sat on a bench and pulled the coat closer to my body, the temperature was dropping every day.

A dark van slowed down in front of me and the passenger window was lowered.

"Hi." The man inside the van had a red cap over his head and eyes.

The situation was making me nervous. I looked up and down the road but the cars passing through were few and far between.

"Can you come here? I need some directions," he asked. The uneasy feeling intensified.

"I'm not from around here." I said, pulling the backpack closer and deciding if I should run. A car slowed down on the other side of the road and I pretended that I knew the driver by smiling and waving my arm in the air.

The man took off just before the girl drove away, too. My brother pulled up soon after. I decided to keep the concern to myself. I could've been making a huge deal out of something inoffensive.

"How were the classes, sis?" Ry asked, as soon as I got in the car, erasing my dark thoughts. I smiled and reassured him that classes were fine. I sure didn't want him knowing about Keith.

"I have something for you, it's a belated birthday gift. Being the last one to give you a present means you're likely to remember it most!" He nodded at the backseat while I chuckled at his logic. I picked up the wrapped present. It looked wrapped by a five year old and that just made me laugh harder. I knew one would be a book by the shape but there was something else. A mug. I turned it around to read 'World's okayest sister'. I laughed so hard that my eyes glistened with tears. The book was about web design.

"Thank you, best brother in the world." I joked.

That night, everyone was home and I got to cook one of my best recipes: lasagna. Cody tried to help, but he gave up shortly after I shooed away my brother, who kept stealing pieces of food. Keith sat on a chair, eyeing my work without saying a word. He hadn't apologized and I hadn't thanked him for the supplies, so we were even.

After we'd sat down to eat, Cody said, "So, baby, how was your class? You were worried about those pens." I choked on a piece of lasagna and drank some water before answering.

"It went okay." As I said it, Keith's eyes shot up to meet mine. He almost looked sheepish. Was he worried that I would tell on him? Never in a million years did I want my brother and the boyfriend I'd never slept with knowing that I'd seen Keith naked. I warned him silently. If you tell on me, I'll cut something precious of yours during the night.

"She didn't give you hell because of that?" Cody was so sweet that I almost felt bad for lying.

"No, not really."

After dinner, Ryan and Cody set the dirty dishes on the counter and went to the living room. I was getting used to this, but it still bothered me that they didn't even ask if I needed help. With Keith, on the other hand, I would never be bothered if he disappeared. He, of course, stayed—not that he helped. He sat on the kitchen island, bouncing his legs and almost kicking me.

"So… you're not going to tell Cody you saw his hot brother naked?"

I didn't need to turn to know there was amusement in his eyes. He was having so much fun with this. "No, and neither will you." I turned so he could see I wasn't joking.

"Oh, I can imagine his face. You didn't do what I told you, though," he said.

"And what was that?" I rinsed the last plate and placed it on the counter, turning to face him.

He jumped to the floor to stand in front of me. "You didn't stand up for yourself. She will never let you go if you don't."

"What should I do?" I asked, exasperated.

"If you tried not looking like a little girl and almost crying, it would help." He followed me to the living room and I was afraid he would continue this conversation in front of his brother. "Let me check your sketches to see if I can help."

I widened my eyes at him and nodded to the boys on the couch, but he just shrugged. "I'm an art student. Elizabeth loved my work. I can help you, you know?"

"He has a point, sis: his work's amazing." Ryan never paid much attention to what I said. Did he have to choose this moment to listen? Cody rolled his eyes, but never commented. What could I say? As clueless as the boys were, they would find it weird if I didn't accept Keith's help.

"Sure, why not?" I threw my arms in the air, defeated.

I stomped up the steps, took the key to my bedroom from my pocket, and opened the door.

"You know, as much as you hate me, I would never steal anything from you. You don't really have to lock your bedroom, Sky."

"It's not you who worries me—it's your friends. I caught a couple the other day having too much fun in my bed."

He grabbed my arm and I let out a shriek. "Why didn't you tell me, Sky? I would've taken care of the situation right away. Next time something like this happens, you come to me. Deal?"

I nodded incredulously. He would have laughed at me if he'd seen my reddening face when I'd thrown the half-naked couple out of my room.

I had left my drawings downstairs, so I had to leave him alone in my bedroom while I got them.

When I got back, Keith was sitting on my bed. Why he hadn't sat at the desk was something I didn't want to start with. He was staring at the photos on my chest of drawers.

There were at least ten, and a couple had Keith in them. Of course, they were from birthdays and other events at which he was required to pose next to his brother and mine. In one of them, he was actually looking at me, and that's the one he was focusing on. He hadn't looked annoyed or angry in that one, so I kind of liked that photo. It was as if the four of us were all friends.

"There: you can check my work and give me some pointers," I shoved, not so gently, the folder into his lap.

"It doesn't work like that, but okay, it's a start." He took an eternity on the boxes' drawings, before he moved on to the sceneries. Finally, he looked at the ones I did today. I sat on the desk, scribbling notes in a book and pretending he wasn't checking my most intimate work ever—of him, of all people.

"Okay, I already know what's wrong."

I jumped back at the sound of his voice. So, he thought something was wrong. If my ego had survived Professor Collins's scrutiny, it would survive Keith's.

"They lack… life." Ouch.

"What? First of all, the only thing alive I drew in that class was you, and second, what the hell are you talking about? Look at that face." I nodded at the first drawing of him.

His lopsided smile greeted me. Oh, here we go. "I already know what the effect of that face on people is. I'm talking about transferring the life to the paper. The essence of what you draw, you know? Representational Drawing is not only drawing what you see: you have to pour your feelings onto the paper. Add what you feel when you see the object of your work. For example, this orange—what did you feel when you were looking at it?"

I shrugged. I felt like I had to draw the skin with those characteristic dimples and get the color right. That was what I answered. He automatically shook his head at me.

"You're doing it all wrong. You have to feel it. Pretend you are in a desert, you're hungry and thirsty, and all you have is an orange—a sweet, juicy orange. Imagine that for a second."

I actually tried. I did like oranges and the picture he was drawing in my head was coming to life better than the one on the paper. I understood what he was saying. I had to pretend we were in a cartoon, in which the orange was surrounded by light and even accompanied by cute music. I had to erase the excessive light and cute music, but I got what he was saying.

"There's one drawing I think that you captured that… energy in: the first one of my face. You got the smile right, and even the light in my eyes. You just forgot everything else." He nodded down his body, lightly teasing. "The one when you actually looked down, you forgot the face and even the body. You stopped getting the energy and just drew on auto-pilot. Am I right?"

"Kind of. You took me by surprise. I had never drawn anyone without clothes on, and in the first nude class, you walk in? What was I supposed to do?" I fidgeted with my shirt. He wasn't making fun of me, really, but I got the feeling that it wasn't that far off in his mind.

"You were thinking about what my brother would think, instead of focusing." His smile faltered, like he was offended someone would think about anyone while in his presence.

The sad reality was that I hadn't actually thought about Cody during class, just about that I was seeing his brother naked before him. If he found out, he would never forgive me.

"That's not what—" I started, but he stopped me with a raised hand.

"That's okay. I don't need to know. You should practice, though: make him pose for you, or something." He averted his eyes and studied the last drawing.

I snorted, "Yeah, right." I didn't want my sarcasm to be that evident, but I failed miserably.

"That would be the obvious choice, and you could practice expressing your feelings." He rolled his eyes.

"No, not really: he wouldn't know how to pose," I gulped, nervous at the direction the conversation was taking.

"It's not that difficult. You would be more comfortable with someone you already know."

"Not like that," I whispered it to myself, but he heard, anyway.

"What was that? What do you mean?" He let go of the drawing he was holding and turned to me. I looked at the door, considering if I should flee, when he placed his hand on my calf. I eyed his invading hand and tried to forge an explanation.

Keith must've felt my raising panic. "Are you telling me that you and my brother have never…" He was so amused that I almost slapped his hand away. Cody was going to kill me.

"It's none of your business," I mumbled, trying to focus on anything but his face. My eyes landed on the drawing of his naked body on my bed and I blushed for the first time since this morning.

"That's so…" His lightened eyes embarrassed me even more, if that was possible. He got quiet and continued, "Strange. Is my brother gay?" He was amused, but he didn't seem to be laughing at me, anymore. He was really considering if Cody was playing for the other team.

"Of course not." I was outraged now. How could we have dated for four years if he was gay? "Please don't tell him I told you—or at least that you figured it out. Please, Keith. This time, I'm asking for real."

He seemed to think for what felt like a minute, before sighing and shaking his head with a small smile tugging on his lips. "I won't, Sky, I promise. But I still can't believe it. You have dated for four years, without…" He trailed off. "My brother is so stupid." He was still shaking his head. "So, you're still…" Not even he could finish the sentence. Yes, it was ridiculous, but not as much as not saying the word. Keith dancing around a word was not something I was used to. Maybe virgins scared him.

"I refuse to answer that. Like you said, Cody and I have dated for four years. Who else would I have been with? Now, let's focus on my work. This has nothing to do with class."

"Of course it does. I'm betting I'm the first guy you saw naked in your life—of course you would be embarrassed in class. You need to toughen up, or Professor Collins will make you pose on that table."

My head shot up, horrified. "Never in a million years."

"She did that to a girl last year. She didn't make her pose, but incited that her drawings would benefit if she did so, just because the girl was red from head to toe whenever someone was posing—me included."

"So you've done this since you took the class?"

"Yeah. It's easy and good money. Besides, I enjoy making them squirm."

"Of course you do." I smiled. Maybe I wasn't the only target of Keith's need to piss everyone off.

"It would be good for you to relax. I'm serious." He leaned on my bed and rested his head on the headboard.

"Can I ask you something? Will you tell me the truth?"

He shrugged. "It depends if I want to or not. Go ahead."

Something has been playing in my head since my birthday and I haven't talked to Keith long enough to ask him about it. "Friday night," I started, and his arms tensed under his head. Yeah, that's exactly what I was suspecting. "It was you." It wasn't a question, anymore.

He sat up again, not smiling this time. "Yeah, and before you get all mad at me, I was just preventing you from waking up with your dress carved into your back. I didn't see anything."

I wasn't just thinking about the dress, but also about the covers over me, and the missing paper and jacket. For now, this was enough.

"Okay."

"Okay? Aren't you gonna yell and tell my brother?"

"I'm not going to tell your brother about that, just like I'm not telling him about this." I nodded to the drawings. "He wouldn't understand." I shook my head.

"You give him too much credit. He's not as perfect as you think. But fine, I'll keep quiet if that's what you want. You should really practice—maybe hire someone to pose for you."

Yeah, like asking a complete stranger to come to my house and take his clothes off would be much easier.

"Or... I could do it." His smug expression almost made me laugh. I already avoided clothed Keith—naked Keith, I'd run for my life. "I'm serious, Sky. It would be completely professional. You need to be comfortable with anyone and I'm going to warn you now that today won't be my last day as a model."

I groaned and let myself fall on the bed. I suspected as much. As I covered my eyes and groaned again, I felt Keith moving.

"I'll pose for you if you pose for me," he teased again.

"Ah, right. In your dreams, naked boy."

He laughed at me, and, before getting up and leaving, said, "Think about it."

Keith was kind of right—about him posing for me, not the other way around. If I could get used to drawing him, any other model would be easy. I couldn't ask my brother or Cody for advice in this situation: it was something I needed to think through on my own. Keith could hold it over me for the rest of my life and even ruin my relationship with Cody.

Two days later, I was, once again, humiliated by the professor. She said my work of the woman on the table looked like a four year old's drawing. This time, I asked her what she meant, and surprise swam in her eyes. Was this what Keith had suggested, or had I just failed this class? Professor Collins actually leaned forward and explained some wrong lines of the woman's hip. She then walked to her table and stayed there for the rest of the class, never coming to check my final work.

I jumped on the couch as soon as I arrived home, yelling to the guys that I wouldn't be cooking tonight.

"Sorry, baby, it's just you and me." On any other day, Keith's fake Cody voice would annoy me. Today, however, I was so tired that I just grumbled.

Keith came to stand in front of me, chuckling, wiggling his eyebrows, and rubbing one hand on the other suggestively.

"Not in a lifetime." I lay on the couch, groaning again. Walking home was getting to me.

"What is it?" Keith seemed much happier and friendlier, lately. This morning, he'd even made me toast and orange juice.

He sat next to me on the couch and pulled my legs over his. I tried to kick him, but my strength ran out and I gave up.

"I'm tired," I slurred the words, whining.

"I can order pizza. The restaurant staff must think we all died this summer, with you cooking, and all."

I shrugged. Right now, anything would be fine. He shifted on the couch to get his phone from his back pocket and dialed a number.

"Margherita with onion?" he asked me, which made me sit up. How the hell had he remembered how I liked my pizza? I started ordering onion on my pizza to keep Ryan away from it, and it was a habit that stuck.

"How did you remember that?" He shrugged and talked to the person on the phone. He asked for mushrooms and meat on his, just like Cody liked. They were not so different, after all.

We waited for the pizza in silence, watching an episode of The Simpsons and laughing.

Keith stopped me when I reached for my wallet and went to the door to get our food.

"I want to pay for mine," I stated when he placed the box on my lap.

"Not in this lifetime," he mimicked me. If it made him happy, I wouldn't complain about free pizza.

Another episode of The Simpsons came on and we ate in silence. I left two slices, as I was full already, and Keith surprised me by taking them. I raised my eyebrows at him, waiting for the punch line.

"Yeah—not a very good combination. But it's not that bad."

He took the second slice and I laughed.

"You're weird." I shook my head at him.

"Oh, you're one to talk. How was class?"

I knew which class he was talking about and I groaned, throwing my head against the couch again. I placed my feet under his leg, to keep them warm. I never thought I would be sitting like this with Keith, without wanting to strangle his pretty neck.

"The usual 'Jane-has-the-worst-drawing' speech."

"She doesn't think that. Like I said, she wants to push you to be better. Was it a woman or a man today?"

"Woman: not as embarrassing, but equally difficult." I was talking about naked people with my boyfriend's brother.

"I told you: it's easier when you feel something. If you don't want to ask Cody, what about Ry?" My disgusted face was enough of an answer.

"Maybe I'll take you up on the offer," my mouth said before my brain could filter my words. He bit his lower lip and shot me an incredulous look.

"Really?" he slurred.

I shrugged and took the remote to change channels. Keith's eyes took their time leaving my face.

Cody arrived at ten again, and sat between his brother and me. He kissed my lips and ignored Keith, who had removed his arm from around my ankles when we'd heard the key turning in the door.

"Hi, baby." I chuckled, remembering Keith's welcome from earlier. This made Cody's brows scrunch.

"Sorry. I missed you." I apologized.

Keith got up, mumbling something about a painting waiting for him, and left for the attic.

"You had pizza? With my brother?" He was as astonished as me. I nodded and nuzzled his neck, smelling his cologne. We settled on a movie, which was about to start—I would worry about drawing Keith another day.

I saw Cody exactly four times the rest of that week. He looked tired every time, and, instead of getting upset by his absence, I felt compassion. My school work wasn't that simple, but studying political science wasn't easy, either.

On Sunday, though, he woke up happier and grabbed me by the waist, ignoring his brother, when he got to the kitchen.

Keith and I had been eating breakfast together, not really talking about anything in particular. He never said anything about posing naked again and I was glad. He was giving me time to think.

Cody kissed me on the lips and then on my neck before grabbing the toast I had made for myself. He knew how irritating I found that. If he wanted me to cook for him, he could have just asked.

"Hello, beautiful," he said, trying to kiss me again. This time, I was still chewing my toast, so I avoided his mouth. My eyes came to rest on Keith's face, instead. His lips were set in a fine line, but, as soon as he met my gaze, the corners of his mouth lifted, as if he were sympathetic.

"Why are you so happy this morning?" I remembered asking Keith the same thing a few days ago, but, this time, I avoided looking at him.

"It's Sunday," he said matter-of-factly. "I was planning on spending the day with my beautiful girl."

"Oh, no study dates today?" I didn't mean for my voice to sound irritated, but I guess that was exactly how I sounded, by the sudden flash of pain in Cody's eyes. He grabbed me by the waist again and kissed my shoulder as an apology. My heart contracted: I was being a lousy girlfriend, as it was and I didn't need to make my boyfriend feel guilty.

"Hey, I'm still here," groaned Keith from behind his brother.

"Never noticed," grumbled Cody, with his mouth still on my shoulder. "What do you want to do today? The weather is still good. We can go for a walk or go out to eat. Whatcha think?"

"You're very good with words, bro. How you're going to survive being a lawyer is beyond me."

Cody never acknowledged his brother, who just chuckled before leaving the room.

"And you say he's behaving when you're alone? I can't understand why you haven't killed him, already," Cody said as he grabbed the milk from the fridge. I was waiting for him to drink from the bottle so I could smack his head, but, at least with me watching, he didn't.

I shrugged at his incredibility. "He's not that bad." I looked up at his eyes and added, "If you ignore half of what comes out of his mouth, that is."

I took a shower and dressed in warm clothes. Despite the shining sun, we were almost into November and it was cold outside.

The rest of the day was pretty good. I hadn't had this much fun in a while and it made my worries about our relationship melt away for now.

Cody was happier than usual, maybe because of the free day or because he was spending time with me. I didn't know which, but I wasn't going to complain.

CHAPTER EIGHT

The next day, when I got home from classes, I wasn't feeling good. Cody had left to study, so I went to bed early. I woke up a couple of hours later to someone shaking me.

"You're burning up." Keith sat at the edge of the bed, first holding my wrist and then checking my forehead. "How long have you been feeling like this?" He pulled the covers away from me and I scrambled to pull them back, shivering.

Keith got up and paced the bedroom for a second, before disappearing into the hallway. I was alone again, but I was kind of used to it, by now. My body ached all over and I just wanted to sleep.

I willed my tears to stay put when I heard footsteps in my room. Keith sat next to me, pushed the covers back, ignoring my protests, and shoved a thermometer in my mouth.

"You should've called for me," he whispered, feeling my forehead again. The thermometer beeped and he checked the temperature.

"103. That's high. I'm going to see what I have downstairs." He disappeared again, but this time I knew he was coming back. Even if Keith was the last person I wanted around when I was sick, I was glad at least someone was.

He helped me sit up and held the glass of water while he shoved something in my mouth. "You're not allergic to anything, right?"

I shook my head, as I didn't have much strength to talk. I couldn't stop my body from shaking.

"I turned the heat up," he said, while placing another blanket over me. "What else can I do?"

He almost looked pained to see me suffering. Any other day, I would laugh it off. Today, though, was different. I just wanted to whine. I curled into a ball under the covers and continued shivering, willing the drugs to take effect quickly.

I stilled for a moment when I felt Keith pulling off the covers again to lay next to me. I was torn between pushing him off or yelling at him, when he pulled up the back of my shirt and pressed his stomach against my back. Any protests from me disappeared.

He was warm—it felt like he was the sick one. I was grateful: my shivering subsided and it took all of my self-control to not snuggle closer.

"I shouldn't be doing this," he whispered, which sent a wave of cold air against my ear. I knew we shouldn't have been this close. Cody would have killed us both if he saw, but who cared? I was comfortable for the first time since this morning and even my headache had subsided.

Keith kept talking and Cody was the last thing on his mind. "I should be cooling your body to lower the fever, not getting you warmer." He was talking more to himself than to me, so I didn't answer. My body was fine as it was.

I dozed off only to be awakened half an hour later. I groaned, displeased. Didn't he know how hard was to fall asleep when you feel like crap? I turned when he got up.

"I'm going to call a friend of mine. His father's a doctor. I need to know what to do."

He left my room again. His face was all scrunched up, like he was really worried about me. Keith had a heart, after all.

"Okay." He rubbed his hands together, like he was ready to perform surgery, which worried me. "He said to check your temperature again. If it's the same, we'll need to cool you off."

I hated that idea. Bring on the surgery. I felt cold already. "No, I'm fine," I said. My voice sounded rough. Keith picked up the thermometer anyway and confirmed the fever hadn't lowered in the past forty minutes. "No, please, I'm cold," I whined.

Keith almost looked more worried. He put his hands through his hair, pulling at the strands, which made him look even more like he had just woken up. Bed hair. Girls at our school called it something else, but I wasn't mixing Keith and sex in the same sentence.

"Let's make a deal: I'll cool you down with towels for now, and if, in an hour, your temperature hasn't lowered, you'll have to hop in the shower, okay?"

No. I didn't want cold water anywhere near me. The first option was better than the last, so I shrugged.

Keith came back with a big bowl of water and some towels over his arm. "You'll have to take off your shirt and your pants. Leave the tank top and underwear." He wasn't even trying to make a joke and that was the only reason I didn't refuse him on the spot. He wasn't trying to be sexy—this was Keith on doctor duty.

"You're enjoying this too much," I mumbled.

"Not at all. You're sick, Jane," he answered, almost annoyed by my remark.

The first towel went to my forehead and, although I cringed, it was bearable. I was cold, but the lower temperature on my head was pleasant. With the second towel, he took more time squeezing out the excess water.

Holding it in one hand, he pulled my tank top up to bare my stomach. This one was going to hurt. He threw me an apologetic look before pushing the towel against my skin. I squirmed and Keith tried to keep me quiet.

"Shh, it's alright. You're going to be alright," he whispered as he caressed my neck, behind my ears.

The next towels were easier. I was getting colder and so tired that my eyes started to shut and I dozed off. When the towel on my stomach was removed, the breeze on my skin made me shiver and woke me up.

"Just one more time, and then we'll check if the fever has lowered." He changed the towels again. I had stopped feeling awkward about the lack of clothes a long time ago: maybe between the cold towel or the scared look on Keith's face.

My shivering never stopped. After Keith took all the towels from my body, I just wanted to curl up and sleep. The sheets were wet, though, as well as my clothes. Keith left for a minute and I opened one eye to see him standing at the door, frowning.

"What is it now?"

"I can't find any clean sheets," he answered. I wasn't feeling good enough today to do laundry, so the other set was dirty.

"Come on. Try sitting up." Keith opened one of my drawers.

"What are you doing?" It was where I kept my underwear. He ignored my protests and took some black cotton panties and a matching tank top and placed them on the bed.

"I'll be in the hallway. Call me when you're done—unless you want my help." His smirk was weak, but I knew he was trying to make me smile. I shooed him out of my room with a wave of my hand and took my time changing out of my clothes. My body hurt, especially my ribs.

"I'm coming in," Keith warned, as soon as I pulled the tank top down. "Can you get up?" I obeyed him, unsure of why he wanted me to get up if I didn't have any clean sheets to change the bed with. My bedroom swung around me and I had to sit back down again. I was too weak to stand. Keith sighed and put his arms under me. I stiffened instantly, not just at the gesture, but also at my lack of clothing. He picked me up and left my room.

"What are you doing?"

"What do you think? I'm taking you to my room. The sheets are clean, I haven't slept there this week, and they are dry, at least." He winked while pushing open his bedroom door with his shoulder. I had been in his room once or twice to bring him his clean clothes, but I'd never taken the time to look around. I wouldn't do so this time, either, as the only light on was from the lamp on his bedside table.

The space was clean and tidy. I imagined all his clutter was in the attic, where he spent most of his time.

I whimpered against his cold sheets. "Come on, scoot over," he said, as soon as he laid me down. I did what he asked and the next thing I felt was his warm body against mine. I gasped at the contact, but scooted back against his chest. I tried to ignore the chuckle that came from him, which shook my body slightly.

His hand came to rest on my stomach for a second before he pulled my tank top up. I was prepared to turn and punch him in the face when I realized what he was trying to do. He lifted his own shirt and hugged my bare back. I sighed, trying not to moan. For the second time tonight, I wasn't cold, as his body was warmer than mine.

"Just so we're clear, in the morning, we go back to not caring much for the other, right?" I asked, more to try and clear the air. I felt him tense before answering me with a weird shrug.

"I guess," he mumbled.

"Why do you hate me?" I whispered. I resisted the urge to put my hand over my mouth. I was never one to speak my mind. Why did it have to start with Keith, of all people?

This time, he not only stiffened, but also pushed away from me. I felt the difference in temperature and shivered.

"I never said I hated you." He looked offended now, and hurt. I would never have guessed I could hurt Keith Hale.

I sat against the headboard and pulled the covers to my chin.

He shrugged again and looked everywhere but at my face. "You're the one that never liked me much."

I laughed at that one. "Me? I can't believe you said that. I tried to be nice many times. You were the one pushing me away." I crossed my arms, letting the covers down to my stomach. Keith's eyes left my face and darted down to my chest. Before I could realize why, they came to rest on my face again, before looking over my shoulder.

He, at least, had the decency to look embarrassed for checking out his brother's girlfriend. I hadn't thought much about Cody tonight and felt a little bit guilty, only to notice how he hadn't come home and it was two in the morning, from what I could read on Keith's alarm clock.

"I don't hate you," he said, sheepishly. I wanted to laugh at that face, but remembered all the times he was a jerk to me and to his brother.

"Yeah, right. I was only six, but I remember how you treated me that first time."

"You have no idea how much I regret that," he mumbled with a faraway shine in his eyes. I sat up straighter at his confession, careful to keep the covers up.

"Why?" My curiosity was too strong for me to care if I was sending this conversation in an unpleasant direction.

"That's a story for another day." He lowered himself back onto the bed. His answer just made me more curious.

"Oh, come on. Just tell me why you disliked me so much that first day. I was just six." The last part of the sentence came out as whimpering. Keith's rejection that day had haunted me my entire life. I just couldn't understand why.

"What will you give me in return?" He asked, wiggling his eyebrows suggestively. I joined him under the covers, trying to ignore the part of my brain that really wanted to know what had happened.

Once again, before my brain could filter my words, my mouth said, "What do you want?"

He seemed amused that I was playing along. "You have to let me get you drunk one night."

"Drunk? Why the hell do you want me drunk?" I asked, suspicious.

"Because I bet you've never been drunk. I would also guess you're one hell of a happy drunk. You need to let yourself go once in a while—live a little." I wasn't going to deny that I had never been drunk. I wasn't of legal drinking age, anyway, and didn't care much for the taste. I turned my back to him and he snuggled against me again. After ten minutes of watching the alarm clock, I turned to Keith and let his hand rest on my hip.

"What if I say yes? Can I ask you whatever I want?"

"Not whatever you want, but I can compromise." His gray eyes glowed in the almost-dark room. There was a full moon tonight, and it reflected some light over us.

"Why did you treat me like that?" I whispered to the silent room.

Keith looked away and turned on his back to face the ceiling. "It's not a happy story, as you might already know." I resisted the urge to roll my eyes. Almost nothing with Keith was happy—not really. His eyes had always been kind of empty, which I couldn't understand. Cody was the exact opposite.

"That day, Carl, my father, had promised he would spend some time throwing balls with me. I had always been a fan of baseball, instead of football, which my brother liked." He paused and I listened to his breathing.

"My father never had the time, so it was a big deal to me. I was in the backyard practicing alone when I saw him leave with Cody. My brother was so happy that I had an idea of where they were going, but I went to ask my mother anyway. My father had taken Cody to sign up for football that afternoon. That's why I was so mad when you came skipping into my yard, so happy and carefree. I regretted yelling at you and pushing you to the ground the moment I saw you falling, but it was too late: you had already run to your house, crying."

He paused and covered his forehead with his arm. "A few days later, I saw you from the kitchen door. I had felt bad every time I looked at your house, but, before I could make up my mind and go to you, Cody stepped out, picked up a flower, and gave it to you." He was still looking at the ceiling, lost in his thoughts. I never imagined he would remember all of it so well. I always guessed that Keith had never paid much attention to me. "When you looked up to him and smiled, I knew Cody had you. I had no chance apologizing, then."

"You're wrong, you know. If you had apologized, I would've forgiven you. Even now, you still have time." I smiled at him, not believing that Keith would ask for forgiveness.

"I'll take you out to get drunk to make up for it. How does that sound?"

I laughed again. "That doesn't seem to be the way to my heart. I'll keep that one for when I need a favor from you." My face turned serious. "Your father was wrong that day, but Cody isn't to blame."

"You want to know what my father said when I confronted him that night about why I couldn't sign up for baseball?" I nodded. "He said, 'If you have good grades next year, you can.' The thing was: I'd had good grades up until then. It was the next year that I rebelled. I stopped trying to earn his respect."

"That's awful. I never saw that side of him. He always seemed fair and nice." Cody's father wasn't the kind of person to throw out hugs and pleasantries, but he was always nice to me and never seemed this cold.

"Well, he isn't to me," he answered.

"So, if I had stayed and asked you why you were so mad at the world, we could have been friends?" I turned to the ceiling, taking my eyes off Keith's face for the first time.

"Nope, probably not. I was eight—much, much older than you. At that age, it's like dog years. You were six and I was nine going on fifteen. We would never have been friends at that age," he trailed. "Come on, we need to sleep. You'll be tired tomorrow. Let me check your temperature first, though."

He grabbed the thermometer from the bedside table and placed it gently into my mouth.

"It's not ideal, but at least it lowered a bit." He turned the lamp off again and snuggled against my back, this time keeping my shirt between us. I fell asleep instantly.

The next thing I heard was angry voices in the hallway outside Keith's bedroom.

"What the hell is wrong with you? You show up at seven in the morning and start waking up the whole house?" Keith whispered.

"Yeah, when my brother's sleeping with my girl." Cody's voice wasn't controlled. He didn't care if he woke me up. I was hot—sweating even—and my legs were tangled in the sheets. My head was pounding.

"She's sick, you bastard. You weren't here to take care of your girl."

"So you jumped in to take my place, right, big brother?"

"Don't be bitter—it doesn't suit you." I heard Cody groan so I decided to step in.

"Cody?" I asked, surprising myself with my rough voice. I covered up with the covers, not wanting to add fuel to their argument.

"Baby, I'm here. I'm sorry I wasn't home last night. I had a study group."

I was getting tired of his excuses, but today wasn't the day to argue with him. I turned away when he tried to kiss me. "I don't want you getting sick." He looked hurt, but nodded, and threw a glare at his brother, who was at the door.

"Why didn't you sleep in your bed?" he asked.

"Long story short, my sheets were wet and I had no clean ones." He opened his mouth to complain more, but Keith put his hand on his brother's shoulder.

"If you're going to keep interrogating her, you can leave. She was awake most of the night. She's tired and probably hurting. Your insecurities can wait."

Cody shoved Keith's hand away and turned, prepared to keep arguing. My head was pounding. "He's right, Cody. I need to rest."

"Fine. I have a class in an hour. I can't get sick now, when I have quizzes every week. I'll text you at lunch." He turned and left.

I felt tears come to my eyes at his cold tone. I blamed it on the flu and on Keith caring for me all night, not worried whether he got sick.

My brother wasn't home. If it hadn't been for Keith, I could have died in this house and my body would have only been found a couple of days later. I shrugged at the thought. I never imagined I could feel so alone in a house in which four people lived, and where, every weekend, there were dozens of party guests over.

"He's a jerk and school's getting to him. You need to rest, so stop thinking about my brother and try to go back to sleep." He wasn't as nice as he'd been last night, but at least he cared enough about my health not to sound pissed at me.

Keith left the room for half an hour, but came back before I could fall asleep. He complained about me still being awake and lay by my side, just like he had last night. My eyes darted to the door, but he shook his head.

"He already left. Try to rest now, Jane."

"Why are you calling me Jane now?"

He looked confused by my question. "You… don't like when I call you Sky?" He spoke slowly, as if it were a question, even though he knew very well what my answer would be. To be truthful, I had missed him calling me Sky, but I didn't comment on that fact. This was already weird, Keith actually being kind to me.

I spent the rest of the day in bed, in Keith's room. I heard the washing machine running, so I supposed he'd washed my sheets. I was probably being a burden. I tried getting up after Cody's text asking about my health, but ended up tripping on a shoe.

"What are you doing up? I told you to stay put. You're too stubborn."

"Look who's talking," I mumbled, getting under the covers again. "I need to go to my room. I don't want you and Cody fighting."

He sat next to me, dropped a pill in my mouth, and pulled the covers to my chin. "Don't worry about us. You don't have any sheets, yet—maybe tomorrow. I'll sleep upstairs, that way Cody can take care of you." He averted his eyes and shrugged.

That night, I felt much better, so Cody didn't have to stay with me. Keith left for the attic soon after dinner. I didn't sleep very well. After being in bed all day, my brain was too rested to shut down.

I was disappointed with Cody, as he seemed so out of sorts lately that it was like he wasn't pleased that I was here. I didn't understand him at all. All summer, he had been excited about having me come to live with him. I hadn't expected to become friends with his brother, though.

Keith was the other surprise. After so many years of being shut down, ignored, and teased by him, I found out that he was actually a good person. Maybe we weren't that good of friends, but sometimes he surprised me in a way I'd thought wasn't possible.

CHAPTER NINE

Ryan's birthday came a week later. I hadn't been with him on the actual day for three years, so I didn't know what to expect.

"So, Ry, what is the plan?" Cody asked three days before.

"I dunno, man. It's on a Tuesday and I know how committed to school you and my sister are, so I was thinking about throwing a party next weekend and just going out for drinks with you guys on my birthday." He pointed at us with his fork while chewing his food.

Ryan had never thrown away a chance for a party, but I was glad he at least had the decency of doing it on a weekend. I was already so tired of classes this early in the semester that I just didn't know what to expect from the next few months.

As predicted by my brother, Cody had to study Tuesday night for a midterm of some difficult subject, which meant staying at his friend's house. I was starting to worry about his so-called "friends." He never talked about them and they didn't come to our parties much.

"I was going to go out with Kelsey and a couple of friends from school. Do you two want to come?" Ryan descended the stairs already dressed to go out, which meant he wasn't waiting on my answer. The feeling of being unwanted that now lived permanently in the bottom of my stomach came to life.

No one here missed me. No one here wanted to be around me much.

"No, go ahead. I'll stay in and watch a movie." I shrugged.

"Oh, come on, sis, you need to live the college life more. This way, I can't tell on you to Dad."

I didn't doubt for a second that he would. Not out of spite, but just to mess with me.

"You owe me one." I jumped a good few feet in the air when Keith's whisper sounded near my right ear. I looked to Ryan, but he was already in the kitchen, eating something, surely. That boy had an infinite appetite.

"What are you talking about?"

I tried looking him in the eye, but, for some reason, couldn't. My heart was still trying to rip out of my chest.

"Remember the promise you made? You said you'd let me get you drunk one night." He balanced his weight on the back of the couch, lingering over me.

"You never mentioned 'night,' and... and I don't really remember making that promise." I should've had turned the sentence around, but it was too late. He laughed at me, picked up his black jacket from the couch, and nodded at the door.

"Oh, for God's sake, at least give me five minutes to put something on."

I didn't know what to wear because I had no idea where we were going, but green sweatpants and an old, white shirt wasn't really an outfit for doing anything outside the house.

I put on some denim shorts, a black shirt with a black jacket over it, and a hint of makeup.

The boys were already waiting for me at the door. They both looked me up and down and, from the looks on their faces, neither was appreciating the view. I could understand why Ryan felt that way, but Keith, not so much. I knew I wasn't his usual type, but couldn't he at least pretend I was somewhat attractive?

"If you weren't leaving this house with us, you would be changing, just so you know." Ryan was always a pain. I had never given him any reason to be protective—or an ass, for that matter—but he was both. I threw him my tongue and Keith laughed behind me, making that little friendship I had with him shrink even more. It had gone downhill ever since he'd pulled the 'get Skylar drunk' card.

I sat in the back seat, of course. From what I could hear of the conversation, this "Kelsey" my brother was seeing was meeting us at the bar. I hadn't mentioned I didn't bring a fake ID, guessing my brother knew I didn't have one.

The ID wasn't necessary. Apparently my brother and Keith came here often enough that they knew the bouncer.

"Happy birthday, Keaton! You haven't been here for a while—and neither have you." He motioned to Keith and they exchanged a weird guy handshake. "Yours?" He nodded at me and I blushed, before looking at my brother, pleading.

"Nah, my brother's. And she's his sister, so watch it," Keith answered, before Ryan could even frown. He was already looking for this Kelsey girl, so maybe he hadn't even heard. "Come on, and watch where you're going: in those shorts, a lot of hands are going to go your way tonight."

As if I wasn't nervous already, Keith always knew how to make me more uncomfortable. I started walking a little closer to him, as the room was packed with men, mostly.

I sat on a chair that was pulled out for me, as I hadn't even realized we had arrived at our destination: a table with at least a dozen unknown faces. Some of them introduced themselves and a few guys smiled warmly at me. Keith elbowed the one on his right and nodded at my brother. None of the girls smiled. In fact, they kind of frowned at me—maybe for being near Keith. Ryan was friends with everyone and they seemed to adore him. What about extending the friendship to me?

Keith ordered me a beer and another after that. He stopped for a while and made me eat a burger with fries. Some of Ry's friends went to the dance floor, but Keith remained by my side the entire time—and not for the lack of invitations. Every decline came with a murderous glare thrown my way.

Thank you guys for the friend magnets you two are. I tried to blend in with the chair, as Keith hadn't talked to me, besides about the food menu, and none of the guys had invited me to dance, courtesy of Keith and Ryan. It wasn't that I would have accepted, but it was nice to be wanted by someone.

After what seemed an eternity, Kelsey and Ryan came back with shots for the four of us and then we got up to leave. I was about to sigh with happiness when I realized we were going to another bar. This one was quieter.

"This is where Kelsey works. It's karaoke night."

"Karaoke?" My voice was different. I don't even think I said the word right. They smiled at me.

"Watch it, Keith. I let you get her drunk, but you better keep her safe." Ryan left us at the door to find an empty table in the back. The couple singing was awful and I almost threw my hands over my ears to prevent them from bursting.

"Some of them are really good, some are fun to watch, and then we have these painful ones." Kelsey nodded at the stage and smiled at a couple of waitresses.

I took one more shot and stopped with the drinking. I felt tipsy, already, and the idea of getting sick wasn't thrilling.

"Hi, Keith. We haven't seen you around." One of the blonde waitresses approached our table and put an arm around him, while dragging a huge, red nail across his neck. The gesture was so intimate that I guessed they really knew each other. He shrugged off her arm discretely and gave her a fake smile.

"Carly. Nice to see you."

Kelsey started kissing my brother and I averted my eyes, trying to find something fun to do, or anything to say to Keith. By the intensity of his stare, it seemed that he was trying to solve world hunger.

"We're hitting a club. Want to come?" Ryan stood, pulling up his girl, who stumbled.

"No, man, I'm going home. I have a class tomorrow morning." Keith was the first to answer, and I had to think for a second. I wasn't having much fun, and I wasn't going to be the third wheel of the night, so that meant I would go home with Keith.

Both guys looked at me and I knew right then that I wasn't wanted by either one of them. The sting in my chest came back.

"I'm… going home, too. I'm tired." I picked up my wallet to pay for the drinks, as my brother was already on the way to the door, but Keith briefly placed his hand over mine.

"I've got this. Stay close to them." He went to the bar to pay our tab. I turned, but Ryan wasn't there, so I started pushing through the dancing people.

I had almost reached the door when a guy pulled me closer. I grimaced and pushed him away.

"Hi, baby. I saw you at the bar." He smelled like beer and was probably drunk. I looked over his shoulder, searching for a familiar face, but the club was packed.

"Please, my brother is waiting for me." I nodded at the door.

"He was your brother?" He thought I was talking about Keith, and he smiled at his friend. "We're lucky, then. He won't mind you having a little fun." My fun had ended long ago. I couldn't believe I was being manhandled by two guys with Ryan and Keith so close to me. The second guy pulled me to him, leaving a red mark on my arm.

"Are we having trouble here?" That voice had used to annoy the hell out of me, but, right then, it was heaven.

"We were just talking to your sister, here." The first guy stood between me and Keith. That was his second mistake of the night.

"She's not my sister." Keith hissed through clenched teeth. He saw the hand on my arm, then, and all the calm left him. He pushed the guy in front of him so quickly that he stumbled over a dancing couple. The boyfriend thought the drunk guy was making a move on his girl and punched him in the face.

The hand on my arm disappeared a second later, and, when I turned to see what had happened, the second guy was already on the floor with blood pouring from his nose. Keith was shaking his right hand in the air.

"Shit," was the only word he said, while pulling me to the door. Security was already approaching the dance floor when we got to the street. Ryan was making out against a car, but, as soon as he saw us, he knew something was wrong.

"What happened?" He pulled Kelsey aside—not very romantically, I must say—and frowned at Keith's hand on my arm. If he thought Keith's hand on me was bad, it was better that Keith had been the one who had come to my rescue: my brother would have killed the two guys.

"Nothing. Your sister was attracting unwanted attention." He motioned for a cab. "See you later?" My brother wasn't convinced, but he shrugged, put his arm around Kelsey, and called another cab.

"Yeah. Night, sis."

I opened the door and sat in the back seat. Keith went around the car and sat in front. Of course he would avoid my presence: I was the reason he'd hurt his hand. I just hoped it wasn't broken.

When we got home, he paid the driver and left me to fend for myself. I wasn't hurt, but now, with the adrenaline gone, I was feeling the alcohol. I stumbled twice before making it to the door.

"I'm sorry about your hand," I said. He threw his jacket over one of the couches and sat on the other. His eyes dropped to my arm, which I was subconsciously rubbing.

"Did he hurt you?" He wasn't mad, this time—he was worried.

I tried to hide my smile and shook my head. "Not really. I bruise easily."

He jumped to get closer. "Bruise?" He pulled my wrist and turned my arm to check the damage. It was red. Maybe I wouldn't get a bruise, but his face made me smile.

"I'm not dying, Keith. He was just an ass."

"I told you to go with your brother." He sat again. "Did you have fun, at least?"

"Not really. I guess I didn't drink enough." I shrugged, not feeling drunk anymore.

"You really shouldn't have told me that." He jumped from the couch and disappeared into the kitchen. I heard a couple of cabinet doors opening and closing and then glasses clinking.

Keith came back with a bottle under his arm, two glasses in one hand, and a lime cut in two and salt in the other.

I wasn't experienced, but I knew what that meant. "Tequila? Do you think it's wise?"

"This night wasn't supposed to be about being wise. It's just the two of us: you won't get in trouble." He paused for a second, staring at the walls in deep thought. He then placed the ingredients on the coffee table. "We won't get too drunk. Do you know how to drink this?"

I nodded. I'd never tasted it, but I saw it in the movies. The first one burned, and the second did, too. I stopped, while Keith kept pouring shots for himself.

After the first shot, Keith had turned the TV to a music channel. He had turned it up a couple of times, since. We were laughing at each other's faces. Of course, he was used to it, but I saw the glimmer in his eyes. We were both drunk. The first time I had ever gotten drunk was with Keith Hale. Who would have guessed?

"You should go to sleep," he slurred, pushing me to the stairs. "Your brother would kill me if he showed up right now."

"Really?" I stumbled on almost every step. Keith grabbed my waist every time and released me after I steadied myself, only to stumble again. I repeated the word because it was funny in my tongue. "Really?" He laughed behind me.

"Yeah…" He was also dragging his words. "Thanks."

"For what?" I had reached my door and turned to say good night.

He struggled for the words. His smile disappeared and he took so long to say anything that I was considering forgetting the question and going to my room. Then he grabbed my face with his hands.

I opened my mouth to ask him what was wrong and he took that chance to lean forward and touch his forehead to mine, with our noses almost touching. I was so astonished that I did nothing for a couple of seconds. He stepped forward, pulled my ponytail, and tangled his hands in my hair. He then leaned over my neck, inhaled the scent from my skin, and kissed my collarbone.

I forgot who was kissing me, and the song coming from the TV in the living room was ringing in my head. It talked about giving up and falling down. I forgot he was Keith and I forgot I had a boyfriend. I let him kiss my sensitive skin. His lips then lifted from my neck to meet mine. We both pulled apart at the same instant, realizing what we were doing.

"Sorry. I'm..." he started, looking panicked. He pulled his hair with both hands, with the tattoo on one of his arms popping up on his muscle. He stepped back, slowly. His eyes were darker than normal, with the gray almost gone. I wondered if he could see the same in mine.

Keith turned without finishing the sentence and left for the attic. Before I could close my own door, I heard his lock turn. The music was still blasting through the house. I had to turn the TV off if I wanted to go to sleep, but I couldn't manage to leave my room.

What the hell had just happened?

I let myself fall on the floor, with my back against the door. Cody would kill me. He would kill his brother. Hell, my brother would kill us. I couldn't say a word to anyone. I hoped Keith had some love for his life and would do the same.

I could blame it on the alcohol or on the crazy night. I could blame it on the way he protected me, the way he held me, the way he tangled his hands in my hair, and the fact that I felt so alone all the time.

CHAPTER TEN

I fell asleep sometime during my confused thoughts on the floor of my bedroom.

I didn't know if what had woken me up was the pain in my lower backside, the pain in my head, or the light coming through my window, which hurt my eyes.

I was definitely hungover: the part I wasn't so thrilled about. I would blame Keith.

Keith.

The kiss.

I groaned and sat back on the floor. What was I going to do? I couldn't pretend it hadn't happened, right? It wasn't right. I would talk to Keith—if I could face him. I wasn't too sure I could. I could pretend that I didn't remember, but I wasn't that good of an actress and he would know. He knew me better than I gave him credit for.

I decided to go downstairs for breakfast when my stomach started to groan and I found all three guys sitting at the kitchen island.

"Morning, baby. Your brother told me you went out with them yesterday." Cody got up to kiss me, while I took in his brother's reaction. It wasn't what I had been expecting: Keith smiled at me and drank his coffee. He said something to Ryan about a game tonight.

"Yeah, but you didn't miss much." I sipped the coffee my brother had given me.

"What happened to your hand, Keith?" Cody's question turned my attention to his brother, who had a bandage around his right hand.

He flexed his fingers, as if he had forgotten about the bandage. "I hurt it last night—don't even remember how." He shrugged and challenged me with his eyes. I wasn't going to tell Cody how he'd gotten it, either.

"Well, I have class in half an hour. Do you want a ride?" I wanted to talk to Keith first, but I couldn't turn Cody down.

"If you want to go later, I can take you," Keith said as he washed his mug, without turning to meet my eyes—my panicked eyes. What did he want? "I have class," he finished. Okay, at least he had a reason to make such an offer.

"Sure. See you later, baby," Cody answered for me and kissed me before leaving. He never waited for my answer, even though I was the one who was deciding.

"I'm leaving too. Bye, sis, Keith." Ryan left behind Cody and I ran to my room. I needed time to process my speech. I was a coward. I put on my favorite jeans, not caring that I was going to have art class. I also wore a black shirt, like my mood.

"I'll be in the car," Keith shouted from downstairs an hour later. I could do this. I could beg a guy to never mention a kiss ever in his life, right?

The wind was freezing, so I hugged my jacket against my body while I made my way to the driveway. I had never ridden in Keith's vehicle. It was a crossover, which suited him perfectly—it was black, of course.

I waited until he was on the road to approach the subject.

"About last night... I think we should talk." I swallowed before facing him.

"I know." He nodded. "I'm sorry, I should never..."

I kept going with my rehearsed speech. "It's okay, I just want to forget it. We can't ever talk about this to anyone. Cody and Ryan would kill us." I guess he was on the same page, but he still scowled and turned to me at a red light.

"What exactly are you trying to say? Did I do something last night?" He looked worried now—more like panicked.

"I-I... don't you remember?" Was it possible? Was I that lucky?

His hand went through his hair a couple of times before he turned to me again. "I haven't been that drunk since high school. I don't remember much after we started with the tequila. Did I do something?"

He was really worried, and for good reason, but I wasn't going to tell him that. I would enjoy the lemons that life was giving me. I tried my nonchalant face. "What do you think happened? I was talking about the tequila. Cody and Ryan wouldn't appreciate knowing about me drinking that much." I peered at him to watch his face. Was it possible that he didn't remember the kiss?

"Sure. But if I said or did something... inappropriate... you would tell me, right?" He parked in front of the art building.

"Sure." I wished my voice wasn't so weak, so I added a smile. "How's your hand?"

He got out of the car, which I didn't appreciate. I looked between him and the building and then we started walking.

"Better. It doesn't hurt that much. Your arm?" He pointed at my shirt-covered arm. It was slightly red, but no bruise was coming.

I forgot to answer when he turned down the same hallway. "Are you..." I never finished the sentence, because he guessed the question by my blush.

"No, not today, but I have to talk to Elizabeth. It's probably about another session, so you should get used to the idea." The smirk I hadn't seen in days showed on his face. Maybe he didn't remember the kiss. He wouldn't be this carefree, walking around with me, if he was as embarrassed as I was.

It would be my dirty little secret.

I shook my head to remove the kiss and naked Keith from my head and went to my stool, while he talked to his "friend." Their relationship annoyed me to no end. I couldn't understand. She was so difficult. Maybe he was right that I worried too much.

Of course that class would be a disaster.

"For God's sake, Keaton, you live in the same house as the best student and model this class has ever had and you can't even create an average drawing. In two weeks, I'll be evaluating your work. At this rate, you will fail."

She couldn't have spoken louder unless she was yelling, and every student was looking my way. Some were considerate about my embarrassment, while others were just pleased I wasn't competition. Her last three words were like nails in my coffin. I couldn't fail—my father would kill me. He would demand that I transfer to another school closer to home, with another major not art-related. I would be miserable and alone—more than I was now.

I dragged myself through the empty streets that afternoon, thinking about what I should do. I knew what I could do to get better: ask for Keith's help. That would be so painful, but it was between failing and asking him.

I couldn't go back to my parents with my tail between my legs, or pretend I did not kiss my boyfriend's brother—pretend he did not kiss me, I mean. I needed to convince myself before I could convince anyone else. I just hoped that day wouldn't come.

I was starting my twenty minute walk through the woods to the house when it started to rain. I looked up. Really? I opened the door, already wet and freezing, just to come home to a living room with strangers playing video games and yelling at each other.

Some of them turned to me and I recognized the one who had made fun of me the last time. I searched for Keith and found him snapping at his pierced friend.

"Hi. Going upstairs." I had no energy to talk or argue, so I just went to my room. Hopefully I wouldn't have to talk to Keith, at all.

After taking a long, hot shower, while trying to keep any unpleasant thoughts from popping into my head, I sat on the bed with my drawings spread around me.

I could pretend to draw someone by memory. Who was I trying to kid? I needed Keith. I groaned against my pillow for a couple of minutes and, when I stopped with the childish screaming, sat back up. I almost fell to the floor when I spotted Keith, leaning against my open doorframe with crossed arms and a smirk in place. Of course he had to watch my meltdown. He just had to.

"Problems in the art department?" He nodded at the drawings.

"No. Yes. Maybe." I could do this. I could ask him to help me with his clothes on.

"I kind of need help." I lowered my voice.

"Can you help me?"

He uncrossed the arms and stepped forward. "What was that? I didn't catch the end."

"Yes you did," I said, groaning. "I need your... advice."

"What kind of advice?" He sat at the end of the bed, still smirking. I wished I could slap that smile from his face.

I sighed before asking again. "I can't fail. Can you help me?"

"I already told you: you need to practice. Your drawings are getting better, and you're more comfortable with nude portraits. You need to capture the feeling behind the painting."

If I captured my feeling behind Keith's drawing, it would be frustration. What would frustration look like on paper?

I fidgeted with the hem of my shirt and heard the clock in the hallway announce that it was eight o'clock. I should've started with dinner half an hour ago.

"Will you pose for me? Clothed, of course."

He smirked and I shook my head. What had I done?

"Sure thing. When?"

My brother was coming home in an hour and Cody had texted me after my shower that he was coming home, too. "Not today. I'll see when it's best, 'kay?" I piled up my drawings and went downstairs to start dinner.

Keith followed me to the kitchen and, silently, helped me cook. Keith was actually a great cook.

"Where did you learn how to cook?" I asked, after starting preparing the meatballs for dinner.

"My grandfather taught me. He said a man has to learn how to do everything a woman does." He dried his hands and leaned against the counter. "At first, I sucked at it, but he never let me give up. I cooked every night and he ate even the burned food. I started getting better. It's the same with your drawings: you just need to keep going, until, one day, they get better."

He was right—that was the rule to most things in life. Practice makes perfection.

Arms came around me, accompanied by a whisper. "Hello, beautiful." I jumped, never having noticed that Cody had arrived. I kissed him back, pushed the stack of plates I was holding into his arms, and nodded at the dining room.

"Hi. Set the table, please. Dinner's almost ready."

I lifted my head and my eyes set on Keith's face. He was studying me, with his arms crossed. "You can take the food to the table," I ordered. I felt uncomfortable under his stare, so I busied myself with the salad.

My brother walked in while we were placing the food on the table. He kissed me on the cheek and sat next to Keith, his usual seat.

"So, how are your classes, sis?"

"Fine. I'm getting better at art," I lied, which earned a raised eyebrow from Keith. "And your classes?"

"They're fine." He shrugged, which made me believe they were not fine. I had given up on helping him a long time ago, though. "Mom asked me if I was going with you for Thanksgiving. Not sure yet." He shrugged again.

Cody moaned beside me. "This tastes wonderful. I knew you cooked well, but not like this." He took another bite and moaned again. I opened my mouth to tell him it had been mostly his brother's doing, but I saw Keith discreetly shaking his head, so I closed it again. Okay, I could take all the credit.

After dinner, Cody stayed with me as I washed the plates. He told me about his quizzes. After drying my hands on the towel, he picked me up and sat me on the counter.

"I miss you, baby." He sniffed my neck, which made me smile. "Me too," I whispered. I did. Not only did I feel alone all the time, but I also felt that I was losing him.

He kissed me, gripping my legs against him, and we made out, right there, in the kitchen, until my brother decided to come in to get a beer.

"Oh, gross. I already told you: none of that while I'm home." Ryan lifted one hand to hide us from view, as if we were doing much more. I laughed at Cody's uncomfortable face. He respected my brother too much. I nudged his shoulder and nodded upstairs. Cody turned around and pulled my legs around his waist, so he could give me a piggyback ride.

"Good night," he said to my brother, while I didn't bother saying anything. In the living room, Keith looked at us and nodded at me, serious. I nodded back, feeling my smile drop. I didn't understand him, sometimes.

In my room, Cody threw me on the bed, making me screech. He shrugged off his hoodie and came to stand over me, serious now. I preferred him to be playful over serious. He kissed my neck again and pulled down my shirt to kiss me lower, while one of his hands gripped my hip and the other started working at the string of my sweatpants.

I let him get it loose, but I wasn't very comfortable at the direction this was taking. The hand on the string had stopped when he felt me tense, so he repositioned it under my shirt, and over my stomach as he kissed me passionately. I could feel how turned on he was against me and already knew I'd have to stop him at any second.

The cue came when I heard my brother shout at the TV downstairs, while Keith laughed. "Cody." I pushed the hand unhooking my bra off of me. "We should stop. Our brothers are downstairs."

"They're distracted," he murmured against my lips and pulled my bra off me. We had fooled around before—if we were alone, I would let him take my shirt off, as well—but, hearing the boys talking downstairs was distracting me. That wasn't the only reason, of course. Cody's patience with me was dissipating and I should stop being a coward and take our relationship to the next level.

"Cody," I said, sternly, "we need to stop, now." I pushed him off me. I could already see the disappointment on his face.

"Okay, baby. Can I stay, at least?" I couldn't turn him down—not when he was making that puppy face.

"Sure." I gave him a brief kiss and stood up to take off my shoes and the unhooked bra. Cody took off his clothes, and, standing only in his underwear, I couldn't understand why it didn't feel right to have sex now.

After locking the door, I turned to the bed. Cody was eying the locked door, confused. I shook my head a little too vigorously.

"It's because of Ryan. He would throw you out if he came inside. This way, we can ignore him."

Cody enjoyed my train of thought and pushed the covers back so I could join him in bed.

"I miss sleeping with you," he said next to my ear. We had camped a few times alone—without my father knowing, of course—and he had also snuck out on special nights, like Valentine's Day or our anniversary.

"Me too, Cody. You're never around," I pouted. He kissed my forehead, nose, cheeks, and, finally, lips.

The rest of the make out session was pretty controlled, especially on his part. He was sweet. I had to at least give him a prize for his restrain.

"Love you," he whispered at my back a few minutes after we decided to go to sleep.

I half turned and kissed him again, not liking the sad way he said it. "Love you, too."

In the morning, Cody had already left when I woke up. I saw a note on my nightstand.

"Had to leave for classes. It pained me to leave you. Love you."

I skipped down the stairs, smiling, but slowed down when I got to the kitchen door, from which heated voices came.

"And are you okay with that?" Keith asked, sounding exasperated.

"What can I do? They've been dating for so long—I can't keep them apart. What's it to you?" My brother asked, getting upset with Keith, instead.

They were talking about me and Cody. I waited for Keith's answer, because that's what I couldn't understand. What did he have to do with us? I leaned against the door.

"Nothing, Ry, it's just weird. I guess I still see Jane as a kid," he answered with a calm and defeated voice.

"Yeah, I know you've never been friends, and that you care about her as a brother, right?" I heard the threat at the end of the question. Keith must've nodded, because I didn't hear anything breaking.

"It's also weird to have a girl around," Keith continued. I frowned. I knew he didn't like me very much, in spite of my brother's comment about him caring about me, but to say that to my brother was strange.

I pushed the door open, trying my best to ignore the conversation I'd just heard.

"Good morning, guys." I picked up a clean cup from the counter and poured coffee. They both took almost a minute to mumble a response, still uncomfortable with my presence.

My brother kept looking at me, trying to find a way to approach the subject of Cody, I'm sure.

"You know I don't like to see you and Cody…" He trailed off.

"And you didn't," I answered, ending the conversation. I smiled at them and went to my room to get ready for school, not wanting either Ryan or Keith to ruin my good mood.

That day, I made a friend. The first one, actually, since I came to college. Shelby was in one of my classes, Composition and Rhetoric, but we had only just met when the teacher paired us for a small project.

She was a bit taller than me, with dark blue eyes and very blond hair. At first, I had my defenses up, as she looked just like the popular girls from my high school, who had used to make fun of me and point out that Cody and I had nothing in common. As the class progressed, however, I started realizing that I shouldn't make judgments based on looks. She was nice and we had similar tastes in art. When we stopped for coffee after our class, I discovered we had similar tastes, in general.

"Want to come back to my place to work on the assignment?" I asked when leaving the coffee shop.

"Sure. I heard you live with Keith Hale. Is that true?"

I sighed internally. Was it possible that she'd befriended me just to get closer to one of the boys? "Yeah, he's my boyfriend's brother."

"You live with your boyfriend? I so want my parents to be that cool." She linked our arms together and walked toward her car.

"We've been dating for a while. Cody was my neighbor, as well as Keith."

"Oh, really? That's awesome. You must have tons of information on him. Do you know if he's dating anyone?"

She looked at me, waiting for an answer. The kiss came to my mind.

"No, I don't think so. Keith isn't one to date, though. He hooks up, and that's it." I tried not to sound bitter and didn't even know why I would have. It wasn't my business, but it bugged me that Shelby was so interested in him.

I gave her directions to my house while we chatted about classes. I tried to steer clear of the topic of Keith, but I wasn't so lucky when we got home. I instantly heard the music coming from the attic. He probably had the door open. My curiosity always got to me, just like the attic also called to me.

"Wow, this house is amazing. It's pretty clean if three guys live here. My brothers are such pigs." She propped herself up on the couch and set her books on the coffee table. I wanted to go to the dining room to close the door and avoid seeing Keith's man-whore demeanor. I asked Shelby if she wanted something to drink and went to grab a couple of sodas.

When I got back to the living room, Keith was leaning on the couch a few inches from Shelby's face, with that panty-dropping smile he'd practiced so much in high school. I cleared my throat and they both jumped, looking at me. At least they looked guilty for flirting with me in the room. For God's sake, he just kissed me. Even if he'd forgotten about it, it was… disgusting.

"Keith, I see you met Shelby. She came to work on an assignment." I wanted him to know that this wasn't recreational. We were there to work, so he just had to back off.

Shelby got up, picking up her books, and throwing him a sexy smile. "After our assignment, we could talk more about music."

I didn't bother saying anything else, and just turned around and went to the dining room.

I never had any real friends. Of course, I had a couple back home, who had gone to colleges far from here, but I couldn't say that either Callie or Tamara were my best friends. I wasn't even sure that we would see or talk to each other again. They were best friends with each other, but not with me. They were the popular girls and I tagged along, but I was the third wheel.

Every other girl either approached me because of my brother, or hated me because of Cody. Now I was adding Keith to the equation. Shelby would be my friend just to get close to him, and the girls in my art classes hated me because I lived with him. I rolled my eyes when I sat down, which Shelby noticed.

"What?"

"I only left for a minute. How could you have bonded with him during that short time?" I yanked the book from my backpack.

"I just said I liked the music that was playing. He did the rest of the talking." Her honey-coated voice told me everything I needed to know.

"Shelby, don't get into his trap. This is how he plays: he'll sleep with you and toss you aside." I hadn't wanted my words to come out sounding the way they did, but at least I hoped she would get the message that Keith was trouble.

"Maybe I don't mind playing a little." Or not.

"Forget it. Let's work."

I tried to focus, but her words and his smile kept playing in my head. Now and then, the kiss would pop into my mind. It shouldn't have bothered me this much, since I knew he was a player. He probably kissed tons of girls and then just forgot about it. This was something normal to him. He probably slept with girls he didn't even know the names of. So why did it bother me this much? I should have been pleased, but I was pissed.

Shelby didn't get to talk to him again, though. He was locked in the attic, so I told her she shouldn't interrupt him and that I could give him the message. Shelby wasn't too pleased, but I was sure that there would be plenty of opportunities for them to hook up. After all, we were talking about Keith freaking Hale.

Shelby would be my friend from now on—at least until she fell into his trap and came to me, either crying rivers or yelling at me for not keeping them apart. I've seen that happen, only it used to be with my brother. At least Keith hadn't been my friend in high school, or I would've been an outcast for the hearts he'd broken back then.

After closing the front door, I stomped up the stairs. I couldn't let Keith ruin college for me. I knocked on the attic door until the music was turned down.

"Yeah?" I heard from the other side.

"Open the door," I demanded.

"Go downstairs. I'll meet you there."

"No. Open the damn door right now." I crossed my arms for good measure. He did open it, but just a crack. There was a lot of light coming from the room. Since it was getting dark outside already, I decided he must have some pretty cool lighting set up there. My artistic side kicked in for a second before I remembered why I was mad.

"We need to talk. Let me inside," I tried.

"Not a chance. Go downstairs, and I'll be there in a second to help you with dinner." He closed the door in my face.

I didn't go to the kitchen, and instead waited at the attic door. He would have to go through me. The door opened and closed exactly two minutes after our talk. I got up when he reached me.

"I told you to wait downstairs. I need to clean up." He nodded at his body. I let my eyes fall to his shirt, which had paint all over it, as well as his arms, hands, and face.

His hair was all over the place and I finally understood why girls said his hair was one of the things that had attracted them in the first place, even if, in high school, it had been shorter. It was all tangled, as if he'd had his hands through it over and over again, like a girl if she was… I'm not going to think about Keith Hale like that. Not going to happen.

Oh, God, I couldn't get the image out of my head. I needed to open my mouth and talk before he thought I was delusional, which he already suspected. I saw one of his eyebrows shoot up. Okay, the eyebrow was the second thing that made girls drop their panties.

"Shelby," I said, sure that it would make my mind start working again. "You were luring her into your… trap." I nodded vaguely at him, but, as he was a couple of steps higher than me, it ended up being at his groin. He laughed at me for the gesture and kept laughing when he saw me blush.

"You've already seen it, baby, don't need to be shy on me." He leaned against the wall and crossed one leg over the other.

What nerve.

"You must be kidding me. 'Baby,' really? What would Cody think about you calling me that?" I crossed my arms over my chest for protection.

"What would he think about his precious virgin girlfriend drawing his brother naked?" He leaned forward, whispering the word like it was dirty.

He must've been joking. Was he threatening me? After all of our conversations, I had thought we were closer to being friends. I guess I had been wrong. I felt something stir inside my chest. Disappointment? Sadness? It was something along those lines.

"I can't believe you just said that." I stepped back and saw regret in his eyes, but it was quickly hidden when he stepped forward and grabbed my arm.

"Shelby is a big girl. I can't promise not to get her into my... trap, if she wants. It's nothing personal." His smirk was no longer fun, nor sexy. It was something made to hurt me. I knew he wanted to hurt me, although I wasn't sure why he was bothering. I also wasn't sure why it hurt, but it did.

I shook my arm, scratching it on the wall in the process, and then locked myself in my bedroom. I let myself fall to the ground.

I couldn't understand Keith. He had this loving and caring side, which was so deeply buried that no one could see it. I'd had glimpses here and there, though. Then he would say or do something to make me believe that my mind had only wanted to see that caring side and had made it up.

Why it bothered me this much that he wasn't that good guy I saw sometimes, especially when we were alone, I couldn't understand. Maybe one day, we would be related by law through Cody, and we would always have this strange relationship—this hate you/don't hate you thing.

I had seen the possibility of marrying Cody more clearly in the past, but now I had a sickening feeling that it wasn't going to happen. The more I pushed him away, the more he pushed away from me. The more he pushed away, the more I didn't want to keep him close. I didn't even know if that made sense.

Relationships went both ways, and I hadn't made an effort to keep him close. I got mad because he was never home, and then when he was home, we would fight. It was becoming exhausting.

CHAPTER ELEVEN

I found time for Shelby a couple of days later, when she asked me about the Halloween party at my house. It was a party I hadn't been informed about, but she had found out through Keith, who had sent her a text message. I had no idea how he'd gotten her number, but that painful pull in my chest came back. He lived with me. He'd seen me that morning in the kitchen. Why hadn't he said anything about what was, allegedly, the biggest party around here on Halloween?

Shelby was as excited as a three year old and jumped all over me. "It's three days away. What are you going to wear?"

Shrugging, I answered her. "I don't know. I haven't thought about it." I didn't know about the party until two seconds ago, let alone have time to think about costumes.

"Oh, honey, we will think about it together." She laced her arm in mine—a habit she had.

"I don't even know if I'll go," I murmured.

"Oh, silly, it's at your house! You can't get out of this one. Won't Cody be there?"

Cody, the bastard: of course he must've known about the party. I was wondering if he had bailed on me last year to go to this party, using exams as excuses to not go home that weekend. I had sat at my parents' while even my younger sister was out, having fun.

My senior year had been kind of lonely. Even though I had still been in the popular crowd, I hadn't felt it, anymore. With Cody gone, people hadn't looked at me like I was worthy enough to be part of their group. They'd never had the courage to kick me out completely, though. I should be used to being left out of the fun plans, but it still hurt. Neither my brother, nor my boyfriend should forget about me. The anger was growing inside and I had to push Shelby away.

"Sorry, can't talk right now. I remembered I told Cody I would have lunch with him."

"Jane, that's on the other side of campus. When you get there, it'll be time for our class." She looked confused. I was a good student, was never late to class, sat in the front rows, and did all the assignments. Bailing in the middle of the day wasn't my usual behavior.

"Don't worry—I never miss classes. I'm sure if I'm late to this one, it won't be that big of a deal." I shrugged and started walking, leaving Shelby standing there with an astonished look on her face.

I walked for almost twenty minutes. I wasn't used to that part of the campus and got lost twice, before I started asking people about Cody's department.

I finally found Cody outside, accompanied by four other students I hadn't met yet. One of the girls had her hand on Cody's arm and was smiling at him in a much too friendly way. If I wasn't mad enough before, I was now seeing red. He wasn't bothered by her hand.

"Cody," I said, when I reached the group. He turned around quickly with a surprised and scared look on his face, as if he had been caught doing something wrong.

"Jane? What are you doing here?" He stepped forward, looking around to see if I was with someone else. I stepped back from his reach.

"I came to have lunch with you. Aren't you happy? We never see each other." I felt his friends' eyes on me. They looked like they were having a laugh at my expense. "Aren't you going to introduce me to your friends?"

He took too long to react, which made me feel even more uncomfortable. I knew he had been avoiding this encounter. All the times he went out, to study or not, he never let me get close to his friends.

"Sure," he finally answered, gulping before turning around. "Guys, this is Jane." My idea of introductions wasn't exactly that. He was supposed to give me their names, as well, but no one bothered to point that out. His friends weren't very eager to meet me, either.

"Can we have lunch?"

"I'm sorry, Jane, I already ate. We were on our way to a study group."

He rarely called me Jane, instead opting for a term of endearment. I never gave it much thought, and didn't even enjoy it much, but, right now, my name pissed me off. He was doing it on purpose, as if he were ashamed of me. I felt tears in my eyes, and, before anyone could notice, pulled my cell to pretend I was checking the time.

"I'm sure you can miss a meeting. After all, you study every waking hour of the day." My voice caught on my impatience.

One of his friends made a choking sound, like I was amusing him. Had Cody been lying to me? I locked eyes with the girl and noticed a bit of pity there, before she averted her eyes altogether.

"Jane, please."

"Cody, I really need to talk to you—right now," I whispered between my clenched teeth, not wanting to give his friends any more reason to laugh at me.

"I'll catch you guys later," Cody threw the words over his shoulder, like he didn't want us in the same space anymore. He started walking toward the coffee shop I'd passed on my way there and didn't try to hold my hand or create any other form of contact.

"What was so important that you had to walk all this way in the middle of the day? Couldn't you wait until I got home?" He grabbed my arm before entering the coffee shop, reminding me much of his brother's behavior from a couple of days ago. I shook off his grip and turned to look him in the eyes.

"Were you planning on going home today, because I never know these days. I haven't seen you in what? Two days? And the way you greet me is with: 'What are you doing here?' Way to go, Cody. Way to make me feel loved." I noticed two couples looking our way; I was clearly talking too loudly.

"Don't pin your bad day on me, Jane. This is where I study. Did you come here to make a scene? Is that it?" he whispered, not wanting to cause said scene.

"I came here to ask why you never bothered to tell me about the biggest party around town." I rolled my eyes. "I get here only to find a girl all over you." I knew I was exaggerating, but that girl gave off a weird vibe.

His laugh had nothing amusing in it: he was mad, and, if I didn't keep my cool about this, I would end up accusing him of something I had no proof of.

"You must be kidding me! Now you're jealous? You came here because I'm too busy with studying that I forgot to tell you about a party, and now you're accusing me of cheating?" He crossed his arms and I knew I had messed up. My pride prevented me from feeling any kind of regret at the moment, though.

"You're never home. What am I supposed to think?"

"You're supposed to trust me, damn it." He threw his arms up, stepped away, and kicked a rock. I had never seen Cody react like that: he was the calmest person I knew. "What if I was home, huh? You don't even want to touch me, anymore. I'm the one who should be worried. Have you cheated on me, Jane? Have you?" I stepped back when he got so close that we could kiss. With his accusation and tone, I was almost afraid of him.

Keith's kiss popped in my head, but that hadn't been cheating: I hadn't wanted it. The reason I wasn't telling anyone about it was because I didn't want his family any more torn than it already was. "Of course not, Cody," I whispered, looking to the ground. A tear ran down my cheek and fell on the dirt. "I don't even know you, anymore." My voice was still weak.

I was waiting for him to step forward, hug me, apologize, and say he loved me, like he always did when we got into fights and I cried, but nothing happened. I lifted my face to his and saw some pain there, but it was mostly anger—as if he had a reason to be angry at me. I had just come to surprise him. Okay, I'd had an ulterior motive, but he hadn't known that until a minute ago, and he had been hostile since the first second.

"Maybe we both changed this past year. Everyone changes at some point." He shrugged, like he wasn't talking about his four year old relationship—like he wasn't breaking my heart.

"We'll talk when you get home. I think we've said enough." I backed away from him and looked him in the eyes, waiting to see the Cody I loved. I then turned around and almost ran to the bus station.

I wanted to get home as soon as possible, lock myself in my room, and cry. I could feel my relationship slipping away from me. I was losing Cody and it was probably my fault. If I had slept with him on my birthday, like I'd promised, maybe this wouldn't have happened. I had been so stupid to try to convince myself that he would wait for me all this time. What guy would?

He said he loved me. That should have been enough.

I arrived home, drenched, because the day was agreeing with my mood and it was pouring outside. I closed the door behind me, hoping I was alone for once in my life.

"Look who doesn't know what an umbrella is." Keith was sitting on the couch, with one beer in one hand, the remote in the other, and a smug smile on his face. This wasn't the right time for him to tease me.

"Why don't you go mess with someone else?" I snapped.

"Whoa! Look who's pissed today."

"Go fuck some random girl and leave me alone." I didn't wait for his remark: his choking sound and huge eyes told me I had surprised him with that one.

After locking my bedroom door, I turned the radio on, turning up the volume to an almost painful level.

I threw myself on the bed and hugged my pillow, screaming into the feathers with all my power. Why had I come here? Why had I come all this way just to stay close to Cody, only to talk to him less even than I had when I was home? If we broke up, I wouldn't have anything else, here. I had no friends, my brother was home even less than Cody, I was going to fail my classes and my father would force me to choose another major. I would be miserable, and, again, alone.

The pounding on my door was getting unbearable, so I got up, marched to it, and opened it with such force that it bounced off the wall and crashed into my forehead.

"Shit, damn it…" I stepped back, hugging my head.

"Let me see." Keith's hands grabbed my wrists to pull them away from my face. "You're bleeding. Come to the bathroom so I can see it properly."

I followed him almost blindly into the bathroom and let myself fall onto the toilet seat. My hands were bloody, so I assumed it was kind of serious.

Keith took cotton balls and washed my wound with a liquid that stung.

"Don't move—it will be worse. I guess your day couldn't have been very good for you to be cussing so much. I've never heard you swear before." He smiled and blew on my forehead. I was mad at him, too: he had been the first one I had been mad at today. Right now, however, after my fight with Cody, it was almost irrelevant.

The sadness was settling in me again. I watched my face in the bathroom mirror, all flustered, eyes bloodshot, and forehead still bleeding. I just wanted to curl up in my bed again. I got up so fast that the room spun. Keith's arms came around me.

"You have to sit down for a few more seconds."

"Let me go," I protested, while I tried to get free from his hands. He just gripped me harder, pushing his fingers into my flesh. "Let me go! Let me go, now!" I screamed. Then, as if all of my energy had left my body, I collapsed in his arms. I woke up a second later, as he was still trying to put his right arm under my knees to carry me out of the bathroom. I had fainted from exhaustion. I wanted to tell him to let me go once again, but my mouth felt like I hadn't had any water in days.

Keith laid me on his bed, since his room was closer to the bathroom, and I saw that his face was contorted with worry. Maybe I was being too hard on him. "Water," I groaned, and he disappeared, only to come back half a minute later with a glass of water. I drank it slowly and then gave him the glass back.

"I'm going to get a bandage for your head." He nodded at me and then left again. I snuggled against his pillow and curled up, shivering. Maybe I had a concussion. That would be the only reason for me to faint, right? And the only reason for me to feel like I had died and gone straight to hell.

"Here it is." Keith sat on the bed and placed the bandage over my small wound. "It's done. Does it hurt?" He lowered his eyes to meet mine, still worried.

I shrugged. No, the wound on my forehead didn't hurt, because my heart hurt all over.

"Have you fainted before? Was it the sight of blood?" He smiled at me, but the expression didn't reach his eyes.

I shook my head. I had never fainted before. I was just tired—so tired of crying—and then I had a freaking door crash into my head. It was understandable that my body hadn't held it together.

"You're not pregnant, are you?" At first, I thought it had been a joke, but his serious face told me otherwise.

"Are you kidding me?" My voice was still kind of hoarse, but I managed to sit up on the bed.

"You're... all worried and sad, and then you fainted. It was a thought that came to my mind." He was embarrassed, but it didn't prevent him from making me mad.

"You know I'm still, you know..." I nodded at him and he sighed, relieved. His hand went through his hair, messing it up.

"I thought—I mean, he slept in your room and, I mean—sorry. I didn't mean to pry." He looked away, uncomfortable.

"You called me 'Cody's little virgin' days ago," I muttered.

"I was mad. I had no right to talk to you like that. Sorry."

Keith got up and paced the room. He looked sorry, but it didn't erase the empty feeling inside me.

"Do you think Cody will tire of waiting?" I whispered so low that I didn't know if Keith had heard me. I wished with all my being that he hadn't. I hadn't meant to ask out loud. I just needed to ask someone—talk to someone—and Keith was the only one around.

I shut my eyes. "Forget what I just asked, please," I begged.

"I can't." He sat back on the bed. "Why are you asking me that now?"

I pried one eye open and swallowed. He wanted me to spill my most secret fears, and to him, of all people. He hated me. We weren't even friends, much less close friends. He was a womanizer, had kissed me against my will, well, kind of, and had forgotten about it.

"You made a lot of remarks about Cody. Do you think he's cheated on me?" Just shoot me now. Maybe I did have a concussion. Maybe I had gone to the other side without realizing it.

He looked away, not helping with my unsettled stomach.

"I don't know, Sky. You see him as much as I do, and last year was similar. I never saw anything, if that's what you're asking. I'm sorry if I planted the thought in your head. It was wrong of me." He didn't look me in the eyes, and I had no reason to trust him, but I did. "About waiting—he would be a fool if he didn't. You just do what you feel comfortable doing, you hear me?" He grabbed my wrist to force me to look him in the eyes. "Never jump into anything you don't want to, okay? Promise me."

I have no idea why I obeyed him. "I promise," I whispered. I didn't know what was with him and this promise, or why he cared so much. It was especially strange coming from someone who jumped from girl to girl without a care in the world. Had he cared what the girls he'd slept with felt?

"What about the girls you sleep with?" He flinched and let my wrist go.

"That has nothing to do what I'm asking of you. I've never been with a virgin before." He looked away before mumbling. "I'm not worthy of that."

That statement left me speechless. He'd said it so quietly that maybe he was the one speaking his thoughts, now. The look on his face told me as much: he didn't want me to hear that last part.

"Why?" My voice sounded incredulous. Keith Hale was one of the most confident people I had ever met. He exuded confidence. He looked like someone who didn't think anyone was worthy of his time.

"It doesn't matter. It's something you need to give to someone you love, who you think will stay with you forever, even if, eventually, things don't work out. At the moment, you need to think he's the one."

"I-I… don't know what to say. I never thought you would be this… philosophical."

He laughed and sat back on the bed. The laugher died quickly. "What happened today? Why were you crying?"

"It's actually your fault." I lowered my eyes to the blanket he had placed over me. "Shelby told me about the party." I glanced up and saw him flinch.

"I'm sorry, Sky, it's—"

"It doesn't matter, anymore," I interrupted his apology. "I went to confront Cody about it and we had a huge fight. He accused me of not caring about him, anymore." That was a messed up conclusion, but that had been one of the things that had me crushed. He'd made it seem that it was my fault we were growing apart.

"Because you don't sleep with him? Is he fucking crazy?" Keith jumped to his feet and turned around to face me. "You're not falling for that shit, right? Is that what made you cry? I'll kill that mother…" I groaned and he stopped cussing. "Sorry," he muttered, but he wasn't any calmer.

"Is not that I'm falling for that crap, it's something I have been thinking for a while. He's never home to talk to, so…" I shrugged.

"You've been cooking this inside your head. He's the stupid one, okay? Now I practically forbid you to sleep with him. He's the wrong one, okay?" He cradled my face in his hands and it was so similar to the night he kissed me that my heart went into overdrive. He just wanted to check how my head was, though, and I exhaled in relief. It didn't go unnoticed.

"What?"

"Nothing. It… stings a little, that's all." I bit my lower lip unintentionally, but Keith noticed.

Oh God, I'm so stupid. Just a few hours ago, my boyfriend accused me of cheating, and, now, here I am, lying on his brother's bed.

I swear I heard a low groan from Keith before he got up again. "I think it's okay—your head. Do you want something for the pain?"

I shook my head, as it was just a light throbbing, now. My period gave me worse headaches. I wasn't going to tell him that, though.

"Do you want to watch a movie?" he asked, removing his laptop from his backpack. I nodded as answer and gave him space on the bed, pulling a blanket over my body.

I didn't need to point out that my brother hadn't come home, and neither did Cody. Cody should have come home to check on me, to apologize, or at least to see if I was okay, but no, his study date was much more important.

Keith brought me a sandwich for dinner and a glass of orange juice. A second after I finished with the sandwich, he picked me up again.

"What are you doing?" I asked, grabbing his shoulders for support.

"Taking you to your room. I need to stay in my bed to check on you during the night." He tucked me in, as if I was still a child, and kissed my forehead so fast that I didn't have time to realize what he was doing. He left the door open and went to his room.

How wrong was it that my boyfriend's brother was more concerned with my well-being than my own brother or boyfriend? This was the side of Keith I liked the most—the one that made him human and that no one else saw. Either he played the man-whore part, or the cold-shoulder part. I guessed my brother was the only one who'd escaped these two sides of him. They had a real friendship.

I thrashed all night. It wasn't the cut that bothered me, it was Cody, our fight, and the fact that he hadn't come home. I got up twice to check his room, before giving up and trying to sleep. I felt Keith's presence a couple of times, to check on me.

The next day, my head throbbed and I groaned every step until I reached the ground floor, where the TV had its volume turned up pretty high. Keith was eating cereal, while bouncing his head. I turned the sound down before he noticed I had arrived.

"Good morning to you, too. The head's that bad?"

"It's like I'm hungover without all the fun of the night before." I sat down slowly to avoid shaking my head while he laughed.

"Next time, you can open the door more ladylike, and not throw it into the wall."

I ignored his remark and changed channels to something with less noise.

"Do you know where Cody is? Did he come back last night?" I asked without meeting his eyes. I didn't want to see the pity in them.

"Nope, didn't see him, and he never called. I'm sure he's studying somewhere."

"Yeah, yeah, no need to defend him." I waved my arm and went to get my breakfast. When I returned, I said, "By the way, our fight started because of the Halloween party. Why didn't you tell me?" I sat back on the couch with the bowl on my lap.

He frowned and turned to me. "I thought you knew. It isn't a secret. I'm sorry if I didn't ask you, but it's kind of mandatory for us to set up the party."

I shrugged, finished eating, and left for my room to get ready for classes. A thought was settling in my head: I would go to the damn party, with or without Cody, and I would have fun. I was going to prove to everyone that I knew how to have fun. The anger that still ran through my veins was pounding with the need to do something reckless—to just let go, for once in my life.

I lied to Shelby that I already had a costume ready. I would use some of my clothes and make a few changes to them. As soon as I got home, I turned my laptop on and connected to the internet. I still needed a couple of things: fake vampire teeth, fake blood, and red contact lenses. I also found out that the natural color of my eyes was so freaky that they made special Halloween lenses in the same color.

The moment I spotted the all-black contact lenses, I changed my mind about the red ones. The teeth were kind of weird, but it was mandatory for a vampire. I was going as a sexy vampire with black shorts, a dark purple bodice, and black boots.

I paid my order and closed the laptop, smiling.

"Hi. Can I come in?"

My smile dropped instantly. I hadn't seen Cody since our fight and the surprise of seeing him in my doorway was clouding my mood. "Sure. It's your house, right?" I crossed my arms.

"Not really—it's Keith's." I frowned, not believing that he was giving me the information he so carefully kept hidden, but he waved me away. "Another story." Cody sat on the bed, uninvited. "We need to talk."

"I waited for you yesterday." I shrugged and looked away to a beautiful picture on the wall, next to the door. It was an oil painting of a green field with poppies and a lady with her back to us, walking hand in hand with a little boy.

"I had a quiz this morning and had to study half the night."

"And the other half?" I asked in an accusatory tone. I didn't want to fight, but he made it so easy.

"Don't start. I crashed in one of the guys' dorm rooms. I still don't know what happened yesterday."

"I was mad because none of you tell me anything that goes on in this house, and then you're never around. You've been so far away from me that I don't know what to think, anymore, Cody. Do you still love me? Do you want to break up?"

"Of course not," he interrupted.

"Do you want me to move out?" I whispered and looked up to meet his eyes.

He shut his for a second and then lowered himself in front of me. "I still love you and I'm sorry about what I said yesterday." He kissed me softly, grabbed my waist, and sat me on my desk, hugging me closer to him and deepening the kiss. If he wanted to keep going, I wouldn't stop him this time. I couldn't, in spite of what Keith had said. I had to give Cody something, and not just hope that he would be there the next day. I needed to show him I loved him, too. Words wouldn't work, anymore.

Cody undid the first button of my shirt and kissed my collarbone, which made me shudder. He undid the rest of the buttons, then, exposing my white bra, and he kissed the top of each breast. I got my hands under his shirt and let them travel up and down, feeling his muscles tightening under my touch.

"You drive me crazy, Jane. Can you feel how much I want you?" he whispered in a ragged voice near my ear and stepped forward to align his body with mine. It still bothered me that he would think about sex so soon after our fight, but I kind of let it go. I tried, at least, to let go of my anger and disappointment. I didn't fight him when he unzipped my jeans and when he helped take them off of me. My shirt followed. I wanted this. I felt that same excitement as when we made out—that tightening at the bottom of my stomach.

A groan escaped my throat and he heard it as encouragement to keep going. He picked me up from the desk and whirled around to sit me on the bed, unzipping his jeans before coming to stand over me. My heart was beating so fast. This was it: I was going to save our relationship. If only that nagging feeling that something wasn't right could have been peeled away, like our clothes.

"Jane," Cody whispered near my neck. He lowered himself to kiss my chest and moved down to linger at my bellybutton. That's when a nice bucket of icy water was thrown over us—figuratively, of course.

Keith's voice sounded in the hallway a second before his head popped into my doorway. Cody had left the door open when he'd come in.

"Sky, how's your head—" He looked at us and stopped talking. Cody jumped back, leaving me even more exposed to his brother. I might have seen him naked, but him seeing me like this was completely different. I pulled a pillow over my lap.

"What the hell, Keith. Don't you know how to knock?" Cody got up and pulled his shirt on, already anticipating that I wouldn't be interested in proceeding after this. He picked up his discarded jeans and left before Keith could say anything or leave.

Cody and Keith bumped shoulders and, a second later, I heard the front door closing. How could Cody leave so fast, and leave me here, almost naked, in front of Keith, who was still staring at me like I had grown two horns.

"That son of a bitch," he cursed, stepping inside my room. I hadn't noticed that a couple of tears had left my eyes.

How could half a minute ruin my life even more? It had been Cody's fault for leaving the door open. He'd just cared about getting me in bed as fast as possible.

I flinched from Keith's hand and he turned around to pick up a quilt from the chair, which he wrapped around my shoulders. "I don't know what's gotten into him lately."

I choked back a sob and squeezed the quilt around me.

"Shit. Shit." Keith leaned over the pillow still in my lap and pulled me against him. "It's okay. He's the asshole, okay? You didn't do anything wrong, Sky. I just don't understand what changed between our conversation from yesterday and today." He grabbed my chin and turned my face to check my forehead. Cody hadn't even asked why I was wearing a bandage. This was messed up.

"He apologized and one thing led to another. Forget it. Maybe it's good you came home. Maybe this was a mistake," I murmured, dislodging my chin from his hand.

"'Maybe?' You're capable of doubt when he leaves this fast, leaving you…" He nodded to me, wrinkling his forehead.

I shrugged. I didn't know what was going through my head, anymore. "I need to take a shower. Can you leave?" I tried to sound nonchalant; I didn't want him thinking I was unappreciative of his concern.

Keith didn't answer. He stood up, looked at me once again—measuring my level of depression, for sure—and then left for the attic. The shower came an hour later, when I finally found the courage to get up from my curled-up position. I had been a few seconds away from losing my virginity to a guy I'd thought was my world. Then he'd left me, without any explanation, to go who knew where with who knew whom. That girl's face popped into my head again. She wasn't innocent in this. I felt it.

Cody and Ryan left me alone all the time, and then claimed some hold on me. Well, not tomorrow. The party would be a new start for me. They had taken my good girl side for granted and they would regret it.

There were a couple of things I still needed to do the next afternoon: some not-so temporary things, like going to the hair salon and the piercing shop. The thought had popped into my head out of nowhere, but I was set on it. I was rebelling, damn the world. I was tired of being the good girl.

Jane was a good girl's name. In my head, I was starting to be Skylar.

CHAPTER TWELVE

The second I entered the hair salon, my confidence started to fade.

"Hello. What can I do for you today?" The hairdresser asked me after her co-worker sat me in one of the chairs.

"I want very thin light blue streaks—somehow discreet—on the lower half of my hair. Do you think that would look good?" I asked, meeting her eyes on the mirror in front of me.

"Sure, honey, that will look good on you. With those eyes, anything would look good, though." I resisted the will to roll my eyes at the comment. If only she knew how freaky I thought the color was.

The result was good and I surprised myself by liking it. I'd never had a rebellious bone in my body, but maybe college was changing me.

The piercing in my nose hurt a little bit, but I liked the outcome, as well. Maybe I could pull it off. The stone was so small that it was barely visible and only shone when light hit my face. I stood in front of the mirror for half an hour before starting my shower. My adrenaline was gone and I was starting to fear my decisions. I had to go home for the holidays and knew for a fact that my dad was going to murder me. He would possibly blame Cody, Ryan, or even Keith.

Keith was going to laugh at me like crazy over my weak display of rebellion.

Ryan and Keith spent the afternoon cleaning up the house and stocking it with supplies for the party. I had managed to sidestep them and avoid showing off my new look before the guests arrived. I guessed that Ryan wouldn't have been so supportive of the way I was going to dress, but I was beyond caring.

Cody texted me that he would be here later and that he would be bringing some friends. Whether he was going to introduce them to me was unknown.

I dressed in black stockings, black shorts, a dark purple corset, and some black boots I rarely wore. I started pinning my hair up in a messy bun. The makeup was the tricky part: I wanted to look sexy, but not overdo it and look slutty.

The teeth were uncomfortable, but I had to wear them if people were supposed to believe that I was, in fact, a vampire, and not a prostitute. The blood on the corner of my mouth affirmed that, but I only used a little bit to avoid looking like I had eaten an entire family.

When I gathered the courage to go downstairs, the house was already packed. As soon as I stepped on the ground floor, my eyes started burning again. I wasn't used to the contact lenses, and the cigarette smoke, which was already filling up the air, was irritating my sensitive eyes. Black eyes with real red around them would be even a freakier look.

The first person who spotted me was Ryan, who was, as I had expected, mad as hell about my outfit. It had taken him a couple of seconds to recognize me. Good: that had been my plan.

"Jane Keaton, come here right now," I heard him yell at me, but I managed to get lost in the crowd. My brother had his arms full of bottles, so he couldn't chase me throughout the entire house.

I felt lost in my own living room. The space had been cleared out to allow people to dance. The music choices were cool, with an edge of darkness, as it was Halloween.

Almost everyone was dressed up in the usual attire: ghosts, witches, famous people, and even a vampire or two. Most of the girls were dressed in as little clothes as me, so I didn't feel out of place—just lost and alone.

The alcohol table had a line formed and two guys I'd never met were serving everyone, not bothering to check IDs. I guess nobody was worried about police coming to end this party, as we lived so far away from town. I asked for a soda and they laughed at me, pouring me a vodka tonic, instead. I shook my head in disbelief, but picked up the cup and cleared the space for the next person.

I drank three more before Cody arrived. The bartender guy must've been pouring me more vodka than tonic, because I was starting to get dizzy.

"Cody." I smiled at him and hugged him, not acknowledging the girl next to him—the one from campus.

He eyed me from head to toe, his eyes popping from his face. He wasn't used to seeing me like this.

"Jane, have you been drinking?" he asked, suddenly upset. "You were never a drinker."

"These are the times to pick up new habits, right?" I asked, looking to the uncomfortable girl next to him. I wasn't planning on being a drunk any time soon, but the line had flown from my mouth, while the corners of his turned down, disapprovingly.

"This is Alexis. You met her the other day." He looked at me, as if asking me not to make a scene—like I usually made him look bad.

"Hi, I'm Jane Keaton, Cody's girlfriend of four years." I extended my hand and smiled politely. I had to add the last part, as it seemed she had forgotten he was taken. She flinched momentarily and I saw the little wrinkle appear on her forehead, before she could plaster a smile and shake my hand quickly.

After they had drinks in hand, we sat in a corner, where there were two empty chairs. I sat on Cody's lap and sipped his drink, which seemed to have even more alcohol than my previous ones. Alexis and Cody made small talk, but the girl avoided looking our way and I started to think she had feelings for my boyfriend, which was not good—at all.

"Come dance with me, baby," I cooed in his ear.

"Not now, Jane. Maybe later."

He hadn't even said that I looked good. What a disappointment.

"Fine, whatever. I'm going to dance alone." I pouted, looking at him for a second to check his reaction. Figuring he wasn't going to backpedal, I got up and searched for a place to dance on my own, like a loser.

I ended up leaning against the table for drinks, nursing my second beer, while sulking.

"I don't really like you all alone in the house, as packed as it is." Keith leaned against the table, as well, while greeting some friends who had come to get their next drink.

"Tell that to your brother," I mumbled, looking away. I'd tried avoiding looking at Cody for the past half an hour, all cozy, and absorbing every word his friend said.

"Want to dance?"

I looked at him finally, raising my eyebrows. Keith looked as if he regretted the words as soon as they'd come out of his mouth, but I didn't care. I wanted to dance and I wanted to be Skylar, not the goody-good, Jane.

"Sure." I grabbed his hand and pulled him to the middle of the room.

The first minute was tense and awkward. He didn't touch me and I kept bumping into his legs. The music changed and a song from one of my favorite bands came blasting through the sound system. I stepped closer when another guy grinded against me. I didn't think Keith noticed, though, or he would have put him in his place.

Keith grabbed my waist, instead, and pulled me to his body. I tensed for a second, but the alcohol was clouding my judgment. The decision of not continuing to be the Jane everyone stepped on all the time came to my mind, so I put my arms around his neck and we started dancing—really dancing, and boy, Keith knew how to dance. His hands came to rest on my lower hips while he moved us along. I could feel the heat between us. I could smell his cologne. I could almost feel his heart beating against my own.

After a while, I lifted my eyes to his face and the serious look there almost made me step away.

His lips were set in a straight line and his eyes were locked on mine, dark in the dimly-lit room. I usually felt exposed when someone stared at me like this. With Keith, even knowing the black lenses blocked my real eyes, I still felt exposed, as if he could stare straight into my soul. I didn't move or look away.

His eyes dropped to my lips, a jolt of electricity ran through my body, and I suddenly remembered we were dancing in the middle of a room. The way our bodies connected and the way my skin tingled under his hands wouldn't please my brother, or Cody.

I looked around, stepping away from the heat of Keith's body, and felt the cold instantly. Apparently no one was looking, and Cody hadn't even been in our line of vision. I looked up to Keith's face and his eyes were cold again. They had lost their intensity, as if he, too, was coming to the conclusion that we weren't supposed to dance like that.

"I'm sorry. I need to look for Cody." It was the only thing that came to my mind. It seemed to be the wrong thing to say at the moment, because Keith's face turned to his usual and fake smirk.

"Sure. I just don't know if you're going to enjoy dancing with him after doing it with me." He crossed his arms, distancing himself from me even more. The way he'd said "doing it with me" sounded like it meant a lot more than dancing. I hated when he played the womanizer—it wasn't him.

"Oh, cool it, Keith. You didn't ruin me for other men." I crossed my arms, mimicking him, and feeling exposed in my lack of clothing.

He moved to get past me. "Yet," he whispered in my ear before going to the kitchen and leaving me in the middle of the crowd. How infuriating. If I was feeling restless before, now I was furious, with both Keith and his brother. I started looking for my boyfriend when Shelby jumped in front of me.

"Jane! I was looking for you, but, in this crowd, it's really difficult." She was slurring her words from the alcohol, I'm sure, and held a red cup in her hand, while gesturing around with the other. She was dressed as an angel in a short white dress and fake feather wings on her back. She sure was attracting attention from the guys around us.

"Hi," was my only answer. We couldn't talk over the music, so I dragged her to the side. "When did you arrive?"

"A while ago, but people kept interrupting my search for you and offering me drinks." She smiled and raised the cup for me to see. She meant guys had been interrupting her and offering her drinks, but I didn't correct her.

"Have you seen Keith? I was looking for him, but I haven't found him, yet." Shelby kept looking around and lifting to the tips of her toes, as if it would help her see better over the crowd. I didn't like that she'd come for him and not because we were friends, but I was already pissed at the only people I knew in this town, and I didn't want to add Shelby to the equation. I just shrugged. Maybe they would miss each other completely.

"Oh, there he is." She beamed. I peeked over my shoulder to where she was looking. He looked over at us and waved, smiling at Shelby. He was such a playboy, and it irritated the hell out of me. Shelby disappeared without a word to me, leaving me, once again, alone.

I found Cody snuggled against Alexis and went to claim my territory. I put a hand on his shoulder and whispered in his ear in the sexiest voice I could come up with, "Do you want to come upstairs?"

"Alexis doesn't know many people here. It would be rude, Jane."

My smile faded and a frown set upon my face. "Oh, sure. I'm going to grab a drink, then."

He grabbed my wrist after I turned away. "Don't drink too much. You're not used to it."

Could he humiliate me more? I couldn't believe he was telling me how to behave in front of his friend, as if I was a misbehaving child. I yanked my arm back and stomped to the stairs.

I was done with this party.

My outfit had gotten me nowhere. Cody hadn't been able to wait to jump my bones a couple of days ago, but, now, with Alexis here, he barely looked my way. Shelby had come to keep Keith company, and my brother was up against a wall, making out with a redhead. I wanted to call my mother for comfort. How childish was that?

I stepped around the mass of people, and it took five minutes just to get to my bedroom door. Before I could unlock it, Keith came out of the bathroom with a pleased smile on his face and Shelby trailing behind him. She winked at me before disappearing into his room.

My mouth was probably wide open, because he stopped in front of me, and, with his finger, tapped on my chin. "We don't want you eating a fly, now, do we?" I just stared at him, not believing that he would be so low as to go against what I'd asked and sleep with my friend. Shelby couldn't give a crap about me, but Keith? He turned before I could come up with something—anything—to deter him from going into his room and closing the door in my face.

His hand stilled on the doorknob. "Oh, and, Skylar, could you change?" He looked all over my body, almost disgusted, and made me shiver. "You look like a whore." After that, he went to his room and left me shaking with rage and embarrassment.

After opening my door and stepping into my sanctuary, I sat against the door and let a few tears run down my cheeks. Was that what Cody thought? Could he have lost his interest in me because I looked so easy tonight? That had been my point, exactly, but I guess it had backfired. I looked ridiculous now, but, not wanting to go out of my room still looking like this, I got up, yanked my clothes off, and went to my dresser. I took out my favorite sweatpants and a shirt, and put them on.

I caught my reflection in the wall mirror. My make-up was running down my face, making me look like a real monster. I had some make-up remover in a drawer, so I didn't have to go out into the hallway.

The black contact lenses were the last to come off. I still stared into the mirror for some time, wondering if I would feel so exposed if that was the real color of my eyes, and not the freakish light gray that stared at me every day. I snuggled under the covers with my childhood teddy bear as company. Everyone made me feel like a child, so what did it matter if I did something childish to make me feel better? Or, at least, to make me feel not so alone.

CHAPTER THIRTEEN

The next day, I woke up to sounds out in the hallway. I peeked through my key hole and saw Shelby leaving Keith's room and going down the stairs, heels in hand. Talk about the walk of shame.

If she wanted to catch something, I wouldn't be the one to deter her. I had already said enough about him as a warning.

I had seen this happen too often at our high school: girls thought they would have a one night stand with him and walk away without a scratch. That hadn't happened often, though.

They'd all wanted more.

Something he couldn't give: love.

I think he was incapable of loving someone. He had even stopped going home to visit his parents, and his relationship with his brother was strained, to say the least.

Love and Keith didn't mix.

I got up and went to the bathroom with some clean jeans and a green shirt, trying to not make a sound. I wanted to feel clean before facing the world.

When I stepped into the kitchen and saw that Keith was already up and standing next to the fridge with a cup of coffee in one hand, no shirt, and just-had-sex hair, I wondered if I could face my day without any food. I had two options: avoid my everyday tasks because of him, or not let him disrupt my life.

"Good morning, ray of sunshine." He understood that I was mad at him, and his sarcasm was turning my bad mood up a notch. I tried to avoid touching him when I went to take out the milk from the fridge, failing for a fraction of a second. I grabbed the cereal box and sat on a stool, ignoring him.

"Oh, someone seems to be in a bad mood. Didn't enjoy the party? It didn't look that way yesterday." He leaned over the counter, getting into my personal space. That personal space, when it came to Keith, was about a foot away, though.

"I am trying very hard not to acknowledge you at all. Believe me: it's for your own good," I whispered slowly, not lifting my eyes to meet his.

"Someone is in a bad mood. What? Didn't get laid?" He laughed.

The anger that had been consuming me since last night came boiling up, now. I stood and stepped in front of him. The smirk on his face was my downfall. I threw my arm back and slapped him so hard in the face that his head bounced back. He'd realized what I was about to do the second before my hand had collided with his skin, but he hadn't been fast enough to stop me.

I heard a couple of gasps behind me and turned to the door. Of course, my brother and Cody would be there to watch. They were so surprised at me that they didn't even move. Jane Keaton, the good girl who never hurt anything in her life had just slapped someone.

Keith was rubbing his face and frowning at me.

Ryan stepped forward and grabbed my elbow. "What the hell, Jane? What's gotten into you?"

I should have given an explanation—something to excuse me—like telling my brother and boyfriend that Keith had called me a whore yesterday and had just hinted at the same thing a couple of minutes ago, but I didn't.

I didn't know why. Why was I protecting him from their wrath? My inner excuse was that I didn't want Cody and Keith's relationship to get even more strained.

"I-I… need to go." I yanked my arm and ran out of the house, forgetting that I didn't have a car to drive.

The first of November was cold with freezing wind that knocked my breath away. I had forgotten my jacket, as well. Could Keith mess my life more than he already had?

I walked for a couple of hours around town, bought and ate a cupcake with the change in my pocket, and started walking back home. When I was at the beginning of the road that led to the house, rain started pouring.

"Great," I screamed at the sky. This was my punishment for slapping someone, even if that someone had offended me profoundly—even if that someone was now stepping out of his black car and walking toward me with one of my jackets in his closed fist.

When he reached me, I turned away and walked a couple of steps in the direction of the house. "Damn, Skylar," he muttered, grabbing my elbow just like my brother had done a few hours ago. I yanked back automatically, which made me lose my balance and fall into a mud puddle.

"Shit! Damn you!" I yelled. Another habit I was acquiring while at his house was yelling and swearing.

"You were the one pushing me." He grabbed my arm again and I shook off his hold. "Stop fighting. Let me help you." He forced his hold this time, not giving me a chance to run.

"You're hurting me," I whined.

He gave a dry laugh. "Well, you marked your pretty fingers on my face. We're even."

I looked up and there they were: the fading red marks on his cheek. "I'm sorry," I blurted before thinking. Understanding my mistake, I covered my mouth, frowning angrily.

This time, Keith did laugh out of amusement. "Yeah, I'm not sure if I'm accepting that apology because it did come from your heart, or if I'm not accepting because your mind wasn't in it." He directed me to his car and I almost apologized again because of the mess I was in. Clearly I was going to get it all dirty, and I had been in it before and had seen that he kept it almost obsessively clean.

"Put your jacket on, or you're going to get sick."

I didn't want to do a thing he asked of me, but I was kind of cold. I didn't have a choice, but to pretend he hadn't been the one reminding me of the fact it was freezing and that I was drenched in mud.

The short ride was quiet, of course, and I couldn't wait for us to get home so I could shower again and cuddle under my covers. The car had barely stopped and I already had one leg outside.

"Wait, please, Skylar." I jumped out and stopped by the door only because I didn't have my key. My pride took another nosedive. I turned to him, crossing my arms, but I didn't meet his eyes.

"Look at me." He stepped in front of me and caged my body with his arms. I looked up, warning him with a pointed look. He still had another side of his face for me to mark up. He held my face in his hands and my arms shot up, grabbing at his wrists to pull him off. I struggled for a second, but he made me step back, against the door and framed my face forcefully. I did look up and met his worried expression. What now?

"I'm sorry," he said, slowly, like I was a frightened animal. "If all you need is to slap me again, go ahead, but, please, forgive me for what I said yesterday. It was... uncalled for." He averted his eyes, then.

"'Uncalled for,' Keith?" I shook my head and he released me. "You offended me when I did nothing to deserve it. You were the one coming out of the bathroom, rearranging your clothes."

He nodded and looked away, sighing to the woods. "I know. I was an asshole and you're right: you shouldn't forgive me. It's better this way." He removed the key from his front pocket and turned for the door.

He went inside and left the door open for me. I took a second going inside and went to take a much-needed hot shower.

After putting on clean clothes and loading the washing mashing with the rest of the laundry, I went to my room. My brother and Cody had started yelling a couple of minutes ago, so I knew they were playing games in the living room. I had yet to talk to Cody, but he didn't seem interested, so I would put off that argument for another time. I was already exhausted. I just needed this weekend to go by quickly, and then classes could distract me.

The deadline for my art class portfolio was closing in and I had nothing worthy to show. If Keith wasn't such a pain, he could've helped me long ago and things would have been much more pleasant in this house.

This was all his fault, but the haunted look on his face when he apologized this afternoon was haunting me. He even made me feel guilty when he was the one in the wrong. I groaned and got up to search for him, but, of course, he would be in the damn attic. I knocked several times before he heard me. The music was so loud that I couldn't hear myself think.

He cracked the door open, not surprised that I was the one knocking. I think I was the only one who disrupted his time up there, because my brother and Cody had learned long ago that he didn't want to be bothered while working.

A smear of black coated half of his cheek, and I couldn't meet his eyes, so I focused on the paint. We stood for a full minute before I gathered the courage to say the words. They would come back to bite me in the ass, I knew. It was just a matter of time before he screwed up again.

"I still don't understand why you said what you said—hell, I can't understand you ninety percent of the time. But," I inhaled a full breath, "I forgive you. I still don't know why, but deep down, I forgive you." I raised my eyes to finally meet his. The dim light coming from inside cast shadows over his face, making him look more dangerous than I knew he was.

What I wouldn't give to have his eye color. The dark gray was much more appealing than mine.

"You shouldn't." Yes, I knew he would screw up again, but not so soon.

Was he making me work for the apology? I mean, for the forgiveness? What a mess. He was too complicated. As if he were reading my thoughts by my deep frown, he added, "I don't deserve it. I am screwed up, I will offend you again, and I will make you mad again. I don't want you to forgive me. I don't deserve that. What I said yesterday was to hurt you on purpose."

I stepped back on that one. What?

He winced at his own words. "I'm not good for you. Not a good friend, anyway. It's best if you hate me. It's easier that way."

"Easier for whom?" I asked, before I could comprehend what he was saying. I knew he'd hated me before, but I thought it had all stayed behind when I'd come to live here. "I thought you were going to help me with my drawings." That was my pathetic way of grasping for something left of our barely-existent friendship.

He scratched his forehead and sighed. "I won't leave you stranded. I will help you, if you still want. Then we go back to the ignoring each other. Agreed?"

No, but what could I say? I couldn't tell him I felt lonely and beg him to not be another friend to leave me behind. I shrugged and went to my room. He was completely right: he was complicated, and didn't deserve my forgiveness or friendship. So why did I feel like someone had punched me in the stomach?

The next day, my brother had work to do somewhere on campus. I think he was working on students' computers for money. I just hoped he hadn't gone to the hacking strategies he'd used to exploit in high school. That would get him in too much trouble in college.

Cody had lunch with me at home, but we barely talked. He didn't seem to think he owed me an apology. What he'd done was worse than what Keith had done, though.

Cody was my boyfriend: he had some kind of responsibility when it came to me. I didn't say anything, though. Apparently I had become kind of numb.

He kissed me goodbye, saying that he would probably crash at one of his friends, because they had to gather to study for one of his classes.

This would be my life if we got married: me, miserably alone at the house, while he worked as a lawyer on other people's problems. Even criminals would come before me.

I curled up on the couch, watching a sappy Saturday movie on TV. A few tears escaped my eyes at the story. It was so stupid, but, at the same time, so sad. Maybe I was depressed—that could be the case.

"What happened?" Keith sat on the couch next to me, with a worried expression on his face. I just shrugged at the TV and he turned and watched for a couple of minutes.

"This is crap. Are you crying over the movie?" His incredulous tone said everything. He wouldn't have bothered sitting and worrying if he'd known I was upset over a stupid movie.

He clapped his hands, which made me jump. "Well, you need to work on your drawings and I promised you I would help. How do you want to do this?"

"I don't know. You would be posing for me, right? I want you to keep your underwear on. I can't work here, in the living room, and the attic is off limits, so…" I trailed off.

"We can work in your room. It's a place you feel comfortable in and that's important. You need to find a place where you can lose yourself. I'm free now, and apparently you are, too." He turned to the TV, on which the credits were rolling.

I got up from the couch slowly, as if I was the one doing a favor for the other.

I gathered my art supplies from my desk and sat on the chair. "Where do you want to sit?"

"I was thinking we could do a simple pose—natural, like it's not forced. That way, it would be easier for you. I can keep my pants on for now. I'll take the shirt off, because you need to work on the muscles." He winked, knowing he was appraising his own body.

With one hand, he gathered up his shirt and pulled it over his head. He sat on the edge of the bed, still thinking about the best way to pose.

"Wait." I'd just had an idea. I picked up the shirt and gave it to him.

He looked confused. "Are you backing off, because I can—"

I shook my head. "No, no, pick up the shirt and let it dangle from your hand. Look down to the floor, like you're thinking, and grab the edge of the shirt in a closed fist. Hunch your back a little, and let your left arm rest on your leg at the elbow, with your hand facing in." I liked the way he was responding to my commands. I just needed one more thing to accomplish my goal. I sighed and he looked up, without moving his body, questioning me with his eyes. "Now think about the way you apologized to me yesterday." His frown deepened. Good: he should have been confused. I was a confusing artist.

"You looked..." I blushed, because I didn't want to voice what I thought about his expression. "You looked pained. That's it," I finally said, frustrated. I paced the room and turned the music to one of the latest bands I was listening to. It wasn't angry music, but it was disturbed enough to set the right mood.

Keith was still looking at me, confused, but then a brief light came to his eyes and he nodded, as if he understood.

I knew now that Keith understood me better than anyone else. He looked at the ground and turned his face to the same expression I'd seen yesterday at the door, when he apologized. I picked up the pencil and started outlining his features. Then I detailed from the torso up, and then to his legs.

Everything came to me easily: every stroke, every time I looked up, some mix of anger and forgiveness came to me, taking up my arm, my hand, and my fingers.

When I finished, I took a last look down and then up to him. He hadn't moved an inch, but his expression had softened over time. To anyone else, he probably looked the same, but, to me, it was obvious he wasn't thinking about the same he had been thinking yesterday.

I took my time examining his tattoos. I hadn't drawn them, which is what my professor had advised in class. It would have been too time-consuming for me and tiring for him. They were a piece of art, themselves. The dragon was amazing, and I bet it had taken him several sittings to get it done. It had probably hurt like hell, too.

He had some other smaller tattoos: some ancient scribbling on his chest, arms, and back. The only one in English was over his heart, and read: "The more you love, the greater the harm." A shiver went up my spine. Had someone hurt him—a girl, perhaps? I had never seen Keith in love, though. I opened my mouth to ask, but thought otherwise. It was too personal, even if he showed it to anyone who would like to see him naked.

"I'm done," I said, my voice rougher from being quiet for so long. I looked over to the clock and saw it was six in the evening. He had posed for me for almost two hours. The movements had come to me so easily that I'd never noticed the time passing. His neck popped when he moved, which made him wince.

"I'm sorry. I didn't realize I'd been drawing for two hours." I rotated my wrist, but it didn't hurt, at all. The movements came so easily that I never stiffened my muscles. I flowed lightly over the paper.

"No problem. Want to show me?" His voice was also rough. He almost looked sleepy and I couldn't blame him. He must've been tired.

Suddenly, I didn't want to show him the drawing. I looked down, while he got up to stretch. It was good, but it seemed to be too personal, all of a sudden. I couldn't understand why, so when he leaned over my sketch pad, I let him, and turned the paper to him.

My breathing stopped while he studied my work. I didn't know until that moment that his opinion mattered—a lot. What if he said I had no talent? This was one of the best drawings I'd ever made, so if he said right then that it wasn't good, I was going to cry for sure—and give up on my art career.

Keith, being Keith, couldn't make it easy for me. He stepped back and sat on the bed with the sketch pad on his lap.

He took so long studying my drawing that my heart started beating faster. Was he about to crush my dream and say what my father had been stating all these years: that my career shouldn't be in art?

His face showed no emotion, good or bad. When he looked up and locked his eyes with mine, never saying a word and sighing deeply, my beating heart dropped to the floor.

Was I strong enough to keep trying, or was I too stupid for thinking about it? This was, after all, my professor's favorite student. He was all she'd dreamed about in a student. If I couldn't please him, I would never please her.

"It's good," he finally said, and that confirmed my suspicions. He was too kind to kick me when I was down, but Keith wasn't usually kind. I looked up, searching for something else in his gaze. What I found confused me. It was the same look from yesterday. He hadn't done it right while I was drawing—it should have been deeper, like it was right now. I hadn't captured all of it in my drawing, because he hadn't given me all of it.

Suddenly, I felt angry. It wasn't that bad. I stood up and crossed my arms. "You don't need to be sympathetic. I can take the truth. Honestly, I thought it was good."

He looked around, confused. "I just said—"

"That it was good, I know, but the way you're looking at me says otherwise. Tell me the truth. That's what Elizabeth is going to do when I show her this." I nodded at the pad, mad at myself for not being good enough.

I was never good enough. Not for my parents, not for my friends, not for my boyfriend, and, now, not even for Keith.

"Sky, stop." I opened my mouth to continue with my rambling, but he jumped up, letting my drawing fall to the bed. He grabbed my shoulder to turn me to him. "It's amazing." I rolled my eyes and struggled to get loose. "Look at me. Look at me."

I turned to him, annoyed, but stopped fidgeting in his hold. He was serious: he liked it. He almost seemed conflicted about it.

"You poured everything into it. What I feel, what you feel…" He let go of my shoulders, leaving me more confused.

"That's absurd. I don't know what you feel, because you seem to be carved out of stone. Your expressions are always so guarded. And me? I felt nothing, I was just drawing." As soon as the words were out of my mouth, I knew they weren't true. I had felt something: exhilaration, peace, anger, and forgiveness, all in one. He knew it. I knew he'd seen each of my emotions all over my stupid, pale eyes. I was so easy to read, and had been all my life. I wished I could be more guarded, like him.

"We both know that's not true. This," he pointed at the bed, "is what you need to do all the time you're drawing. Don't detach yourself. Make your heart pour onto the canvas—or paper, as in this case."

"Oh, right?" I laughed sarcastically. "Is that what you do? I would love to see your paintings, then." I crossed my arms, probably to protect whatever sanity was left in me.

Keith's expression changed drastically. He almost looked panicked, which just increased my curiosity. Was he guarding his emotions just to pour them into his art? I had seen some of his work, and he worked with landscapes and abstract, mostly.

That was something I didn't understand. Professor Collins said he was one of her best students and we drew mostly human form. If he was so good at that, why had he resorted to inanimate objects? That was another of Keith's mysteries to add to the huge pile.

"If it's that good, how come you look so disappointed?" I asked, lowering my arms to hug my stomach.

He sighed and shook his head. "I'm not disappointed. I'm surprised."

I laughed dryly. "Oh, now you tell me you didn't think I was capable of—"

"No, you're putting words in my mouth," he interrupted me. "I knew you were good. I've seen your work all these years." He winced, as if that had been too much information. It kind of had been—I'd always thought he'd ignored me. "I never thought you could read me like this." He picked up the pad from the bed and studied for another minute. He had to have been kidding. Me? Reading him? He was like a motionless rock when it came to feelings. I never knew what to expect. Maybe, this time, he'd let me in, but it was a one-time event.

We gave up on our argument to cook something for dinner. Now that the artistic time was over, my bodily needs, like going to the bathroom and eating, were coming back. We didn't talk much, and just said what was necessary to help one another around the kitchen. Keith had made it perfectly clear that he didn't want anything to do with me. No friendship— just a little mentorship in art.

"You still need to work on your nude portraits." I had just taken my first bite and his statement made me choke. Of course, he had to laugh. "Exactly. You need to feel comfortable drawing human form, in any form, clothes on or off."

I placed the fork down on my plate. "I'm not drawing you naked, Keith Hale." He smirked at me.

"You wish, baby." He joked with Cody's term of endearment. "I would start by drawing you."

"What? No. No way am I going to—"

"No, I don't mean me drawing you, not that it's not a pleasant thought, but I was talking about you drawing your own body. Stand in front of the mirror and sketch yourself. You wouldn't be the first self-portrait in the history of art. You are comfortable with your image, so it's a start. After that, you should really draw someone else." He turned his attention to his food and I tried to do the same.

He was right, though: I needed to work on nude portraits, and who better to start with than myself? I just needed to hide it well after it was done.

The next afternoon, I was lying on my bed, staring at the white ceiling and thinking about Keith's words. I should have started working on my self-portrait. After making sure the door was locked—twice—I took all of my clothes off and turned the lamp on, casting a dim light over the bedroom, like in Keith's drawing from yesterday.

It took me almost half an hour to find the best position, but I was pleased with the outcome. I sat on the floor, with a comforter between me and the hardwood floor, and a body length mirror in front of me against the wall. One of my legs was bent and the other was on the floor. I wouldn't make the drawing pad disappear—on the contrary, I was going to make the fact that I was drawing myself the main theme of the portrait, like Keith's pained expression from yesterday.

The most I would be revealing of my body would be my naked breasts. The rest was covered by a slight twist of my bent leg.

My drawing took as long as Keith's and I'd gotten to the place where I could focus on my work and forget the entire world. The music coming from my phone was the only thing that poured into my brain here and there, when a song I really related to played.

When I was pleased with the outcome, I dressed in a robe and sat on the bed, staring at it. After staring long enough, I turned the page back to the previous one and ripped Keith's drawing out to place it on the bed next to mine.

Something in them related to each other, not only because they were both made by me, but because some of the hollow vibe I'd gotten from Keith was present in my eyes, too. I had never noticed it before.

CHAPTER FOURTEEN

had always been a happy person—not outgoing or exuberant, but optimistic and smiley, even with the ever-present pressure my parents exercised over me.

I was the middle child: the one they'd thought was salvageable. My brother had always been a trouble maker who had never gotten good grades, and who'd had detention every other day. It had come as a surprise when he'd received a couple of college acceptance letters.

Ryan was only good with computers, and my parents were the kind of people who still thought computers would get you nowhere, no matter how many millionaires they saw on TV who got rich from them.

Matilda, our little sister, was Ryan's female version. She'd gotten into trouble as often as he had, and, being a girl, got on my father's nerve every day. She was his little girl no matter what—his youngest—while my brother was his only son. This left me, literally, in the middle. I didn't feel less loved, but I'd always worked harder for their love.

My brother and sister had received attention every day—almost never for a good reason. They had been such troublemakers that, no matter how many As I'd earned, or how many recommendations letters I'd received from teachers, it was never enough to get their attention on me. It didn't help that I hadn't had their talent to connect with people, captivate everyone around them, or make friends with a simple greeting.

My father was just waiting for me to fail my art classes so he could convince me to go to medical school. He thought this was my rebellious phase and he was giving me a semester to get it out of my system—his words. I was supposed to think about a way to earn money from my work, even before the end of the year. At this rate, I wasn't even sure I would pass my Representational Drawing class.

What had turned Keith, though? Had it been his father's indifference toward him? I knew how much that could hurt, not that my father had been indifferent toward me. On the contrary, his pressure for me to always be better had almost been asphyxiating. I never thought that Carl could favor Cody over Keith, as they had always been so different from each other. One was all shine and light and the other was dark and mysterious. They were even different in their appearances.

I left the drawings, got dressed, and went to see if either my brother or Cody had arrived, yet. They crossed the door at the same time, shaking the rain from their coats and laughing. The scene gave me a ray of hope: this was my family now, at least while I was in college.

"Hi, guys," I said, rubbing one foot against the other to keep them warm. Walking with only socks on my feet when, outside, it was freezing, wasn't smart, but I had always been a sucker for walking with only socks on my feet.

"Hi, baby." Cody hugged me gently, trying not to get me wet, and placed a light kiss on my lips, which made Ryan grumble.

"Watch it, Hale."

Cody rolled his eyes, still hugging my waist. "Oh, come on. That was the chastest kiss ever."

Ryan threw his coat over the couch, not bothered by the water seeping into the fabric, and jumped to the next one. "She's my sister: even if she was in a convent, it wouldn't be chaste enough."

I laughed at that one. It was so true. Curiously, with Matilda, he didn't get so bothered. Maybe he was so used to her being friendly with boys that he didn't mind, anymore.

There was something warm in the look he gave me that made me jump to his lap and hug his neck. Maybe it was because I missed home so much. "I love you, Ry. You know that, don't you?"

He laughed and hugged me back. "What's the matter? Are you PMSing or something?"

I slapped his chest. "Can't your sister tell you 'I love you' without you thinking it's period-related?" I jumped before he could hug me again.

Okay, sentimental moment over. It just got on my nerves when he thought every emotion I felt was related to that time of the month. If I was mad, sad, or emotional, it didn't matter. Come on.

"Everything about you chicks is period-related." Of course, that statement could only come from Keith, who was coming down the stairs, still pulling a shirt over his torso.

"I don't want you walking around the house naked with my sister here." By Ryan's tone, he wasn't joking. He didn't even use the bored voice he'd used earlier with Cody's kiss. This time, he was serious, and Keith knew it. He waited for Cody to sit next to my brother, focused on the TV, to silently laugh. I smiled, too—it wasn't possible not to. I had drawn him naked in front of a class. If Ryan and Cody found out, all hell would break loose.

I almost forgot to reply to Keith's comment, but a comeback surged. "And everything with you guys is dick-related." I turned and went to the kitchen, laughing at the cough my brother couldn't hold back.

I started taking ingredients from the fridge, almost missing Keith's approach. I should have been used to him helping around the house, unlike Cody or Ryan.

"What's for dinner today?" He propped himself against the counter, crossing his legs at the ankles.

"I was thinking homemade lasagna. What do you think?" I looked over my shoulder, watching him grin and nod in approval. I turned to the task at hand and smiled, pleased with his appreciation. I wasn't a professional cook—not by a long shot—but I could manage alright in the kitchen.

After we ate, I was given several minutes of praise over the food from all three boys, which made my ego grow an inch or two. It was good, and they complained that I didn't make enough to have thirds. I swear I didn't know how they could eat that much and not get fat.

Cody helped me wash the dishes, surprising me with his loving glances and kisses. I was still mad with what he did on Halloween but, when he invited me to go watch a movie upstairs, I couldn't say no. After all, I was always complaining about the lack of time he had for me. When I got to my bedroom door, though, I remembered the two drawings on my bed. It wouldn't sit well with my boyfriend to see his naked girlfriend beside his brother's almost-naked body. Even if they were on different sheets, they were both made in the same room: mine.

"Let's go to yours today," I suggested. He looked surprised, but shrugged and walked in front of me.

His bedroom was a mess and the bed wasn't even made. At least he felt sheepish. "Sorry. This is a guy's room, you know."

Cody threw me to the bed, stood over me, and kissed my neck. I should have still felt mad about Alexis, but I couldn't gather the passion to fight when Cody was trying to make up for lost time.

It was that pathetic. I couldn't find the passion to fight, just like I couldn't feel that tightness in my belly I'd used to feel in the past. I loved Cody, but I was starting to believe I wasn't in love with him, anymore. That thought scared me endlessly.

He was part of my plan—my plan of living in this city, in this house, and majoring in art. If I lost him, I would probably lose everything else.

After the movie ended, I decided it was time to go to bed—alone. Cody groaned and rolled in his bed, but never got up to say goodnight. On Friday night, I would have gone all the way with him. I'd felt brave, even though I was mad because of Alexis. Tonight there wasn't enough passion—love or hatred—to get me in the mood.

I brushed my teeth in the bathroom and dragged my feet across the hallway, noticing my bedroom door was cracked open. A dim light cast under the door. I hurried the rest of the way and shoved the door open.

Keith was standing next to my bed, with his back to me, staring at both drawings.

"Keith, what the hell are you doing here?"

He jumped and turned to me, looking guilty. "Sorry. I came here to tell you something, and…" He looked down to my neck and turned his head. I buttoned up the two buttons that Cody had undone and crossed my arms over my chest before remembering I was in my own bedroom: he was the one who should leave.

I scooted both drawings and placed them inside the sketch pad. Keith hadn't moved. He'd only turned when I groaned out of embarrassment and eagerness for him to leave.

"Your portrait—it's really good," he whispered. If I didn't know better, I would say he was embarrassed. When he turned around to face me, I saw a little blush over his cheeks, but also some darkness in his eyes, as if he wanted to say more. We had a staring contest for a minute before the pressure inside me became too much.

"You should've knocked. Leave." I crossed my arms again.

"I did knock. I didn't know you were with my brother." That condescending and disgusted tone had gotten on my last nerve. He had no right to feel upset.

"I'm not a little girl, anymore, despite what you and Ryan think. I'm eighteen."

"I know, believe me," he snickered, rubbing some invisible dirt on my floor with the toe of his black sneakers. "Your drawing is really good, as I said. You should show it to Elizabeth."

I jumped to my feet. "No way am I showing this to anyone. I'm already mortified that you saw—" I clapped my hand over my mouth. He wasn't supposed to know that. His usual smirk was his answer. Of course he would enjoy my shyness.

"You shouldn't," was his only answer, before leaving me standing in the middle of the room, wondering about the meaning of his statement.

That was one very restless night. I kept waking up, turning, and dreaming about Cody and then Keith. I kind of woke up feeling grumpy. I didn't say good morning to anyone in the kitchen the next morning, which granted me a lifted eyebrow from Ryan. I had always been the polite one, obeying all the rules, including acknowledging people.

"Morning, sis. Ready for school?"

"Ugh," was my answer, while I poured milk all over my hand and cereal on the counter. In a few minutes, I would be losing toothpaste to the sink and stumbling on the stairs, for sure. This was going to be one of those days.

"Keith, will you give Jane a ride? I have a test in a few minutes and I'm already late." Cody didn't even ask me. After a quick kiss, he left the house without waiting for his brother's answer.

"Sure, little brother, I have nothing else to do," Keith said to the empty living room.

Ryan chuckled beside him, but said nothing. He didn't even offer me a ride. He patted Keith on the back and kissed my temple before following Cody.

"Guess it's just the two of us," he said, picking up my empty bowl and rinsing it. My face must've been so surprised that he laughed out loud. "Don't be that surprised, Keaton. Not all men are pigs."

"Keaton? That's your new name for me?" I felt a little sting of pain—I would miss being called Sky.

"Nope," he brushed against my side. I was sure he was about to shoot his good deed out the window with some remark. "You will always be my Sky." He left to his room, probably to brush his teeth and pick up his books, although I never saw him carry anything to his classes.

I sat on the stool for a minute longer than I needed to, thinking about his words. I should have felt outraged by his assumptions, but I wasn't. I caught my reflection in the living room mirror when I went by it, and a smile was plastered on my face.

This wasn't good—I knew that smile. I'd seen it before in dozens of faces. I tried to keep thinking about all the times he'd been a jerk to me. He had called me a whore two days ago and now I felt giddy with his sweet words?

I didn't see Shelby that day. I needed to confront her about Keith and advise her, somehow, that he wasn't someone who she should be having a relationship with. I didn't even know if he was capable of such a thing.

Professor Collins critiqued all my drawings, but today I wasn't even making an effort, so I didn't blame her. I still had the feeling of worry at the bottom of my stomach. About what, I had no idea.

That afternoon, I ended up staying late in one of the classrooms, talking about a group project. Cody had texted me around seven to tell me he was staying in the library, so I decided to surprise him there to see if he could drive me home. It was late and dark outside: not a good combination for an empty campus.

I was crossing the patio that lead to the library when my phone started ringing. It was my common ringtone, so I knew right away that it wasn't home, Ryan, or Cody. I took a couple of seconds to decide if I wanted to search in my backpack for my phone.

Since it kept ringing, I decided it was better to get it over with than to keep receiving calls in the library. I paused in front of the door, phone in hand, wondering what Keith wanted.

"Hi," I answered.

"Sky, I got home a few minutes ago and you're not here." He sounded upset—demanding, even. Since when did he start checking my schedule?

"Keith, I don't owe you an explanation." I leaned against a wall, willing the call to end, as it was too cold to be outside any longer.

"I-I wasn't demanding…" I heard him groan on the other side. I could

145

just picture his hand messing up his hair impatiently. "I was worried." It might've taken him some years of his life to say something sweet like that. I softened a little.

"Okay, I'm at the library. I was just saying hello to Cody and asking him for a ride home."

"He texted me an hour ago saying he was staying there. I'll pick you up." There was such finality on his part that I didn't have the courage to say no. If he wanted to bother driving all the way here, I wasn't going to complain. Cody would, so this would make for less of an argument for us. I ended the call and went in search of my boyfriend.

I found his friends at one table, talking in whispered voices, but I could sense it wasn't work-related. Cody wasn't there, but, in one of the empty chairs sat his coat—the one I had given him last Christmas. I smiled and turned to search for him in the aisles. I didn't know his friends, so going to them to ask for him would make me sound like too much of a clingy girlfriend, even though I wasn't one—not by a long shot.

I turned the corner and jumped back. Cody was leaning against the books and Alexis was all over him, with her hands on his shoulders and a pleading look on her face. I should have run to them and tackled her to the floor, but I did nothing. I wanted to see Cody's reaction.

"Alex, stop. You know we can't." His voice was barely a whisper, but, in the silent library, my ears caught every word they were exchanging. "I have a—"

"Girlfriend," she answered, with a disgusted voice, as if they'd had this argument before. I didn't like that, at all. "I know. It didn't stop you last time."

I stumbled against the shelves and they looked around. They didn't see me, however, because the books were hiding me completely. "It was a mistake." He sounded like he didn't want it to have been a mistake.

"Don't tell me I was a mistake."

He silenced her. "Not you, but sleeping with you was a mistake. We should get back to the table."

The blood in my body had frozen me in place. I couldn't move a muscle. When they turned the corner and Cody's eyes met mine, I did something I was so used to doing: stayed quiet when someone was stomping all over me.

Cody looked so panicked. He'd thought I would never find out. He had been hoping for it.

"Jane, God, you heard…" He scratched the back of his head in a way that wasn't so different from his brother. "Alexis, go." He stood between us, like I would turn into a cat and scratch her. I wished I was capable of that. I wished, at that moment, that I was one of those people who could scream and make a scene anywhere. That way, I could humiliate him in front of his friends and probably ban him from the library. I wasn't one of those people, though. My mother had taught me well.

I crossed my arms and faced him, waiting for the excuses to start.

"I'm so sorry. It happened just once, I promise you. Jane, don't hate me. I love you."

Those three words woke me up, as if a lightning bolt had descended upon my body. I jumped back, hitting the shelves behind me.

"Don't ever tell me that. Never again." I was consumed by hate. The tears hadn't even started, yet. It was better this way: hating him was much easier than hurting.

He went for my arm, but I stepped aside again. I was disgusted by his touch.

I had almost slept with him—I had almost lost my virginity to him—and the bastard had cheated on me. I had thought for a long time that we were it, forever.

"Don't say that, baby, please." He had the decency to look ashamed, hurt, and apologetic. A tear was forming in the corner of his eye. Yeah, he loved me, alright, but he'd betrayed me in the most horrible way I could think of. Even if, one day, I would be capable of forgiving him, I would never be able to forget. This moment would chase us forever.

"Don't call me that, ever. It's over, Cody." I gulped, trying to block out my own tears.

He shook his head and tried to reach for my arm again. "No, Jane, you're upset right now. Let's talk." People were starting to look our way. Some were annoyed we were interrupting their study time, while others were intrigued by our argument.

"No. I need to be alone." I ran outside, ignoring his pleading. After bumping into someone and even gathering my voice to apologize, I pushed the door open and ran to the road. Only then did I remember Keith's ride offer. He was probably around campus, waiting for me.

I wanted to be alone, but I couldn't let my argument with Cody get in the way of my safety. A car stopped by my side and I looked quickly to the driver to confirm that it was Keith.

I threw the door open and jumped into the seat.

"You should've waited outside the library, not started walking along the road. Do you know how dangerous—"

He stopped talking when my sobbing reached his ears.

"Skylar, talk to me. Did someone hurt you?"

Keith was slowing down the car and I managed to tell him to go somewhere, but not home. He just nodded and stopped questioning me. He'd probably discerned the truth: that I'd had a fight with Cody.

He stopped in a clearing on the outskirts of the forest that surrounded the house and turned off the car, facing me. He respected my silence.

Was it normal that Keith's presence helped, even when I wanted to be alone so badly? He felt like home.

A depressing song came up on the radio, and Keith asked me if I wanted him to change stations. I shook my head. I brought my knees to my chest and hugged them tightly. The tears came down almost instantly when the lyrics mentioned pain.

I was feeling pain, alright.

When my breathing slowed, I heard Keith's low voice singing the lyrics.

I turned to face him, placing my cheek on my bent knee, and stopped crying while he murmured the song. I wanted someone to take it all away, but knew it wasn't possible. I knew I would have to suffer for a long time before everything would be less painful.

Cody was a big part of my life. The betrayal was too deep. I knew I hadn't been a good girlfriend. We'd been apart for too long. But cheating? If someone had asked me a couple months ago, I would have placed my hand over fire before ever thinking he could do something so cruel to me.

He had been my first love, my only love, my best friend, and now my roommate. How was I going to face him now? Keith must've sensed my panic, because he touched my elbow, making me wince.

"I don't…" My voice felt strange in my throat, as if I had been screaming for hours. "I can't live there, anymore, with him."

"Are you going to tell me what happened?" he asked. I shook my head vigorously. I didn't want to voice the words out loud. Cody had cheated on me. Even in my head, the words hurt so much. I closed my eyes tightly, trying to erase the last hour. If I pretended it didn't happen—no, I couldn't. I couldn't be one of those girls who pretended not to see what their boyfriends did when they turned their backs.

"Well, if you want him gone, just say the word."

My head snapped up. "What?"

He looked out the window to the trees around us and shrugged. "I already told you: the house is mine. I say who lives there."

I was appalled. "You would choose someone you are not even friends with over your brother?" My voice came out too high-pitched and coated with astonishment, while I turned to face him. I waited for a reply, which came a couple of minutes later.

"If he hurt you in any way, then yes, I would choose you over him." He raised his eyes to meet mine and looked sheepish, as if that had been too much information. I didn't have a doubt it was true, though. If I told him about what had happened with Cody, he would turn his back on his brother.

Why? I had no idea.

And Ryan? Oh, Ryan would kick Cody from here to the next century. He'd warned me endless times before. He told Cody on a daily basis that, if he hurt me, he wouldn't live to see the next day. I didn't believe he would hurt Cody too much, but he would absolutely beat him up and ask Keith to kick him out. One thing I'd learned over the years was that Keith had a much brotherly relationship with Ryan than with his real brother.

I couldn't do this to them. Right now, I hated Cody with a passion, but one thing I treasured most was family, and Keith was his family. I would do anything to protect their fragile bond.

"We," I stammered, thinking quickly for an excuse. "We had a fight. It was no one's fault." I had to stop there to gulp some air. That lie had hurt so much to utter. "We broke up." A single tear escaped my eye and rolled down my cheek.

"I'm sorry, Jane." He was sincere but that name on his lips seemed wrong. It was as if he were talking about someone else.

My eyes shot up. "Don't call me Jane. It's weird." I winced.

Keith laughed, making me smile slightly. "Now you think it's weird? It's your name."

I fidgeted on the seat. I wanted to be honest about something in our conversation. "Yeah, but not for you," I whispered. It was my turn to look out into the woods. "I kind of got used to your nickname, although I have no idea why you started it, other than to get on my nerves. No one calls me Skylar. Most people don't even know that's my middle name."

He opened and closed his mouth a couple of times before honestly answering my question. "When I met you, I looked into your eyes and the first thought that popped in my head, before I shoved you to the ground, of course," he winced, "was that your eye color was just like the sky, when it's clear and you can sense a storm approaching, but it's not there, yet."

I nodded, even though I had no idea what he was talking about. I was still mesmerized that his first thought of me had been about my eyes: a part of myself I didn't really appreciate.

"I don't like my eyes," I answered, not sure why I was sharing such an intimate thought with him, of all people. He looked surprised, which made me laugh again. At least he could take my mind off Cody.

He was still shaking his head when he asked why I had such a dislike for something everyone seemed to find attractive.

"It's not that I find them ugly, it's just… they weird me out. How can they not weird other people out? They're so light that I feel conscious of them when someone stares, and people do that a lot." I looked at him sideways, daring him to correct me.

Keith kept shaking his head, and started the car to get the heating system on. "People stare because they're beautiful, not weird. They envy your eyes, Sky."

I was mute after that. Beautiful—my mother had always called me beautiful. Cody had frequently called me beautiful. Even some of my friends had done so. Keith Hale called me beautiful, when his only adjectives for women had used to be "hot," "smoking," and some other words I dared not to pronounce, I'd heard them all, but "beautiful" wasn't among them. Should I have felt special, or was he just trying to make me feel better? For the rest of the way to our house, I pondered both hypotheses.

Keith opened the door for me when I didn't jump right out—and not because he's a gentlemen, because he was not. I had to remind myself on a daily basis, or, as of recently, on an hourly basis.

I hugged my arms to keep me warm and shook my head when Keith offered his jacket. After all, we were only ten steps from the front door.

"Don't confront Cody, okay? I will talk to him tomorrow." I wanted to talk to my ex-boyfriend before he could talk to Ryan or Keith. I shivered at the thought of Cody being my ex.

I didn't want to cry more in front of Keith, so I said a quick goodnight and skipped the stairs two at a time.

I didn't even bother taking my clothes off: I just snuggled under the covers, hugging Mr. Teddy, and cried myself to sleep.

CHAPTER FIFTEEN

Cody kept calling my cell every hour that night, including at two in the morning. I got up from the bed and turned my phone off. I didn't want to talk to him this soon, especially not on the phone. Was he stupid? He didn't even bother to come home to see if I was okay.

The next day, I woke without any desire to get up. I wanted to stay under the covers and ignore the world outside, but Keith didn't let me. He came to my room with a glass of milk and a French toast and sat on my bed, removing the protection of the covers from over my head.

"Ugh," I mumbled, peeking over the green cover. "I'm sick. Not going to school."

Keith chuckled and pulled the cover off of me. His smile dropped when he saw I was still in yesterday's clothes. "I'm not your mother. I know all the excuses to not go to school. Breaking up is not one of them."

It was my time to freeze. I hadn't thought about Cody since I'd opened my eyes. I didn't have a boyfriend, anymore. Four years ago, this wouldn't have bothered me at all. I had never been one of those girls who couldn't live without a guy hanging on her arm. But now, having lost the only boyfriend I'd ever had hurt like hell. It wasn't that I wanted to get another one, though: I didn't imagine I would be thinking much about guys in the near future.

Guys wouldn't look at me, anyway, especially here, where I was still Ryan's little sister, Keith's best friend's little sister, and Cody's ex.

Guys had codes. They wouldn't come knocking on my door any time soon. I was destined to be a virgin forever.

Keith shoved the food to me. "Come on. Today, you'll have the exceptional opportunity of drawing me in class."

My bugging eyes made him laugh. "Now I'm not even going to get up. No way!"

He shoved the toast into my mouth. "Yes way. Don't be a baby. Try to think of this as a way to get back at Cody. You'll be drawing his hot brother." He wiggled his eyebrows.

I snorted. "He wouldn't know, so it's not a good way to get back at him." I shrugged.

"Do you have reasons to get back at him?" he asked, serious all of a sudden. He was fishing for more information on our breakup.

I ate quickly before pushing him out of my room. "If you stop asking questions, I'll go to class." His weak smile didn't reach his eyes. Keith claimed that he didn't want to be my friend, but he kept placing his nose in stuff that was none of his business.

I wanted to cry again, but, right now, I was still so mad that I just wanted to do what Keith said: get back at him. What better way than to use his own poison? I just needed to find a guy who wouldn't cower before Ryan, Keith, or Cody. Where the hell was I going to find him?

At least my plans kept my mind working, until Keith and I reached the classroom. Now I was panicking again about drawing Keith naked. I just needed to pretend that we were at home, with him sitting on the bed, dressed, like the last time.

Professor Collins greeted Keith as she always did: with a kiss on each cheek. This time, she looked over at me, as if to grasp my reaction—like I would have any reaction, at all. She probably thought I wasn't immune to his charms, like everyone else. I shrugged involuntarily and stormed to my stool. I just wanted this class to be over.

The teacher made Keith pose with his clothes on and we had to create quick drawings in succession. It was good for us to manage our time, she said. My sheet looked like a blur at the end. Most of the drawings were unfinished. I couldn't possibly understand how this would help us, but she looked pleased with the outcome.

Keith smiled at me when he got down from the table and started my way. I must've looked around, panicked, because he frowned, following my eyes. He shrugged, believing I had no reason to feel embarrassed, and continued to my easel. I closed the sketch pad and we both silently fought for a hold on it.

"Not here, please," I mumbled when he'd won the sketch pad.

Keith ignored me and inspected my work, not giving any hint about what he thought. How he could say I read him well, I had no idea. I couldn't read him, at all.

"They're good. You just need to work on the time, though. If you know you just have a couple of minutes, you need to take advantage of that. Don't worry about the details: grasp the whole picture and draw light, vague traces of what you see. Get it? I can pose for you at home, so you can practice."

I didn't think he meant to say it so loudly, or to embarrass me even more, but every ear in the room had caught the last part, and almost everyone snorted. I felt my cheeks burning with the spreading blush. He looked confused, first at my face, and then, as if he'd woken up and realized we weren't alone, he looked around.

Everyone shut up immediately. Even Professor Collins busied herself with the papers on her desk, maybe not wanting to displease her favorite model and lose the opportunity to gawk at a twenty one year old, hot, naked body a few times a year.

I would have felt proud, if it wasn't for the fact that everyone though Keith would be posing naked for me later, in the privacy of our house.

I gathered my stuff and almost ran out the door. It took Keith a minute to catch up to me.

"Wait, Skylar." He grabbed my arm as soon as he reached me and spun me around to face him.

"I'm sorry. I didn't mean it like that."

I shook my head to clear the air. "Never mind, they're just stupid. I don't have a boyfriend, anymore, so I shouldn't even feel guilty for drawing you naked," I said bravely. Keith looked confused with my outburst and he shook his head.

"Why does that have anything to do with me posing for you?"

I shrugged and kept walking, while he trailed along, still waiting for an answer. That's when we bumped into Shelby and it couldn't have been more awkward. Keith froze beside me, while Shelby gave him her most endearing smile. Here we go.

"Keith, it's good meeting you here. You didn't call..." she trailed off, playing with a strand of hair.

"Sorry, Sarah," he apologized. Ouch.

"Shelby," she corrected, letting her smile drop. A frown set in on her forehead.

"I think I lost your number." Keith placed his hands inside his pockets and shrugged, uncomfortable. By Shelby's face, I could tell she was about to yell from here to next week.

"Shelby, I need to talk to you. It's kind of important. Can you leave this conversation for another time?" I played with my bag while managing to keep hold of the sketch pad.

She turned to me, almost as if she had forgotten I was there, and her expression softened. "Jane, what happened? You look terrible."

That wasn't what friends were supposed to say when you were feeling down, but I guessed she was taking my still-bloodshot eyes, dark circles, and pale skin as signs that I wasn't feeling well.

Keith took the opportunity to flee to the parking lot, probably to go home. I still didn't know what his class schedule was. He seemed to be home all the time.

I took Shelby's arm, like she usually did, and started walking to the class we had together. She eyed me curiously. I had been the one practically claiming to have a life-or-death situation and now I didn't know where to start.

"Cody and I broke up," I blurted out. It was like ripping off a bandage.

"What?" she yelped. I tugged on her sleeve to keep her quiet. I didn't want everyone to know about my problems.

"I need you to promise not to tell this to anyone. Not even Keith, got it?"

"He doesn't know?" she asked, incredulous. I lived with him, after all: it wasn't possible to keep this a secret. That wasn't what I was asking, though.

"No, he knows about the breakup. He just doesn't know why." I paused for a second, took a deep breath, and continued with the next hurtful part. "He cheated on me."

Shelby at least had the decency to look surprised. In high school, everyone had always said he was too much for someone like me. They wouldn't have been surprised, at all. They would have just commented on how long it had taken to get to the end.

"I don't know him very well, but, by what you tell me, that's very strange. Are you sure, because sometimes you see—"

I shook my head, interrupting her. "No, I'm sure. He admitted to it after I caught him talking about it with her," I answered, disgusted. I still couldn't believe he'd slept with her. He'd given her something that was supposed to be mine.

Shelby transformed her face instantly from upset to ecstatic. "I know what you need: to get shit-face drunk and hook up with some random guy. He was your first boyfriend, right? I bet he was the only guy you've ever kissed! You need to expand your horizons."

She kept going on and on about how much I needed to use other guys to forget Cody, as if it was possible. She was right about kissing only Cody, apart from that one time with Keith.

I wasn't going there with Shelby, though. She'd just gotten the brush-off from him, and I wouldn't throw ashes into that fire. I would have never considered that kiss as a betrayal of Cody, either. Keith had been drunk—he never would have done such a thing, otherwise. I had been just as surprised and inebriated, too, or I would've pushed him away sooner.

Later, when we got to class, Shelby was beaming and clapping her hands. I awoke from my thoughts only to realize I had agreed on a girls' night out this Friday.

CHAPTER SIXTEEN

When I got home that evening, Cody was waiting for me in my room, which bothered me to no end. How dared he? This was my personal space. I should have been able to avoid him in my own room, at least.

"Jane," he pleaded, getting up from my bed.

"Cody, stop right there," I extended my arm to keep him from getting closer. I could tell Keith was upstairs, because I could hear his music blasting. I didn't want to cause a scene.

I lowered my voice, while shutting the door. He took that as a sign that I was forgiving him and stepped closer. "Stop," I said between clenched teeth. "I agree with talking, but stay away from me."

Cody looked pained. He even looked worse than me, in yesterday's clothes with purple bruises under his eyes and messed up hair.

"I'm so, so sorry, baby. I never meant to hurt you. That's why I never told you," he started. I didn't want to hear his apologies or the excuses that would come. I wanted to end this, clean and forever. I had thought enough about us during the nightmarish night I'd had. The only conclusion I'd come to was that I wouldn't be able to forgive him for this—at least not enough to continue dating him. There was the possibility of becoming friends in the future, but not right away.

"No, stop right there. I don't want to hear you. I want to talk, now."

He sat back on the bed and stared at me, expectantly, probably waiting for me to bend to his mistakes.

"You hurt me, Cody." I started. He opened his mouth to say something, but I shook my head. "There isn't anything you can do or say right now that could make me forgive you. I said we were over and I stand by that decision. Don't say anything. I don't think it would do us any good."

I sat on the chair in front of him, suddenly tired. "We had a good thing going for us and you ruined it. I want to keep this clean, though." I gestured between us and he looked confused by my train of thought.

"I don't want to have to yell at you or have you begging for forgiveness. I want to be able to one day look back and see how sweet you always were— how we were best friends for all these years, because we were friends, before. I want to be able to be your friend again in the future."

Cody got up and started to pace the room, angry. I thought this was going well. I wasn't throwing a fit. Isn't that what guys wanted: girls that stayed composed, even when all they wanted was to throw the glass on the bedside table at his head and punch him, until there was nothing left to feel?

"How can you say that?" he asked in a strained voice. "How can you throw away our relationship this quickly?"

Now that glass was calling to me to pick it up. I crossed my arms to keep me from doing something I would regret.

"Throw away?" I asked, calmly. "Are you kidding me? I'm not the one who slept with someone else, Cody," I said between gritted teeth. "Alexis was more important to you than me at one point. You should think about that."

I let my voice get louder and the music upstairs ceased playing. I needed to finish this talk with Cody before either my brother, or Keith found out he was here.

"We don't need to tell anyone about why we broke up," I said, quickly. "If Keith or Ryan find out you cheated on me, they will get mad. I'm not spiteful enough to want that, okay?"

He was confused as to why that was important in our conversation, but it was. I didn't want him getting hurt because of me.

"We'll tell them we just decided to break up, okay? No one needs to know our business," I said, hearing Keith coming down the stairs.

"But I don't want to break up, Jane. I want you to forgive me, please, baby." His voice was louder, as well, and, from the look on his face, he was starting to panic. He reached for me and I bumped the desk, trying to get away from his hold, which made a few books fall to the floor.

Keith opened the door, then, not bothering to knock. His face scrunched up when he saw Cody, and I could tell he hadn't known we would both be in here.

"Cody? What are you doing here?" Keith asked.

"I could ask you the same thing. What are you doing in my girlfriend's bedroom?"

Cody couldn't fight me—he knew he didn't have a reason for it—so he was going to turn on his brother. I couldn't let that happen.

"Ex-girlfriend," I stated.

"He doesn't know that, does he? Have you gone behind my back, now? You always want what I have, don't you, Keith?"

He was being ridiculous now, and Keith saw that he just needed to lash out at someone. He didn't fall for his trap.

"Give her time, Cody. I know you're mad at each other right now. Give her time and talk to her another day, okay?"

Cody shook his head and left my room, shoving his brother back and looking murderous. "If you touch her with a single finger, I'll kill you." He left, but paused in the hallway to turn back and smirk at his brother. "And so will Ryan, the only person who still cares about you." He then left the house, leaving both his brother and me staring at the empty space.

What an awful thing to say, especially to your own brother.

"I'm sorry you got in the way," I apologized, feeling like it had been my fault they'd fought. This was what I had wanted to prevent by omitting the truth about the breakup.

I hadn't noticed that tears were running down my face until Keith pulled me into a hug. "You know you just need to say the words and he'll be out of here," he whispered into my ear.

I disentangled myself from his hold and shook my head vehemently. "No, I don't want you fighting—not because of this. We'll figure out a way to coexist. He's never home, so it won't be that difficult." I shrugged, trying to sound nonchalant about my breaking heart.

It didn't surprise me that Cody was absent the rest of the week. I went to classes and did the required work, all on auto-pilot. I had shut down my heart and, consequently, my brain. Everything was robotically made—even my drawings, which were worse than ever.

Our evaluation was just after Thanksgiving and, if I wasn't careful, I would be in a big predicament with my parents. I could pretend for a few days, but not for the rest of the semester.

"Did you forget what day it is?" Shelby beamed beside me, after our classes.

Oh, right: Friday. Alcohol, guys, blah, blah, blah.

"Right," was my only answer. I didn't have the strength to even complain that I wasn't in the mood to party. Maybe it would be good. Maybe I would find a guy who would be agreeable about my revenge plans—or Shelby's revenge plans. I didn't know, anymore, and I wasn't feeling very vengeful. My mind just screamed to be kept blank for as long as I could pull it off. If it was up to me, it would be for a very long time.

"I have an outfit that will be a killer on you." She eyed my body, taking measurements. I wouldn't have thought so, since she was much taller than me, and had a bigger chest perimeter and more curves. I would look like a potato bag in her clothes, but I didn't point that out. I shrugged and let her take me to her dorm room.

I hadn't been in one before, so I took a good look around, taking in the place in which I would probably be living in the near future—if Cody started to spend more time at home, that was. If he didn't, I wouldn't bother moving. I liked the house, even if it was far away from our classes. I took pleasure in the quiet of it. I loved my beautiful room and I liked cooking in that kitchen.

I kind of even enjoyed Keith's small presence. I'd been shutting myself in my room, but he always managed to get me cooking for him. I didn't think it was because he didn't want to do it, himself, but because he knew I needed to occupy my mind, even if for just a few minutes.

We didn't talk much. He continued with his hot and cold demeanor and I never knew what mood he was in. When Keith felt that I was okay, he didn't pay much attention. When he knew I was feeling down, he managed to keep me talking, even if, most of the time, it was about classes.

Shelby threw a couple of outfits to the bed and I didn't see much fabric for covering either of us. "Try the skirt and the tank top," she said, and I picked up the pieces, like they would bite me.

"Shelby, it's freezing outside. They say it will probably snow in the next few days. Do you think this is enough?" I asked, not wanting to take off my tight, warm jeans and comfortable hoodie.

Shelby kept skipping around the room, choosing accessories and clothes, and ignored my remark. I sighed and changed.

I never cared much for taking my clothes off in front of other people, but, right now, it didn't bother me much. Whether it was because of my shut-down mind, or the fact that I drew naked people on a daily basis, now, I didn't know. I changed and stood in front of the mirror, feeling cold and ridiculous.

The skirt was too short and the top was too tight. I had no idea how they fit Shelby. It wasn't me, and I stated as much.

"That's exactly the point, Janie-girl. You need to get out of your comfort zone."

The comfort zone talk reminded me too much of Keith, when he'd talked about my drawings. They were probably right. I had kept myself locked in my comfort zone for too long.

Maybe this would be step two in the Skylar makeover. The piercing in my nose shone in the mirror, almost taunting me. It was saying, "Do you think I changed your personality? Think again, innocent child."

My brother asked me twice to take out the piercing, I ignored him both times and he stopped caring. If only my parents were that manageable.

"You know what I've been thinking?" Shelby asked, stopping with one hand on her hip and a strange look on her face. "You could invite Keith to come with us."

I turned around to face her. I had been expecting this, but was starting to hope it was just my fears talking. Shelby had only wanted to take me out in the hopes that I would bring Keith along. Well, like she said, I needed a change. Janie-girl, who everyone stepped all over, was going to say no.

"I don't think so, Shelby. We don't get along, and, with him, I won't meet new guys. Believe me: he's almost as bad as my brother."

She frowned, but the upset look didn't last long, so I kept hoping she was taking me out as a friend and not only as a way of bringing Keith along.

After a painful half an hour of brushes being poked into my eyes, while she attempted to make me look older with make-up, Shelby went to the bathroom to change. I decided I needed to let Ryan know I was out with friends. He was always complaining I was too homey for my own good, but he just couldn't make up his mind. Either I was too homey, or I needed to be locked in to save me from the world.

Ryan already knew Cody and I were no longer together, and, surprisingly, he hadn't said anything. He'd just stood in the middle of the kitchen for a full minute, staring at the cupboards. Then he'd said, "Okay," shrugged, and left for his next class—no questions asked. I suspected Keith had talked to him before I had and that was the reason he didn't jump with joy or yell about him being a bastard.

"Come on, Jane. Let's get you a stud to keep your mind occupied."

I looked at her sideways. "A stud? Really, Shelby? I just want some quiet time with you."

"Oh, baby, nothing about this night will be quiet," she said, wiggling her eyebrows and worrying me.

We ended up going to a club nearby. The bouncer asked for my ID, but Shelby was able to convince him to let us in without seeing any of our identification. Let's just say it involved showing off her cleavage to an almost indecent level. I just rolled my eyes and stepped inside close behind her, before he decided he wanted me to rearrange my clothes, too.

We sat at a table in the middle of the room, something I never liked. I enjoyed being able to engage the room in front of me—not being in the spotlight.

The music was so loud that we gave up on talking almost as we sat down. Shelby found a couple of friends that bought drinks for us. I didn't give it much thought when she chose mine. I didn't know any sophisticated drink names, anyway. It was easier to let go and let her decide, even if that was against my decision of being independent and not just a sidekick.

Shelby pulled me to my feet after our third drink to get us to the dance floor. I was feeling my inhibitions flying out the window, and, somehow, in the pit of my brain, I knew it wasn't smart, even though that was the main purpose of this whole night.

A couple of guys invited us to dance. Later, we went to their table, where they gave us more alcohol: beer; it was probably the cheapest drink, but I was beyond caring.

One of the guys asked me to dance and I stumbled around to meet him in the dance floor. I was feeling even drunker than the last time, and, considering I'd made the huge mistake of letting Keith kiss me last time, I should probably have just called it a night now. I couldn't find Shelby, though, and I had no ride home. We had hopped in a cab to get here and that's the way we were supposed to go back.

I let Tony cling onto me and kiss my neck and chin, getting closer to my mouth. He was good-looking and seemed nice and not too pushy. This was a good opportunity to do what Shelby had suggested: let go. I would be someone other than good, old, plain Jane. I put my weight on his forearms, as I was feeling dizzy, all of a sudden, and my stomach started to turn. Last time, I hadn't gotten to the part of throwing up. I guess, this time, I wouldn't be spared.

"I need a bathroom."

"Sure, baby," he cooed into my ear. Was he so drunk that he didn't realize I was about to throw up on him?

I pushed other people aside, while stumbling to the bathroom. When I spotted it, my stomach clenched again and I barely had time to get near the toilet before my dinner came up. After a couple of minutes of throwing up, Shelby appeared by my side.

"Are you okay, honey?" she slurred her words, but didn't seem to be as drunk as I was. She was probably used to drinking regularly, but I wasn't.

"Not really. Can you call a cab?"

Her face stilled and she looked away, setting her lips in a firm line.

"I kind of asked Keith to meet us here, using your phone."

I had left my purse with her when Tony had asked me to dance. I couldn't believe she had done something so wicked. She was using me to get to him, after all.

My stomach was settling, so I decided to look for Tony. I found him near the girl's bathroom, waiting for us. He had been the one who called Shelby for me—he really was a good guy. I just regretted doing to him what Shelby was doing to me: using him to forget Cody. I should have suggested to him for us to be just friends and was about to, when he pulled me against him and dragged me to the dance floor, again.

"Are you feeling better? Do you want me to get you home?"

The world was still spinning around me and I was about to take his offer when someone yanked him out of my reach, making me stumble back and look for something to support myself with.

"What the hell, man?" Tony wasn't pleased and I was about to protest, too, when the guy turned and Keith's fuming eyes met mine.

"Keith," I greeted him. "Shelby wanted you here. She wants to fuck you," I said, getting closer and trying to say it like a secret, even though I was yelling to be heard. People around us looked my way, as if I were crazy.

"She sure does, and apparently so do you." He pulled me away from a couple of drunk guys who were dancing around, while Tony tried to decide what Keith was to me. I was shocked by his words.

"I do not," I said, appalled by his bluntness.

He shook his head. "Not me, him." He nodded at Tony, who was deciding if I was good enough for him to stick around and defy Keith. I guess I wasn't, because he turned and went back to his table.

I set my face so Keith wouldn't see the hurt. I couldn't have cared less about Tony, but knowing I wasn't good enough for somebody so soon after being with Cody still stung.

Keith grabbed me, digging his fingers into my arm, and pulled me to the side, looking for someone. I guess he wasn't just taking me home: perhaps he would use this opportunity to hook up with Shelby. At least it was payment for coming to get me.

"Let me go. If you want to leave with Shelby, do as you please, but let me have fun with my friends."

He released me, which made me lose my balance momentarily, and then he crossed his arms over his chest.

"What friends?" he spat, nodding at the two guys we'd met tonight, who were already cozying up with two other girls. Okay, maybe Tony wasn't that good of a guy.

"I'll make new ones," I said, spiteful. It sounded more like whining. Keith shook his head and his expression softened slightly.

"Keith!" Shelby came barging through the crowd and jumped right into Keith's arms. Maybe she was as drunk as me. He didn't shove her back, but gently set her on her feet.

"Let's go." He grabbed both of our arms and dragged us to the street, nodding to the bouncer and yelling through the line.

"Garett, if you ever let these two inside without me present, I'll tell your boss you're letting underage girls into the bar."

The guy, who seemed like a beast to me, just nodded, ashamed, and turned to the next customer in line. He asked, rudely, for the girl's ID.

"Oh, you come here often? I asked Jane to invite you earlier, but she didn't want to, so I sent you a text. Did you like my text, Keith?" Shelby shoved me to the side so she could sit shotgun and cozy up with Keith, who groaned while covering his eyes.

"So it was you. I should've guessed," he mumbled. He started driving to her dorm. My eyebrows shot up: he was taking Shelby home? That was a surprise. I'd thought he would take us both to his house.

I guess he was the kind of guy who didn't take advantage of drunk girls. He had slept with Shelby at the Halloween party, though, when she was drunk. He'd kissed me while I was drunk, too.

After helping Shelby up the stairs, he got back inside the car and turned it around.

"Are you okay, there? If you need to throw up, ask me, or I'll make you clean it up tomorrow." He started the car. I waited for him to peek in the rearview mirror so I could flip him the finger. Who did he think he was, my father?

Keith parked the car in front of the house, but didn't get out right away. I stayed behind, too. I was too comfortable, lying in the backseat, to get up any time soon. He picked up his cell from the back pocket and dialed a number.

"Yeah, it's me. I've got your sister."

He called Ryan? How immature was that? I shot up and glared at him through the rearview mirror and he mocked me. "She's okay—a bit drunk, but everything's fine. Sure. See you tomorrow."

Without another word, he got out and slammed the door, startling me, and then came to help me out. I shoved his hands away.

"Calling Ryan? Really?" I glared again, but it didn't have the desired effect, as I stumbled on the gravel and fell over his arms.

"He was worried. He tried to call you, but you didn't answer. When you sent me that text, I knew something was wrong."

When I got my full bodily functions back, I would check my texts to see what Shelby had written. It must've been pretty forward for Keith to think it was strange.

I said multiple times during our long walk to my room that I was fine by myself, but he ignored me until I had my pajamas in hand. Then he left, claiming that he was getting something to prevent my hangover the next day.

I realized I was still very drunk when I tried to get up from my seated position on the bed to go to the bathroom.

"You okay?" Keith placed the glass of water and the pill on the desk to help me up. "Why the hell did you go out to get drunk?" he asked, exasperated, while I jumped forward to get to the toilet and throw up again. This time, I didn't have much in my stomach, so it just hurt my throat. "Exactly my point. If you wanted to get drunk, you should've asked me. I know how to properly get you drunk without the sick part."

"Well, last time didn't go so well, did it?" I shot up, stumbling again against him, as I tried to brush my teeth by myself.

"What do you mean?" Keith asked, leaning against the door.

I took my time brushing every corner of my mouth, while searching my brain for an answer and avoiding his stare in the mirror.

I dried my hands on the towel, shrugging. "You know, I was hungover the next day, too."

"You didn't throw up, though. I don't think that's what you meant when you spoke a few minutes ago, anyway." He stepped forward to help me to my room.

"I did." I raised my chin petulantly at his attempt to call me out. "You're the one who doesn't remember." I taunted, giggling. I could play this game. As soon as I saw the confusion and panicked look on his face, I changed my mind. He didn't deserve that. Even if he was a pain in my butt, he kind of had gone looking for me tonight. I wasn't convinced that Tony had the best intentions, anyway.

"I liked being drunk with you better," I mumbled, before falling asleep almost instantly.

CHAPTER SEVENTEEN

Of course, I had to wake up with a raging headache and an unsettled stomach. The smell downstairs was making me nauseated, so I decided to find out if Keith was trying to punish me or if Cody or Ryan had come home.

Lucky for me, all three guys sat at the kitchen table, sipping coffee and eating Keith's pancakes—he was the only one who knew how to make them, so I assumed they were his.

"Morning," I mumbled, annoyed that they had to be here, in the front row to my humiliating moment.

"Coffee, sis?" Ryan pulled the stool out for me and got a mug to pour my coffee. People say coffee helps with hangovers—I just hoped it was true.

"You went out yesterday?" Cody asked, annoyed, as if he had any right to ask for explanations, especially after his week of absence.

"Shut it, Hale. I'm the only one here who can be mad," Ryan intervened, looking behind his shoulder to warn Cody to keep quiet.

"Don't fight because of me." I cradled my head in my hands. "I went out with my friends. I still have a life, you know." I peeked between my fingers to see the hurt in Cody's eyes and pushed the guilt away. He was the one who'd cheated.

"So, Jane, are you going home for Thanksgiving?" Ryan asked, sitting next to me and trying to block me from Cody's stare.

"Yes, aren't you?" I looked up at my brother. My mother had always complained that he never visited, anymore. He looked away and shrugged.

"I don't think so. I have a couple of jobs on those days."

"Jobs? Ryan Keaton, if you get in trouble with hacking again, Dad won't be around to bail you out." My head throbbed and I regretted raising my voice.

"All legit, sis, don't worry. I don't want to see a cell anytime soon."

I doubted "legit" meant the same thing to both of us, but he was old enough to know what he was doing. I shouldn't have worried—but that was me, plain Jane, worrying about everyone, before herself.

"You can't go home alone, though. Are you going, Cody?" Ryan asked, and my heart skipped a beat. I didn't want to spend a minute alone with Cody, much less several hours. But, of course, Cody had somewhere to be. He looked like he was making an effort to search for a way of postponing whatever he would be doing, but, after a minute of deep thought, he dropped his head and shook it.

"Sorry, I have a huge assignment for the next Monday. I really can't."

He shouldn't have looked so pained. I wasn't sure I would have gone with him, even if he had been able to.

"You can't drive by yourself," Ryan stated, as if it was his decision to make.

I rolled my eyes, which made me wince. "You're not Dad, remember that. I can always go by train or bus."

He was already shaking his head and Keith groaned beside me. He was the one to state what they were all thinking. "It's too dangerous. If Cody isn't going, you can't, either."

He had been so supportive these last few days about me and Cody. He knew how upset I was, so how could he say something like that? He was less entitled to an opinion than Ryan was, and I told him that.

Cody started arguing that Keith had nothing to do with the conversation, Keith answered him by swearing, and Ryan tried to make them both shut up. I slipped away from the kitchen and went to lie down for the rest of the morning.

The next few days went by quickly and I hadn't found a way of going home without upsetting Ryan, Keith, apparently, and my parents, who were also apprehensive of my choice of transportation.

I wanted to drive, but the bus was much easier and safer, even with Ryan mentioning murders and rapes at every waking moment of the day. He even searched for news on the internet to show me how irresponsible I was being.

Shelby had gone home earlier that week, missing the last couple of days of school because her parents had a huge anniversary party she had to attend. I actually missed her for those two days, and, on the evening of the last day of school, I found myself panicking, because I had no transportation for getting home. Ryan had actually managed to spook me about the public transportation and refused to lend me his car.

My father called to ask about the trip and I had to let him know that, if Ryan wouldn't lend me his car, I couldn't go. Of course, my father had to bring Cody into the conversation. He got even more upset at my refusal to tell him why we weren't going home together.

"He has to study, Dad. No, he can't get the day off." I rolled my eyes and went to the kitchen to start dinner, while putting my father on speaker.

"What's going to be ton—"

I jumped back and waved my arms at Keith, who was strolling in the kitchen, still towel-drying his hair. I looked like a maniac, pointing to my phone and making gestures for him to be quiet.

There was a strained silence, and then my father asked, "Who was that, Jane?" His strained voice met the quiet kitchen.

I slumped my shoulders, feeling defeated, already. "It's just Keith, Dad. He lives here, you know."

"You said you never see him. I thought you two didn't talk?" He was using his don't-mess-with-me voice, now.

Keith leaned on the counter, frowning at the phone, as if he could shoot my father through it.

"We don't, Dad, but he still lives here." I put the pasta in the boiling water.

"Jane, he's not a suitable person for you to deal with. I already told you to stay away from him. I was against these living arrangements, but—"

I jumped back and tried to retrieve the phone from the counter to prevent Keith from hearing these ramblings, but Keith stepped in from of me with one hand over my waist to keep me from getting closer. If I said something to him, my father would hear on the other side, so I kept making faces and gestures to threaten him to let me go. He didn't need to hear this.

"I hear Carl talk all the time," my father kept going, and I struggled harder, warning Keith that this wasn't funny. "He's a bad seed, Jane—not good company to have. I'll tell you this: if he lays a hand on you, I swear to God, he's—"

"Stop, Dad," I almost yelled. "You're being irrational, now. Keith has never made me feel unsafe. You're making him look like a monster. Don't talk about what you don't know."

My father wasn't used to me stepping up and confronting him, so the kitchen was silent again for what seemed an eternity, before he continued. "See? He's already making you a rebel. Jane Keaton, we'll be having a little talk when you're home, be sure of that. We are paying that punk rent for you. If you're not safe there, you'll be moving to a dorm, do you hear me?"

Keith finally let me go and I jumped to get the phone, but I pushed it away instead, and it fell to the floor, separating the battery from the phone. I hung up on my father. When I'd ended the call, I managed to shut off my phone, too. I could blame the battery, which would give me a couple of minutes before I needed to redial.

"'Punk,' really?" Keith tried to downplay the situation, but I'd seen the pain that he almost immediately covered up. He wasn't immune to what other people thought, no matter how much he tried to make everyone believe it.

"He doesn't know you. You haven't been home in three years, so he doesn't even know how you look, anymore."

Which wasn't a good thing: he looked more like a punk now, with all the tattoos and piercings, than he had three years ago. "I came down here to suggest something, but now I don't think it's a good idea, anymore." He nodded to the phone in my hands.

I looked confused and my face showed it. I took the pasta from the boiling water before it became inedible, and set it on the counter, turning to face Keith.

"What do you mean?"

"I," he stammered, which increased my curiosity. "I just thought I could give you a ride home. It's snowing and no one will let you go by yourself, but I don't think your father would agree." He shrugged, like it was no big deal.

Well, I was eighteen and I could make the decision on my own. Right now, it was the only way of me to go home this weekend. I missed my parents and Matilda so much that I wouldn't complain about hours alone with Keith in a confined space.

I turned the phone on and dialed my father, while Keith waited, confused.

"Hi, Dad. Sorry, the battery died and I was cooking, so I couldn't get to the charger right away." I might have been eighteen, but I still needed Daddy's money to stay in school. Keith muffled a laugh beside me.

"I found a way of getting home." He waited for me to continue and I struggled for the right words. "Keith will take me," I rushed saying it, almost hoping he wouldn't hear.

It was wishful thinking. Of course he would be outraged at the prospect of his little girl driving around with a punk.

"Dad, listen, it's the only way I can go home. It's either that, or I don't go."

Almost half an hour later, after listening to advice and threats to Keith's life, while we both sat on the couch, eating my bolognese, he agreed, and we set the time I would arrive the next day, around dinner time.

My mother was so happy that she started making plans in the background, shouting out for me to hear. Her only advice for our trip was to control the speed at which Keith would drive.

"Did you hear my mother's speed limit?" I asked Keith after hanging up.

He laughed. "Roads also have minimum speeds. Does your mother know that?"

I shrugged, faking an innocent smile. "It's my mother: she's an old lady when it comes to driving." I shrugged.

I went to bed early, feeling tired after the week I'd had. Professor Collins had given us assignments for over the holiday, but I couldn't find the will to pick up my sketch pad.

I would have to pack it and take the assignment with me, which meant I had to have someone pose for me. The first person who popped into my mind, as soon as the professor said the words, wasn't either of my parents, or Matilda. It was Keith. Now I could ask him, as he was going to be there.

Keith and I didn't talk much that last day. My brother mumbled something when we gave him the news. He didn't seem happy with the situation, but I didn't even know why. He was the first one to say I couldn't go by car on my own; he should have been happy someone had offered.

I would've been miserable without my mother's food.

"Make sure you, at least, call home tomorrow night, as it is Thanksgiving, and our parents are paying for your college, 'kay?" I warned Ryan, while he hugged me goodbye. He then pushed me inside the car and pulled Keith aside.

Their conversation lasted a few minutes. Ryan looked upset and he was upsetting Keith. They both argued and nodded to the car several times. I was pretty sure Ryan was talking about me.

He was such a hypocrite. He left me alone almost every night, knowing full well that Cody was away, too, which left me with just Keith. Now, for just a few hours' drive, he was worried? I groaned to the empty space and turned the car on to start heating it. They both jumped and ended their argument.

Keith was mad for the next two hours, grumbling about my choice of music every time I changed the radio station. Then, giving up, I pulled a CD from the glovebox and shoved it in.

As soon as the song started, Keith started singing—probably without realizing it. I hadn't heard him singing since the day I broke up with Cody. He had such an amazing voice.

After three hours, I was starting to feel tired. We weren't even midway, and the prospect of driving much longer was tiring me, even though I wasn't the one driving.

"You can sleep, you know," Keith said, still upset, after my tenth yawn.

"What the hell did Ryan say to you to keep you in that mood this long?" I turned to him, crossing my arms over my stomach. He was infecting my mood.

"Nothing worth repeating," he mumbled in response. I gave up on cheering him up.

An hour later, the real storm began. We had been driving through heavy rain and then light snow, but, when we were just two hours away from home, the car slid twice. Keith swore profoundly each time.

The second time, the first thing he did was place his arm over my chest. I was so scared that I even forgot to complain about the fact that he was feeling me up.

Keith was trying to protect me, and, even though he'd done it countless times before, with every time he'd stopped a guy from hitting on me at a party, or when he picked me up, drunk, at the club, this was the first time I realized he cared about me. It wasn't only because I was Ryan's sister, or Cody's girlfriend, because no one had that reflex when the friendship was an obligation.

He stopped the car and turned it off, leaving the hazards on to warn other cars.

"We can't continue in this weather. It's too dangerous."

"What are we going to do, then? Sleep here?" I looked back at the road. It was still dangerous, and another car could slip and hit us.

His hands went through his hair several times before he looked at me. "We can drive a little bit further and see if we can find a motel." He looked scared, which was the only reason I hadn't refused on the spot. That didn't mean I wasn't going to complain all the way to said motel, though.

"We can't: my parents are expecting me. What do you mean a motel? I'm not going to sleep in a motel, especially not with you."

He groaned, while trying to control the car in the snow. "Exactly: your parents are expecting you. If you want to get home ever again, we need to stop, Skylar."

That shut me up.

Okay, a motel wasn't my first choice but, as he said, I wanted to survive the night.

We stopped at the first motel we spotted. It had that shady appearance I'd seen in movies and it didn't surprise me.

What did surprise me was the amount of cars in the parking lot. There were just a couple free spaces and Keith maneuvered the car into the spot closest to the lobby. It was still snowing and I had to gather the coat against my neck to protect me from the cold.

Keith opened the front door for me. The interior had red walls, and a strange smell, besides tobacco, which filled my nostrils. It was a mixture of grease and insecticide.

There was a line for the reception desk, which I hadn't expected. With the cars piling up in the parking lot, though, there must've been a lot of people trying for a room.

The man in front of us asked for a room, paid, and met his three friends outside. They fitted this place perfectly, with long hair, leather jackets, and motorcycle helmets in hand. When I looked back, they were staring at me and smiling sickly. Keith pulled me to him while the receptionist searched his computer for empty rooms.

"I only have two rooms: one on the first floor and the other on the second," the old, bald man said. Keith shook his head automatically.

"No, they need to be next to each other," Keith counteracted.

The man looked bored and glanced over our shoulders to the customer who had just come inside. He looked just like the other men outside. Keith pulled me again, this time between him and the counter.

"Okay, we'll take the one on the second floor."

I looked back at Keith. We weren't supposed to share the same room. I still felt a little bit relieved—the men were starting to creep me out. Keith wouldn't be able to protect me from four or more of them, but at least I wouldn't feel unsheltered.

Keith wasn't pleased, either, by the way he was holding my arm. He took some bills from his pocket, paid the man, took the key, and turned me to leave, never releasing the grip on my arm.

"Stay close to me," Keith said, before we reached the car to get our backpacks.

I snuggled against Keith all the way to the second floor. The icy wind and sideways snow was freezing me. The clientele was making me wary, to say the least.

As soon as Keith opened the door, we went inside and locked the door. The first thing that hit me was the same smell from the lobby. It was nauseating. The second thing I noticed was how cold the room was. I wasn't expecting it to feel like Hawaii, but, it at least should have been warmer than outside.

Keith grumbled, while dropping both backpacks on the bed and turning to the heater over the door. After ten minutes of trying everything, from pushing the on button to getting up on a chair and opening the machine, itself, we gave up. We knew going to the bald man downstairs to complain wouldn't be fruitful.

"If you're so upset with me, you should've asked for two rooms," I said, crossing my arms, after his fifth curse about this nightmare.

"And leave you downstairs alone? I don't think so." He turned to the heater again, kicked the chair, and continued cursing, while I tried to hug my body to keep me warm. The bed had only a white sheet and a thin blanket. It wouldn't do much for warmth. "This place is a shit hole. Maybe I should've kept driving. Your brother will kill me," Keith kept rambling.

I snorted at his train of thought. "I think Ryan would kill you if we had an accident. You did the right thing. Now we just need to figure out a way to keep us from dying of hypothermia."

Keith stopped with his temper tantrum and focused on me and my clothes.

"How many clothes did you bring?" he asked, eying my small backpack. I hadn't packed a single piece of clothing, since I had clothes at home: just toiletries I wouldn't have at my parents' house.

That's exactly what I told Keith. It was followed by another string of curses from him.

"I brought a thermal shirt. Take it from my backpack, change into it, and put your hoodie back on. I'll give another try with the heater."

I took my time obeying him. I didn't want to dress in Keith's clothes, but I was so cold that my lips were turning purple and goose bumps were a permanent feature on my skin. The shirt was black, with no patterns or logo. I sniffed it: at least it was clean. Why I expected otherwise was beyond me, since Keith never smelled bad. In fact, he always smelled like soap, deodorant, and, sometimes, cologne.

After returning to the bedroom with a new layer of shirts, which helped just a little with the cold, I saw that Keith had given up on the heating system. He looked disappointed with himself and I felt responsible. I didn't think he would bother this much if he was alone. I was a burden he had to put up with.

"You should call your parents to let them know we aren't going to be there tonight." Keith sat on the bed, looking around, upset.

I rummaged through my backpack, only to find my phone dead. I had left the charger on my bedside table.

"My phone's dead," I told him, panicking. My dad was going to kill me after dying with worry overnight.

"Use mine." He threw me his cell and I dialed the number.

"Hello." His business voice reminded me that I would need to explain whose phone this was.

"Hi, Dad, it's me." I sat near Keith on the bed and he turned to look at my face.

"Jane, what's wrong. What happened? Are you okay?" He was already freaking out with the phone call.

"No, everything's fine. My phone died, so I'm using Keith's. I just needed to tell you that I'm not going to arrive tonight."

"What? Why?" The worry was quickly leaving his voice, giving its place to annoyance.

"There's too much ice on the roads. We thought it would be better to stop." I heard some yelling on the other side, but the connection was quickly deteriorating, probably because of the storm, which was getting worse. "Dad, I can't hear you. Did you understand?"

"I understand that punk made up your mind, that's what I understand. Where are you going to stay?"

I nudged away from Keith, who was listening to every word. "At a motel." I should have lied and said we were at a hotel, but he probably knew very well that, on these roads, there were only motels.

Sure enough, he yelled, "What? Jane Keaton, you are not going… if he lays a hand…" The connection was so bad that I thought it would be better to end the call. I was only wasting battery, now. My father had already gotten the message.

"I was planning on sleeping on the floor, but, without the heating, I don't think it's smart." Keith got up from the bed, scratching the back of his neck, while eying the bed and rest of the space.

The only thing I'd removed was my sneakers—and my bra, when I'd dressed in Keith's shirt. My jeans would be staying on, though—not only because of the cold room, but also because Keith would be sleeping right beside me. It wouldn't be the first time sleeping next to him in my underwear, but the last time I'd had a fever and it hadn't bothered me much. Somewhere, at the back of my mind, was the fact that I was single now. I didn't think Keith would make a move, but I felt self-conscious for different reasons.

"Scoot," he said, so I would move to one side of the bed to give him space on it. It was nine o'clock and still early, but there wasn't anything to do, and the thin blanket was looking much more appealing by the second, even if there were some dirty spots on it. I carefully pulled the sheet between my body and the dirty cover. I just hoped the sheets were clean.

Keith stayed on his side of the bed for a few minutes before seeing that my shaking wasn't going to subside any time soon. I was shaking the entire bed, making impossible for either of us to fall asleep.

"Come here." He pulled me to him, gathering me in his arms. He rubbed my arms and the cold started to feel bearable.

"Th—thanks," I stuttered between clattering teeth.

After a while, my body began heating up again and I was able to doze off, cradled by strong and warm arms.

CHAPTER EIGHTEEN

The light coming through the window woke me up at around seven and I noticed two things at once: I wasn't cold and Keith was aroused. My legs and arms were tangled with Keith's. I was facing him with my head on his right arm, and my own arm was resting on his stomach. My leg was hugging his body. When I noticed the second thing, I jumped off the bed and got stuck in the sheets, which made me fall to the floor with a loud thump.

I knew it was normal for men to wake up aroused, but feeling Keith hard against my knee had been startling, to say the least.

He sat up in the bed, looking around with wide eyes. "What? What is it?"

I winced. Of course I'd had to squeal when I fell. Now he was going to believe he'd shocked me. If Keith hadn't made fun of me before for being naive, he would now.

He realized why I'd jumped off the bed and surprised me by looking shocked, himself. He ran to the bathroom and shut the door without another word.

He took half an hour with his shower, and I wondered why the hell he was taking so long. I thought maybe he was taking care of his little problem—or big problem, really. I snickered to the empty room. I had seen him naked before: this shouldn't have surprised me.

What was surprising was the fact that he hadn't actually had a lot of girls over to the house. The only girl in three months that I'd known for a fact he'd slept with was Shelby.

Keith didn't leave the house often, and, when he did, it was usually only to go to classes on campus. I had to assume he wasn't as much of a player as everyone had him pegged for—that, or he'd changed after high school. I supposed it was probably the second option, even though I recognize that high school had a lot of gossip fabricated by teenagers' minds.

Knowing he hadn't been sleeping with anyone lately made me believe he was feeling a little bit on edge. This was something I should have thought about last night, when I was snuggling against him for heat. I knew he would never hurt me like that, though, nor want me like that.

The thought ripped the smile off my face. I wasn't his type, even if Keith had no type, at all. I believe he still saw me as an annoying little girl that he couldn't shake off.

He emerged from the bathroom, letting the steam escape into the room and warm it. He was avoiding making eye contact—embarrassed, maybe? That was something I would have never guessed he had in him. I tilted my head and studied his body language.

"Are you ready to leave?" he asked, after zipping up his jacket. I hadn't moved a muscle. I had been checking him out for the last few minutes and this made me blush. I used his method: jumped up and ran to the bathroom.

I took my time brushing my teeth, washing my face, and putting my hair into a braid to get it away from my face. It was so cold that I wouldn't be able to take a shower. We were almost home, anyway. In a couple of hours, I would be hugging my parents and my sister, snuggling into my own bed, and eating Mom's food.

Keith knocked on the door and asked me to hurry up. He had been allowed to take his time, but I couldn't? This irritated me.

"What? A girl has to take her time," I spit, opening the door and crossing my arms. He threw me my backpack, and it almost fell to the floor.

"You're not that kind of girl. Now, hurry up, so we can get on the road before the next storm."

He said it so matter-of-factly that it froze me in place. I wasn't "that kind of girl?" What the hell was that supposed to mean? I wasn't sure I wanted an answer, though, so I shut my mouth and followed him downstairs. The weather was better: a positive sign on this upsetting day.

I moped for the rest of the ride, crossing my arms, and staring at the landscape through the window.

As soon as we got to our hometown, my mood got better. I was going home, even if only for a few days. I needed my family, right now.

"The hell drive is over," Keith said, as soon as he parked on our street. It had been snowing here, as well. It wasn't as bad as it had been last year, but there was enough to leave a few inches on the lawn and roofs. It was a beautiful sight.

I turned to Keith before opening the door. We would see each other again during the holiday. It wasn't uncommon for our families to gather together for Thanksgiving dinner. I had to say something to lift this cloudy feeling from my chest, though.

"I'm sorry if I'm that unbearable. I'm sorry I'm such a burden to you, Keith," I spat, "and that my brother feels the need to make you babysit me. As you well know, I was fine with the idea of coming alone. You were the one opposed to it, as I recall. You were the one who offered to drive me. Have a nice holiday."

I ignored his stunned face and got out of the car. My plan was to get my backpack from the trunk and stomp to my house, but of course, things wouldn't be that easy. The car was locked, which meant Keith either unlocked it from the inside or had to get out and open it for me. He took his time, probably mulling over my words in his head.

He took out my backpack and handed it to me, but, before releasing his hold, he met my eyes.

"I'm sorry if I made you feel unwelcome. That wasn't my intention.

You're right: I offered, and I wouldn't take it back, especially after the night we had."

He meant the storm. If I had driven here by myself, I would probably be lying in a ditch, somewhere. I had little experience in driving in the snow, much less in a full storm.

"Okay. Bye." I didn't feel any desire to forgive him just yet. My house was just a few feet away and I was dying to hug my parents.

The road was slippery and I made an effort to not fall on my butt in front of Keith. I didn't look back. I was sure my mother was in the kitchen, waiting.

The snow was undisturbed, so I knew my father hadn't come out to shovel, yet.

"Jane!" My mother opened the kitchen door, still drying her hands on the towel, and I jumped into her arms. She hugged me tightly. "I missed you so much, baby. I was so worried last night."

"I would like to know what that was about last night, Jane." My father came into the kitchen with open arms, despite his words.

"Dad. I missed you, too." I hugged him and stepped back to answer his question. "I told you on the phone: we had to stay in a motel because of the storm. The car was skidding on the ice."

"I don't like that one bit, miss—staying in the middle of nowhere with that punk."

"Keith. His name is Keith, and he was being responsible by stopping."

My father paced in the kitchen, while my mother started the oven. He wasn't giving up any time soon.

"So, the motel was his idea. I knew it! I'm going to kill that—"

"David, that's enough. We'll talk about this later; she just got here. Have you eaten anything today?" she asked, grabbing some blue strands of my hair. The streaks were dissipating.

I answered my mother by shaking my head. We had gotten away from that motel so quickly that neither of us had remembered breakfast. Mom had made a ton of pies and cakes, luckily.

"I want to take a shower and rest for a little while. Is that okay, or do you need help?"

My parents both looked distressed and I started worrying that something was wrong.

"Oh, honey, we are having some problems with space. Your grandparents came to visit, as well as your aunt and uncle. They are staying in yours and Ryan's rooms.

"Oh, come on, Mom, I can't sleep with Matilda. I'll wake up with a black eye."

My sister couldn't sleep with anyone: she thrashed so much and punched like a boxer all night long.

"We were thinking you could stay in Cody's room, since he didn't come, and all." My mother looked sheepish. I had come home for Thanksgiving after months of being away and now they were shipping me off to the neighbors. I loved Samantha and Carl, but I missed my old room.

My father still looked upset. Staying in Cody's room, even with him absent, was against his rules.

Before I could open my mouth, my father grabbed my chin and turned my head toward him. I had completely forgotten about my nose piercing. I had convinced myself it was so small that most people wouldn't even notice it. Not my father, though. He'd seen it pretty quickly.

"Jane Keaton, what the hell did you do? First the hair and now this? Who talked you into—"

Keith chose that exact moment to knock on the door. The three of us turned to look at him on the other side of the glass doors. I felt my mother tensing on one side, and heard my father hiss on the other. Keith's eyebrows shot up at the hand still on my chin.

I pulled away from my dad and opened the door for him. I tried to see Keith as my parents did. He hadn't come home for the last couple of years, and the piercing was new, along with the tattoos peeking out around his neck and wrists. He looked so delinquent that I feared my parents wouldn't let me leave with him, let alone continue living in his house.

"Hi, Mr. and Mrs. Keaton." He nodded at my parents and turned to me. "You forgot your sketch pad in the car." I looked to his hands, but they were empty. He expected me to go with him.

"Keith." My mother startled both of us with her incredulous tone. He was very different from the Keith who had left at eighteen.

The look my father was giving us was terrifying. He was about to kick Keith out, for sure. I could almost see the smoke coming from his ears.

"Jane, you are not going home with him. There is no way I am letting my daughter live with a delinquent."

I rolled my eyes, "Dad, you're being rude."

"Rude? Rude? You have no idea! And you," He was fuming and stepping closer to Keith, "are the one who convinced her to pierce her nose? What next? A tattoo?" At that mention, my father spun around, shocked.

I shook my head. "No, no tattoo. And Keith had nothing to do with it—I swear."

My mother was shocked, still, and glued to the floor. She was cautiously eying Keith and strangling the towel in her hands. While my father shouted everything he thought, my mother dwelled internally, which sometimes was much worse. Maybe I would be getting my room back for the weekend, after all.

Keith seemed to pretend that nothing being said bothered him, but I could see past that. I was learning to see beyond his walls. The fact that he was actually building walls told me he wasn't fine.

My father's yelling had to come to a stop when he called Keith a criminal.

"Just stop, Dad! You're being ridiculous. Keith isn't a criminal, and he doesn't even party as much as Ryan, so if you want to consider your own son a punk who doesn't do anything for a living, go ahead." I turned to a stunned Keith and motioned to the door. "Come on. Let's get my stuff from your car." I pushed his arm for good measure and went outside.

My house's warmth was already comforting my body, despite the fact that my father's cruel words were as cold as the snow under my feet. My parents weren't this shallow, were they? They hadn't even let Keith talk—how could they assume anything about him, and, worse, tell him to his face?

"I'm so sorry," I said, as soon as we were out of the house. "They shouldn't have said those things."

He just waved a hand between us and shrugged, composing his face and clearing his throat. "It's fine. You don't have to apologize for them." He opened his car's door and bent to get the sketch pad.

I clutched to it as soon as it was in my hands, hoping it would protect me not only from the cold, but from the indifference pouring from him.

"I'm fine. Go ahead, go home." He motioned for my house before going around the car, getting in the driver's seat, and driving away faster than he should have in the residential area.

Was he going all the way home to his house? Was he leaving me here alone, hurt and without a ride? Why the hell was I hurt, I had no idea, but, after living with him and seeing him every day, even if for just a few minutes, had gotten me used to his presence.

I dragged my feet to the kitchen door again, bracing myself for another cruel speech from my father. I was too upset to let him do it again, though. I always hated when he talked to my brother like he was doing everything wrong with his life, but I rarely confronted him or defended Ryan. Maybe that was why Ryan teased me so much: to get back at me for not standing up for him. He never showed that he hated me or anything, but sometimes the face he made when my father compared the two of us made me cringe. It wasn't hate, but it was definitely resentment.

CHAPTER NINETEEN

My father was nowhere to be seen when I got inside. My mother was busy at the stove, so I told her I was going to take a shower and pack some stuff to take next door for the night. She turned to me, searching for something in my eyes, but she didn't open her mouth. If she found what she was looking for, I didn't know it. I just hoped they would stop attacking Keith and threatening to take me out of that house. It was home for me, now.

I spent so many days there, missing my parents' house. Now that I was here, I was missing my room there. I missed the green comforter, the picture on the wall, the trees rustling outside, and the silence at night with only the occasional song of the crickets or the call of owls.

My grandparents weren't home: they'd probably gone for a walk in the park or to fetch something for the holiday, so I got my room to myself for a while. I grabbed several changes of clothes and placed them in my backpack.

The hot water warmed my chilled bones, which hadn't recovered from the night. Even if Keith had been hot enough to replace a blanket, he hadn't been enough for the low temperatures that plagued the area.

After blow-drying my hair and putting some makeup on, I went downstairs to help my mother—or, at least, to spend some time with her. That was why I came home this weekend.

I let myself fall on the kitchen stool and picked up some apples to peel.

"So, is anything new around here?" I started, hoping she would let the subject of Keith go.

After a couple of seconds of silence, she turned to me. "Matilda's doing well in school. We were afraid she wouldn't adapt to high school this quickly, but maybe she'll get the message that education is important."

The news she thought I wanted to hear was about my sister's grades. I smiled anyway and nodded. "That's good. Is she still dating Michael?"

With my mother, this wasn't a touchy subject: she never really minded us dating. She did talk to us about precautions, though—not only with our bodies, but also with our hearts. She'd taught us to respect ourselves, and all that.

Matilda had dated since she was eleven, to my father's horror, and had changed boyfriends as quickly as a punk rock singer changed her hair color. My mother worried she wouldn't respect herself. My father worried she would come home pregnant with triplets—that's how tragic his imagination was.

"They had a falling out a couple of weeks ago, but I think they're back together. You'd have to ask her—she doesn't talk to me about it." She looked sad about the fact that the only child still at home didn't confide in her.

She probably missed my brother's bluntness over everything. He opened his heart up all the time, and I'd always gone to my mom for help and advice. She had been the first person I'd told about Cody. She'd assured me that my brother would come to his senses about us and support me when we had to tell my father. My dad hadn't been enthusiastic, but he'd always cared about Cody as a son, so Cody was the least bad candidate.

"You know she cares about you. You're our mom, though: she won't tell you everything."

Matilda had just turned fifteen. I sure hoped she didn't have anything too daring to talk about.

"Do you tell me everything?" She stopped washing the plate and my heart skipped a beat. What was she getting at? Keith's drive, or something else?

I played dumb. I was confused, after all.

"What are you talking about? Of course I do."

"Of course you don't," she answered, annoyed, but she resumed washing the plates. "That's okay. I don't want you telling me every detail of your life. You could, at least, tell me about some life-changing moments, though."

She had no idea that I hadn't had many life-changing moments. I was still a virgin, but I couldn't tell her that. In my case, it was better if I made my parents believe that everything was okay with Cody and that I had a sex life—at least, with him.

"There is nothing to tell, Mom." I averted my eyes so she wouldn't call out my lie.

"Is everything okay with you and Cody?" Of course she had to ask. She would be devastated when she found out. Our mothers had been planning our wedding since we'd gotten together. Secretly, so had I.

"I know you are still young and I want you two to finish college first, but have you thought about the future?"

This hurt. Knowing we wouldn't have any future together was painful. I might've been pretending to be over it by now at home, but, here, pretending we were still together, brought out the pain all over again. I swear my mother had caught that as soon as I'd stepped inside the door, too. For now, I was saved by my sister, who delayed an answer I didn't have.

Matilda ran from the door and threw herself into my arms, barely giving me enough time to put down the knife.

"Sis, I missed you so much. Mom and Dad are giving me hell here, by myself."

My mother rolled her eyes at us, but still smiled, pleased to see at least two of her children together. Ryan hadn't come home in a while.

"You're exaggerating, as usual."

"No, I'm not. 'How's school, Matilda?' 'How was the test, Matilda?'

'Have you missed school this month, Matilda?' They go on and on about it every day." She pouted, sitting next to me, as if those weren't every parent's worries. "You're not here to get them in a better mood. At least they don't compare us, anymore." That stung. I knew she and Ryan had suffered from it, but turning it into a good reason for me to be away hurt. I just nodded and resumed peeling.

"How's Michael?" I asked, so our mom would be able to participate in the conversation.

Matilda slowed down her rambling and looked between me and Mom. "Everything's okay," she answered, before getting up and leaving. She claimed she wanted to take a shower before lunch. I hadn't even noticed that it was two o'clock but apparently my mother had a meat pie in the oven for lunch. The other stove was already occupied by the huge turkey. How that thing fit inside, I had no idea. The Hale family was probably also invited to have dinner with us.

After setting the table, I went to Matilda's room. She had just gotten out of the shower and was wrapped in a pink towel. She dismissed my presence and let the towel drop to the floor. My sister had no decorum. I looked away. Although I was used to seeing people naked for class, my sister was on a different level.

"So, about you and Michael: it seemed like you wanted to tell more about it," I started.

She waited until she had her underwear on before coming to sit beside me. "Yeah—it's just weird, now."

I didn't like that. "Weird how? You haven't—"

She shook her head. "No. He doesn't want to."

I didn't expect that answer. It wasn't usually the girl who was ready first. I looked into her eyes, waiting for her to continue.

"I want to, but he wants to wait. He says I'm too young." She got up from the bed and searched for the rest of her clothes.

"That's why you broke up with him?" I asked incredulously.

She turned to me as she buttoned her jeans. "How do you know I was the one who broke us up?" she asked, surprised.

I could see the whole scene in front of me: my explosive sister thought he didn't care about her and broke up with him, only to realize she missed him and that he actually loved her and wouldn't back off. This was exactly what she explained to me.

"You are too young, Matilda. You just turned fifteen, and he's what? Sixteen? You should wait. Been there, done that."

I had been there. Cody wanted to wait and I thought he was so sweet because of it. I just didn't know he wouldn't tell me when he didn't want to wait, anymore.

Matilda must have read something in my face, because she changed from upset to worried. "What is it? Is it something to do with Cody?"

I was so sick of keeping my feelings bottled up and not confiding in anyone that the dams opened and tears started falling to my face. I wasn't able to wipe them away. My baby sister came to sit with me and hugged me, until I cried out every tear I had kept inside me these past few weeks.

"What happened? If you don't want to talk, it's fine. I didn't want to, either, when Michael and I broke up."

I shook my head. I wanted to tell her, but, right then, my mother called us to eat. My sister went downstairs first, claiming I had a bathroom emergency, which wasn't far from the truth. I splashed cold water on my face and had to wipe the mascara running down it. I was a disaster, and there was no way my mother—or even my father—wouldn't notice I had been crying.

As I suspected, even though my face was almost composed, my mother caught it. "What happened?"

I had to come up with an excuse fast.

"A friend from school had an accident, but I think she'll be okay." It was awful to lie like this, but I needed to be convincing. I couldn't have my mother knowing I had broken up with Cody. I suspected she had worries

195

about me and Keith, even if that was preposterous.

"I hope so," my father muttered, believing my lie.

"Where are Grandpa and Grandma—and Uncle Tom and Aunt Sarah?" I asked, trying to turn the attention off of me.

Apparently they'd gone to another town for the day. My aunt had wanted to buy some stuff and my grandparents had gone with them to distract themselves. They lived in a small town a couple of hours away and didn't do much during the rest of the year, since they were retired, except for cultivate the land around their house. My aunt saw them even less than us, so they'd decided to spend the day together.

When my mom spoke about her sister, a happy smile crossed her face. "What is it?" I asked.

"Oh, nothing." It was definitely something, though, and what else could it have been other than a baby? Aunt Sarah was ten years younger than my mother, had married three years ago, and had been trying for a baby ever since. I knew that they were having a hard time and that, lately, my aunt was thinking about giving up.

A smile spread on my face, replacing the previous tears. I was already opening my mouth, but my mother shushed me. "Don't you spoil the surprise." My sister caught up with the secret and she, too, smiled, but we kept silent. It was Aunt Sarah's secret to tell. I just wished I was right. She would be the coolest mother ever.

I spent the rest of the afternoon hanging around the kitchen and living room. My father and sister were watching a movie that both had seen many times. My mother was still cooking. She hadn't learned from previous years that there would be so much food left at the end of the weekend that not even distributing it to the entire family would be enough. I guessed I would be delivering Cody and Ryan a Thanksgiving dinner, after all.

At five, my grandparents arrived, followed by Uncle Tom and Aunt

Sarah. I automatically eyed her belly, but she wasn't showing. They could have been adopting a child. I looked forward to the announcement tonight.

They all hugged me, claiming to miss me more than the other, even though I had seen them on the Fourth of July. Aunt Sarah tapped my pierced nose and winked. Yeah, she would make the coolest mother ever.

"Come on, Matilda and Sarah. Help me set the table? Jane, go next door and see if Carl and Samantha are ready."

I had no idea if she'd purposely left Keith out, if she'd forgotten, or if she believed he wasn't invited. I wouldn't let them leave him out. He already felt that his parents didn't give a crap about him—I wouldn't let my parents do the same. He'd welcomed me into his house, even if he had been an asshole about it, at first. He'd helped me, he cared about asking about my day, and he cared enough to pose for me when I needed him to. The least I could do was make him feel welcome into my house—my parents' house.

"Don't forget Keith's coming, too," I shouted to the room before leaving through the kitchen door.

The Hale's kitchen had lights on, but no one was there. I made myself at home and went inside, tiptoeing around the kitchen and calling for Samantha. I didn't want to catch my ex-boyfriend's parents doing anything romantic.

"Hello, honey," she greeted from the stairs, as she put beautiful earrings on. She hugged me tightly. I had missed her, too—she had been a second mother to me, after all. She made me miss before, when I could come inside without asking for permission and slip upstairs to meet Cody. I could invite myself for dinner, or let them know when Cody wouldn't be having dinner with them. Those times were now lost forever.

Willing the tears to stay in my eyes, I stepped away. "I missed it here, too." Yes, that defined my feelings.

"Carl will be down in a second, and then we'll come over, if you want to go ahead."

I wanted to wait, but, most of all, I wanted to ask about Keith. I searched for something to say that would allow me to linger without being obvious.

"My mom told me I needed to stay here for the night. Did she ask you?"

Samantha was taking a cold dessert from the fridge—as if we didn't have enough food, already. "I was working all day and only had time to make this yesterday. I know your mom probably bought all the food available at the grocery store." She eyed me, smiling.

She knew my mother too well. She tried to help out around Thanksgiving, even if my mother always dismissed her efforts, claiming that she had everything under control.

"Of course, honey. Your mother mentioned it yesterday. You're always welcome here. Cody didn't come home, unfortunately, so you can have his room." She sprinkled something on top of the desert and picked up a bottle of wine from the counter. "Carl, come on. We're going to be late," she shouted to the ceiling. "I swear, they whine about us, but men take much more time getting ready."

"Don't I know it! I live with three guys. Ryan takes an hour getting ready every time he goes out," I told her. Ryan had always been like that, ever since he'd found an interest in girls. Cody wasn't so bad, but sometimes he'd taken more time than I did. I still had no idea about Keith. He didn't go out much, and he had his own bathroom within his bedroom, which made it impossible for me to know his schedule.

"How are the boys?" she asked. I guess Keith hadn't talked about home with his mother. If he had told his mother about Cody and me, she wasn't giving any hints.

"It's fine. We all work hard for school. Cody studies and Keith spends his time painting." I didn't know if he wanted his parents knowing about it, but, since that was his major, I guessed it was a good thing.

Samantha's smile faltered. I guess she hadn't liked the news about her son, which was damn weird. I had never heard them talk about Keith, so I didn't know what their opinion of his chosen major was. Maybe they didn't approve, just like my parents. They would just have to suck it up, because he was damn good at it. If there was a person in the world who had to be a painter, it was Keith.

"Where's Keith? Isn't he coming? My parents are expecting him," I added, to make him sound more welcome than I knew he was. I looked around, as if it would conjure him.

"I wouldn't expect it," said Carl, as he came down the stairs. "I missed you, girl." He gave me a sideways hug. "How's that boy of mine?"

I knew he was talking about Cody. The smile, the pride in his voice, and the change of tone from talking about Keith said it all. It bothered me so much that my blood was boiling. They didn't notice, because they were busy adjusting Carl's tie. The question had kind of been rhetorical, too. I held my fists down, willing my heart to settle. I wanted so badly to tell him that his pride and joy had cheated on me. He would probably dismiss it and say I had it all wrong, despite the fact that Cody had confessed.

I didn't answer and they didn't insist. Carl stayed behind to lock the door and I made a point of not touching him as I passed him. I was still angry when we sat down at the table.

After eating vegetable soup, my mother asked for help with taking the bowls to the kitchen and bringing out the rest of the meal. Curiously, all the women got up to help, while the men stayed and talked about upcoming games. Even with the world evolving, some things didn't change.

I was the one to pick up the last platter of mashed potatoes, when I glanced through the window and spotted light coming from the window of the Hale kitchen. I should have told Carl about it: it might have been a burglar. I had a feeling, however, that it was just Keith coming home. It was too cold outside to wander the street, and, as far as I knew, he didn't have close friends around.

I left the mashed potatoes on the counter and went next door.

I didn't knock, but pushed the door open and tiptoed inside. If it was a burglar, I wanted to find him, first. The door hadn't been broken in, so I must have been right. The soft music coming from upstairs confirmed it. I went up the stairs without calling for him, which I knew was an invasion of privacy.

As soon as I was at his door, I called his name. He jumped so high that it was a miracle he didn't hit the ceiling. He was cradling his chest and I hoped he was too young to have a heart attack.

"I'm so sorry—I didn't mean to scare you." I stepped forward, but didn't go inside the room. I didn't feel welcome there.

He sat on the bed, still massaging his chest. "You creeped up on me, of course you would scare me! God, Skylar, way to give me nightmares."

I placed my right hand on my hip. "Gee, thank you for making me feel ugly."

He just looked at me under his lashes, rolled his eyes, and got up. "What are you doing here? Aren't you supposed to be at your Thanksgiving dinner?"

I didn't miss the "your." He didn't feel invited and no one could blame him.

"Oh, come on, everyone is waiting for you." It was the overstatement of the year and we both knew it, even if he didn't comment on it.

He looked around for a shirt: he had just come out of the bathroom wearing only jeans. "Not feeling like it."

I was on borrowed time—someone would be coming here at any time to look for me. I didn't want them to hear me beg Keith to come to my house—or to even see me so close to him, without a shirt on.

"Come on, we came for this dinner, and now you're bailing on it. Your mother wants you there. She misses you."

"Oh, right. She didn't even call today to see if I had died on the road." He shrugged a shirt over his head: black, like his jeans, and probably like his mood, too.

It was my turn to roll my eyes. "She knew I made it home and she was working today. Don't be like that, Keith. Come on." I stepped inside his room and grabbed his forearm. "My mom made so much food," I whined.

He was thinking. That was progress, right? I tugged harder on his arm and he followed me without putting up much of a fight. Along the way, his stomach groaned, and I laughed while he eyed me sheepishly. He was used to my food at home, and he had probably gone the whole day without eating.

As I suspected, when we got back to my house, my mother was already putting her coat on to look for me. "There you are. I was getting worried," she started, until she saw Keith behind me. Her eyebrows shot up and she looked between us.

"I saw Keith get home, and went to get him for dinner. He misunderstood the time." Keith was about to correct me, but I managed to nudge him without my mother seeing. "Come on, you already missed the soup." I pulled his sleeve, but let go before reaching the dining room.

His seat between Matilda and my aunt was still empty, and I silently thanked my mother for not removing the plate. The second thing I noticed was the look of horror on his parents' faces. They hadn't seen his piercing or tattoos. Shit was about to hit the fan, so I had to intervene.

"Aunt Sarah, is there any news?" I tried. Of course, my aunt understood my meaning and looked at my mother, reproachful.

"Oh, you couldn't keep quiet." She was smiling, though. She placed her hand over her flat belly, confirming my suspicions. "We're going to have a baby. We were waiting for the second trimester to announce it."

We all cooed and congratulated them, diverting the attention from Keith successfully. I didn't miss the sour looks, though, especially in his father's eyes.

After a while, my grandfather asked about college, and it was my father's turn to look sour.

"It's going well. I really like my classes." I didn't want to dwell on the subject, but my father had other ideas.

"I gave you a semester to find some place related to your major to accept an internship for the summer—don't forget that."

How could I? People kept telling me I needed to find my place and to grow up. How could I do that while my father was always around, reminding me that he paid my bills? I kept quiet for the rest of the meal, not missing Keith's glances in my direction. He wanted to speak up for me—or he wanted me to speak up—but, on Thanksgiving, I didn't feel comfortable enough to do so.

After finishing the deserts, Keith was the only guy to help in the kitchen, much to our mothers' astonishment. They kept looking at him like he was the enemy, which was pissing me off. I knew that, as soon as his parents were alone with him, they would grill him because of the way he looked.

In the end, it was just the two of us in the kitchen. I could hear my family talking loudly and laughing in the living room.

"I should probably go," said Keith, drying the last glass.

"I don't know if anyone told you, but I'm going to sleep in Cody's room," I said, not wanting to catch him by surprise later.

Keith turned to look at me, frowning, and I knew I had to explain. "My grandparents are staying in my room, so my parents asked yours if I could stay there." I shrugged, like it wasn't going to be too hard to be in a place I had so many memories in.

He understood, though, and looked through me, as if I were made of glass. He opened his mouth to say something, but my sister chose that moment to poke her head in the kitchen.

"Hey, you two, come on—we're going to play that drawing game and I want you two on my team. We're so going to win this. Mom, Aunt Sarah, and Samantha are on one team, against Dad, Uncle Tom, and Carl, and they can't draw shit."

"Language, Matilda," I warned—she was still my little sister, after all. I looked at Keith, who was ready to decline. Maybe this would be good for him. The game was fun: we always ended up laughing like crazy at everyone's drawing attempts.

"Come on, we can win this." I nudged his shoulder and pulled him to the living room. Before we sat on the floor around the coffee table where everyone already was, I caught my sister eying me curiously. She nodded to Keith's back, but I ignored the unspoken question. That was just what I needed: Matilda making up stories about me and Keith.

The first game didn't take long. Our team got every word right, while our parents and my uncle and aunt couldn't draw anything. We ended up laughing more than guessing words. My father's castle was a cake and they couldn't get it right, even after the one minute had long since passed.

Keith had relaxed beside me. After the first game, the other two teams decided it was unfair to have me and Keith drawing, so they got Matilda to do it while we guessed. Matilda wasn't that bad at art, either, and we ended up winning, again.

After the second game, Keith got up, saying he was going home. Everyone agreed that the game had lost its appeal. The men gathered around the TV, watching reruns of football games, while the women gathered around Sarah, asking about baby names, clothes, and everything that was attached to an expecting mother.

I got up, feeling misplaced in my own house. "I'm tired, too. We didn't sleep much last night, so—" My father's eyes shot up angrily, and he looked between Keith and me. "With the weather and sleeping alone in a motel room," I added, not wanting another argument.

I went to my room to pick up my backpack and took my sketch book, as well. I didn't want my grandparents to have heart attacks by seeing drawings of naked people. They were old-fashioned.

When I got downstairs, Keith had already left. I caught up to him while he was pouring himself some milk in his parents' kitchen.

"Goodnight." It was the only thing he said. I nodded and poured some water for me.

I stayed in the kitchen a while longer, eying the backyard and staring into my house's lighted windows, so full of life. I missed my family. They had been on my mind for weeks after I'd moved, and then less and less when classes started occupying my mind—even less when Cody broke my heart.

Now, staring at the house I missed so much, another feeling crept up inside me: the feeling of not fitting in. I didn't feel like this was my life, and what bothered me the most was that I didn't feel like this in Keith's house. Sure, for a few weeks, I had been self-conscious about living there, but now I found myself missing it more and more.

Of course, the prospect of sleeping in Cody's room tonight had me shivering. I so didn't want to step inside his room—not even for a minute, much less to sleep there for the night.

CHAPTER TWENTY

I had so many good memories from this house and from his room, even before we started dating. I had spent so much time there that now my mind started playing games with me, making me remember stuff I didn't want to recall. I wasn't thinking about the betrayal, I was thinking about my best friend, my first and only boyfriend, and about how his face would light up every time he spotted me in the school hallway, or when he opened his bedroom door to come play with me. I remembered how much I enjoyed cuddling with him on his bed, watching movies on his laptop.

This feeling was suffocating me by the time I actually made to his room to change into my PJs. I wouldn't be able to close my eyes. I was so tired after the previous night's adventure that I picked up the blanket and went to curl up on the living room sofa.

I felt my body relaxing, but my eyes refused to close. Keith's parents came home around one in the morning, and I prayed they would go upstairs and bypass the living room. They took their time getting a glass of something from the kitchen and giggling like teenagers.

I really didn't want to hear Cody's parents making out.

They stumbled up the stairs, probably having drunk too much. I didn't want to imagine my parents doing the same.

Afterward, I took a long time falling asleep. What was probably just a few minutes later, someone shook me awake.

"What?" I jolted and almost fell to the floor, but Keith's arms stopped my fall.

"What are you doing out here?" he asked, sitting on the couch where my head had been just seconds ago.

It took me half a minute to gather my breath and my surroundings, which gave me time to come up with an excuse.

Keith picked me up by placing an arm under my knees and the other behind my back. I yelped, but he advised me to be quiet, otherwise I would wake up his parents. That was the last thing I wanted, especially in the compromised position I'd found myself in. I wasn't expecting him to carry me to his room, but that's where I stood, moments later, staring at his unmade bed with a confused frown.

"I understand, Sky: it's his room." I couldn't turn to him, so I stayed still, willing the lump in my throat to go away. It wasn't difficult to put two and two together, but, for Keith to understand was unexpected, to say the least.

"I'll stay in my brother's room. I'll come wake you up before my parents, and then we can switch, 'kay?" he asked. I didn't want to stay here, either, as it was too personal and intimate, but I couldn't refuse the offer.

My body was complaining after the restless night I'd had yesterday and I really wanted to sleep in a comfortable bed, so I nodded. After Keith mumbled something about not snooping in his stuff, he disappeared into the hallway, with his sketchbook under his arm.

I didn't lose time wondering about the arrangements, and snuggled under his covers to become enveloped in his scent.

Keith didn't use much cologne, but he always managed to smell good. It was either his natural scent or his aftershave—or a mixture of both. As I inhaled the scent on his pillow, I felt safe. It was stupid, really, but being under his warm covers and feeling as comfortable as I did made me feel strangely safe. I slept through the whole night, which was something I wasn't used to doing lately.

Around six o'clock in the morning, Keith came to wake me up, stating that his parents would be up in an hour or so.

I felt so comfortable and tired that I whined. "Oh, come on, just a couple more minutes." His chuckle made me open my eyes.

"My parents won't be checking my room, but they'll go to Cody's to wake you."

I snuggled in even more, which granted another chuckle. "Then stay and give me one more hour." I pulled the blankets back and motioned for him to climb in. His smile dropped instantly and a frown replaced it as indecision played on his features.

I rolled my eyes. "It's not a big deal, Keith: just one more hour." He thought for a couple of seconds and then turned the lock on his door before joining me.

We kept our distance and I went back to sleep. When I opened my eyes again, Keith was staring at me.

"What?"

"My parents are downstairs, you need to go."

I groaned, but finally got up. Keith turned over on his back, crossed his arms under his head, flexing his muscles, and watching me leave. That man knew how to be sexy and the problem was that he knew it.

I got dressed quickly and went to meet Keith's parents in the kitchen.

"Hello, sweetie. How did you sleep?" Samantha asked as she gave me a sideways hug. I smiled politely and answered.

"Great, actually. I was really tired last night. Thanks again for letting me stay here."

Keith never joined us and I went to my house to spend the day with my family. I helped my mother by gathering all the leftovers and making new dishes. My grandparents went to the park, and Matilda disappeared all day, only returning for dinner. Once again, the Hales joined us, but Keith didn't show up. I wanted to send him a text, but restrained myself. He'd probably had enough family time for the rest of the year.

Matilda joined me in putting the garbage outside after dinner, while giving me updates on her relationship with Michael.

Before turning to go inside, she grabbed my arm and pulled me aside. "What about you and Keith?"

I spun around and stared at my sister. "What about me and Keith? I hope that you're not insinuating—"

She cut my sentence, "Oh, come on, I saw the exchanges yesterday at dinner. You won't get any complaints from me: he's a fine piece of man."

I couldn't believe what I was hearing. She was my baby sister and he was, well, Keith.

"Oh, Matilda, he's… Keith." I didn't want to sound disgusted or outraged, but I guessed it sounded that way, because she laughed.

"I'm not saying you should marry the guy—he's a huge player, everyone knows that—but, as a rebound, he would be great. Jane, think about it. It's what guys like him are good for."

I wanted to defend Keith and say that he was much more than that, but my tongue was tied. I couldn't believe my baby sister was suggesting such thing. She just laughed at my shocked face and turned to our house.

I waited to go to the Hales' house at the same time as Cody's parents, trying to be polite, even though, at eleven, I had been yawning like crazy. They both bid me goodnight and left for their room. I stood outside Cody's room, wondering if I was welcome to switch with Keith again.

I paced the hall until I felt ridiculous for not knocking on his door.

"Can I come in?" I whispered, after pulling the door open. He hadn't answered and I wondered if he was even home.

The room was dark, the bed was made, and I started when he jumped from behind the door, pulled me in, and shut it, while placing a hand over my mouth. My heart was pounding, and fear curled up in me, despite the fact that, deep down, I knew he wouldn't hurt me.

I could see the gleam in his eyes from the light coming through the window. This was cold Keith staring at me—the one I didn't like. I struggled in his hold and he stepped forward, aligning his body with mine to touch me everywhere from my chest to my toes.

"What?" His rough, angry voice told me what I already suspected: he was doing this to scare me. "Isn't this what you want?" He almost spit in my face as he pushed his forehead into mine. "A rebound?" He groaned against my cheek.

My eyes snapped up to his as realization set in. He'd heard my conversation with Matilda. I wiggled to get myself loose. I wanted to explain and apologize for my sister, but he had me in such a strong hold with his hand over my mouth that I couldn't.

"What, you don't find me suitable enough to replace my brother? Isn't that what guys like me are for: to scratch an itch, Jane?"

The more I struggled, the stronger he held on, so I gave up. He let go of my mouth and now held my waist on both sides, sinking his fingers into my flesh. The surprise on his face told me he'd thought I would scream the moment he'd let me go. Feeling stronger for not falling for his games, I searched his eyes.

"You heard my sister. It's her opinion, not mine," I answered calmly. The hold on my waist loosened.

"You didn't say otherwise," he countered.

"I was surprised, Keith. I would never expect my sister to think that way. She usually isn't judgmental."

He let me go all of a sudden, which made me stumble over my own feet. "Then I'm right: I'm not good enough to replace my brother."

A frustrated sigh left my mouth and I waved my arms in the air. "You're not replacing anyone. It's not about being good enough."

He seemed to have lost his fight, and he pulled his hair and paced the room. "It's stupid. It doesn't even matter," he mumbled, not making much sense. "Stay here. I'll sleep on the couch." He didn't even let me answer, before he stormed out of the room and closed the door on his way out.

Like hell did I want to sleep here after all of this, but the prospect of sleeping in Cody's room gave me chills, so I sat on the bed, thinking about the outburst Keith had just had.

I was starting to believe that the cocky boy I'd always thought he was, was more insecure than anyone thought.

It took me a long time to fall asleep and my night became occupied by nightmares.

The next day, I went home before breakfast, trying to avoid seeing Keith so soon after his ridiculous outburst. I was missing Ryan, so I called him around noon.

"Hi, sis." His sleepy voice made me smile. Of course he would be asleep at noon on a Saturday. "Everything okay there?"

I swallowed the lump on my throat. "Yeah, it's fine. I just wanted to check on you," I answered.

His chuckle made me smile again. "We went two years with a couple of phone calls a month and now you're checking after, what, two days? Come on, what's up?"

I could hear a female voice in the background, Ryan's muffled response, and then some clothes shifting. "Is it Dad?"

He knew me well, even after being apart for two years. I never had many reasons to be upset, but, now, with everything that had happened with Cody, and with asshole Keith back, it was getting hard to stay sane.

Ryan was silent on the other side, giving me time to answer. "It's just... all that happened with Cody." I stopped, afraid I wouldn't be able to keep the tears at bay.

My brother groaned on the other side. "That's exactly what I didn't want to happen when you two started dating. Did you tell Mom and Dad?"

"No," I stuttered. "I can't. In twenty-four hours, I'll be gone, and then, maybe during Christmas break, I'll tell them. Well, I just wanted to say hello. I'll let you go back to your girl."

He laughed again. "My girl? Don't be mad at me, but I don't know if her name is Marissa or Larissa."

I rolled my eyes, finding it both amusing and sad for the girl. Who the hell slept with a guy who didn't even know their name? "You told me you were going to call Marissa this weekend, so that's probably her name, Ry. Don't forget she has a heart, even if her brain is probably missing." I said goodbye and hung up.

My mother wanted to gather the remaining food and go to the city shelter and I decided to go with her. It would be great to take my mind off my problems and do something useful for those in need.

She ended up driving to the mall after we took the food to the shelter and dragged me through several stores. She bought me two pairs of jeans and several sweaters for the winter.

"How are you feeling there? Are you helping out at the house?" We sat at a table, eating an ice cream.

"Of course, Mom. I do almost all of the cooking, I clean my part, and I try to force them to do the same." I smiled at the memory of the state the house was in when I had first gotten there. My mother would have had a heart attack. The boys had been behaving, but it didn't mean it would be approved by my mom.

"Your brother can't cook to save his life, and, from what I remember, Cody doesn't, either."

I knew what she was doing: fishing for information about Keith. I could satisfy her curiosity—after all, it would be a compliment.

"Keith learned how to cook from his grandfather, and he cooks pretty well." I didn't elaborate, but, by my mother's frown, I knew she wasn't happy that I spent time with him.

Later that afternoon, my mother asked me to go over the Hales' house to call them over for dinner. I knocked on their kitchen door, but, after hearing heated voices in the living room and predicting they couldn't hear me, I pushed the door open. Before I had reached the living room, I was second-guessing my decision. It would have been better if I had waited outside for things to calm down.

"Don't talk to your mother like that, you disrespectful punk. I told you

I wouldn't be tolerating that tone in this house." Carl's cold words chilled my bones. Keith could be a pain most of the time, but he didn't deserve that from his father.

Samantha's voice was weaker, but she was also angry at her son. "Carl, let go of his arm. Do you think I deserve that, Keith?"

His grunts got closer to where I stood and I knew I was just seconds away from being discovered.

"I should've known: you always side with him." The hatred coming from him was even worse than his father's. I just couldn't understand this family.

"Carl's not wrong, you know. I didn't raise you to be like that." I had never heard Samantha talk with such disgust. "You look like a felon and you talk like one. I'm always waiting for a call informing me you've been arrested." She was angry, but I could detect some hurt in her words.

"You're wrong," he answered quietly, sounding like a boy. "I've changed since I moved there. You would know, if you ever bothered to ask or visit, but I guess you're so busy…" he trailed off, still with a low voice.

He was a lost boy asking his mother to give him more attention. I hadn't been wrong last night: he was insecure, and his parents were to blame for that.

I guess his father didn't hear his plea, because he just continued, as if Keith hadn't tried to defend himself. "You sound like a child," his father spit venom with his words.

I heard footsteps and some shuffling. "I haven't been a child for almost seventeen years and you damn well know it."

"Stop it, Keith. I swear, if you so much as raise your arm at Carl, you're out of here—for good."

Keith breathed hard. "You would choose him over me, right? It wouldn't be the first time." I guessed he was leaving, because his words got even louder.

I chose that moment to step forward and pretend I had just arrived. For a second, Keith stopped, looking at me, surprised, but his mother continued.

She hadn't noticed my arrival, since Keith blocked her view of me.

"Each day that passes, you look more and more like him."

You could have heard a needle fall to the floor after that statement. Keith's face changed—not exactly to anger, but more like to emptiness. I'd seen his cold demeanor before, but this was different. Samantha had broken him at that very moment. Even Carl had turned to his wife, with surprise marring his features.

Keith closed his eyes for a second, inhaled, and went past me to leave the house. Samantha had the decency to look ashamed when she saw me there.

I'd never felt as angry at someone in my life—not even at Cody for cheating on me—as I felt for Samantha right then. I hadn't understood a word at the end, but I knew she'd had the intention of hurting her son, and that was despicable, especially if the argument was about the way he looked. No one would mistake Keith for a punk, or whatever they'd called him. He had a huge tattoo on his torso and a piercing in his eyebrow—nothing more. He never got into trouble anymore, and he barely got out of the house.

"I have no idea what your argument was about, but… you're his mother, and, the way he looked just now—no mother should put that expression on her son's face. Keith's a good person. You just don't bother to look closer. My mother asked me to come get you for dinner, but I just lost my appetite."

I left their house without another word. I didn't want to go home, but it was cold and I hadn't picked up a coat. I went inside and told my family I was going to lie down for a while and didn't feel well enough to eat.

I didn't want to miss the last meal with my family, but I couldn't face anyone, as angry as I was. Our families were too alike. My parents didn't bother to look past Ryan's actions, or Matilda's: they just wanted good grades and good behavior, or, at least, whatever made them look good to the world. They didn't care about what really made us happy.

I stayed lying on my bed while they talked downstairs. The view from my window was just black sky. I missed my bed, with my view over the forest. When I had bid them goodnight, I'd promised my parents to have breakfast with them before leaving. I still had to talk to Keith about the trip. It was going to be really uncomfortable to be in the car for hours, just the two of us, after what had happened.

I dragged my feet to the house next door. I probably wasn't welcome there, but I had nowhere else to stay. If they hadn't mentioned the argument to my parents, they wouldn't have a problem with me staying there.

The living room light was on, as well as the TV. It was getting late, but I guess Samantha had felt too guilty to sleep peacefully.

"I'm going to bed. See you tomorrow," I said, poking my head in the living room. She just nodded and kept sipping her tea.

I went to spend time in Cody's room, waiting for Samantha to go to hers before switching. Midnight rolled around, however, and Keith was still absent, which probably meant his mother was still awake. I went downstairs to her.

"He's still out. What did you mean by what you said?" I asked, leaning against the door.

She answered me by shrugging. "It's… nothing."

My feet moved by themselves a step closer. I could feel the anger boiling up again. "It's not nothing, Samantha. You meant something. He was hurt when he left. Do you even think he's coming back tonight?"

Samantha's sad and tired posture changed and she leaned over her knees. "You have no idea what kind of trouble that boy stirred over the years. He's disrespectful toward us and I can't let Carl be subjected to that."

"Carl? You're worried about your husband? What about your son? It's past midnight and it's freezing outside. He didn't even have a coat with him when he left. Do you care?" I was the one being disrespectful in her house, but I was beyond worrying about that.

"He's my son, Jane, you—"

"That's right: he's your son. I'm going to look for him." I turned to pick up my coat from the hanger, as well as Keith's.

Samantha followed me to the door. "Jane, you can't. It's late, and it's not unusual for him to do this. You'll have no idea where to look."

I turned to her, gathering the courage to say the next words, which would come back to bite me later. "If you spent less time berating Keith and looked more closely at Cody, you would see he's not as perfect as you think he is. At least Keith says exactly what he thinks about people. He doesn't deceive anyone."

I turned the doorknob and stepped outside, leaving Keith's mother standing on her doorstep, looking astonished.

CHAPTER TWENTY-ONE

It was cold, and any place that came to my mind wasn't within walking distance, so I went to my house and quietly took my mother's car keys.

I spent the next half hour driving through our relatively small town. I covered all the places he could be. I'd tried calling him as soon as I left my house, but, of course, he wasn't picking up.

After visiting a couple bars, I started wondering if he'd just left me here and went back to his house.

Either that, or he was with a friend. I didn't want to call Ryan to ask who he thought would be on that list, because my brother would just send me home and get pissed at Keith for worrying me.

I was starting losing all hope of finding him when I remembered a place he'd used to go with Ryan. It was almost out of town, but lots of people went there, as it was between three towns that had a relatively younger population. It had always been too country for me, with wood walls and one or two animals hanging on them, but they had refurbished it four years ago to attract high school students with a mixture of country and rock appeal.

As soon as I opened the car door, I could hear the music coming from inside. A dozen people lingered at the door, smoking and laughing with each other.

A couple of pick-up lines were directed at me, before I got inside. This was definitely not my type of place. It took around two minutes to spot Keith, sitting on a stool, sipping a drink. He had a barely-dressed girl hanging all over him. Some of the anger I'd felt toward his mother diverted to him and I stomped in his direction.

"Keith," I started. I had no idea what I could say to make him leave with me.

He slowly turned to me, not letting go of his drink or the girl's waist. She stopped ogling him and turned a snide frown on me.

"Well, if it isn't Janey, here, slumming with the crowd," Keith slurred, confirming that he was drunk. It would probably make it easier to get him away from here.

I tapped a foot on the floor and put one hand on my hip. "Let's go," I ordered, which got a good laugh from Keith. The girl looked uncertain for a second, but, after hearing him laugh, she joined and snuggled closer to him, thrusting her cleavage toward his face. He didn't look down.

"Get lost. He already has company for the night," she warned.

This just pissed me more. Here I was, worried sick about him, and he'd just wanted to go to a bar, get shit-faced, and sleep with a random girl.

"Whatever, Keith," I mumbled, as exhaustion got to me. He left me feeling like I'd been on a rollercoaster of emotions. One moment, I wanted to protect him and show him he was a good person. The next, I wanted to knock him in the head and tell him to grow up.

Our staring contest lasted for a minute before I turned to leave. I hurried outside, trying to keep my presence as least obvious as possible to the guys at the door. As soon as I reached my car, another thought popped into my head: what if he drove drunk? He could get into an accident and kill himself or someone else. I rubbed my eyes, not believing I was going back inside.

I heard the same pick-up lines as I went back inside. Either they didn't have any imagination, or they didn't even notice I was the same girl.

I was three steps into the bar when I almost collided with Keith as he was coming out.

We had another staring contest, but, this time, he was the first one to speak. "Why did you come looking for me?" I couldn't understand if he meant right now or earlier, so I stayed silent. "It's late," he continued. "You should've stayed home."

I bit my lip, searching for an explanation. I didn't want to flat out admit that I was worried about him. It looked like he wasn't as drunk as I'd thought.

"I was worried," I admitted, fidgeting. The girl caught up to him and latched herself to his side. He shrugged her off, never taking his eyes off me.

He looked confused or pained—I couldn't figure out which. "Why?"

It was my turn to be confused: why wouldn't I be worried about him? We lived together, he was Cody's brother, and he was my brother's best friend. I'd known him for so long and was just now understanding the kind of feelings he could inspire in me. Some of it scared me to death.

"Can we go now?"

He just nodded, shrugging the girl off, once again. Some people couldn't take a hint.

As we were opening the door, a group came inside, making us take a step back.

"Jane Keaton? What are you doing here?" I knew that voice. It was the queen bee, my fake friend through high school. She'd gotten especially fake after I started dating Cody.

"Courtney," was my only greeting. I didn't want to chat—I just wanted to leave this place.

Of course, Keith couldn't go by unnoticed. As soon as Courtney and the three girls she was with noticed him, sighs and moans reached my ears. How he could inspire such sex-driven desires everywhere he went was beyond me. Sure, he was hot, but couldn't they keep themselves in check? We weren't animals, for God's sake. We had to have some self-restraint, right?

"Keith." The snarky tone Courtney had while greeting me was gone and she purred all over Keith. I had to give him some credit, as his bored expression didn't change while he nodded at her and her friends, who had probably warmed his bed at one point or another. A shudder went through me at the thought of him with one of these brainless girls. He should have had more respect for himself, too.

"I didn't know you were back." She stepped closer to him, stretching her back like a cat in heat.

"I'm not. Skylar, let's go." He grabbed my elbow to sidestep the girls and head for the door.

Courtney didn't hide her sneer, an expression I'd witnessed on a daily basis in high school. I just waited for the punch line.

"Where's Cody? Does he know you're here with his brother?" She leaned back, swirling a strand of her long blonde hair between her fingers.

I didn't bother answering: her only goal was to get on my nerves. When the chilling cold from outside hit my body, a shiver ran up my spine; Keith pulled me against him. I remembered the jacket I had in the car.

"I brought your jacket. It's in my mother's car." I started in that direction, feeling him behind me. "It's better if I drive us home. Tomorrow, we'll get your car."

After we'd gotten into the car and turned the heating system on, Keith leaned his head back. "Can we go somewhere else before going home?" His voice was low and soft, as if he was tired and the night was catching up with him.

"What do you have in mind?" I asked. Now that he was with me and the worry was out of my mind, I was kind of tired. I didn't, however, want to go home just, yet, either.

"Don't know… maybe the park? I haven't been there in years. I've missed ice skating in sneakers."

I smiled and drove to the park on the outskirts of town. I'd used to play there all the time when I was younger, and, after that, I'd walked with my friends or Cody there. Maybe going to the park wouldn't be the best idea if I was going to be assaulted by memories.

After I parked the car—the only one in the parking lot—we got out and zipped our jackets closed to keep the chilling wind away.

"Come on." He tugged at my arm and pulled me in the direction of the frozen lake. I wondered how thin the ice was. In fact, a couple of years ago, a girl who fell into the water had to be taken to the hospital with hypothermia. I wasn't keen on going anywhere near it, much less even step on the ice to skate. I'd seen other kids do it, and it seemed fun. I'd even seen Ryan and Keith do it a couple of times.

Keith let go of me before we reached the lake and stepped on the ice. I held a breath, he was still drunk, didn't matter how much drunk. If he fell I would never be able to pull him out.

"Keith," I warned, "This is dangerous." I looked around to search for help, if needed, but we were completely alone.

He just threw his head back and laughed. He smiled and raised his arms out to the sides, while clumsily skating away. His sneakers didn't work very smoothly.

"That's exactly why it's fun! Come on."

I was shaking, not only with the cold, but with fear. I stepped on the ice, anyway. After a couple of steps, I got the feel for it and skated toward Keith.

"So, what's the verdict?" he asked.

I mimicked his smile. "It is fun." I twirled around him and he pulled my hand to him. His hand was freezing, and so was mine. "We should go. It's cold—we'll get sick. Race you back?"

We were thirty feet from the edge of the lake and racing back was kind of stupid, but I was having a good time, and it seemed like the best way to end the night.

I was completely beat by Keith, obviously, but that didn't change my determination. A couple of steps away from the end of the race, my foot slipped forward and I ended up on my butt on the ice. I was starting to laugh it off when pain erupted in my left hand.

"Skylar." I heard footsteps hurrying to my side and Keith slouched in front of me, reaching for my hand. I protected it against my body with wide eyes warning him to keep away. "It's probably not broken, but it may be sprained. You need to go to the hospital."

I whined all the way to the car, but the half of my brain that could still think beyond the pain remembered that Keith was drunk—or at least he'd had too much before I'd picked him up. I struggled with the driver's door.

"You're drunk: I'll drive. I can drive with one hand."

Keith seemed to think about it for a couple of seconds before giving up. He knew we would get in trouble if someone at the hospital noticed he wasn't able to drive.

After what seemed like an eternity, we were out of the hospital. The conclusion was that it wasn't broken, but they wrapped it and gave me ice. I guess it could've been worse: it could've been my right hand, which would have made it impossible for me to draw for a few days.

Now I just needed to find an excuse to tell my parents as to why I'd been out in the middle of the night in a park with Keith, of all people. It wasn't going to fly well with my father—not at all.

As expected, as soon as I pulled the car into the driveway, my parents came barreling through the front door. It was five in the morning, but I guess Keith's mother had told them we weren't home, yet. It really hadn't been necessary.

"Jane Keaton, what the hell are you doing out at this—" My father stopped talking to glare at my hand. He narrowed his eyes at Keith. I stepped closer to him so I could, somehow, shield him from my father's rage. "What did you do to my daughter? I'll kill you, you little punk."

By the end of the sentence, I was in front of Keith, preparing myself to defend him.

"It was my fault, Dad. I fell on my hand, and we took a long time at the hospital. I guess with the snow, the staff was..." I stopped mumbling, because I realized my father wasn't listening to me. He was still busy glaring at Keith.

"And what were you doing with my car in the middle of the night?" My mother was hugging her robe tightly around her.

I guess I couldn't get away with that one. "I took it to go look for Keith. He had an argument with his mother and left. I was worried." Now it was my turn to hug my jacket against my body.

My father's murderous glare moved between me and Keith. "You are not going back with him. I won't have my daughter driving with a reckless punk."

I was done being the good girl trying to defend myself. I was eighteen and the only wrong thing I had done was take my mother's car without permission.

"That's enough, Dad. Keith's not to blame for my sprained wrist." The gasp my mother let escape told me I should have kept the extent of my injury to myself. "I'm leaving tomorrow morning with Keith. I'm eighteen, now, and I need to make my own choices."

"Let's get inside, David. We'll talk better without freezing. Keith, go home. I'm sure your mother is worried about you."

I didn't want to face my parents alone, but I didn't want to subject Keith to my father's scrutiny, either, so I followed my mother. I threw a glance over my shoulder to let Keith know that everything was okay with me and with us.

Of course, as soon as we got inside, the argument started all over again, and I could only sigh and listen to my father. I was tired and the pain killers they'd given me at the hospital were getting to me.

"You've changed, Jane, since you went to live there. I don't like it. Maybe you should come closer to home and go to pre-med, like we talked about."

I couldn't take that conversation, anymore. It was as if my father hadn't listened to a word I'd said.

"I didn't change," I lied. "I want to major in art, just like I've always wanted. I need to go to sleep, please."

My mother caressed my father's shoulders to help him drop the argument. "Maybe it's better if you sleep here, on the couch."

Instead of answering, I went to the living room and collapsed on the couch. I was so tired all of a sudden. I didn't know if it was due to my arm, the drugs, or the argument, but I felt my life turning upside-down.

I'd always had three constants in my life, until now: my family, good grades, and Cody. I'd lost Cody, my grades were just short of failing, and my parents were so disappointed in me that I didn't know if I could get our relationship back. I fell asleep, plagued by the haunted expression Keith had shown on his face after his mother's words.

The next morning, I woke up to noise in the house. Sleeping in the living room meant I would have to get up as soon as the house came alive. My grandparents were the first to come downstairs. They tried to stay quiet, but I was a light sleeper. After a couple of minutes, I had to get up to go to the bathroom, anyway.

The pain in my wrist had become a light throbbing, and it was uncomfortable. After washing my face, I joined my grandparents in the kitchen.

"Oh, honey, up so soon? What happen to your arm?" My gram asked, getting up from the kitchen table to inspect my arm. I didn't want to worry my grandparents with the argument of last night, so I just shrugged.

"It's nothing, Gram. I fell last night—just a sprain." I fell on the chair next to my grandfather, who was watching me with knowing eyes. He had the same distaste for Keith as my father and was probably coming to the conclusion that he'd been the one to hurt me. I loved my family, but was so ready to get out of there.

The rest of them woke up within the next twenty minutes, including my sister, and I had to tell the story about my arm several times, leaving Keith and the park out of it. My parents didn't correct me. Apparently, no one had heard a thing last night when I'd gotten home. If Samantha hadn't called my mother, my parents wouldn't have known, either.

I tried to avoid being alone with my parents, but, eventually, my mother cornered me in the kitchen.

"Tell me just one thing, Jane. Are you romantically involved with Keith?"

What? Where had that come from? "You can't be serious, Mom." I think she'd gotten her answer from the shocked expression on my face. She finally exhaled and leaned against the kitchen counter.

"Your father's right: you've changed, a little, at least, especially when it comes to Keith. It's like you are prepared to defend him against the world. Samantha told us what happened yesterday. You turned against her and then your father, for... him. We don't like it."

I tried crossing my arms, but it just ended up in an awkward shield. "He's my friend. You don't have to have an opinion about all of my friends."

The frown on my mother's face told me I should have kept quiet. "At least you're not cheating on Cody with his brother. That would be disgusting, and I didn't raise my daughters to be like that." My mother's words were like a punch to my gut.

"You can rest, Mom: you raised me right. I'm not going to cheat on anyone." Before she could continue attacking me, I stepped outside, not bothering with a jacket. I walked into the Hales' kitchen without knocking. The only one in the kitchen was Samantha, the last person I wanted to see.

"Good morning, honey," she greeted me. "Do you want something? Tea?" She nodded at the cup in her hands and I shook my head.

I knew I should apologize for last night. It hadn't been like me to confront people like that. Keith's face popped into my head just then. The hurt his own mother had put in his eyes kept me from saying anything but a short greeting in response. She didn't ask about my arm, as she had seen it from her door last night, and had probably grilled Keith about it after.

Keith showed up on the hallway just then. His hair was still wet and falling over his forehead, and he'd barely put his shirt on before he came to a stop in front of me.

"Hi. How's your arm?" The way he looked, with his tousled hair, faded black shirt, tattoos peeking out from his collar, and the slight guilt I saw in his eyes, turned my stomach. The unexpected feeling was so strong and sudden that I stumbled. Keith jumped to grab my good arm to hold me in place, with worry marring his face.

My heart was all over the place and the shocked expression must've been scaring him, too, because he let go of me slowly, as if I was a wild animal. Where the hell had that feeling come from? Butterflies at the sight of Keith? That was what was missing in my crappy life right now.

"It—it's fine," I stuttered, stepping away from him to get my sanity back. "When do you want to leave?" I patted my hair and looked away, trying hard to pretend nothing had happened.

Still wearing a frown, he went to the kitchen and faltered when he saw his mother. "'Morning," he mumbled. From the stern look she gave him, I could tell they'd probably had another argument last night. "I was thinking about leaving before lunch so we can get home early."

Home. That word had used to mean this place, but when he said it, I felt it was my home, too—which was strange, since I felt alone all the time there.

I went upstairs to Cody's room to get my backpack and then went back to my house to say goodbye to my family. I would be back in a month for Christmas, so the goodbyes weren't all that tearful, especially not with the recent fights.

My sister, surprisingly, hugged me tightly and whispered in my ear. "Don't be afraid to show what you feel for him. He might surprise you." I jerked away from her, alarmed. Our parents were in the same room, and if they'd heard her, they would never believe I didn't have feelings for Keith.

He was waiting in the car when I went outside. His father was nowhere I could see, and his mother was at their door, hugging her body. Whether it was against the cold or out of worry for her son, I couldn't decide.

"Be careful, honey," my mother warned, hugging me again, while my father walked around the car and tapped Keith's window. I was so tired of all of this that I just got into the car and pulled the seatbelt over me.

"That's my daughter, there. If she doesn't arrive today, in one piece, you'll have to deal with me. Got it?" Keith stared straight ahead and nodded. As if he wouldn't be careful—that was the whole purpose of him driving me.

My father rested his forearms on the window to be at Keith's eye level. "If you so much as touch her with a single finger, I will kill you." This part was said much more quietly, but I could still hear him. I watched in horror as he uttered such words. My mother was too far to hear, or she would have been shocked, as well.

Keith finally turned to my father, who was relaxing and stepping away from the car. "Don't worry, sir: I'm not the brother you should be worried about." His tone had as much venom as my father's had.

The look on my father's face told Keith to start the car and drive away before starting another argument. "Cody is the good brother. I trust my daughter to him. You would never be good enough for her."

Keith's jaw set and, finally, he started the car. I was worried he would say something back, but he didn't. We drove away and I had a bitter taste in my mouth. I wanted to say something back. I wanted to defend Keith. I would have, if he'd waited, and I wanted him to know that, but the icy gleam in his eyes suggested that I should keep quiet, for now.

After two hours of silence, I couldn't take it, anymore. "Can we stop now? I need a restroom and some food." My stomach was starting to make uncomfortable noises. My mother had packed something for lunch, but I needed to stretch my legs.

We stopped after five minutes and I practically leaped from my seat and ran to the restroom, while Keith got out to get gas.

The small diner had character, but the smell of grease trampled my hunger. When the burgers we'd ordered arrived, however, they were surprisingly tasty.

"So, can we talk, or should we keep silent for the rest of the drive?" I asked between bites.

Keith stared out the window for a while before lowering his burger. "What do you want to talk about?"

I raised an eyebrow. Seriously? "What about the elephant in the room?

My father was out of line with everything he said. It's like he's a different person."

He snorted and stopped eating altogether. "That's because you were always Daddy's little girl. You have no idea how protective he is of you."

I was puzzled. Keith had never spent much time in our house. In fact, it was usually the other way round, with my brother going to his. "What do you mean?"

He was suddenly regretful, as if he just noticed what he'd said. He shook his head. "Nothing, just that he loves you and wants to keep you safe."

I instantly shook my head. "No, don't do that. Tell me exactly what you mean. Don't bullshit me."

"Wow. I am rubbing off on you." I rolled my eyes at him. Was he? Or was I just letting go, like he'd always suggested? "I just meant that he never liked me and he made sure I knew it."

My mouth was hanging open. Had I been so blind all these years? My father had a temper I didn't know about, Cody was actually capable of cheating on me, and Keith, the only person around me who I'd thought wasn't worthy of my friendship, was the only decent and honest one?

"Even when you were a child?" I asked.

Keith paused. Hurt flickered briefly though his eyes. "I was never a child."

I refrained from rolling my eyes again, because I could feel he really meant it. "Oh, come on, you were nine when we met."

"I wasn't a child, anymore, by that age—not where it counted." He tapped his temple and drank the rest of the soda. "Your father was right by keeping me away from you. I didn't deserve you then and I definitely don't deserve you now. Your friendship, I mean," he added. I was baffled with everything he was saying. Something or someone had hurt him so much before we'd even met, and then his parents and mine had only made it more unbearable.

I got up from the table—the room was closing in on me. I was mad at everyone, and even at him, for treating me like a child. I wasn't a porcelain doll who didn't know what was good for myself; I knew how to defend myself, and I did not need anyone to get in my face and dictate who I should or shouldn't befriend. I paid the bill on the way out, before he could protest. If he wasn't good enough to be my friend, he wouldn't be paying for me.

"That wasn't cool, Jane," he stated, when he got back into the car.

"You and my family telling me what I should or shouldn't do isn't cool, either, and none of you give a damn about what I feel." He was definitely rubbing off on me. I couldn't give a damn.

After another hour of silence, I turned the radio down. "Cody told me he loved me." I paused when Keith's relaxed form changed and his fingers gripped the steering wheel tightly. "He also said that I was the only one—that we were forever." I paused again, taking in Keith's reaction to my words. It was as if he hadn't wanted to hear them.

"Then he cheated and lied and kept promising things he had no intention of fulfilling. You were always a jerk to me, true." He turned to me, briefly, with a frown on his face. "But you never lied to me. You never pretended to be something you're not. So, on my deserving list, Cody's way below you, right now."

I turned to the window again, eying the still-white fields around us. The day was sunny, and the bright light made my eyes hurt. Keith didn't respond to my confession. I didn't even know if he believed it, but it was the truth.

I dozed off for a couple of hours, and then we stopped again to eat and use the restroom in silence. I didn't feel like he was mad at me. He had no reason to be, anyway, but the weekend had given us both some things to think about, and I was actually appreciating the silence after a couple of days of being crowded by people who dictated what I should do with my life.

"Ryan doesn't like us being friends, either, does he?" I asked, maybe half an hour from home. It was a rhetorical question, but I wanted him to answer it.

Keith looked at me from the corner of his eye, making me aware that this was a subject he'd thought was closed. After a few minutes, he answered. "Ryan is your father's son. Besides, he wants to protect you. Anyone who loves you wants to keep you away from me, as they should." Once again, my mouth was hanging open. I turned all the way to him, pulling one leg up onto the seat.

"What the hell is wrong with you? Keith Hale, almighty Keith Hale, the most I-don't-give-a shit-about-anyone, I-can-get-any-girl-I-want-by-snapping-my-fingers, Keith Hale is, in fact, a fake." He looked at me, surprised. "Yeah, a fake. You don't have a drop of self-esteem. You were supposed to be the most confident person in the world, yet you keep giving me that cryptic, rehearsed shit. And, yeah, I can cuss. I just didn't feel like it, before."

Keith swerved the car to park on the side of the road, which made the car behind us honk. He turned it off and got in my face, anger pouring from him.

"Is that before/after shit I don't want, Skylar. There is no before. We're still not friends, got it? I can get any girl I want. I could get you if I wanted, but I don't." The last word hung between us for a few seconds. I should have been mad for what he said, like some pathetic girl who'd fallen for him that easily, but, sadly, I was just hurt that he wanted anyone other than me.

He started the car and we kept driving for the next half hour, which seemed like six hours. I didn't open my mouth the rest of the way. As much as I wanted to be a stronger girl, Keith kept crushing my chances.

No one was home when we got there, and the kitchen had a pile of dirty dishes in the sink. I didn't feel like cleaning today, so I grabbed a bag of chips and a soda and went to my room, shutting the door with my foot.

CHAPTER TWENTY-TWO

Monday came too fast. I had spent the rest of the evening in my room as I didn't feel like talking to anyone. Cody and Ryan poked their heads in to greet me, but that was the extent of my social interactions. Keith's words played around in my head.

I didn't work on my drawings during the holiday, which, of course, granted me extra work and extra worry that I was about to fail this class. Today, we were drawing an older woman, and I swear even the model's expression was condescending.

Later, I had lunch with Shelby, and I wished I had a friend I could confide in and tell all about my strange feelings for Keith and his disregard for me.

The rest of the week was uneventful. I didn't see the boys much, which was good, because I decided to stop thinking about any of them and focus on my drawings. I also had finals to worry about for other classes, soon, so I had to bury my nose in my books.

Studying for theoretical classes was easier than drawing, which was really strange for me. I always preferred the latter, and my father's words popped into my head from time to time. Should I think about changing majors? If I was falling for Keith, leaving was best for my sanity. I hoped it wouldn't have to come to that, though. I didn't want to be in so deep that Keith would dictate my life choices.

The first evaluation in my drawing class was at the end of the first week of December. I got a C. It was disappointing, but not a complete fail. I didn't have the courage to tell my father that day, though, as it would be a victory for him. How could I make a living with something that I'd gotten a C in?

Later that night, I couldn't sleep, so I went downstairs to warm some milk. I then sat on the couch, warming my hands around the cup. My wrist didn't hurt, anymore, and I had already taken the wraps off. The house was still warm, but, with the heating turned down, it was colder in the living room. I hugged a blanket against me and leaned back, staring out the window and at the storm outside. I'd always loved storms, thunder, and heavy rain while snuggling on the couch.

Footsteps on the stairs startled me a few minutes later and Keith's face was lit by lightning. He must've seen me at the same time, but, unlike me, he hadn't known anyone was up. He jumped back and hit the wall.

"Jesus Christ, Skylar. Do you want to give me a heart attack?" He put his hand to his chest and came closer.

I finished the milk in one gulp. "You're too young to have one," I mumbled. I was finally relaxed. Either the milk or the storm had calmed me down, and Keith wasn't going to ruin it.

"What are you doing up? Are you okay?"

I lifted my eyebrow at his concern. He hadn't talked to me since our trip back. "Yeah." I bit my lip, wanting to wrap up the pleasantries and go to bed. "Just couldn't sleep. Milk helps, along with the rain."

It was his turn to lift his brow. "The rain? You like watching?" He stepped closer and leaned against the couch. He was wearing shorts and no shirt. The room was dark, but I could still make out the tattoos on his torso. I had seen him naked too many times now, but the effect his body had on me was changing. It now made me uncomfortable.

The lightning increased outside, just leaving a few seconds between thunderclaps. Keith pushed away from the couch and extended his hand. "Come here. I want to show you something." I eyed his hand suspiciously. He was being nice, but that could change any second, and I didn't like to be played. "Come on," he insisted. I followed, without touching him. He surprised me even more when our destination became clear: the attic. He'd forbidden me to step inside, but now I was about to discover his secrets?

"Wait here a minute." He didn't wait for my reply as he retrieved a key from his pocket, entered, and left me in the hall. I waited for two minutes, and almost decided to go back downstairs when he opened the door. "Close your eyes."

I shook my head. "Nuh, uh." I was not going to shut my eyes anywhere near Keith.

He let out an exasperated sigh and popped his neck. "Come on. It will be worth it—before the storm ends." He extended his hand, once again, and this time I took it and closed my eyes. I kind of trusted him—physically, but not emotionally.

We stepped inside. "Lie down." I still didn't know if it was the thunder outside, the request, or the whisper, but I did what he asked. There was a soft mattress on the floor. The butterflies in my stomach terrified me. I should have been running out the door, but I obeyed.

Turning to the ceiling, I placed my free hand on my stomach, while the other was still interlaced with Keith's. After what seemed an eternity, he whispered against my ear to open my eyes.

The ceiling had a huge skylight through which I could see the dark gray clouds. As if on cue, a lightning bolt crossed the sky. The storm was far away, but it felt like it was just over us.

"Wow," I started, turning to Keith. "It's... amazing."

My thoughts were all over the place, and I envied this place. It must have been wonderful to paint here, with all the natural light. The most prevailing thought I had, however, was that I was in his attic. He didn't bring anyone up here, but he'd brought me. Me.

After a few minutes of watching the lightning, I looked around the room for the first time. It was too dark to see anything and Keith automatically placed his hand on my chest and pushed me down again.

"No peeking, or you'll have to leave." Okay, maybe I wasn't that special, if he wouldn't let me see the room, itself.

I turned to him and whispered back. "What secrets do you keep up here?"

He looked at my face, lingering on my lips. The tight feeling in my belly was back.

"My heart," he whispered.

My eyebrows shot up in astonishment and he didn't explain any further. We kept watching the storm above us, until it turned to rain. It was almost as beautiful. The rain was loud, so, at first, I didn't have any idea how he could have slept there. After a few minutes, however, it became a lullaby, and my eyes started closing.

I must've fallen asleep, because, after a while, Keith picked me up and took me to my bedroom. He placed me gently under the covers, tucking me in and kissing my forehead.

The next day, I woke up like I hadn't in a long time: relaxed and rested. The events of the previous night kept playing in my head and my heart fluttered in my chest.

I could not fall for Keith. He would ruin me. I wouldn't have a chance of getting out with my heart whole.

After taking a long, cold shower to clear my head, I headed downstairs, where I found Keith and my brother having breakfast in the kitchen. I bid them a good day and got a mumbled response from Keith, who was focused on his coffee mug.

He was already on cold mode. Maybe this was better. If he kept switching from caring Keith to the asshole version, I wouldn't fall for him. He'd made it clear that I was no one to him—not even a friend. I couldn't think any romantic thoughts about him. They wouldn't take me anywhere.

"You want me to drive you to school? I have to go into the office," Keith said. I pondered it and looked outside. It was still pouring and I did not want to walk to the bus.

I nodded, looking at my coffee. "Sure."

After brushing my teeth and getting my bag, I walked outside, expecting him to be in the driver seat of his car. Instead, he was on my side, drumming his fingers on the dashboard.

Without knowing what to do, I opened the driver's door and got inside. It was raining too much to linger at the door. "What?" I asked, frowning at him. My brother had already left, and, as far as I knew, Keith didn't let anyone drive his car.

He lowered the radio's volume. "You need to drive the car so I know if I can trust you with it."

"Huh?" I wasn't very eloquent this morning.

He sighed and messed with his hair: it was getting too long to keep tidy. Every time he wove his fingers through it, some strands stood upright. It was so distracting that I needed to shake my head to take my eyes off of him and listen to what he was saying.

"I want you to take the car to school. I'm going to have too much work the next few weeks and can't take you. I won't let you walk in this weather, though."

I was shocked. Not even my father or brother trusted me with their cars. "Okay, but what if something happens? I'm not used to driving manuals." And you treasure your car too much for me to wreck it. I looked at my shaking hands.

"That's why I want you to drive with me." He crossed his legs at the ankles and leaned back. My first attempt to start the car failed. I hadn't driven a manual since I'd gotten my license. Keith had the patience to instruct me, and, when we arrived at the college parking lot, I was already used to it.

"See, it's not that difficult. I'll come by at the end of the day to get you, 'kay?" He didn't wait for my answer and left in the opposite direction I was going.

Professor Collins was in a special mood that morning. She not only criticized my drawings, but also every other student's. She ended the class by yelling to us that we were below average, and that, at this point in the semester, we should be getting better, not worse. The last part was directed at me, and I shuddered at the thought that she was about to fail me.

I didn't want to cry because of a class, but I kept playing her words in my head for the rest of my classes. At the end of the day, at the sight of Keith in his car, waiting for me, drumming his fingers on the steering wheel, and bouncing his head to the rhythm of the music, my heart contracted again. Said tears were about to fall. Keith's eyes connected with mine and he instantly frowned, stopping the drumming and lowering the radio's volume.

"What happened?" The concern in his voice was the last straw, and I started crying like an infant. My father's words were playing in my head, mixed with my professor's. I wasn't good enough to be there—to compete for a place in Keith's world.

His hand came to rest on my shoulder, hesitantly, and he squeezed lightly. "Tell me," he whispered, worried.

After calming down enough to answer him, I turned, not meeting his worried eyes. I couldn't get his caring side now, or I would break even harder. I had never been good at being consoled.

"It's my drawing class, as usual. I think I'm going to fail." I bit my lip to keep the trembling to a minimum, and Keith surprised me by tracing it with his finger, which released the pressure I was creating. I met his eyes, then, and was confronted with a torturous expression, which was quickly covered by his usual blank one.

His hand retracted quickly. "No, you won't. I'll make sure of it." His eyes returned to the road in front of us and he started the car, taking us home.

I didn't ask right away, and willed my heart to calm down both from having his hand on my lips and from the mixed emotions I'd been experiencing all day. It had started great, but had turned awful. Apparently, however, it was becoming better again.

"What do you mean?" I finally came up with.

"I'll help you—this time for real. We'll work it out." He turned the car off. Before I could get out, he stopped me with a hand on my elbow. "But you'll do what I tell you, no questions asked. You draw what and who I tell you."

I was about to open my mouth to complain, but his eyes told me I should be doing otherwise. He wouldn't budge this time, and, defeated, I shrugged, finally nodding. "'Kay."

That night, Keith didn't come downstairs to have dinner with me and the boys. I tried not to read too much into it. He already agreed on helping me. If he needed time to process all of this, it was fine with me.

My thoughts were all on him, however, until I fell asleep that night.

The next Friday, we, apparently, had a party scheduled. When I got home at the end of a long and complicated day, there were a dozen strangers in my living room with red cups in their hands. My brother came barreling out of the kitchen with more beer and a goofy smile on his face.

"Sis, how was school?" His arm came around my shoulder while I tried balancing my backpack and sketchbook.

"School's good. Another party?" Truth be told, they hadn't thrown a party in two weeks. I was already used to the quiet. Ryan just shrugged and kept distributing beer among his friends, while I made my way upstairs.

Sleep was hard to come by that night. The music was loud and I had a ton of work for the weekend: two papers, not to mention that I should have been perfecting my drawings. It was almost eleven when I woke up, confused, and feeling like I was late for something. This had always happened in high school when I was stressed, and it left me grumpy for the rest of the day. Never bothering to change from my pajamas, I went downstairs to eat something, as my stomach was making itself painfully aware. After all, I had skipped dinner last night.

Keith was sitting on the stool. He said "good morning" and was about to add something when my brother came in with his backpack on his shoulder. "Hi, guys. I'm so late." He mumbled with his head already inside the fridge.

I sat next to Keith, watching my brother rummage through the cabinets. "For what? It's Saturday." My brother never bothered to hurry for school, so I doubted that was where he was headed.

"I have a convention a couple of hours from here. It's today and tomorrow. The guys and I will stay there." He stopped completely and looked to where Keith was seated. "I'm so sorry—I completely forgot." He opened his mouth several times, and then glanced between me and Keith. "Will you be okay? Do you want me to stay?" I had no idea what they were talking about, but it seemed serious, by the look on Ryan's face and his tone.

"It's fine, Ry. Go ahead and have fun." Keith wasn't as serious as my brother. In fact, he was almost nonchalant about whatever had gone on between them.

"You sure? I'll stay. Just say the word." My brother waited by the door, but Keith shrugged and gestured for him to go ahead.

After a couple of minutes of silence, I couldn't hold it in any longer. "What was that about?"

"Nothing." He shrugged again and got up from the table to wash his mug.

I joined him at the sink, but he retreated a step to avoid touching me. "Please, I've never seen my brother that serious about anything. Are you sick, or something?"

My stomach was in knots at the prospect of Keith being sick or hurt. He didn't seem upset about anything—he was just quiet. That wasn't strange about him.

"Drop it. It's nothing that concerns you. We should start on your drawing lessons if we're going to have the house to ourselves." He dried his hands on the towel and left me alone in the kitchen.

I ran after him. "Okay, you'll pose for me, but you have to tell me what that was about." I nodded to the kitchen. He looked between me and the kitchen door, and then laughed.

"You're negotiating with me without giving me anything in return, if you haven't noticed. One: you're being nosy. Two: I'm helping you."

He was right, but I wasn't going to give this up so soon. "Pretty please," I pouted, which only made him laugh harder.

"Oh, come on, baby, pouting, really?"

His term of endearment shocked both of us. He dropped his smile and I stood there, blinking. He had called me hundreds of names before, which almost never included Jane, my first name, but "baby?" I could pass it off as sarcasm or as teasing, as he'd used it in the past, but this time he'd meant for it to be endearing. He quickly covered his own surprise.

"It's my birthday." Being shocked twice in the span of just a few minutes at eleven in the morning wasn't a good omen for the rest of the day. "But I don't celebrate it, ever. So drop any ideas you have of a happy day with cake and candles and shit, okay?" I just nodded, still frozen in front of him. "Promise me, Sky, that you won't do anything stupid."

If he didn't want a birthday party, I wouldn't go against it. It was still sad, though. I decided to bring up the subject later.

After our strange conversation, I headed to the shower, where I stood for a few minutes, letting the water clear my head. Then I dressed in comfy leggings and a long shirt that ended at my thighs, and planned what I was going to cook for lunch.

Keith ended up helping me make bolognese and we ate in front of the

TV—something I'd always loved to do, but rarely could back at my parents' house.

"How's the hand?" He nodded to me. After chewing the last bite, I looked over at him.

"It's fine. Don't worry."

The mood around us was becoming uncomfortable. The atmosphere was thick with tension and we ended up watching a movie, while eating, until the credits rolled on. Keith had never been nervous for posing for the entire class, and he'd been pestering me for weeks to let him help me. Now that the moment had arrived, he was the one looking uneasy.

"You," his voice faltered, and he tried again, with his hand already through his hair. "You want do this?"

He sounded as if he was proposing something much more intimate than just posing, but I guess that, for the both of us, art was intimate, especially if he wanted me to pour my feelings into my work. I was starting to fear that he would see me through my paintings. If Keith suspected I could fall for him, he would back off completely, and might even go as far as asking me to leave.

"My room?" The question made me blush deeply, and he looked away, thinking.

"No." He shook his head. "Mine. We'll have good lighting there, and more space." His expression told me he needed that space to be between us. I murmured my reply and headed upstairs to prepare my materials—and my mind—for the task ahead. I was getting used to drawing naked people in class, even Keith. It shouldn't have been much different.

His room was well-lit by the light coming from outside, even though the day was cloudy and gray. He had discarded his shirt and shoes, but was looking around his room for something. I looked around, too, as if I could help him.

"Let's do a sequence of quick drawings to warm you up. I'll stay dressed." Dressed was stretching it, as he had only jeans on. It was, however, hard to mimic the denim.

For the first couple of drawings, everything was stiff. Keith wasn't at ease and I couldn't concentrate, even with the easy poses. "Okay, we need to change something." It was my turn to look around for something, and my eyes landed on his docking station. "Music." During class, our professor let us listen to music, if the volume was low. I never had the courage to do it because it looked disrespectful. It was something I loved to do while drawing, though.

Keith was the one to set the playlist. It wasn't quite classic, but it was still dramatic and without distracting lyrics.

The music helped, but it took a couple more drawings to set the mood to the point that I could forget everything and lose myself in my art.

Without warning, Keith took off the rest of his clothes and I stiffened again, trying my best to avoid looking at him.

"Relax. Breathe, Sky. You can do this. It's just like in class."

No, it wasn't—not for me, and not for him, either. I tried to focus on the task, though, and it ended being that: a task. This meant the drawing ended up being crap.

Keith put his boxers on while he studied every drawing I'd created that afternoon. The last ones with him dressed were okay, but the one without his clothes on was kind of robotic. He didn't need to tell me that: I could see it with my own eyes.

"I know. Awful. It's such a disappointment." I was so tired—not only physically, but also emotionally—that I could cry.

He dropped everything on the bed and grabbed my hands, which were now covering my eyes. "Stop. You're not a disappointment and neither are your drawings. What was wrong today? I thought you'd gotten more comfortable with me naked." He flinched and tilted his head. "Sorry. You know what I meant."

The mood was playful now, so I tried a smile. "I know, but it's different with just us." He could feel it, too, even if he didn't agree with me.

Then, Keith surprised and shocked the hell out of me once more, by placing my hands on his chest. My first reaction was to tug my arms away, but he tightened his hold.

"Relax. I don't bite." The smirk I'd hated so much was now showing fully. Maybe for the first time, it didn't bother me. The feeling it enticed was very different, and I was afraid he would sense my quick pulse through my wrists.

"Come on. If you don't relax, I'll make you touch all of me." He was playful, and the threat was empty, but, even knowing that, my heart beat faster. I didn't know if I should feel outraged, scared, or excited.

I lifted my eyes to meet his, and, whatever he saw there—probably the three complex feelings inside of me—made him let go of my hands and step back. He cleared his throat.

"Okay, let's go downstairs, drink something, and try again."

When he said "drink," I hadn't expected it to be alcohol. That was, however, exactly what he placed on the kitchen counter.

"You think I draw better drunk? Am I that bad?" I teased, but I picked up the tequila, anyway. The kiss was playing in my head on a loop now, and I feared and yearned for it to be repeated. Keith just served us a second time before placing the bottle back into the cabinet.

I followed him upstairs, and my eyes lingered at the place the kiss had happened. Weeks ago, I had been so mad at him for kissing me. Now I just wanted it to happen again.

"You coming?" Keith asked, ending my daydream.

We had to change positions. Before, he was too stiff as he stood up, away from me, and then sat awkwardly in the chair. We needed to make this more intimate and more relaxed.

"You need to sit on the bed. Let me choose the setting, this time," I said. He had been the one in charge of that before, but I needed to take the lead. After all, the work was mine. I was the one who would be evaluated by it.

Keith ended up sitting with his back to the headboard of the bed with one arm over his head. The muscles on his arms and chest contracted, giving me good texture for the drawing. Of course, like this, he was completely exposed to me. That had to be the point, though. I sat on the chair this time, and placed the sketch pad on the foot of the bed.

This time, I did lose myself, and everything came easier. The lines blurred together, the music was loud in my ears, and my hand travelled over the page much more easily. His face was set in stone, while I traced the general lines. After maybe fifteen minutes, he groaned and my eyes snapped up to his, bursting my bubble. He had always been the perfect subject to draw because he never complained or made a sound.

"What?" I asked, irritated that he had interrupted my concentration.

"You need to stop biting your lip, Sky."

I looked at him confused, and frowned. Was that really an important thing right now, if it would destroy the chance of a perfect drawing? He noticed my annoyance and sighed.

"If you don't stop doing that, there'll be a lot more of my pose to mess with your work."

I was still confused, and it was only when he nodded downward that I understood. The realization made me snap my pencil, which went flying through the air. I turned to pick it up, only to let the sketch pad fall to the floor, too. Keith chuckled from the bed.

I knew I was blushing deeply by the heat radiating from my cheeks. He was having a laugh at my expense.

The concentration was long gone, so I had to grasp something quickly to distract myself. I was almost curious enough to keep biting my lip, but it didn't work if I forced it, and I was afraid to look like a lunatic.

"Talk to me," I said.

He waited a few seconds before replying and already sounded cautious. "About what?"

I shrugged. "Anything. Tell me what the best memory you have is."

Keith took a long time answering and my heart constricted in my chest.

He could be deciding whether to tell me, but I was already afraid that wasn't the case. He was really looking for a good memory. What kind of person was I? I'd lived next door to him since we were kids and I'd never noticed he had been that miserable.

After what seemed like an eternity, he opened his mouth. "Remember Ryan's birthday, when we went to a baseball game?"

I nodded, vaguely remembering being upset that my father didn't let me tag along. He said it was something he wanted to do with my brother, like father-son bonding.

"We were around eleven or twelve. Ryan never liked baseball and was always a fan of football, like my brother, but I'd been through a rough few weeks, and out of the blue, he asked your father to take us to a baseball game for his birthday. I remember the look on your father's face when his eyes landed on me. He knew Ryan was doing it for me, so he kept insisting that he choose something different. Your brother put his foot down and said, 'That's the present I want. If you can't take us to the game, then I don't want anything else.'"

My hand had long gone still, and his eyes were fixated on the window as he recalled the memory. I gripped the pencil harder. I just wanted to go back in time and hug that boy tightly.

"In the end, your father ended up taking us both, and I remember having the time of my life. I don't even know if Ryan knew the rules to the game by then, or any player's name, but he cheered all through the game, alongside me. Your father had a friend somewhere who had gotten him passes to the locker room, where all the players congratulated Ryan and signed T-shirts and even a ball for us. I remember being so happy that I wasn't even jealous Ryan was getting most of the attention. When we got home, you had baked a chocolate cake with your mother."

"Oh my God, I remember that!" I said, outraged. "You laughed at me for having chocolate all over my face, and then you licked my cheek. So gross." I faked a disgusted shudder.

We had ended all pretense of working. My sketch pad was lying on the bed, and I was leaning forward, trying to look menacing, which only made him chuckle harder.

"Not as I remember it—not gross at all. You were very sweet, then." He was sitting straight now, with a pillow over his lap. "Best cake ever."

I stuck my tongue out at him, and, after a good laugh, he became serious again, got up, dressed in his jeans, and reached for his bookshelf.

"A week later, your brother went to your father and confessed that he had lost the ball playing with it. Your father was so mad that he grounded Ryan for a while. Only after his punishment was over did he come to me to give me the ball, asking me not to tell your father." He took his arm from behind his back so I could see the baseball in an acrylic box. It looked worn from a game, but the signatures were impeccable. He had cherished it all these years.

Ryan had always seen something in Keith that I was only just starting to understand. He was worth it—worth the punishment and the risk. I got up and went to him. I ended up fixing my eyes on his.

"Your best memory is with my brother?"

"I remember talking about a chocolate cake somewhere during the story." I gave him a weak smile. I'd almost forgotten about that day. What I remembered, was feeling that he'd been teasing me back then. What if he wasn't? What if that had been his way of playing with me and of telling me he'd needed me to be his friend, too? I had been too wrapped up in my happy childhood to see that he needed someone other than Ryan.

"I'm sorry," I blurted out.

He set the ball back on the shelf and turned to me. "For what?"

I was too emotional these days, and tears were already threatening to pour from my eyes. "For not being there for you."

His frown deepened and he shot his arm forward, as if he was contemplating caressing my cheek. He changed his mind, though, and dropped his fist along his tense body. "You have nothing to be sorry about.

You were a kid—a girl—and much younger than me."

I shook my head vigorously. "It doesn't matter. I should've never stopped trying to reach you." This time, it was my hand that reached him. I traced his forehead, while he closed his eyes tightly. I moved down his right eye and to his chin, trying hard not to touch his lips. If I did so, I would lose it. Before I could back away from him, he grabbed my wrist forcefully and pulled me against him. My heart was beating furiously and I kept my eyes on his chest, which was heaving slightly. With my free hand, I traced the dragon's face, with its bared teeth sinking into his flesh. It looked so real.

"I owe my sanity to Ryan, Sky, which means I owe him everything. If he says to jump, I'll ask, 'How high?' If he says to stay away, I'll stay away."

My eyes landed on his, finally, but I took too long answering him. He turned and grabbed a change of clothes. "I'm going to grab a shower, and I'll meet you downstairs to cook dinner, okay?"

I just stood there, dumbfounded, without knowing what to do or say. Had his words meant he cared about me, but that Ryan was standing between us?

After he turned the water on, I decided to leave for the kitchen. I needed to do something for his birthday, even if he didn't want it. The day he'd been born was worth celebrating.

The first thing that popped into my head was chocolate cake, but I didn't have enough time to make it before he ended his shower. Something told me he wouldn't appreciate it today, anyway. For dinner, I still had no idea what to make. I decided I would ask him out. He couldn't decline if the main purpose wasn't to celebrate. I skipped up the stairs and opened his door without knocking.

Keith was standing in the middle of the room, still pulling his boxers up. I stopped and blushed. "No knocking now? Rude much?" he asked.

Okay, his mood had gotten a bit darker. "I spent the afternoon watching you naked, so… modesty is long gone by now." I rubbed one foot with the other, feeling embarrassed. "I—I came here to ask you out to dinner." The question started out weak, but I tilted my head up and ended with more confidence.

Keith started shaking his head. "No birthday, I told you."

I interrupted him before he could complain more. "No birthday, I promise. I just don't feel like cooking, and I really want Indian. Pretty please."

He groaned while putting his shirt on, and grabbed a belt from the other jeans on the chair. There was something kind of erotic about seeing a man getting dressed—maybe even more than drawing him naked.

"It's the second time today you're pouting on me. Don't, please." He turned to give me an intimidating look. A while ago, it would've worked, but not today. I just rolled my eyes.

"I won't pout if you come." My voice was joyful, but that didn't seem to deter him.

"Don't pout, don't mention our previous conversation, no presents, cake, or happy birthday, and I'll go with you, okay?"

I jumped up and down in front of him, clapping my hands, which seemed to improve his mood. "I'm going to get dressed, then." I ran to my room and spent the next fifteen minutes searching for something to wear that would be nice, but not date-nice, nor birthday-nice. It wasn't easy. I ended up choosing tight dark jeans and a dark blue shirt. When I made my way downstairs, Keith was already waiting by the door, wearing his black coat and a frown.

"Don't be a baby. It'll be fun," I stated, satisfied that he hadn't backed out.

CHAPTER TWENTY-THREE

We arrived at the restaurant at eight. Keith parked, still silent, and we walked through the restaurant door together. We ordered quickly and I placed my head in my hands.

"You'll have to do a better job at amusing me, or I'll start doing all those things you asked me not to." A small pout started forming on my face, and I started humming the birthday song. He finally smiled.

"Fine. What do you want to talk about?" He had ordered red wine and I served myself a small portion. I didn't really appreciate the taste, but it looked sophisticated to drink it.

"What about your art? We're always talking about me." I chewed the first bite and almost moaned. It was really good. Last time I'd been in the restaurant was with Cody, on my birthday, and I'd been so nervous that I didn't appreciate the food.

From what I could see on Keith's face, he, too, enjoyed the food. Maybe he'd have a good time, even if this was not a real celebration. "There's nothing special about my paintings. Maybe one day I'll take you to one of the galleries." My head shot up and I dropped the fork.

"Galleries? As in exhibitions? More than one?" I had no idea that he was already having shows—that was huge.

"I've had two, so far. At the first one, I sold half of the paintings, and, at the second, I sold them all. I'll have another one at the beginning of the year, so I have too much work right now to be going on dates with you."

I just shook my head. "Don't be tedious; you're the one always telling me I need to go out, have fun, and experience the world to be able to make art." I finished my dinner with a satisfied pat to my stomach.

Keith didn't reply right away, but he was eating his own words. "You're right. What do you want to do, now?" He crossed his arms and tilted his head sideways.

I pondered his question. I wasn't much for going out, but it was his birthday, and, even if he didn't want to celebrate, I could ask him to go to a bar or a club to have a couple of non-celebratory drinks. "Take me somewhere—a place you like to go alone to have a drink."

Keith took a couple of minutes thinking, and, after paying for dinner and not letting me pay for mine, he finally got up and motioned for me to follow him outside. "There's a place I like to go. It sometimes has live music. Tonight probably isn't so calm, because it's Saturday. You stay close and don't walk around alone—I'm sick of chasing drunk guys off of you."

Keith was exaggerating big time, but I didn't want him backing off on his decision, so I just shrugged, tightened my jacket, and followed him to his car. This night was so not about me, but he wasn't supposed to know that.

The club was packed. Quiet time wasn't in the cards tonight, but we could still have a good time. Keith knew the bouncer, who didn't card me. We took a seat at the only two empty stools at the bar, and were immediately crowded by two of the waitresses. They beamed, giggled, and hung onto Keith much closer than I had been all night.

"Keith, baby, it's been ages since you came here." The first platinum blonde rolled her eyes, while the second one nodded so enthusiastically that I was waiting for her neck to break.

He just shrugged and looked around, as if they were bothering him. Maybe he would have the decency to look ashamed around me for his previous womanizing behavior. I bet that, if he had been alone, he wouldn't give them the cold shoulder.

"I've been busy," he answered, shrugging again. He then ordered for the both of us: a beer for him and a girly drink for me.

I should have been mad at the assumption that I wouldn't know how to order for myself, but I just wanted him to have a good time. If being controlling was the way, then, for tonight, I would endure.

The girls left, but not before giving me a sour look, as if it was my fault Keith had such a hot and cold demeanor. I was sure they were about to spit in my drink.

"I know how to order for myself, and, for someone who gets so pissed at me for drinking alcohol, you sure know how to get me drunk." I had no intention of sounding bitter, but I guess that was the way he interpreted it, because he turned with a frown in place.

"I don't like you drinking when you're alone and with those friends of yours." He sounded spiteful. "I keep you safe, and, besides, I won't let you get drunk." He turned to the crowd and crossed his arms, while I stood still. I had to open my big mouth.

"Are you that sure?"

Keith heard me, but didn't bother turning. He kept admiring the dancers stumbling around us. "About what?"

"Keeping me safe." My voice was getting weaker, because I knew I was moving into dangerous waters. If he sensed I was keeping something from him, he would pester me, until I gave him what he wanted. He knew how to be persistent.

He turned and leaned forward. "What are you talking about? When didn't I keep you safe?"

The bartender placed our drinks in front of us, saving me. "Hi, Keith. Long time, no see." The guy was older—maybe in his thirties—but that didn't stop him from looking at me from head to breasts. He couldn't see anything else, with the counter between us. If he could have, he would have done the whole creepy thing from head to toe.

Keith groaned and pulled me against him. "This is Ryan's sister. Don't even think about it." He added, "I've been busy." He picked up his beer and sipped, never letting go of my waist, especially now that two other guys had sat on my left.

The bartender gave him a smirk, and, before turning around, muttered, "I can see that."

The whole conversation turned Keith's mood down even more, but, at least, it had distracted him from the track our conversation had been headed down. After my second drink, I turned to him, bored. Two guys had asked me to dance, but, at the growl coming from beside me, as if I was some territory to claim, they backed off without waiting for my reply.

"I want to dance. If you don't let me go with anyone else, you'll have to do it." I pulled on his shirt and he didn't offer much resistance.

The music was loud and angry, much like it had been at the Halloween party. After a couple of minutes with us conscious of the other's presence, we started letting go. I'd never been much of an outgoing person, so I'd only danced at school's functions, before, usually with Cody or my friends. Every time, it had felt constrained, like I didn't know what to do with my limbs without looking like a madwoman. With Keith, all of that disappeared. We connected like I hadn't connected with anyone, before.

The music beat loudly in my ears and I was able to close my eyes and trust Keith with myself. His skills helped, of course—the boy could dance. From time to time, I opened my eyes and saw girls watching us, envying me. I was so mad before, when girls got mad at me for no apparent reason, because of my connection to Keith or Cody.

Right then, I felt like the prettiest girl at that club, as if a guy like Keith found me hot enough to hook up with. I didn't know if it was the alcohol clouding my judgment, or the whole club vibe, but I wanted Keith so badly. I grinded myself against him and heard his intake of breath, but he didn't push me away. In fact, he tightened his hold on my hips, pulling me almost painfully against him.

Keith leaned forward and nuzzled my ear with his nose. I could feel sweat running down my back, so I probably didn't smell very good, but I knew Keith was sweating, too, by the way his shirt clung against his skin. The only thing I could smell on him, though, was his unique scent, with a hint of deodorant.

The music changed, and this song was calmer. Keith stepped away, but didn't let go of me completely. I knew his wheels were turning, and, in a few seconds, he would realize what a mistake this had been. I didn't want him to regret this. We had a connection, even if he would never admit to it. I didn't want us to go back to being cold roommates.

"I need to pee and get some water. Do you want to chaperon me?" I smiled. Nothing could stop his train of thought like talking about basic body needs. He nodded and followed me to the line of girls at the ladies' room.

"I can't understand why girls have lines and guys don't," I said, before he could talk about what had gone down on the dance floor.

He chuckled. It was a good sign. "You don't, really? They go in pairs, talk nonstop, and apply makeup, even if they don't need it." I shrugged. My friends at school liked to go to the bathroom and do all those things, and I ended up tagging along, but I never understood it. Bathrooms usually smelled bad, especially at clubs.

The girls in front of us were openly ogling Keith by the time that it was their turn to go. "Hi, I'm Cara. This is my friend, Janice. Do you wanna have a drink?" This one was also blonde. What was with Keith and blondes?

I saw him check her out discreetly, but he looked bored. "Sorry, not tonight."

That bothered me. As soon as he'd said "sorry," I had been about to smile triumphantly. Then he'd disappointed me with the "tonight" part, as if tomorrow would be okay. Of course, the girls beamed at that, understanding the same thing I felt: that I was just tonight's entertainment and would be discarded after a hook-up. I couldn't even stomp away angrily to never see him again, like I would have done with any other guy. The first reason was that Keith actually lived with me and was my ride. The second was that I really needed to pee.

After they left, but not before slipping their numbers to Keith, who didn't even move or protest, I finally got the bathroom to myself. I didn't want to linger to see if he read the paper or went to speak to them.

I did my business and washed my hands, looking at the aged mirror in front of me. What did he see when he looked at me? His best friend's annoying little sister? His little brother's girlfriend? Or did he see someone else, entirely? Did he see a plain girl who didn't know how to have fun, who couldn't draw very well, and who had overbearing parents?

I wasn't ugly—I knew that. My hair was shiny and my eyes were freaky, even though everyone said they were my best feature. My mouth was simple: not too big, and not too small. The rest of my body was okay. I was neither skinny, nor fat, but my muscles hadn't seen a gym since junior year, so they weren't as toned as they'd once been. I'd always thought my breasts were normal, but, from what I'd seen around me since I'd come to college, I realized they were probably on the smaller scale, especially when Keith was concerned.

I'd seen the girls he had hooked up with. I rarely wore makeup. Tonight, I had put on mascara and a bit of lipstick, which was long gone by now. I looked washed up.

We had gone out to make Keith feel better, and I'd just ended up taking a blow to my self-esteem. I'd never felt very attractive, even with Cody by my side. Keith had just taken it to another level.

When I finally got out of the bathroom, the first girl in line looked annoyed, before shoving me to the side to get in.

"What took you so long? You were alone, and, as far as I know, you don't wear makeup," Keith stated. I just wanted him to be quiet.

"I'm on my period," I blurted out, shutting him down. I wasn't, but seeing the discomfort on his face was worth it.

I made my way to the exit, but, before we could reach it, Keith grabbed my arm. "What's wrong with you?"

"I want to leave." I pulled at my arm, but he tightened his hold.

Keith didn't bother answering. He led the way to the car, shut the door angrily, and turned the engine on before speaking.

"I don't know if it's that time of the month or not, but you were fine before going inside that bathroom. Now you look mad."

He started driving us home, and I inhaled deeply a few times, searching for an excuse. I could just say I was tired, but my blood was still boiling, and I had to lash out.

"Did you have to do that?" My voice came out much weaker than I intended. I didn't want him thinking I was hurt, just mad.

"Do what?" He was genuinely confused, and that just pissed me off more.

"Give hope to those girls." Now I just sounded like a jealous girlfriend.

"Hope? I turned everyone down." He was still confused as we started on the path to our house. In a couple of minutes, I wouldn't have the dark and the distraction the ride provided to state my most private thoughts.

Turning to the window, I kept going. "The ones in the line. They slipped their numbers into your pocket and you gave them the impression that you would be done with me by tonight."

"First of all, I'm not committed to anyone, so I can hook up with anyone I want. I would never do that with you by my side, but that doesn't mean I won't get together with them another night." He sounded irritated, now, and, even though I had my own reasons, he wasn't completely wrong. I was starting to feel like a third wheel. I had taken him out so he could have fun. Maybe he'd wanted to go out alone and find some company for the night. I had ruined his chances by tagging along.

Even knowing I was exaggerating, I couldn't stop the words. "Well, you have their numbers right beside your dick, so you can drop me off and go meet them." I opened the door and slammed it, rushing to get inside before he could see the tears that threatened to spill over. It was irrational, but I knew I was falling for him, and this was exactly what I was going to get, until I finished college and moved out. It would be much worse, actually, because Keith had been holding himself back. He respected me and stopped bringing girls home, but that wasn't the same as stopping being interested in girls, altogether.

I went directly to my room, straining to hear the engine to see if he was going to follow my suggestion. He must have decided it was too much work, because, not a minute later, right before I slammed my bedroom door, I heard the front door closing and a loud sigh.

I hadn't bothered locking up, because I hadn't expected him to come barreling into my room, just after I took my shirt off, which smelled horribly of tobacco. I was inside my closet, searching for a clean one. I had decided I would just take a cold shower, even though it was two in the morning.

"Sky," he said, startling me and making me drop the shirt to the floor. I was standing in front of him in just my jeans and bra. I wanted to scream and cover myself, but the confused, embarrassed, and heated look on Keith's face stopped me from covering myself.

"What? Too skimpy for you?" I asked defiantly, tilting my head.

He just gave me a dark laugh and that smirk that I just wanted to slap off his face. "You have no idea," he muttered, tousling his hair before striking out for me. With his hands on my waist, he slammed me against the closet door—not too gently. "What's wrong with you?" he hissed. "You're all hot and bothered on the dance floor, and then you come out of the bathroom all jealous, like a clingy girlfriend. What's gotten into you?"

I tried to pry his hand off of me, but, after giving up, I pushed against his chest, instead. "Get off me. I'm not one of your fan club's sluts."

He laughed again, but there was no amusement in his voice. "Why do I get the impression you want to be one of them?"

That had done it for me. I pushed him away with all the force I could muster. "That's the second time you've called me a whore and the second time I want to slap someone. Maybe you should just leave and never speak to me again."

Regret showed on his features, but I couldn't give in so easily, so I shoved him to the door. He stopped me before I could close it on his face.

"I didn't call you a slut. I asked if you wanted what they want: a piece of me, of my body, just to leave in the morning and never look back. Huh? Is that it, Sky? Maybe I'm not the only one who has self-esteem problems around here."

With that, he left for the attic and slammed the door, before I could even move.

The next day would have been the perfect opportunity to continue our drawing lesson, but I had a feeling he wouldn't be up for it.

The morning went by quickly. At lunch, I cooked for myself, not expecting him to come down the stairs when I was about to sit on the couch to eat my pasta. His hair was still wet from a shower and he was only wearing sweatpants.

"Sorry I woke up so late. I was up until eight."

I dropped the fork into the bowl and turned to face him. Maybe he had forgotten last night completely. He hadn't had much to drink, so it was unlikely.

"I didn't cook for you." It was the only thing that left my mouth.

Keith just shrugged and went to the kitchen. I had the urge to follow, to see if he was the same person who had yelled at me last night. Maybe he thought we were even. I'd yelled at him, so he'd yelled back. If that's how he wanted to act, it was fine with me. I had woken up much calmer. I stayed on the couch, though, eating my warm meal, while he made something in the kitchen.

When Keith was done preparing his lunch, he sat beside me on the couch. I was done with mine, and I had to resist the urge to get up and put some distance between us.

"Are you really on your period?" he asked, which made me cough in surprise. Was that the first thing we would be talking about? Maybe he was seeing if that would explain my behavior last night.

"Don't blame my hormones for what I said yesterday. You made me feel bad, and I stated so. You're the one who's always telling me I need to grow some calluses. Wasn't that the expression you used?" I turned to him. "And no, I'm not. So, no crazy hormones are to blame." I crossed my arms, waiting for the surprise that was about to come, for sure. Keith never did or say what people expected of him.

"And I love to see you mad, even if I get slapped in the process." He didn't seem pleased—on the contrary, he believed in what he was saying, which didn't give him any satisfaction. It was kind of sick to love getting me mad. As if sensing my confusion, he added, "You get so passionate when you're mad, or when you're focused on painting or cooking." He seemed to shake his thoughts, along with his words, but they still lingered in the air. I was still focused on them when he dropped the next bomb. "I want to draw you nude."

I took a few seconds to process everything, from the moment we argued yesterday, to the moment he proposed something like this. "You're crazy," I muttered, not having the energy to shout. I was still hoping the words had been only in my head.

My parents had seen me naked, my siblings, and even my doctor, but no one else, including them, had for a long time. Not even Cody. We might have fooled around, but we'd never taken our clothes off completely. Now, Keith, who was practically a stranger, wanted something so private from me.

Strangely, even with my brain shouting at me to refuse and be outraged, some deep part of me wanted to do it. The sane part resurfaced, then. I had nothing special for him to draw. There were models in our class who were much more beautiful than me. He wouldn't have any special connection like

I did with him, and that would crush me.

"I see the wheels turning in your brain. Stop thinking," he said, placing the bowl on the table and grabbing my hand in his. I tried to pull back, but, like last night, I was weak against him in every sense. "If you want my help with your work, you need to trust me. You need to have confidence in yourself, even with your body."

"I—I don't know." He smiled, knowing full well that I was done for. He just needed to push a little more and I would agree. "My brother, he'll…" Keith shook his head.

"He texted me, saying he wouldn't be home until late tonight. They have some kind of dinner to attend."

Keith stood up and pulled me with him. "It won't be that painful, I promise."

He sounded like he was promising something entirely different, and the butterflies in my stomach didn't calm down. "Let me take a shower," I said, thinking that, if I was going to do this, I was, at least, going to shave and wash every part like crazy, even if he wasn't going to touch. Oh my God, what was I getting myself into? There would be no going back—ever. Keith would always be the first guy to see me naked.

I was scared and thrilled at the same time. It wasn't like when I'd thought I was going to sleep with Cody. It felt so different. Even if there would be nothing sexual about this, it felt so intimate at the same time— more intimate than sex, even. Painting was looking at the model and really seeing them. He would be trying to piece me together and see past my body, like I did with him.

The shower was warm while I shaved and washed, but, at the end, I turned it to cold. I needed some clarity as to what I was about to do.

"Don't dry your hair." I almost knocked my head on the counter at Keith's voice and instinctively tightened the towel around me—as if he wasn't going to see everything in a few minutes. I didn't know what I was supposed to wear, but leaving the bathroom with just a towel was ridiculous. I fished an old shirt that reached my thighs out of the laundry basket. It was baggy enough to conceal my body and was still clean.

I had no idea why Keith didn't want me to blow dry my hair, but I supposed he didn't want me wearing any make-up, either, so I went in search of him, feeling ridiculous in just a shirt. I found him in his room, looking around for something. I stayed at the door as an idea formed in my head.

I coughed to get his attention and paused, waiting for him to turn to me. His eyes darted from my face to my legs and back up. A deep frown formed on his face and, before I could make my demands, he blurted out, "Is that shirt Cody's?"

I mimicked his frown and shook my head. His face softened and I gathered up my courage.

"If you want me to do this," I paused for emphasis and rubbed one foot against the other. Keith's eyes shot down to the shirt's hem and I saw my opportunity. "We'll do it in the attic." His eyes met mine and his face scrunched up again. "What's the problem? I've been there. Nothing weird shot out of the shadows to bite me." Keith opened and closed his mouth twice. His hands shot to his hair and he looked around, searching for something. I tried to explain further. "I don't feel comfortable here in your room, or in mine, so... please."

He finally turned to me, still angry. "Rule number one: you do what I ask. Rule number two: no snooping around."

It felt like such a victory to be going upstairs, and in the middle of the day, nonetheless. It was a place so sacred that not even Ryan had been there. I nodded enthusiastically and turned to go upstairs.

"Not so fast." Keith grabbed me by the back of the shirt and pulled me behind him. "Give me five minutes, and then you can come upstairs, okay? It'll be a test. If you obey the five minutes, we'll do the drawing upstairs. If not..." He left the sentence hanging.

I sat at the last step and watched the minutes on my watch go by. After five and a half minutes, for good measure, I went upstairs and knocked softy on the door, wanting to start this whole thing on his good side.

I opened the door and the room was much more different than what I'd seen at night. There were windows all around, casting sunlight into the room. The mattress was in the same place, with crumpled sheets on it. On the other side of the room, dozens, if not hundreds, of canvases lined the wall. Most were covered with white cloth, while others were turned around.

As the bed was still messed up and the work table was filled with dirty brushes and rags, I guessed he'd spent the five minutes covering the paintings. I had no idea what kind of work he did that he couldn't show me. It would be good for my own drawings.

"You can sit on the mattress, if you want. The sheets are clean—I just slept there last night." I stopped with my examination before he categorized it as snooping around and crawled to the middle of the bed. I was about to pat the sheets into place when he asked me to sit on them as they were. I slumped and waited for further explanation. I had sat on the messy bed with my leg bent under me and hadn't taken the shirt off, because I wanted to do it at the last minute.

Keith started to close the curtains on the windows, confusing me. Someone who had this kind of light shouldn't be covering it up, after all. When almost the entire room was dark, he turned a lamp on. The light was strong enough to light up half of the room, but it had a yellowish color that created a more romantic environment than the sunlight. The butterflies were back in my stomach. I was nervous, already, and I hadn't even taken off the only piece of clothing covering me.

Keith turned some music on: rock, not too hard, and not too soft. It kind of suited the mood. "Are you ready?" Keith asked, sitting on the floor with a sketch pad on his lap. I guessed he wouldn't be painting on a canvas, but would create a detailed drawing on paper. This was much more intimate.

"You need to promise me you won't show this to anyone," I pleaded, with my hands at the edge of the shirt.

Keith gave me a lopsided smile. He could lie, but I knew him too well by now to know he would never do that to me. "Only if you're the one who gives me permission."

I nodded and slowly took the shirt off. I heard Keith's inhale, as if he hadn't seen dozens of girls naked before—as if I was something special. I wanted to believe it, but I wasn't that stupid. I wouldn't make the same mistakes the girls at my high school had. I couldn't feel special around him: that was his way of luring us in. I didn't think he could control himself.

Without lifting my head, I threw the shirt away from the bed and turned to Keith, not meeting his eyes. "Now what?" My voice was weak, but, at the same time, I sounded mad. It wasn't my intention.

Keith coughed and scratched his head before answering. Maybe he was nervous, too. I was, after all, his friend's sister and his brother's ex. "Relax. Turn just slightly to the light and rest your arms in your lap."

The light was placed so expertly that I envied his imagination. My right side was almost completely dark, while the left was lit by the warm light. It would be a difficult, but entertaining piece of work for him. Maybe I would be able to draw him like this. He would owe me big time.

Time was going by slowly and it seemed like an eternity before I heard the pencil hit the paper. He was studying me, which was normal for a drawing. This didn't suppress my anxiety, though. Keith was seeing all of me, inside and out. I lifted my eyes to him. The light had been placed close to him, so it hurt my eyes and prevented me from see him very well. His hands were moving, though, and the sound of pencil skirting across paper told me he was immersed in his work, so I relaxed. I knew he wasn't really seeing me, now—he was in his own head.

Every time his head snapped up, I turned my face to the side. "You need to stop moving. You can keep looking at me." He smirked and continued working. I shifted and then settled on a position. Every now and then, he messed his hair with his free hand. The strands were pointing everywhere. It was so sexy watching Keith draw that the first feeling that crept up on me was jealousy for the models he surely hired.

"Do you do this often?" I asked, my voice rough from being quiet and nervous.

He kept working and I almost believed he hadn't heard me. Then he asked, "Do what? Paint?" He looked up, confused, and met my eyes, focusing on me and not on the drawing. I didn't want that: I wanted Keith focused on his work. I just couldn't back off, now, though.

"Hire people to pose for you?" He kept his confused expression, until he shook his head.

"No, I draw from memory, mostly. I haven't drawn anyone live since my drawing classes."

It wasn't the answer I was expecting, but it calmed my jealousy. I needed to keep it bottled up—for both my sake and for that of our kind-of-friendship.

My back was starting to hurt, even though I was finally relaxed and less self-conscious, when Keith muttered that he was finished.

My first instinct was jump up to get the shirt, but it would look ridiculous. He had spent an hour looking at my body, so I took my time reaching for it, only to have Keith snatch it from under my hand.

"I've seen everything there is to see, Sky. Relax." He was looking into my eyes, not my body, but I covered my breasts, anyway.

"I mentioned that yesterday, and you covered yourself, anyway." He surprised the hell out of me when he took his own shirt off and extended it to me. He threw mine to a pile of laundry in the corner.

I sat straighter, gaping, until he placed the shirt over my head, himself. It smelled so good that I had to fight the impulse to sniff it. It felt so intimate to wear his clothes while I had nothing else on underneath. I guessed that was exactly his intention.

Keith was about to close the sketching pad when I jumped from the bed. "What? No, no. You're going to show it to me." I placed my hands on my hips, telling him that I was going nowhere, until he showed me the drawing.

Keith looked embarrassed, and I was sure his work would be perfect, so I couldn't understand why. He placed the sketch pad in my hands. I sat down to look at it better in the light.

It was perfect. It was like looking in the mirror, but there was something else to it. It was my eyes—the way they were looking at him. I was so surprised that I looked up to Keith, but he had turned around and was messing with his art supplies. I wasn't sure I'd been covering my feelings very well, by what my eyes were showing. I took my time appreciating his work and tried to calm myself. His smell around me, on his shirt, and on his sheets wasn't helping.

"It's… perfect. I just don't know if it's really me. She looks much prettier." It wasn't a complete lie. She looked like someone else—someone sexier and more confident. Keith sat on the bed and placed the pad on the mattress, behind us. He took my hand. It was his turn to have part of his face shadowed, which made him look more mysterious and more dangerous, which I knew he was—at least, for my heart.

He turned my hand palm up and traced the line that went up to my wrist. "You don't see yourself," he whispered, turning my skin into goose bumps. His dark gray eyes met mine and I finally understood the gut-wrenching knowledge that was a goner. I had fallen in love with him, against all of my protests—against everything everyone kept warning me about.

I was in love with Keith Hale.

CHAPTER TWENTY-FOUR

I ended up rushing downstairs and shutting myself in my room. I slid down to the floor with my back against the door, trying to keep my heart from leaping from my chest.

I needed to backpedal and return to when I wasn't stupid enough to fall for a guy like Keith. I had to think about Cody and Ryan. I wasn't very good at keeping my feelings hidden—blame it on my freakish eyes, or the blush that appeared on my face, but I was as clear as water.

When my legs and butt were as cold as I felt, I got up from the floor and threw some clothes on. I had to start dinner and form a plan to distract my heart. I needed a rebound, like my sister said, and it couldn't be Keith, period. Even if he was up for it, I would never recover from him—not with any rebound in the world.

Keith was already in the kitchen, with wet hair and fresh clothes, as if he had taken a second shower. He was chopping garlic and I leaned against the door, silent, and watched him cook, while he hummed a rock song.

He turned to pick up a frying pan from the island counter and met my eyes. "You could've said something."

I pushed forward, met him at the other side of the counter, and sat. "What can I do to help?"

Keith looked around, chose an onion, and placed it in front of me. "Here: chop this."

We ended up sitting on the couch, watching documentaries on TV, as we waited for dinner to be ready. We didn't talk and never bothered to get up to turn the lights on, so the night fell and enveloped us. The house was warm, but it still gave me chills after the sun set and no longer warmed the house.

The timer buzzed, announcing that our dinner was ready. Keith picked up two plates, but I took them from him. "No—your dish deserves the dining room. Take the table cloth from the top drawer."

We sat across from each other with our meal steaming between us. Maybe having eating in front of the television would have been a better idea, but I missed sitting at the table. Since Ryan and Cody stopped coming home for dinner, this room hadn't seen much use.

"Was it that painful posing for me?" Keith asked, smirking.

"Let's not talk about it, okay? It was embarrassing." I focused on the food.

"We should do it again," he said. I shook my head violently.

"No. No way. You had one chance—that was it." I ate the food noisily, making him chuckle.

We finished our meal with polite conversation about art. We had similar taste in artists.

My brother arrived late that night and I went to bed right after. Sleeping was hard when my mind was in overdrive with the day's events. I still couldn't believe I was capable of doing something like posing for Keith. I still couldn't believe I was falling for him.

I needed a rebound—for real, this time. I couldn't trust Shelby with this, and I didn't think Keith or Ryan would allow it. Maybe I could ask Keith for help. It would be safer, but it was unlikely he would help me.

The next day, Keith drove us to school, as he had a class in the morning. I spent almost the whole ride trying to come up with the courage to ask for his help.

"Keith," He turned to me at a red light. "Can I ask you something… without you flipping out on me?" He frowned, but nodded. "I want to go out." I made an effort to find the right words. "And find someone. You know, a rebound."

He parked the car and faced me. "What?" he asked incredulously. "I thought you were fine by yourself? You never pegged me for a girl who needs a boyfriend hanging on her arm all the time."

I grabbed my backpack from the floor. "I'm not—I just need to do something to take my mind off of—" I didn't want to lie and say Cody, because that wasn't who I needed to shake from my thoughts. I couldn't admit I was developing feelings for him, though. "Off of everything," I finished, waving my hand around us.

Keith wove his fingers through his hair, got out of the car, and slammed the door. "I don't like that idea. It's not you," he said, moving around the car to stand beside me. "But, if you're doing this, I'm coming with you. I don't trust your friend very much."

"You're very quick to judge said friend, after all, you had sex with her," I retorted, annoyed.

He opened and closed his mouth, and messed with his hair a bit more. "I didn't sleep with her." This made me stop and turn to him.

"You don't have to lie. I saw it."

"You didn't see me fucking her." It was his turn to be annoyed. A couple was passing us and the guy frowned at Keith, who remained unapologetic.

I flinched and blushed at his crudeness. "No, but she slept in your room."

He sighed, exasperated. "Nothing happened. She kissed me in the bathroom, I invited her to my room, and she fell asleep in my bed. I don't take advantage of drunken girls."

I stood still, digesting this news. A pleasant feeling took over my stomach and this was exactly what I'd wanted to avoid: feeling anything but friendship for him. Keith motioned for me to go to the art department, while he went the other direction. The stupid boy had made me believe the worst about him this whole time. He'd made me believe the worst about Shelby, as well, who probably didn't even remember that night.

Today was my last day of classes, except for Drawing, as the classes would be used to build our portfolio for evaluation, so tonight would be the best time to make my move. I would go to a bar and make out with someone. My mind was clearer, and I knew it wasn't safe for me to sleep with some random guy. I still needed to kiss a guy who didn't have "Hale" as the last name on their birth certificate.

When I got home that evening, the house was quiet. I took my time in the shower and choosing my clothes. It ended up being black skinny jeans and a white shirt. I would need a warm jacket, but I was sure the place we'd be going would be warm enough.

I still needed Keith's approval to go out. There was no way he wouldn't tell my brother if I didn't let him tag along.

When I went downstairs to eat something, even though my stomach had such a knot in it that I wouldn't be able to eat a proper dinner, Keith was already at the counter, pushing against his cell phone's screen.

"What did the phone do to you?" I asked, grabbing a carton of juice from the fridge. He mumbled something, annoyed, and finally looked up at me. I had pulled my hair into a bun and applied some make-up, but his eyes didn't go to my head, first. He looked at my legs and the small amount of cleavage I had, and slowly lifted his gaze to meet mine.

"Damn. You still want to go out?" He frowned.

Disappointed, I nodded. I'd thought he was checking me out, but he was just confused as to why I'd cleaned up like this. I just shrugged and turned to the cookies on the shelf. "Yes, I was hoping you would come with, but, if you have plans..." I trailed off, not admitting that I was too chicken to go out alone.

"No, I don't." He put the phone in his back pocket. "Where do you want to go?"

I shrugged again. I had no idea what the best places to hang out were. I never did this—try to pick up a guy at a bar. Keith was right: this wasn't me.

He nodded before grabbing a cookie from the package in front of me. "I know a place." He gave me five minutes to brush my teeth and grab a jacket, and then we got into his car and went to a different town twenty minutes away. This was good: maybe there, people wouldn't recognize him or me as Ryan's sister. A girl could hope.

The bar wasn't dark and shady, as I feared. It had white furniture and a lot of lights. The music was loud, but not so loud that people couldn't talk to each other. People around me looked like they were in their mid-twenties. Maybe an older guy would be better for my purpose. He would be more mature. On the other hand, he might request more than I was willing to give. I just had to breathe and be myself.

Keith's heat and smell wasn't helping to calm my nerves. After we grabbed a table and ordered two beers, I was realizing this wouldn't work. Any decent guy in the room would assume I was with Keith and would back away. I had to dance alone, at least.

"I'm going to dance—alone," I added when he started getting up.

It took me some time to stop feeling ridiculous on the dance floor. Keith's eyes were on me the whole time.

The first guy who approached me was tall and slim, with a hipster vibe. He was nice, but didn't show a hint of attraction to me and I didn't feel one, either. He was a good dancer, and, after a couple of songs, he stepped away to meet his friends. I didn't even catch his name.

The second guy showed his attraction toward me long before I felt any toward him. I saw Keith shaking his head at me and I just shrugged. Brody wasn't being disrespectful—just annoying. He sensed my lack of interest and turned to another girl.

The third guy was cute, like boy-next-door cute. He had blond hair, caramel eyes, dimples, and all. He was also a good dancer and had all the right moves. He whispered his name, David, asked for mine, and then placed his hands in safe places on me. I was starting to think he was the one, when a screeching redhead pushed me away from him and got in my face. The music wasn't very loud, so everyone turned to watch the scene.

"You think you can take my boyfriend from me? You slut! Go find an available guy," she screamed, while pushing me back. I'd never fought with someone other than my siblings, so I didn't know what the appropriate behavior was. David was just standing on the sideline, looking amused at his girlfriend.

"I didn't do anything," I tried pleading, but she just got more aggravated.

"You think a guy like David wants anything to do with you?" she sneered, looking me up and down. She was prettier than me and way more curvy—exotic, even, with all the red hair around her face. I felt like shrinking in front of everyone. It wasn't the first time I'd felt plain, and it certainly wouldn't be the last. I just wanted a friend right now, and Keith was nowhere to be found. Why had he wanted to be my wingman just to up and leave? He was probably with some girl. Of course he would have much more luck than me when it came to seduction.

I was then pulled back by two strong hands, and, before I could complain, Keith's cologne reached me and I instantly relaxed. "Is there a problem here?" he asked, calmly, but with that tone of his that sounded like a threat. His arms remained around me and I snuggled into him, seeking comfort.

"She—she was trying to hit on my man." The redhead stammered, looking between Keith and me. She was attracted to him, alright, and I couldn't blame her.

Keith sneered from behind me, pulling my back flat against him and leaning over my shoulder. "I don't think your guy could handle my girl. Don't you think I satisfy her enough?"

I tried not to blush at his words, but I was beaming. I felt the heat from him mix with the smugness inside me—even if what he'd said had been a lie.

It made me feel desirable and special. The girl didn't even bother answering. She knew I had the upper hand, now. No one would trade Keith for the clean-cut David. They left and everyone else returned to their activities. Keith's hands were still on my wrists, his heat was on my back, and his stubble was against my neck.

"I can't leave you for five minutes without you getting into a catfight." I felt his amusement, which calmed my nerves. I didn't like confrontations.

"You left me. I thought you were supposed to be my wingman." I looked over my shoulder to read his features.

His smiled dropped, but his grip on me intensified. "I never liked this plan of yours. I was watching how you handled the situation."

I disentangled from his hold and turned to him. "You were watching? What about stepping in sooner?" I crossed my arms over my chest and his eyes lowered to my cleavage for a fraction of second before coming to rest on my face again. He didn't look apologetic.

"I wanted to see your reaction. You were the one who wanted a night out. This kind of stuff happens." He shrugged, like it was no big deal. His gray eyes were sparkling with amusement.

I looked around, embarrassed. "Yeah—to you, not to me. I don't usually go out to find... company."

His expression turned to disgust. "You sound like you've been preying on innocent guys to have a one night stand with. I agreed on finding a guy so you could have a good time, not a one night stand. I wouldn't leave your side, anyway."

I pondered what he was saying. I would never make out with a guy with Keith as the audience. I wouldn't be able to, anyway. This had been his plan all along: agreeing to my terms without revealing his own. This night had been condemned from the start.

"Let's go home," I said, feeling the failure weighing on my shoulders. This wasn't important, but I still felt like I wasn't good enough. I would go through life feeling half-accomplished.

We were silent all the way home. I felt deflated, while Keith seemed bored. He'd been counting on having fun and ended up babysitting me and driving me around.

Before I could get to the stairs, he grabbed my elbow and spun me around, bringing me closer to him. "You didn't believe that girl, did you?"

Keith wasn't as oblivious as I'd once thought. He could see through me, but there was stuff I would prefer him not knowing, like how insecure I was. Being cheated on by my only boyfriend and being attracted to the biggest player I knew could hurt anyone's ego.

He shook his head like he was reading me again. "You're the most gorgeous girl I ever seen—and, believe me, I've seen and hooked up with a number of them."

I didn't know if I should feel flattered or jealous—maybe both. He'd called me gorgeous: me, plain Jane. I had never heard Keith say anything he didn't mean, so I didn't dismiss his compliment. I knew in my heart that he was speaking the truth, and I could see it in his eyes. The vulnerability he rarely showed was cracking through them.

"Can I draw you again?" he asked, before I could open my mouth to address the compliment. Saying "thank you" seemed insufficient. I felt my head nodding before I'd processed the request.

"Now?" I shrieked, when I saw the gleam in his eyes and the energy emanating from him.

"Why not? No one's home." He shrugged, pulling me up the stairs.

I tried to come up with a valid excuse, but I couldn't think of anything. "It's one in the morning, and—and, do you mean nude?" I knew what he meant, but I still needed the reassurance.

"Is there really any other way? It's not the first time. Come on Sky, I need this now." I could see the urgency in his eyes and sense it in his voice and through the electricity running from his fingers to mine. Like an addict, he pulled me upstairs, to the attic, and the butterflies in my stomach fluttered in anticipation. I needed this, too, but for reasons other than art. I needed him, but I also knew he would crush me.

I wouldn't survive Keith Hale.

CHAPTER TWENTY-FIVE

This time, Keith hadn't given me any warning. I had no time to shower or put on a robe, like a professional would do. He rushed me upstairs and into the attic. The first thing I noticed were the covered paintings, as he'd left them from the last time. The bed was made, so maybe he'd expected me to come back here—or hoped, at least.

Keith turned on the small lamp on the floor and turned off the main one, like last time.

I hadn't had enough to drink to take the edge off, so I was feeling very self-conscious in the middle of the room. Did he expect me to strip in front of him? He answered for me.

"Leave your underwear on, for now." He turned to set up the material for the painting. Apparently, this time, he was going to use canvas and paint, instead of pencil.

I hurried up before he turned again: I didn't want him to see the clumsy way I needed to jump on one foot to take off my skinny jeans. I didn't know how people could make taking their clothes off sexy. I always made a spectacle of myself with jeans or stockings, and I had no idea how people took off skinny jeans without making fools of themselves. Keith turned and stopped for a second, eying me—or rather, my body. He had a way of looking at me that made me feel pretty, like I was more beautiful than his hook-ups.

"Sky." His voice cracked and he tried again, this time looking around to avoid my eyes. "Can you sit on that stool, with one foot on the floor and the other leg bent with your right foot resting on the bench? Try to look relaxed."

Yeah, right; that was easy for him to say. I fidgeted on the stool. There wasn't much space for my butt and foot, but Keith came to me and helped by scooting me back and placing my heel on the stool. My other leg was slightly bent, so just my toes were touching the floor. I kind of felt sexy, but relaxed. I understood why he hadn't asked me to strip naked or to sit on the bed: the atmosphere was sizzling too much to do so. The way he looked at me seemed different than the last time.

He did something unexpected, next. Just before he sat on the floor, where he placed the canvas on a box to draw me from a lower angle, he took his shirt off. Sure, it was warm in the room—he had turned the heating on right when we'd gotten home—but I suspected he had other reasons, like making me blush, or making my eyes shine and darken at the same time. His crooked smirk told me how right I was.

Keith needed to rush this painting, because the position was tiring. My leg fell asleep halfway through it. It took him almost an hour, and, just as I was about to beg him to hurry, he put the brush down and stared at the painting, tilting his head, like he'd done all through the sitting.

"Help me down. My leg fell asleep," I said, not daring to move and risk falling on my head.

Keith jumped to his feet and rushed to my side, placing one arm under my knees and the other behind my back. I squealed when he lifted me up and moved me to the mattress. He got up to turn the canvas to us and sat beside me, pulling my sleepy leg over his. He started rubbing from my toes up to my thigh, while staring at the painting.

Everything seemed so automatic to him that I didn't know if he realized what he was doing: touching me in a lot of places. At first, it hurt, because my leg was still tingling, but the massage quickly helped, and I almost jumped up when he spoke.

"What do you think?" He turned to face me, as if he was seeing me for the first time since the painting ended. He then looked to the canvas, and I realized I hadn't even looked. I was so enthralled by him that the cause for my discomfort, just a few feet from us, had been long forgotten.

The painting was beautiful, but I'd never doubted him. He captured the shadows like an expert, as he always did. This time, however, the colors made everything more magical. Although I wore a simple white bra and matching panties, even the white against my skin looked sexy. He'd painted my hair in its bun, but I hadn't noticed that a few stands had fallen over my face and neck. I looked kind of sleepy—kind of... turned on. Oh, that had been the exact reason he'd taken his shirt off. He'd wanted me to look at him like that. That could only mean he knew how I felt.

I tensed in his hold and he noticed. "What? What's wrong?" It was freaking beautiful and perfect, and he saw me, Skylar Keaton—not plain Jane. His hands rested on my bare thigh, while he looked between his painting and me. A frown marred his beautiful face.

"Keith," I said, my rough voice calling his attention to me. "It's perfect." His eyes shot to my lips.

He didn't respond, but his attention shifted from the painting to me, and I couldn't bear the stare. Instead, I started tracing his tattoos. Without conscious thought, I had leaned closer. He pulled me flush against him, leaving just enough space for me to keep tracing the dragon's head on his shoulder.

"It's so amazing, the way the artist captured its essence. I would love to have one, but I would never be able to decide on something I wanted inked on me forever." Keith's skin was warm and soft against my fingers.

"If you want, I can draw you one. I did mine."

My eyes shot up to his, and surprise was evident on my face.

"No," He chuckled, "I didn't ink it. I sketched it on paper, and Fred did them. He's the only one I'll let near me with a needle. A tattoo needs to mean something. You just ink your body with something that touched your life."

My fingers traced the dragon's head and teeth, and I was about to ask what it meant, when my finger bumped a light scar on his shoulder, exactly where the dragon's canine was sinking in and pulling at the skin. I knew without asking that this small, round scar was the reason for the enormous dragon hugging his torso. The question was on my lips, but Keith's face shut down and he was pulling away from me emotionally, tensing under my touch.

"I won't ask. Don't end this just yet," I whispered, letting my hand fall onto his back to lightly scratch him with my short nails. He almost purred at the touch and I brought my other hand around his neck to do the same. He relaxed again and shifted to pull me closer. I ended up straddling him, because that was the only way I could keep scratching his back. I felt him harden under me, but I tried not to squirm at the sensation.

"What is this?" he asked after what seemed like an eternity. His eyes were clouded and dark and his own fingers tightened above my hips, pulling me to him, even though there wasn't an ounce of space between us as it was.

"I don't know. I just don't want it over yet. You feel good." I guess that was both the wrong and right thing to say, because he groaned and pulled me against him with sorrowful eyes.

"Sky, we should stop," Keith said without moving a muscle, except to grind against me again. I felt my own desire build up. If he kept going, I would end up embarrassing myself by coming just from sitting on his lap.

After a couple of minutes in silence, I leaned against his neck, resting my lips there. "I don't want to."

He let out an exasperated sigh. "You don't mean that. You want a rebound. I'm not the guy for that."

I kissed his neck and ran my nose behind his ear, which smelled incredible from the cologne he'd put on earlier. His fingers dug into my skin and he pushed me back enough for me to face him.

I didn't have an answer for him. He couldn't know that the rebound had been meant to keep me from doing exactly this—he would run like the devil was chasing him. I didn't answer, and, when I felt like he was about to end all of this and send me to my room, I kissed him.

I crushed my lips against his and he returned it with equal passion, pulling me against his warm skin. His tongue mixed with mine in a frenzied dance and I couldn't get enough of him. I lifted myself up and sat back down even closer to his hard-on. He moaned my name and shifted to be on top of me. He was the one doing the grinding, now. It felt so good that I threw my head back and curved my body to meet his.

"Sky," he pleaded, as if I was the key to his self-control. I had none, so I wouldn't be able to help him out. My hands reached his neck so he wouldn't talk, just kiss.

We made out for a while and it should've calmed us, but the more we kissed, the more I needed him—all of him. I'd never felt this way with Cody. Sure, we'd fooled around, but he had never ignited this desire for more. I needed it to feel complete—for my sanity.

"I want you, Keith. All of you." His head jerked back so his eyes could fix on mine.

"You're not thinking straight. You've been saving yourself. You deserve much more, Sky," he said, as sadness poured from him. He'd hinted so many times before that he didn't think he deserved me.

"I've been waiting for this. You want me, don't you?" I asked, sheepishly, as self-doubt grew inside me. I felt his attraction, but maybe that was just a reaction to the half-naked girl on top of him.

His smile was shy and sad and he leaned forward to touch his forehead to mine. "Like a man wants water in the freaking desert—but that's not the point. You deserve more. You just want me because I'm here. I can make you feel good and end at that." While he spoke, his hand reached the latch on my bra and unhooked it, letting the fabric fall from my body.

He wouldn't be seeing me for the first time, but I still felt unsure. He was used to slimmer girls with big assets—nothing like me. His eyes darted down and the gleam there destroyed any doubt. He liked what he saw. He kissed my neck and licked down my body, lingering at my breasts for a while.

When I started squirming, he stopped, and I gave him a disappointed groan. Keith chuckled, but looked at me, maybe asking for permission to slip my panties off. I lifted my butt from the mattress as an answer and the gleam in his eyes intensified. The unsure feeling was back, but it didn't stay long.

I was extremely turned on, and Keith's hand moved between my legs almost immediately. He didn't need any more reassurance that I wanted him there. I came quickly as his fingers played with me, and his smirk was quick to show.

"Someone was eager." He kissed my stomach and slid up to my face. He kissed me again, slower and sweeter. I didn't really want sweet right then, though. I might've come already, but I wasn't done. I still felt wound tight.

I whispered to the silent room, "I want you. Please." I wasn't beyond begging. I understood then why girls couldn't control themselves around him.

"Sky, you don't mean that." He saw my complaint coming and cut me off. "Say what you like about me, and then we'll see."

I searched around in my foggy brain for words that could describe what I felt right then, but I came up empty. I tried for trivial things, instead. "You're hot, you're gorgeous, you make me melt with your kisses, and you have incredible fingers." I smiled, but was faced with an annoyed Keith. He pulled away from me and I clung to his shoulders. "What?" I asked, not understanding.

"Everyone feels that way with me. I wanted to know why it would be different with us. I guess it isn't."

He was the one feeling self-conscious, now. I understood exactly what he meant. He'd told me before that girls also used him—it wasn't just the other way around. He felt that I was being one of them.

I pulled him tighter against me. "You know you mean much more than those superficial compliments. You're one of the kindest people I've ever known. You're always worried about me, my brother, and even yours. You are an amazing cook," I smiled when I felt him relax. "If I'm not careful, I'll end up gaining weight here."

I paused, because the list was still missing the biggest reason.

"And you see me—the real me. You're the only one. You see my doubts about art, about myself, and about my parents' approval. You see the loneliness and the girl who never fit in anywhere. You see me, and I think I'm starting to see you: the broken boy, searching for his own place in the world, who had been ignored by his father and who feels shadowed by his brother. You jump from girl to girl, looking for the one who will touch your heart. You drown in your work to fill the void. You dropped everything to take care of your dying grandfather."

I wanted to say much more, because I had much more to say, but my chest felt heavy. His eyes shone with more than passion—my intention hadn't been to make him cry. He stared, and, after what seemed like an eternity, his mouth crushed against mine in a heated and frenzied kiss. I knew I had him. I needed to be sure about this, or we'd both part, hurt. There was no turning back.

His clothes were on the floor when he stopped and turned to me. "Are you sure? We can stop whenever you want. Just say the word."

I nodded and smiled at him. I wanted him to be into this, too—I didn't want him to just be doing me a favor. He relaxed and leaned over the mattress to the bedside box and fished out a couple of condoms. He stared at them for too long, making me chuckle.

"I don't think they have instructions." I teased. Things were becoming too real, too fast.

He returned to me and nuzzled my neck. "I was checking the expiration date, smartass. I've never brought a girl up here." I was divided between feeling special that I was the first one he'd brought up here and feeling crushed that there had been other girls—something I knew too well.

He put the condom on and was over me again. I might've been holding my breath, because he stopped and looked me in the eyes. "Are you sure, Sky? You can't go back from this." I didn't know, at this point, if he was asking for me, or for him. Keith was all I wanted in the world right then, though.

I kissed him back and he slowly entered me. I was waiting for the pain the girls at school had described. I knew it wouldn't be good the first time, but it wasn't that bad. For the first couple of minutes, it stung, but I quickly recovered, and the pleasure was more evident than any pain. Keith was moving slowly and he lifted his head to look into my eyes. I felt so at ease, as if this was where I was supposed to be: in his arms. His eyes met mine and I knew I wasn't just a notch in his belt. He felt this, too.

"You feel too good. I'm not gonna last, baby." The term of endearment melted my heart.

"Let go. Don't hold back," I said, digging my fingertips into his neck. He shut his eyes and leaned against my neck, murmuring my name as he came. My heart swelled with pride. I had done this. I had made him lose control like this.

He took his time catching his breath and calming his heart, and so did I. Without a word, he removed the condom and I saw a smear of blood.

His concerned eyes met mine. "Are you okay? Did I hurt you?"

He looked so much younger right then, as he sought approval, that I just wanted to hold him and never let go.

I scooted forward and leaned my forehead against his. "It was perfect."

He snorted and picked up some napkins to clean us up. "That was not my best performance by a long shot. I think I lasted longer my first time." He sounded disappointed, and then I was the one feeling self-doubt. Was it me? Involuntarily, I pulled my knees against my chest to cover my body and rested my chin on them. Keith must've seen the hurt, because he quickly disentangled my limbs and pulled me to him to roll us over on the mattress.

"That was a compliment to you, Sky. I've never lost control like that. It might've been short-lived, but it was the best sex I've had in my life." I pushed myself up to rest on my elbow and eye him, not believing him. "It's true, Sky. I wouldn't lie to you." I smiled triumphantly and he smirked at me, pulling me against his chest again. There wasn't any place in the world I'd rather be.

"I like when you call me 'baby.'" I said against his skin, kissing the dragon's head on his shoulder.

"You've always complained about that," he joked. "Are you sore?"

I shook my head. I felt a bit of a sting, but that was nothing he needed to know about. He kissed the top of my head and pulled my chin up so he could kiss my lips.

This time, we moved as one. The kissing lasted much less and the actual sex lasted a lot longer. At first, it stung, but, after a while, the pleasure built up, and I managed to come at the same time as Keith. He seemed much more sure of himself, this time: less lost, less afraid I would break. This made it much more pleasurable.

We fell asleep right after, snuggled together and tangled in the sheets.

The sun came up too soon and shone through the massive windows, waking us both.

"Morning," Keith mumbled, scratching his neck awkwardly. Uh oh—I knew that face. He was thinking he'd done something wrong and he regretted it. Had I been wrong to believe I'd meant something more to him?

"You need to go to your room. We have no idea when the boys are coming home."

I guess I knew we wouldn't be announcing to the world what had happened between us, but if he believed we could keep a lid on this for very long, he's wrong. Neither of us would be able to go back to the relationship we used to have.

"Sure." I managed to keep my voice even and strong, despite the fact that, inside, I was crumbling. I didn't want to cause a scene or plead, although that was exactly what I felt like doing.

I quickened my pace and picked up my clothes as I went. I left and rushed to the bathroom. The water couldn't get hot enough to calm my nerves or replace the arms that had held me through the night. I should've known from the start where this would go. I was always going to end up hurt. There was no other way with Keith. I had been a fool to believe otherwise.

CHAPTER TWENTY-SIX

After my long shower, I went to my room for leggings and a comfy shirt so I could snuggle in my bed and sleep for a while longer. Said sleep never came, and I just lay there, watching the sun get higher and listening to the house become noisier. First, it was Keith's shower, which lasted as long as mine. Later, around ten in the morning, my brother's voice boomed against the walls that there would be people coming over tonight. Keith must've complained, but I didn't hear his voice.

"Not many people—just a small gathering," said Ryan, right outside my door. I wasn't in the mood to party or have people over, but it wasn't my place to complain. My stomach chose that time to let me know I needed food.

I couldn't hide forever. Keith and I lived together, after all. I chose the moment my brother was going to the kitchen to come out. He could serve as a buffer, even if he didn't have a clue of what had happened.

"Good morning, sis. You look like crap. Did you sleep at all?" I guess not covering the dark circles under my eyes with make-up had been a mistake. Keith was next to my brother, feeling guilty as he looked around the room to avoid my face.

"I just went to bed late." I was about to add that I'd had some nightmares that had kept me up, but I decided to be the bigger person. "Good morning, Keith," I said over my brother's shoulder. His reply was barely a whisper.

"What crawled up your ass and died there, dude? Chill and prepare yourself for tonight. You need to fu—" Ryan stopped midsentence to glance at me before continuing, "You need to get laid. You've been lonely lately."

I didn't want to hear Keith's response, but I couldn't leave the room without raising questions from Ryan.

"Yeah, sure," Keith said, crushing my heart once again. He could have at least pretended I was special and leave some time for his sheets to cool.

I prepared French toast, but just nibbled at it. After Ryan left the kitchen, Keith sat on a stool across from me. I thought he had waited for Ryan to leave so he could ignore me. Wasn't just that what he wanted?

"We need to talk." The words left my mouth without meaning. I wanted to talk, but my heart couldn't take any more blows.

Keith looked anxiously between me and the door. He whispered, "Not now, with Ryan in the house." It was as if that would have been the greatest tragedy of all. Maybe it would have been, but he didn't need to get mad at me.

After washing my plate, I went back to my room to rest. I had a class later, but I didn't think I was sane enough to go. My body was sore in places I didn't think I even had muscles as a constant reminder of the previous night.

The pictures of Keith in my room taunted me. The sadness in that child pulled at my chest. Who the hell had broken him? Not his father—he wouldn't have had the power to affect him like that. Keith had seemed hurt that his mother hadn't defended him. He had radiated indifference toward the man who'd fathered him.

A light knock sounded around four in the afternoon, when I was just starting to focus on the subject I was studying. "Yeah." I assumed it was my brother, as Keith was probably avoiding the talk. Those beautiful, gray eyes met mine across the room, though. He looked much more tired than me, as if he hadn't slept at all. The circles under his eyes were purplish and the whites of his eyes were bloodshot. I sat straighter on the bed and pushed the books aside.

Whatever he'd come to say was hurting him, and this was the first sign since this morning that he cared about me. If I wasn't indifferent to him, then I could fight for us. I would.

"Ryan went to pick some beer. I'm afraid the 'small gathering,'" He made air quotes with his fingers, "Is turning into an epic party. You know your brother." He shrugged, trying to clear the air between us. I just nodded. I wasn't interested in Ry's party.

"What happened between us was a mistake, Sky." The words seemed to hurt him as much as they hurt me. I turned to the window to avoid his eyes. "I care too much about you and your brother to do this—not to mention Cody." His voice was small and defeated.

My head snapped up to him. "This has nothing to do with our brothers. Cody and I broke up, and Ryan has no say in who I date." I flinched at the word. We'd never mentioned dating, and I had known from the start that Keith wasn't the relationship kind of guy. At least he could man up and admit that I meant more to him than the girls before me. "It's fine, Keith. It's done. Just don't pretend it was just a casual fling—we both know it wasn't. Doing so would betray the part of me I gave you last night. I don't regret it, no matter what you say." I picked up my book and leaned against the bed frame, trying my best to look composed.

Keith got up, sighed, and went for the door, but, before opening it, he turned. "I said it was a mistake—not that I regret it. Those are different things, Sky." He left me and my heart squeezed inside me.

How could this hurt more than breaking up with my long-term boyfriend? I was wrong in the head, that's for sure. I had an adoring boyfriend who had worshiped me and given me anything I asked, but I hadn't been able to find in me the desire to sleep with him. Now, in a matter of hours, I had released my feelings for his brother, slept with him, and got

287

turned down.

I had lost my virginity last night. Instead of beaming with happiness with a healthy gleam in my eyes, I was the saddest I'd been in a while. My eyes hurt from exhaustion and tears. I had told Keith the truth: I didn't regret him. It still hurt.

The party started at nine and I didn't bother going downstairs. I had cookies in my room and that was my dinner, which I ate while watching some comedy show on my laptop. I didn't laugh once through it. My bladder let me know it needed release, even though I could hear the party right outside my door. I locked the door behind me and saw the line to the bathroom—my bathroom.

I was so sick of Ryan's parties. It was my stuff in there. The line wasn't long, but I had already waited until the last minute to leave my cocoon. I couldn't wait for the four people in front of me.

Peeking through Keith's cracked door, I saw no one inside. Everyone knew his room was off-limits, so I tiptoed across the floor to his bathroom. It was much cleaner than the other one would be—that was for sure. After washing my hands, I watched my reflection in the mirror. I looked so tired that it had put five years on my shoulders.

I was still patting my hair when I left the bathroom and almost collided with the desk. Keith was casually leaning against the doorframe, with his door shut behind him.

"I saw you come in here."

"The line to my bathroom was..." I nodded my head to the closed door. He had seen it. He didn't need an explanation.

He rushed to me and gathered me in his arms, pushing me violently against this desk. The table lamp rattled against the wall, but I didn't have time to assess the damage before his lips were on mine. This time, he was more aggressive, and I loved every second of it.

After we discarded our clothes, he picked me up and sat me on his desk. One of his hands searched for a condom in a drawer, while the other came between us and hit me in the right place. I buckled against him, while he muffled my screech with his mouth. I was almost coming by the time he got inside me, and then the stars behind my eyes were almost too much to bear. I wanted him closer and farther away, at the same time, as if it was too much and too little. Keith picked me up and turned me around to face the mirror, he kissed my neck while eyeing me from over my shoulder.

Keith took his time making me come a second time, and then he crashed with me, leaving us both panting and sweating against the other.

I snuggled against him. I felt his brain working and feared what was coming next. If he said we had made a mistake again, I'd punch him where it hurt the most.

"You're the best thing that's ever happened to me and you don't even realize it," he mumbled against my back, clinging to my body like a lifeboat. I tried to turn, but his hold tightened. I relaxed again. I decided his comment was supposed to be heard and not addressed.

What did he mean? Ryan was the best thing that had happened to him: he had been by Keith's side all through his childhood, when he'd needed friends the most. Ryan was his lifeboat, not me. If what we'd done ever came up, it would destroy their friendship.

We'd been doomed from the start. I understood his side, then. I couldn't be the one to break this house apart—or our families apart, really, because our parents wouldn't remain friends after my breakup with Cody. Ryan and Keith's breakup, or Keith and I getting together to become their worst nightmare.

Tears escaped my eyes without my control and I clung to his hand on my stomach, trying to feel his heartbeat on my back.

"We can't do this again." I found myself saying in a frail voice. Keith stiffened against me, but didn't say anything. "It will hurt us both in the long way if we keep this up." I managed to turn to him and kiss his lips lightly. I picked up my clothes and got dressed quickly.

The next day, I was even more tired, if that was possible, and I had drawing class in the morning. I got dressed quickly and met the boys downstairs. Ryan had a major hangover and Keith was silent at the counter.

"So, K-man, any luck last night? You disappeared early, but I didn't see a walk of shame this morning."

"Ry, dude, your sister is right there," Keith argued, upset. "And no, no girl last night," he said, staring hard at his mug, like the coffee had done something to him. "I'm focusing on my work right now."

"Sure—the art show in February. How's that going?" Ryan asked, while I poured my own coffee.

Keith shrugged and went to the sink to wash his mug and Ryan's. "Slow, as usual. It'll pick up in the end—it always does." His eyes flickered to mine for a second.

My brother nodded. "Will you let me come see it, this time?"

His comment surprised me. Ryan was Keith's best friend and he hadn't seen his work on display? That was certainly strange, but I chose against getting between them.

"Do you need to go to school today?" I asked after a couple minutes of silence. Apparently Keith wasn't going to answer my brother.

Keith nodded and picked up his car keys. "I'll wait for you outside."

I kissed my brother on the cheek, grabbed my stuff, and met Keith outside. I was giddy. I had no idea how I was supposed to react to last night. Ignore it? Mention again how wrong we were for each other? I'd let him choose.

Keith chose the former. He drove in silence and parked the car in front of the art building. "I'm sorry I didn't mention it before, but I'm the model in today's class." His hand went through his hair and his eyes didn't meet mine. "I just found out this morning."

"Okay," I mumbled, because what else could I say? I don't want anyone else ogling your glorious body? I grabbed my backpack and shut the door behind me. A few feet away, a hand grabbed my arm.

"It's the last time. I'm going to tell Elizabeth I'm quitting the modelling thing. I don't need the money, anymore, and it's kind of tiring." His eyes searched mine for approval.

I heard the reason he didn't share: I don't want to face you, naked, in a room full of people. Not knowing if I should feel flattered or not, I shrugged and gave him a small smile.

The class wasn't as difficult as I expected it to be, with Keith there, and I finally got praise from the professor.

"Well, well, Keaton, you might have some talent, after all. That's the best drawing of the class. Keep up the good work." I hadn't even noticed her come up behind me to check my work, but my heart swelled with pride, and my day got a little bit better. Keith's eyes met mine and he winked. This was why we'd started drawing each other at home: so I could improve. I guess it had worked. It was a pity we couldn't keep up with it, though.

I went to study in the library for a couple of hours. I was already tired from being there when I received a text from Keith asking me to wait for him for another hour. The sky was clear, the sun was shining, and it wasn't too cold for a December evening, so I decided to take the bus and walk the rest of the way home. I texted him my decision, which brought about half a dozen protests.

When I started up the path to our house, a man appeared in front of me and startled me. He could have come from our house, but we usually didn't have visitors, except for the parties. He stopped a few feet from me and tilted his head to the side, like he was studying me, and smirked. It was so similar to Keith's smirk that I felt shivers run up my body. I could turn and run to the street, but, if his intentions were to hurt me, he could easily catch up with me. He had some fat on his belly, a buzz cut, and he was probably covered with tattoos, from what I could see on his neck and hands.

"Hi, there. Don't be scared." When someone started with that in the middle of a forest, it was reason enough to start running. I didn't, though, because I knew it wouldn't be enough. I prayed for Keith to come home soon, but I knew he was still in a meeting. "I know Keith and I knew his grandfather."

This offered some kind of relief, but not much. This man gave me the chills and I wanted him to leave. I didn't have an answer for him, so I just nodded. I wanted him to step aside, so I could go home, but he just stared, smirking, and made me feel disgusted.

"You Keith's girl? Jane, something?"

The fact that he knew my name alerted all parts of my brain. Should I have been relieved or freaked out?

"Keith's will be arriving any time now."

"I should wait for him and have a reunion, but, I'm afraid I don't have much time, now. I'll be back another day. Bye, Skylar."

Not many people knew my middle name. The fact that only Keith called me that made me shudder. Were they friends? This man seemed to be in his forties or fifties—not the kind of crowd Keith hung out with. Was he in trouble with the wrong people? I was scared and not even the lock on the door behind me calmed my nerves. That man had trouble written all over him.

I decided to keep the visit to myself. If he wanted to talk to Keith, he'd try again. Maybe he was just passing through, though. I texted Keith to let him know I was home safe and I settled in my bedroom to study.

Keith got home late and brought take-out with him, reminding my stomach that it had needs. My brother joined us a few minutes later.

"Family dinner? How cozy," Ryan said, sitting on the couch between me and Keith, and stealing a box of Chinese food from the coffee table. We spent the entire dinner talking about the classes Ryan had and laughing about the shenanigans my brother had gotten into. This time, he'd been caught making out with a girl by the college president. It wouldn't have been a problem, if the girl hadn't been his daughter. In the end, everything ended up okay, but I always worried about him and the messes he seemed to get himself into.

"This is fun. I like hanging out with my sister and best friend. I'm glad you worked out your differences," Ryan said, licking the chopsticks before throwing them into the empty box. I eyed Keith from across the couch and saw his smile falter before he replaced it with his fake one.

"Sure, bro. She's annoying, but bearable."

I knew he was joking and doing it for Ryan's sake, but my insecurities always came to the surface around him.

Ryan messed with my hair, pulled me to him, and kissed my temple. "We have a week until Christmas. Are we all going home?"

Keith shifted on the couch, but I wouldn't let him miss Christmas again. "Sure, the four of us," I answered, disentangling from my brother's hold. "You two need to go, too." Keith didn't seem convinced, but I wouldn't have it any other way. First, I didn't want to spend a week apart from him, even if we weren't together. Second, family was important, no matter how he felt at the moment. If something happened to his parents, he would feel devastated that he'd missed the last few Christmases with them.

"Sure Jane, we'll go—but only if you buy the presents. I have no patience for that Christmas spirit shit. I'll give you money and you can write my name on the cards, deal?" Ryan said.

I don't think Ryan had ever bought a gift for anyone; he'd always guilted someone into doing it for him.

"You're so lazy, but... sure, if that's your condition..." I trailed off, not happy.

"I can take you to another town tomorrow that has some trendy shops."

Keith said, picking up the TV remote and turning up the volume. I nodded, not finding my voice steady enough to respond out loud. He wanted to spend time with me alone? Was that wise? No, but I didn't care. The butterflies in my stomach wouldn't let me say no.

Next day came too quickly. I had so much to study for finals that it hadn't left me any time to make a list—something I needed every Christmas.

"You plan too much, Sky. I'll go to the grocery store to buy those Christmas cookie boxes: done, no trouble, and no one gets jealous of anyone else' presents." He said, when we got in the car.

I rolled my eyes and turned the radio down. "You're a guy—no one expects much effort from a guy. But a girl? Women always have to think about a million things at the same time, which, during Christmas, means presents for everyone... and from everyone, because Ryan always lays it on me on at the last minute, Cody wants to split my presents with him, and Matilda always forgets about someone. For years I've had to have a couple of presents as a backup plan."

Keith surprised me by laughing and hitting the steering wheel. I hadn't said anything funny. "Oh, I see," he said, taking a breath. "I never noticed before, but you're one of those Christmas nuts. You know, people who have to have the holidays completely planned to the tiniest detail."

I crossed my arms over my chest and narrowed my eyes. "I'm not," I said petulantly. "I just want everything to go as planned." He continued to laugh and I realized I'd just agreed with him with other words. Whatever—I liked Christmas, with the smell, the cheesy songs, the food, all of the family reunited, and, of course, the presents.

I always liked to give away presents and watch everyone's reactions the most. I never had an answer when people asked me what I wanted for Christmas: I had everything I needed. Well, this year, I would have liked to have Keith, but that would have been a miracle, not a present.

Years of practice of present-shopping had made me an expert, and I'd almost finished my list by the end of the day, with just a small break to eat a burger with Keith. True to his word, he walked back to the car with bags filled with cookie boxes. I shook my head at his shrug.

"I just hope you're not going to ask me to wrap those." Almost all of my presents had come with the shop's gift bags, which would save me hours of work.

"I'll just give them like this." He shoved everything in his trunk.

"That's so—so un-Christmas-like," I said, wondering if he was going to write the person's name with a sharpie on the metal box before shoving them under the tree.

"Says the Christmas elf. I don't have time for this shit. They're lucky enough to be receiving a gift, at all. I might just throw the cookies on a plate and offer them to Santa." He said. I spent the rest of the ride wondering about Keith's present. I had spent the last hour roaming the shops, trying to come up with something suitable, but nothing caught my eye.

Over the weekend, I asked Keith for his car to go out and buy the rest of the presents I still needed. I found a cover for his phone that he would like: it looked like it had been spattered by paint of every color. It would suit him. When I got home, however, and thought about it, I realized it was such an impersonal gift. He deserved more. My eyes drifted to my sketch book. He'd liked the drawing I'd made of myself. I picked it up and smiled. He would never place it on the wall, but maybe, from time to time, he could think about me. I turned the page and picked up a pencil.

You see me.

I see you.

With love, Sky.

Maybe it was too much, especially the "love" part, but it was what I felt: the truth. I always wanted to be honest with Keith, even if we couldn't have each other. I searched my drawers for a cardboard to place on either side of the drawing and wrapped it with blue paper with white stars on it. I just needed to keep it hidden from everyone before Christmas Eve. I had a feeling he wouldn't receive many meaningful presents. Ryan had asked me to buy him a CD of a band they both liked. It looked like a present for Ryan, instead, but I didn't comment.

The next week dragged on with the last finals. Some were practical, like drawing, in which I had a B+, while others were theoretical and required me to study harder than ever. I needed to balance the B+ with some As for my father's approval.

The weekend before Christmas, we packed Keith's car with our luggage, which was half presents, and settled inside. My brother rode shotgun, while I had to share the backseat with Cody.

Cody hadn't been home much. He'd come home to sleep for a few days between finals, but that was it. He looked tired: his skin was grayish and his eyes were red, as if he hadn't had much sleep in a long time. After Keith got on the highway and turned the radio on, I turned to Cody.

"Are you okay?"

He jerked in surprise and turned to me like he hadn't noticed my presence. His eyes were cautious, like those of a scared animal. "Yeah, just tired. Sophomore year's hard—too many night groups and exams. I think I'm going to sleep through Christmas." His smile didn't reach his eyes.

I didn't have any lingering feelings for Cody, positive or negative. I wanted his friendship back, but I feared it wasn't going to happen any time soon.

The drive was uneventful, and we got home before dinner. My parents met us in the driveway, hugging each one of us. They paused, awkwardly, in front of Keith. My father gave a head jerk for acknowledgment, but my mother kissed his cheek. At least one of my parents hadn't lost their manners. I wouldn't let them treat Keith the way they had last time, even if that meant I had to face their wrath.

"Your parents went to pick up your grandparents, so you're going to have dinner with us." My mother spoke to Cody, while Keith started toward his parents' house. Before anyone could notice, I grabbed at his shirt.

"No way. You're coming with us," I whispered. He faltered, but gave a slight nod and followed my parents and his brother.

That's when I noticed Ryan's expression. He'd seen the exchange and had found it strange. I smiled at him and picked up one of the bags, dismissing any of his thoughts.

The table was set for everyone, to my relief. Keith was about to sit between me and Ryan when my mother rushed Cody to that chair, not so subtly. This confused Keith, Ryan, and me, before we all realized: my parents still thought we were dating. We needed to address that subject, but when? Before or after Christmas?

CHAPTER TWENTY-SEVEN

I stayed in my room that night, but my grandparents were coming the next day and would need it. I expected they'd want me to stay with Matilda. My mother surprised me during breakfast by pulling me into the kitchen to have a word with me.

"Honey, your father and I were talking, and I made him see reason. So, if you want to stay over at the Hales' with Cody, we're okay with it." I was so taken aback that I didn't answer right away. My father was okay with it? No, he wasn't, but I was starting to suspect they wanted me with Cody more than they didn't want me with Keith. Solidifying my relationship with Cody was the best way for them to do that.

"No, Mom, we're not sleeping together there, so it would be stupid to do so here." I picked up the butter and turned to return to the table.

My mom sidestepped. "You're not?" She frowned. Any mother would have been pleased, but not mine, which only confirmed my suspicion. I shook my head and hurried to the dining room.

The next couple of days flew by, as I helped my mother with cooking, decorations, and last minute presents. My mind was on Keith the entire time, though. I missed him with such force that it brought tears to my eyes at night. How could I go on with my life, ignoring these feelings for him, if forty-eight hours seemed like forever?

That night, the Hales were able to come have dinner with us, but Keith wasn't with them. Ryan surprised me by not asking about him. I had seen light coming from his bedroom window, so I knew he was home.

My parents were laughing with the Hales, my grandparents and Cody's and Keith's were exchanging stories from their younger days, and my sister, aunt, Cody, and Ryan were discussing movies. I felt so alone and my heart physically hurt for Keith. I was suddenly so mad at all of them—at the hypocritical Christmas mood, the decorations, food, and presents. The only thing that should have mattered was family and being together. Were they forgetting they had another family member alone next door? Were they the ones who had asked him not to come—to keep the mood positive?

I got up silently without anyone noticing and went to the foyer, and picked up my coat. That was when another thought popped into my head. I went to the kitchen, picked up a plastic box, and went to the dining room. Everyone noticed me, then. I had my coat on and was shoving Ryan and Cody away from each other to reach the table.

"What is it, honey?" my mother asked, confused. That only increased my bad mood. I kept my mouth shut and shoved enough food for two into the box, as I hadn't eaten anything.

"Jane," my brother pleaded when he realized what I was doing. "He likes to be on his own."

I closed the lid and turned to my brother. "Is that what you really think?"

I didn't wait for the answer and went through the kitchen door. No one followed. I made my way to the Hale's house and up the stairs, listening to the music coming from his room.

The door was slightly open and I nudged it with my foot. Keith was on his bed with his shirt off, furiously sketching on his pad. Before he noticed me, I peeked over his shoulder and gasped. He jumped off the bed, almost hitting me with the sketch pad.

"Jesus, Skylar, you scared the fuck out of me," he muttered, rubbing the knee he'd hit on his bedside table.

I tried to catch my own breath as I placed the food box on the table.

I crawled over the bed and picked up the sketch, before he could protest. It was a drawing of the two of us—at least, it seemed the two of us. A girl, presumably me, was facing the viewer. A guy was behind her, circling both arms around her: one was around her hips, covering her up and the other was around her chest. He was kissing her neck and her head was thrown back with closed eyes. It was the most beautiful and sensual thing I'd ever seen.

My eyes shone with unshed tears, and Keith took the opportunity to take the drawing from my hands. "You weren't supposed to see that," he said.

"It's us, isn't it?" He looked around, embarrassed. "Why are you drawing us? Why are you here, alone, drawing us?"

"Because it's the only part of you I can get, okay? I won't show it to anyone, but no one would get that it's you, anyway."

I laughed. "You're very good at what you do: of course they would know."

"What are you doing here?" he asked.

I picked up the plastic container and the two forks I'd brought. "I brought you dinner," I sat on the bed.

His frown showed me his confusion. "Dinner? Aren't you supposed to be next door?" He tilted his head to the window, but sat next to me.

I shrugged. "I left. You can't be alone on Christmas."

"Christmas is tomorrow," he said, as he picked up the fork and shoved it into the food. "Besides," he said, as he put the fork in his mouth, "Don't you think they'll be suspicious?"

It was my turn to fork the food, so I shrugged again, taking my time swallowing before answering. "I don't care. My parents are smothering me again. My mother asked if I wanted to sleep here with Cody, for God's sake. Talk about pushing."

Keith froze beside me, but didn't comment. I hoped he knew how over Cody I was. I had slept with Keith, after all.

The drawing sat on the bed, taunting us the entire time we were eating.

I knew I shouldn't bring it up again, but I couldn't not comment on it. I handed the food to Keith and placed my fork on the table, while he still ate. He had been hungry.

"It's the most beautiful drawing I've ever seen." I nodded at the couple. Did I look like that, having sex? Did he see me like that? Passionate? "It is me, but I don't look like that," I muttered, envying the girl on the paper.

Keith placed the lid on the box and turned to me. "Yes, you do. I didn't imagine that." He nodded at the sketch. "I saw it."

At my confused stare, he explained further. "The mirror in my room. That second time, you looked like that at one point." My mouth was hanging open and I must've been turning bright red, because he laughed and pulled me closer. "Don't shy away from me. I like you exactly like that." He nodded at the drawing, but didn't take his eyes off of me.

His gaze lingered on my lips and my belly tightened in anticipation. I so wanted him to kiss me, but sounds from the stairs made us pull apart from each other. Keith turned the page of the sketch book to a drawing of hands: two intertwined hands. In my head, they looked like our hands, but, now, I could have just been making that up. They could have been anyone's.

Ryan's head popped into Keith's room. "Hi," he said. We pretended he hadn't just tiptoed up the stairs without announcing his presence.

"Hi. Your sister was kind enough to come feed me," Keith said, with a smile on his face. "I was exchanging food for art advice." He nodded at the hands on the paper, but shut the sketch pad closed and put it on the other bedside table, away from my brother.

"Yeah. You should go home, Jane. Mom's worried about you." I noted my brother's tone, but there was no way I was going to let him ruin Keith's improving mood.

"Nope. She knows where I am." I crossed my arms. To prevent an argument, Keith suggested we head downstairs to play some games. I sat next to them, but, after a while, it started getting boring. I looked around and found paper and a pencil. Using a thick book as a surface, I sat a few feet from my brother and Keith, and turned to them.

I spent the next hour drawing their faces, their smiles, and the carefree position they were in. It was so beautiful, in the end. It showed how much they loved each other. It hurt to know that this love was keeping me away from Keith.

Later that night, I lay in Matilda's bed. I kept turning, but sleep didn't come.

"You can sneak out, you know, and meet him in his room." I almost fell from the small bed at Matilda's suggestion. There was no doubt as to who she was talking about. "Go down the trellis outside my window, and text him to open the door."

I turned down the idea immediately, but it was so tempting. I missed him, and, even if it was just to talk or cuddle, I wanted to see him. I picked up my phone and texted Keith. "Are you awake?"

While I waited for the reply, I turned to my sister. "How did you know?"

She smirked at me. She was so much like Ryan, but, at the same time, much different. "It's all over your face whenever you look at his house, or when your face falls when his family showed up without him. Did you two hook up?"

I bit my lip, thinking about me and Keith. It had been much more than hooking up, but I didn't know if Matilda would understand. I nodded, but didn't offer an explanation. She smirked again, but turned her back to me, knowing I wouldn't tell her anything more.

"Yes, why?" Was Keith's reply. I could just picture his eyebrow shooting up in confusion and apprehension.

"If I came over, would you open the door?"

"Why?"

"You know why." It was the only thing I could come up with.

After a few seconds, he answered with a simple, "Yes."

I smiled and jumped from the bed. Matilda laughed at me. I could break my neck going down that trellis, but it would be worth it. I stopped as I pulled my jeans up, realizing that I'd never felt this giddy with Cody. I had never felt this much excitement about going to meet him, or that I wouldn't be able to breathe without him. I quickly finished dressing, knowing that I would have to be quick outside, because my coat was downstairs.

Keith was already outside, pulling the door open so I could come in. He placed his finger over his mouth, as if he needed to tell me to be quiet. I didn't want anyone finding us any more than he did.

When we reached his room and closed the door, we turned to each other, not knowing what to do. I stepped closer and placed one freezing hand over his shirt. He pulled my hand between his.

"What are you doing here?" he whispered.

I answered with the truth: "I have no idea." I leaned my face toward his and his lips found mine. His kiss felt like a feather. It was the quietest kiss, so far, and the most romantic, yet. It wasn't about passion, now—it was about love. I felt it coming from him, even if he wouldn't admit it.

We didn't make love that night, but held each other until the morning sun showered the room in light. He followed me to my house, through the kitchen, and then left in his car. I had no idea where he was going, but I hoped he would be alright. Tonight was the Christmas Eve dinner, and I wanted him there. We would open presents afterward, and I thought we should be with our families.

I spent the day in the kitchen with my mother, Samantha, and the rest of the women in our families. Talk about equality.

"So, Jane, how's school? I hadn't had the opportunity to ask." Samantha sat next to me. I didn't know if this was casual conversation or if she was fishing for something.

I shrugged. "It's fine. I think I'll have good grades on my finals."

She smiled. "That's good, but grades aren't the only thing in life."

"I keep telling her that." My little sister butted in, eying me knowingly.

I warned her with a look.

Samantha and the rest of the women laughed. "And how are my boys?" My eyebrow shot up at the plural use of the word. She had been so detached from Keith lately that I'd never expected her to bother asking about him. One look at her anxious face told me she meant it—she honestly wanted to know about her older son.

"They're fine. Cody's studying so much that he'll end up sick. Keith's the same, but he sticks to the house to work on his paintings." I paused, noticing some disappointment in Samantha's expression, and some sighing from the stove—probably from my mother. A sense of protectiveness washed over me and I smiled, proudly. "Keith's making some serious money with his paintings. He's very well-respected by the professors and galleries. He's already on the path to becoming famous." I was stretching the truth, but I believed in my words.

Samantha's smile told me she wanted that for her son—she just didn't believe in him. It was so sad. We had that in common: my parents didn't believe in my art career, either, even though I wanted to be a designer, not a painter. They still had the misconstrued notion that art didn't feed anyone.

I texted him when I took a break from the kitchen. "Please come to dinner. I need you here."

"Will do," he replied. I sighed in relief. I was starting to feel so lonely without him near, even in a house full of people. He was the only one who really saw me.

We were setting the table when he arrived with my brother, laughing and shaking rain from their shoulders. I smiled at them, and, when I turned, found my mother frowning at me. I kept the smile—if I didn't, it would confirm any suspicions she had.

"Go wash your hands and help me with the table," I told them both. Ryan kissed my forehead and Keith messed up my hair when they went past. The feeling of being whole settled over my heart.

I was so screwed.

CHAPTER TWENTY-EIGHT

I sat between Cody and Ryan, with Keith in front of my brother. We exchanged a couple of glances, but kept them to a minimum. We knew if we kept at it, someone was bound to figure us out. No one engaged Keith in conversation, and I didn't try, either. He was happier to be a bystander.

After washing the dinner plates and placing deserts on the table, as a buffet, we gathered around the TV and fireplace. The room was packed, so we had to sit on the floor, close to each other. This time, Cody gave me space and sat on the other side of the room, while my sister squeezed me between Keith and her, even though there was more space on her right. This forced me to be almost on his lap. This wouldn't go unnoticed by my father or mother.

The presents started to go around the room. A mess was created with paper everywhere, and everyone was laughing. I felt Keith's heat, and, based on his posture, he was relaxed at last. A small smile decorated his handsome face.

Everyone loved my presents, as they should have, after the trouble I'd gone through to find something perfect for everyone. They also loved Ryan's presents, which everyone knew had been bought by me.

"Sure, I'm the Christmas master! I knew you would love that CD, Dad." Ryan winked at me in front of everyone, and we all just laughed.

Matilda snickered. "Oh yeah? What did you buy me, then?" She was opening her present, but hid it behind the paper.

Ryan was thoughtful for a moment and then he had it. "What else? Something pretty for your ugly face!" Matilda threw him the ball of wrapping paper and gave him the finger. My parents yelled at her to not be crude. The grandparents in the room just laughed, knowing how those two behaved.

Keith received some random, non-meaningful presents, but he didn't seem to be bothered by it. I was. After all, I was a Christmas perfectionist. He loved the cell phone cover I gave him and the CD Ryan made me buy for him, and he thanked everyone for the other gifts. His cookies were being delivered, and, a few minutes later, we were all eating them. It wasn't a bad gift, after all.

We scattered after the last gift was delivered. Some picked up their presents, while others tidied up the mess in the living room.

I took that chance to whisper in Keith's ear, "I have another gift for you, but I can't give it to you here. Maybe later, like last night?" I asked. His brows shot up and I smiled, shaking my head. "Not that kind, pervert."

We had to endure a long movie with our families, once again squished next to each other on the floor. When the fire died down, my mother distributed blankets, and I snuggled under one that I shared with Keith. He first shook it off, but, after a few nudges from me, he understood the meaning. He shot me a worried glance, anyway. I grabbed his hand under the blanket.

That night, I needed Matilda's help to get Keith's present down the trellis. She was just so amused that she didn't even complain about the cold getting inside.

Keith ushered me to his room and closed the door, enveloping me in a warm embrace. He kissed my temple and moved me to the bed, eying the present. I handed it to him and waited… and waited. He took a long time, just looking at the wrapping. I was about to make a snide comment about the present being on the inside, but he started pulling at the tape, carefully, as if it was precious. My heart swelled.

His eyes met mine when he opened the card. His eyes warmed and darkened, and then they lowered to the drawing. I waited even more.

"I love it. Thank you." His muttered voice was interrupted by me, as I turned the drawing around. He looked up, with realization on his face, and he moved everything aside to pull me to his lap. His lips met mine with much more ferocity than last night. His parents were at the end of the hall and Cody was in the next room, but, at that moment, I didn't care about anything else. He suppressed a moan by biting my lower lip.

"I have something for you, too, and it's really coincidental."

He went to pick up a similar cardboard piece from his wardrobe. It wasn't wrapped, of course, and I didn't wait as long to open it. I also wanted to savor the moment, though. I understood him, then. Every moment between us felt like it could be the last, and we both wanted to frame each one in our brains.

It was the drawing he'd made yesterday, of the two of us. I wanted to frame it and put it over my bed, but I knew that couldn't happen—at least, not until I had my own place, and maybe not even then. He'd completed it some, by shading and working on our faces. His eyes were now looking at me on the paper, so beautifully drawn that I felt them through the paper, like it was a message to me. He didn't need words in his drawing, like I had in mine. His eyes were the unsaid words between us.

"I want you," I whispered, leaning down to kiss him, while pulling the shirt over my head. His eyes darted lower, to my breasts, and then to the door to make sure it was locked.

"We need to be extra quiet," he said, before pulling me over him once again. We quickly took off our clothes, not bothering with foreplay, this time. He made sure I was ready for him before pulling a condom from the nightstand, and then he moved me to be on top of him. I'd never been in control before and it scared me. The part of me that had always felt self-conscious was surfacing. He had been with dozens of girls. I couldn't compare.

"Stop worrying. I'm here. It's just the two of us, okay?" he whispered against my lips, erasing some of the worry. I started moving and it wasn't difficult to let go. I felt powerful, being the one here with him—the one he'd made a drawing for. I was the one who put that satisfied, smug smile on his face. He pulled me next to him to cuddle.

"You're perfect. Never doubt that, Sky. Perfect. Too much, for someone like me."

"No. If I can't have self-esteem problems, you can't, either, okay?" I kissed his chest and snuggled closer.

I felt complete.

The next morning, we woke up a little later than was prudent, so we had to dress in a hurry. Our parents would wake up early, as it was Christmas day.

We left the next day, as Cody had some internship business to attend related to some politician campaign, and Ryan had something to do on a friend's computer. I just wanted to be closer to Keith without the entire freaking world watching. We had stopped saying we couldn't do this. It was inevitable. Maybe we would tire of each other, eventually. Oh, who was I kidding? Eventually he would tire of me, but I was ruined forever.

The house was cold as we each dragged our suitcases inside, along with the present bags. Ryan had barely stepped inside the house when his friend called—again, for the hundredth time in six hours.

"I need to go. Don't wait up." It was already ten in the evening—of course no one was going to be up by the time he got home. Keith went upstairs, because he'd been the one driving, again, and just wanted to crash. He brushed his arm against mine in acknowledgement. I went to the kitchen to prepare something to eat before bed, and Cody followed me, looking exhausted. He didn't look like he'd gotten much rest these days.

"You really need to rest, Cody, or you'll get sick." I looked over my shoulder to see him sitting on a stool with his head on his arms.

"Why are you worried about me? I was shit to you."

I wasn't expecting a meaningful conversation at this time of night. "You made a mistake, and you hurt me. I can look past that." I sat next to him, drinking a warm cup of milk and offering him a sip.

He looked so young and sad. "I miss you." I stiffened and he shook his head. "No, not like that. I miss you. I miss knowing you, and knowing what's going on." He took the mug from me and sipped, knowing I'd put honey in it, just the way he loved it.

"I miss you, too. Can we still be friends?" I asked.

He averted his eyes. "Maybe not right away, but I would like that. I want you in my life." He stood and leaned close for a hug.

Tears rushed to my eyes, because I'd felt such loss when we'd broken up. Now I knew it hadn't been because I'd lost a boyfriend: it was because I'd lost my best friend.

He kissed my forehead and went to the door. Before pushing it open, he turned. "Be careful. I don't want you to get hurt." He looked down. "I won't say or do anything, but I know you won't be fine after him, like you were with me."

I stood there, gaping, long after he'd gone to bed. The milk was getting cold in my hands. Cody knew? How? I hadn't wanted to hurt him, even though he had been the one to mess up our relationship.

I stayed away from Keith for the next few days. Ryan and Cody were around a lot. If we couldn't get it past Matilda and Cody, we wouldn't be able to keep it from my brother for much longer. He wasn't as oblivious as Cody, and Cody had already figured it out.

The party we were attending on New Year's Eve was, thankfully, not at our house. It was at a nightclub that apparently held great New Year Eve parties, so I tagged along. I put on the green dress I had bought for my birthday and shrugged on the warmest coat I had, because it was freezing outside.

We gathered in Keith's car to leave together, but found out during the ride that Ryan and Cody had plans to meet their own friends at the party. That would have pissed me off on another day, but tonight I felt relieved. I would have the night with Keith. The New Year's kiss would be mine.

"What do you want to do?" whispered Keith behind me.

I half-turned to smile at him. "We can stay until midnight, and then we'll leave and have our own party." I suggested. He just smirked and nudged my ear, but not before checking that my brother and Cody were out of sight.

"I'd love that, Miss Keaton."

We danced, until we couldn't anymore. Then people just watched the countdown screen. My brother and Cody had left for another party a while ago, and I didn't think about them for the rest of the night. My New Year's wish was obvious, and, for tonight, at least, it would be reality.

Later that night—or, rather, morning—we were cuddling on his mattress in the attic. Sleep was not on our minds.

"I would like a tattoo," I said, after long minutes of silence, while Keith traced small circles on my bare shoulder.

He shifted his body to loom over me with a raised brow. "And what would that be?"

I averted my eyes. "I want something that represents my present situation." I felt his body tense and added, "The recent feeling of freedom. You know, feeling like my own person." It wasn't completely true.

"Not the bird flying out of the cage, though, right?"

"That would be pretty, but no... something less obvious." We turned to the ceiling again, thinking. The thought had been playing in my mind for a few weeks, but I needed the opinion of the expert.

I chose my words, before asking, "What about an anchor?"

"Wouldn't that be the opposite of being free?" he asked.

Sighing, I shook my head. I didn't want to go there with Keith, but now was as good of a time as ever. "It's not just being free, but also belonging somewhere, you know?" I looked away as the confession weighed on us. I belonged here—not just with him, but on my own, studying what I liked, making my own choices, and not being pushed to be someone I wasn't—or to be with someone I didn't really love.

After a while, he gave me his opinion. "It is common and cliché, but it makes sense. Where?" I shrugged, because, honestly, I hadn't thought that far ahead. Now, however, knowing Keith approved of it, I had more courage.

Two days later we stood in front of the strangest tattoo shop I'd ever seen. The window at the front was all white with color splashes across white fabric hanging on it. It didn't have a name or any designation of what was going on inside. I started to feel dizzy—maybe this wasn't a good idea. Maybe I trusted Keith too much. If he thought some random dude was going to put a needle in my skin, he was very much mistaken.

When we stepped inside, I didn't feel better, but I had to agree that the place was beautiful. The walls and furniture were white, and the floor was a checkered white and gray wood. The longest wall had a drawing on it, with every color possible. It was breathtaking. I could make out forms amidst the chaos.

I was admiring the view when a guy stepped from around the corner and startled me. He was wearing a black shirt and denim jeans and I could tell he was covered in tattoos.

"Hi, man. Long time, no see." He hugged Keith, and I could see that they got along well by the smile on Keith's face. It was a rare view. "What brings you by? Another tattoo?" He noticed me and nodded to Keith, as if I wasn't a person of my own and needed him to introduce me.

"Nope, this time is for my girl, here."

My stomach back-flipped and my eyes bulged out of my head. Keith didn't flinch at his own words, while my world came to a halt.

"She wants a tattoo."

The guy studied me top to bottom, just the way I hated, and shook his head. "You know I'm booked, man." What he really wanted to say was there was no way in hell he was going to work on a clean-cut girl, like me.

Keith stepped closer to me and hugged my waist. "I'm the one asking, Fred. You still owe me, remember?" He nodded to the wall next to me and everything made sense: the art on the wall was Keith's.

"Oh, no, I did the dragon—we're even. I don't have time—"

Keith cut him off. "It will take you minutes. It's just a tiny anchor on her finger."

The tattoo guy laughed and crossed his arms. "You know I don't do that shit."

"I won't credit you on it, then. I just don't trust anyone else to do it. Come on, it's ten freaking minutes."

The guy laughed again. "If she made you stop swearing, you're done, man, hooked. I never saw that coming." He turned and motioned for us to go inside. I stopped Keith before going to the back.

"Are you sure we can trust him? I don't think he's licensed, and all that." I waved to the space around us.

Keith smiled and shook his head. "No, it's all legit. He's not advertising because he's always booked and very specific about the type of work he does. It's easier, this way, since no one knows what's going on here. No one asks for stupid stuff."

I shrunk at the thought. "Do you think my idea is stupid?" He shook his head immediately.

"No, not at all. It's common, yes, but I know what inspired you to do it, so it fits." Before we walked to the back, he stepped forward, took my chin in his hand, and kissed me softly—probably to calm my nerves.

My girl. He called me his. That would take my mind off the pain.

The tattoo hurt, there was no denying it, but it was relatively quick, as it was just inside my ring finger and very small. I inspected the raised and reddish skin, admiring it. My family was going to kill me, but maybe I could delay that until spring time, or even summer. By then, I'd have my thoughts about everything going on in my life sorted out—hopefully.

CHAPTER TWENTY-NINE

A week passed and neither Ryan, nor Cody noticed I had a tattoo. It was for the best, because I was in need of some peace and quiet.

Everything was kind of good—even Keith kissed me here and there. We hadn't slept together since New Year's Eve, though, and I couldn't see us going anywhere, no matter how much it hurt every moment we weren't together.

I was wandering through the house, thinking about what to prepare for dinner, and ended up in the attic. The door wasn't locked, so I pushed it open to find it empty. Keith was probably showering to help with dinner. I started to close the door, but thought otherwise. I shouldn't have been doing this, but Keith's secrecy was starting to get on my nerves. What the hell did he paint that no one could see?

I stepped inside, closed the door behind me, and went to the nearest canvas. When I turned it around, I gasped. I hurried to turn every canvas, and then I sat on the mattress, catching my breath. What the hell?

The door opened to reveal a fuming Keith. "What the hell are you doing here? Didn't I tell you a million times?" He came closer and saw the damage was done.

"What is this? Why is every painting about me?"

His hands went through his hair and he pushed the closest canvas back. He turned around so I couldn't see his face. I was so tired of being lied to that I got up, went to him, and pulled him around.

"Why? I—I don't get it."

"What do you want me to say? Huh? You have nice features to paint."

"Don't bullshit me, Keith. There are so many paintings here. Some are abstract, but I can see myself in them, too. They must've been painted before I came here." I tried to get to the corner where the oldest painting must've been, but Keith grabbed my arm and spun me around.

"What don't you get?" he whispered, before crushing his mouth on mine. We stumbled to the mattress behind me. He wasn't sweet—we weren't sweet—and it was a struggle to rip our clothes off. There was no time for foreplay. As soon as he was inside me, I arched my back to get closer. I didn't want an inch between us. I begged him to not be gentle with me, and we didn't take long to finish.

As soon as it was over, Keith jumped back. "I'm sorry, I didn't... did I hurt you?"

I sat up and grabbed my clothes. "I'm not made of crystal, you know." I was trying to make light of the situation. "I'm fine. Better, yet, I'm great. Now, talk about the paintings." I nodded at the canvas behind him.

Keith's eyes didn't meet mine and he shuffled through his clothes. "I'm not a creep." He looked embarrassed and I didn't get it. I'd never thought he was.

When I thought he wasn't going to continue explaining, he sat next to me and we both faced one of the paintings. It was black and white and I was naked, with my back turned and my face peeking over my shoulder. There was a shy smile on my face.

"I've been in love with you for years, Sky." I jumped and turned to him at this confession. I was dreaming—it had to be a dream. "Drawing you is the only way I can really have you."

It wasn't the first time he'd said that and it broke my heart.

"That's not true, You have me, Keith. I'm in love with you, too." I tried to kiss him, but he leaned back, placing his thumb over my bruised lips.

"There are things about me you don't know—stuff you won't like. Stuff that will taint you."

"Tell me, then," I whispered, intertwining my fingers with his. Keith just shook his head and leaned against me.

"I can't."

I pretended to let go of the subject, but it still lingered in my mind every waking hour of the day. I went through time in a haze. Keith kept himself locked upstairs, and, now that I knew what he painted, I kept imagining all the ways he would perpetuate me. Us.

A few days before the next semester started, I needed to go to the office to get some papers signed and get the list of materials I needed to read before classes started. Keith was busy with his work, so I called Shelby to ask if she wanted to go with me and stop by the coffee shop. We haven't talked to each other in a while and I needed to get out of the house.

Later that afternoon she dropped me off on the main road. It wasn't raining, so I said I would walk the rest of the way. As soon as I got out of the car, though, a weird feeling crept up on me. I dismissed it and started my walk home. A few feet ahead, a man stepped out from behind a tree. I was startled, but I recognized him from the last time, when he'd claimed he knew Keith.

"Hi, there," he said. His voice made my skin turn to goosebumps. His unshaven face and dirty clothes should have made me run, but I knew I had nowhere to go.

"Do you remember me?" I stepped back, but he quickly reached me and grabbed my arms. While I tried to pry him from me, he pulled his arm back and punched me in the face so hard that I fell to the ground. I tried to catch my breath amid the pain. My lip must have split, because I tasted blood in my mouth. I was still trying to get back on my feet, when he pulled both my arms to my back, which made me yelp in pain again. He was about to dislocate my shoulder when he stopped pulling and wrapped something around my wrists so tightly that it cut into my skin.

"Who are you?" I coughed, wrestling against the man who was now dragging me to a van parked on the quiet street, I recognized the van as being from the man who had asked directions months ago. I thrashed and kicked him, but his hold on me was too strong. I tried to scream but he placed one hand over my mouth.

"Your worst nightmare, dear." He whispered on my ear while pushing me inside a van, placed a piece of tape over my mouth, and closed the door. I guessed the best thing to do was kick the door to make noise, but I could hardly control my movements with my arms tied behind my back. The erratic driving crashed me against the doors and other stuff inside the van.

I couldn't control the images in my head of him raping and murdering me. No one would find my body. I kept picturing my parents' faces. Then those of my siblings. Finally, I imagined Cody's and Keith's. Keith—he was going to murder me if this man didn't. He had specifically told me to not walk around alone. Why did I have to be so stupid?

The man finally parked the van and pulled the door open. I knew it would be useless to scream, not only because of the tape over my mouth, but because we were in a deserted area of town. A block of abandoned industrial buildings surrounded us. He pulled me out and pushed me inside, bringing my backpack with him.

The man dragged me up the stairs until we get to the second floor. There were several structural columns dividing the spaces, chairs and desks had been thrown to the floor, but there wasn't much else. He kept pulling me with him until we reached a corner. He pulled the tape from my mouth and threw me to the ground, scraping my knees in the process. He opened my backpack and emptied it. He picked up my cell phone from the pile and then started texting.

"What are you doing?" My shaking voice didn't match the certainty of the question. If he thought my parents were loaded, he was in for disappointment. His laugh gave me chills much more than his rough hands did, because it showed how crazy he really was.

"I'm texting your boys. We're going to have a party here."

I was confused. Which boys? He must've seen the puzzled look, because he continued, "My son and his bastard brother. Who else?" The only brothers we might both know were Cody and Keith. His conversation didn't make much sense, but I was starting to believe my suspicions about Keith's father were true.

His laugh was much darker this time. "Oh, this is going to be better than I imagined. You have no idea who I am, do you, sweetheart?" I hated hearing that word from his mouth. I gave a little shake with my head, even if I had an idea.

"I'm Keith's father." He smirked at me just as my phone got a new text message. As soon as he said the words, a dozen images came to my mind, along with the words from Thanksgiving: "Each day that passes, you look more and more like him." Keith's shocked expression when his mother had uttered those words made more sense now.

The man's face reddened at my surprised expression. "That man is not his father. I am. He stole my son. Maybe today, I'll steal his." I was starting to fear for Keith's and Cody's lives. This man was crazy.

He pulled a gun from his waistband and I scurried away. "While we wait, I can tell you a little story. How about that?" He waved the gun around and I feared he would pull the trigger accidentally.

"His bitch of a mother ran away from me when he was two years old. Who does that, huh? Who takes a son from his father?" I didn't understand what Samantha had seen in this crazy guy to begin with. "I found them sometime later, and what did I find? My lovely wife cozying up with a lawyer. She hired him to divorce me and then had a bastard with the guy. Taking my son away wasn't enough—she had to have another. So, I made her choose."

I couldn't follow everything he was saying, because the gun kept turning to me and he was getting more and more agitated.

"What do you mean?" I whispered, curious about the story. I also wanted to keep him talking; if the guys were coming, maybe they could hear him from down the stairs.

"I showed up on Keith's birthday and made Sammy choose: either Keith, or the bastard. She put herself in front of the other son—Cody, right? I guess they both live with that day's consequences." The man pointed the gun at his own shoulder, right over the place Keith had the scar. "I bet Keith hates his mother as much as I do. She chose the bastard over him."

I couldn't believe what he was saying. First of all, Samantha wouldn't have ever been able to choose between her two sons. Second, Keith probably didn't even remember. When I thought about that, though, I decided maybe he did. After all, he hated his birthday.

"He doesn't hate her," I answered, despite the fact that my brain was telling me to keep quiet. The man, whose name I had yet to know, stepped closer and pointed the gun in my direction. He was about to open his mouth when we heard noises from the stairs. Both Keith and Cody had come— probably to their deaths—and it was my fault for being so stupid.

"Please," I whispered, "Don't hurt them." The man laughed and pulled the gun to his lips to gesture for me to keep quiet. I wanted to scream at them to run, but I knew that would just make them come faster.

"Sky." Keith was the first to see us and he came to a stop as he put the pieces together. His face turned red with rage and his hands curled into fists. "You. If you so much as touch a strand of her hair…" He started toward us, but the man pointed the gun at me as he grabbed my arm and pulled me to my feet. Then he shoved the gun against my forehead.

"Tsk, tsk. Stay where you are, or your girl's brains will be splattered all over us."

"Peter, your problem is with me, not them."

Keith placed his arm in front of Cody, who was trying to understand the situation. His wide eyes were confused and they stayed focused on mine. Peter held me in front of him, with the gun still pointed at my head.

"Cody, tie your brother against that column, tight—and believe me, this one will be the first to go if you mess up." He threw a couple of plastic zip ties at Keith and nodded at the column near us. "The princess, here, will tie her boyfriend—or, should I say, ex-boyfriend." He wiggled his brows, disgusting me.

I tried to keep the plastic zip ties as loose as possible without Peter knowing and hoped Cody had done the same with Keith's.

"Now the party is complete." With both boys tied up, Peter seemed to relax a bit, knowing I wasn't much of a threat to him. My shoulder hurt, as well as my cut wrists and split lip.

"I have an idea." He tapped his chin with the gun, while stepping around the boys, probably inspecting our work with the restraints. "What if we make our princess choose, huh? Between you two." The gun waved around the boys' heads, as its aim was alternated between the two.

"No! Leave her alone!" Keith struggled against his restraints and his father aimed the gun at his forehead.

"Stop!" I jumped forward. I couldn't watch them die. "Please, let them go." Peter pushed me away so quickly that I stumbled back and hit the floor with my butt. I winced in pain, while the boys I loved—and who I knew loved me back—yelled for him to stop. I knew this wouldn't end well for any of us, but I would fight for them—for both Hale boys.

"Oh, princess, this will end as quickly as you want. Tell me which one to shoot."

He couldn't honestly think that I would be able to choose. "No." I lifted myself to my knees, looking pathetic. I wasn't beyond begging.

"Okay." He answered so nonchalantly that I wondered if he was going to let us go. He raised the gun and shot over my head. I screamed so loudly that I'd missed which one he'd hurt. I spun around, trying to not lose my balance.

Keith had his head down and his eyes shut tight. His left shoulder, in about the same area as his first scar, was bleeding. The color red was staining his shirt rapidly.

"Please, don't hurt them!" I begged again. Cody was also begging for us, but I tried not to look at him or I would lose it.

"Then choose!" He aimed the gun at his son again, which brought more begging from the boys. I needed to get Keith out of here—he needed a hospital. "Who do you choose? Your sweetheart, or the guy you're fucking?"

I had no idea how he knew this stuff, but it wasn't the time to be worried about their feelings. It was their lives that mattered right now.

"Choose," he repeated, this time kicking me in the ribs. I stumbled, but quickly got on my knees again.

"Me," I whispered, trying to gain control of my emotions. Cody and Keith heard me first and started begging both me and Peter.

"Jane, baby, don't." I could hear the desperation in Cody's plea, while Keith's string of swear words against his father told me that he was dealing with the situation with anger, which wasn't ideal with this man.

"What did you say, princess?" Peter stalked me, slowly, like a predator.

"Shoot me." I thought he was going to laugh, tell me no, and extend this whole nightmare. What I didn't expect was for him to shrug, raise the gun, and shoot. I felt it hit my stomach, throwing me off balance, and making me fall backward. I turned over and tried to steady myself with a hand on the floor.

Peter slowly walked away, whistling, while Cody and Keith called out to me. I wanted to get up, help them, and end this, but the pain in my torso was increasing to a burning fire. I stumbled, supporting my weight with my hand, and watching the blood drip to the floor. I turned to Keith, who was closer to me, and saw him struggle with his restraints. He was saying something, but all I heard was a buzz—probably from the gunshot.

At least the man was gone. He wouldn't hurt them—they'd be safe.

I was losing strength, but, before collapsing to the floor, arms held me back. The world was slipping from me, and the pain was too much for me to stay awake.

Keith was shaking me awake, while Cody had the phone against his ear.

"Forget it, we'll take her." Keith said to his brother, while trying to pick me up. The movement sent pain through my body and I screamed. "Shh. You'll be alright. Just stay awake—please, baby. Cody, you need to carry her, I don't have much more strength left." Keith asked his brother.

When we finally reached the car, the pain suddenly turned to a light throbbing and I was losing focus of the world.

"Please, Jane, don't die." Cody kissed my face, but his brother pushed him to the driver seat.

"Drive. I'll go in the back." He was trying to put pressure on the wound.

"I—" I needed to get the words out. There were so many thing I needed to tell them if this really was the end.

"Shh. Don't struggle—rest." Keith whispered over me. His face was getting fuzzy.

"I love you," I finally whispered. I needed to say the words.

"I won't say it back," he stated, surprising me, "Until you wake up in the hospital." I wouldn't argue with him. If I died, at least I would know that he loved me, even without saying the actual words.

Cody stopped at a red light and turned to us. "Keith," he begged, not sure of what to do.

"Drive! Honk and drive, damn it!" Keith shook so hard that I tried to soothe him, but I realized it was probably just in my head.

"Promise." I managed to get the word out and get his attention. "Take care of your brother. Take care of each other." The last thing I wanted was to die and leave their relationship more strained than before.

We arrived at the hospital as I was losing consciousness. Keith placed me on a gurney and the doctors started working on me. I still managed to look sideways at the two boys, who were being blocked from following me. The look on Keith's face gave me the strength to fight the darkness, which was trying to seep in.

I saw lights and movement, and people were talking to me and about me, but soon the world shut off.

CHAPTER THIRTY

I woke up, disoriented, to a bright room. It took me a few minutes for reality to sink in. My body hurt everywhere, my eyes were sensitive, and I felt cold. I tried to move, but a hand stopped me. I looked up to meet my mother's worried and bloodshot eyes.

"Hi, sweetie. You're in the hospital. Try not to move or talk too much—you're still recovering."

The events from the warehouse came flashing back and a sickening worry about Keith and Cody seized me.

"Keith," I managed to whisper.

"Shh. Everyone's okay—you had surgery to remove the bullet. I'm going to call the doctor." My mother stepped back to reveal my Dad and Matilda, who were weakly smiling at me.

"Hi, sis. You look horrible." I tried to laugh, but everything hurt.

My father scolded my sister before resting his hand on my ankle. "Hi, baby."

Matilda sensed my unasked questions and sat in the chair that had been previously occupied by my mother. "They're fine. Keith was shot in the shoulder and he sprained his wrist and two fingers, but he's already home. Cody hasn't left the waiting room." I nodded, relieved they were okay, but confused about why Keith wasn't here.

My mother came back to the room, followed by a doctor. After inspecting the stitches, he offered a detailed account of the surgery and what kind of care I would need in the following days and weeks. I was sleepy by the time he was finished, so I closed my eyes and must've fallen asleep.

The next time I woke up, it was already dark outside. Now only Matilda sat by my side.

"Tilda," I whispered her childhood nickname, "Tell me what happened."

She stepped closer. "You were shot, Jane." She seemed confused by my question, so I just shook my head.

"No, after. Cody and Keith." I was cursing the pain that talking caused.

My sister held my hand in hers. "Keith looked like hell—they both did. When we got here, the doctors had already stitched his arm. Apparently he didn't want to leave the room, before getting any news about you, but he passed out. He was so torn up, Jane—I've never seen anyone looking that desperate. He had blood all over him. We were even more scared when we saw him." Matilda stood up and went to pick up a glass of water. "Cody is outside. Do you want to see him?"

I nodded enthusiastically.

The sight of my ex-boyfriend made me flinch. I'd never seen Cody this unkempt. He hadn't shaved for a few days, which made me wonder how long I had been out. He had dark circles under his eyes and a faraway look in his eyes.

"Hi," he whispered. "How are you feeling?"

I shrugged with one shoulder. "Been better." He winced at my attempt at humor. "Tell me what happened after I got here."

His face fell and he took the chair my sister had vacated. "The hospital called the cops and we were interviewed. Keith passed out, because he refused to be treated before knowing how you were. Your parents arrived, then, and it was a mess, trying to explain it to everyone. Waiting for you to wake up—" he faltered.

I tried to talk, but coughed instead, and took longer to formulate the question. "How long was I out?"

"A couple of days," he answered.

I found the courage to ask my most relevant question. "Where's Keith?" Cody looked away and sighed.

"He's home. He was pretty injured, and then, with the arguments with your family... Ryan punched him, you know?"

No, I didn't. I tried to sit up, but the pain shot through me immediately. "What?" I asked, outraged. My brother had no idea what we'd gone through in that warehouse.

"He kind of put the puzzle together and figured you two out, especially because Keith talked some when he was under anesthesia. He moved out and Keith refuses to come here. I think he feels guilty." He thought? It wasn't that hard to figure out. "He was pretty hurt on his shoulder, but I think he's healing okay," he continued.

Suddenly I remembered that his exhibition was in a couple of weeks. He wouldn't be able to paint. The work he did have was mainly based on me.

"Let me call him." Cody's apologetic wince advised me against it, but it was something I had to do. "Please," I begged, extending my hand. He punched the screen until the call connected.

The raspy voice on the other side informed me Keith had probably been asleep.

"Hi," I answered. "Don't hang up, please." I rushed the words before he could shut me out. "I just wanted you to know that you can use the paintings you already have for the show. I know you feel like they are private, but I'm giving you permission. This is an important gallery. You need your best work displayed."

There was a pause on the other side and then a weak, "Okay." Then there was another long pause, but I still could hear him breathing on the other side. "How are you feeling?" Keith sounded unsure, and it was a side of him I didn't appreciate. I loved when he was confident.

"I'm better. I think I'm being released in a couple of days. Do you think you'll stop by?" My voice sounded hopeful. He was talking to me, after all.

"No, sorry. Bye." He hung up and I lay there a couple of seconds, staring at the phone in my hands. I handed Cody his phone, avoiding his eyes. He probably didn't feel very comfortable with his brother and I being together—if we were still together, which I doubted.

I caressed the tattoo on my finger, feeling the meaning of it changing. The anchor seemed less like a newfound purpose in life and more like I was sinking. Cody's eyes snapped down and he frowned, but he didn't comment. I could still feel the disappointment and judgment in his inhalation, though.

"He was arrested last night—that man. I don't think he'll ever get out again. The prosecution is looking at attempted murder."

The information caused conflicted feelings. I wanted him in jail for the rest of his life, but, at the same time, it hurt knowing Keith would never have a normal father. Carl sure wasn't one.

The doctor released me a few days later and we went home—well, to my parents' house. I didn't talk during the ride, and even went as far as pretending to sleep to avoid confrontation. I knew my parents were happy with this outcome—me going back home—but, I just felt like the attack had changed my life permanently, and not in the obvious way.

When we arrived, I went directly to my room with the excuse of being tired. I was just heartsick, though. I missed Keith, my room, my paintings, and my newfound life.

The days dragged on and I was feeling more and more depressed. I didn't have anything to do here. I tried calling Keith a couple of times, but he just ignored my calls.

Tomorrow was the day of his exhibition and I had been formulating a plan to go see him. Every idea was cut short by some unexpected outcome, though. I didn't feel like I could drive the entire way. Even if I did, my parents wouldn't lend me their car. By morning, I was starting to freak out. I couldn't miss it. I needed to see his paintings on the wall, and, most important, I needed to see him to try to make things right—or at least end our relationship properly. I didn't want his last visual of me to be of me all bloodied and dying in his arms.

After crossing the hallway silently, I knocked on my sister's door. She was still in bed, but already awake, which wasn't common for her on a Saturday.

"Hi, Jane. How are you feeling?" she asked, pulling the covers back so I could snuggle with her. I was in need of some cuddling.

"I need to go see Keith tonight. It's his gallery opening and I have to be there, but I have no idea how to make that happen."

We stayed in bed for almost an hour, brainstorming. The only conclusion I came to was that I had to ask my parents to drive me there.

After getting dressed, I approached my sister at the bottom of the stairs, so we could make the request together.

"Dad," I started, "I need your car tonight." I tried to keep my voice steady, but it must've faltered at the end, because my parents stopped eating their breakfast and turned to me. I'd closed myself off since I'd been released from the hospital, so I understood their curiosity, or fear.

My father sipped his coffee, before asking, "For what, honey? I can take you wherever you want. You're still too weak to drive."

I wanted to state that my external wounds were healing fine, which just left my heart to break every morning without knowing how Keith was.

I fidgeted with the tattoo that was yet to be discussed. "I need to go home—to see Keith." My mother flinched at my mention of home being anywhere, but here.

My father just stood and crossed his arms, with a menacing expression set in place. "For what?" he spat.

"Today is the art show he's being preparing for. I want to be there." I stepped forward, preparing myself for a fight I wouldn't lose.

"No way," my father answered.

I needed to bring everything to light, but I didn't know if right then was the best occasion.

"I'm going, Dad, with or without your approval—or your car. I'll find a way."

"You almost died, because of him," my mother said, surprising me, but just voicing what they had been thinking all along. Even Samantha and Carl's visits had been less, lately. They'd felt guilty, and my parents were probably adding to that guilt.

"It's no one's fault, but Peter's. Keith didn't ask to be born." I sighed, tired of being on my feet. My wounds were healing properly, but I'd stayed in bed so long that my body was weak. "He's a good person. He would have given his life for me, if the situation had been reversed." I sat on the chair my mother pulled out for me. "He's not what you see, and you'll have to trust me, Dad." I got up, already thinking about finding transportation, when my father answered.

"I'll take you. We'll all go. You visit the art show and say your goodbyes, and then we'll come home and begin the process of transferring you to a college closer to home."

That wasn't my plan—not at all. I wasn't leaving my college. Even if Keith didn't want me in his house, I'd find another place to rent, or try the student residences. No one was going to dictate my life any longer, especially not that Peter guy. He might have killed something in my life, but it wasn't my will to live.

I would fight for Keith. I'd promised myself long ago that if he felt for me what I felt for him, I would fight. Now that I knew Ryan was at odds with him because of us, it would make things easier.

We no longer had any other people between us. We just had his stubborn guilt.

We spent the morning in a daze. My mother packed some lunch for us, but no one spoke. I showered quickly and chose a black dress that hugged my body, but which was also warm for the February cold. Matilda and my mother also put dresses on. My father didn't bother much, but he always dressed nicely, so he wouldn't seem out of place in an art show. That was, if they went inside. I was conflicted about that. On one hand, it would disclose everything about my relationship with Keith. On the other, if they made a scene, they could ruin something that was very important to the boy I loved.

I tried to approach the subject when there was only an hour left of the drive. "Dad, I want you to promise me something," I said, playing with the hem of my dress, while my sister placed her hand in mine. "I don't want you to make a scene in the art gallery, please."

"Why would I make a scene?" he asked.

I pondered my next words. "Because you're going to see stuff you won't like. I want you to control yourself, until we're alone, after the show. This day is important to him." I paused, not wanting to give him an ultimatum, but feeling the need to stress the issue. "If you ruin this, Dad, I won't go home with you… ever." His eyes shot to mine in the rearview mirror and my mother turned to face me, taking in my serious expression. She always could see past my words. She'd sensed a long time ago that something was going on with Keith and I. Everything that had happened since just confirmed her suspicions. Tonight, they would discover everything.

They both kept quiet, while the car traveled the roads I'd come to know well. I knew the address to the art gallery by heart and gave my father instructions. It was half an hour from our house—or Keith's house, for the moment. As soon as we approached the building, I saw cars parked on the side of the road. My heart squeezed for him. This would be a good night, even if the outcome wouldn't be what I was expecting.

As soon as I stepped out of the car, anticipation slammed into me—not only about my parents seeing their daughter splashed across canvases for the world to see, but also about seeing Keith. He might love me and not want to be together, and that would hurt. If he forgot about me and was indifferent, though, it would crush me.

We stepped through the gallery doors and my thoughts left me. My fears were replaced with wonder. The first paintings were of a young girl. I could see that the art was older—the lines weren't as sure as his were now. The girl always looked happy, and, in some of them, there were more people—probably Ryan and Cody. Here and there, the paintings were just landscapes, but, somehow, he'd managed to make them related to the others.

As I walked, the girl aged. Her smile wasn't as wide, and her eyes did not sparkle as much. I could see myself in there and knew my parents would, too. The eyes were mine, definitely.

Then came the nude paintings and sketches. Most of them were blurred, and not as defined as the previous artwork. My parents were putting the pieces together and I realized they were beside me when Matilda said, "Holy shit." She didn't say it as low as she'd thought, because she had to apologize to a couple next to us.

I turned sideways to take in my father's face. He was livid. I wasn't as worried about a fight as I was about him having a heart attack—he wasn't young anymore, after all. I turned and my thoughts evaded me.

The paintings had definitely been done by sight. The lines were sure of themselves, as if there had been no doubt about how my body worked. In the middle of the room stood a wall separated from the others. On it was a painting featuring the both of us, as the rest of the paintings after that. I could see Keith standing in the far corner, with his back to me. He was in a dark gray suit that I knew would match his eyes perfectly. As if sensing something, he turned, and my world came to a halt.

He was breathtaking. It was as if I had forgotten how good he looked. The light stubble on his face, his mussed hair contrasting with his put-together clothes, and the broken expression he threw me, all did me in.

My feet moved on their own, closer to where he stood. The man at his side went away, and then we stood in front of each other, both lost in our own world. I wanted so badly to jump into his arms, for him to squeeze me tightly, to forget the external injuries, and to take care of the ones that hurt the most.

"What—" He cleared his throat. "What are you doing here?"

"I couldn't not come." My reply was weak. I didn't dare look back at my parents, but Keith's gaze rested over my shoulder and he winced. I guess my father must have looked as murderous as I feared.

"Please, not here—this is important," he pleaded and I wanted to hug him, but I didn't. I wouldn't have my father ruin the most beautiful exhibition I'd ever seen. "We'll talk later," he said.

"When?" I asked and he averted his eyes. He was trying to come up with an excuse to not talk to me and I wouldn't let that happen. "After the show," I answered my own question. "I'll wait at the house and we'll talk." He nodded and shoved his hand in his pocket, retrieving a set of keys. He handed them to me. I had totally forgotten that my parents had left the key behind.

I was turning away, already feeling the loss of his presence, when my eyes rested on the remaining paintings, one of which was on the other side of the middle wall. They were dark, depressing, and made me question everything.

I should've come sooner. He needed me, and I'd just sat at home, taking in his silence as indifference. He was hurting as much as, or more than, I was. The drawings on that wall scared me. He had given the tale a depressing ending. My eyes found his and the darkness in the canvasses was in them. I wouldn't go anywhere without fixing this—without fixing us.

CHAPTER THIRTY-ONE

As soon as we were in the car, my parents started shouting. I was so tired. The drive, the nervousness and anticipation of seeing Keith, and, now, after watching our love story unfolding like that, the energy was leaving my body.

"You are coming home with us right now. I'm not going to let you stay and talk to that—that pervert."

My father's words snapped me from my slump. "No, I'm not. Take me to his house. I'm going to wait there for him."

"You're crazy if you think I'm going to let you be alone with that—" I cut my father off, wanting to avoid further deprecation from him.

"Yes, you are, or I'll jump from the moving car." I knew I was being overdramatic, but it was the only way to grasp the essentiality of my feelings. "You don't seem to realize that I'm eighteen, Dad. I can make my own choices, and I'm choosing Keith. He's not a pervert. We're in love with each other." I whispered the last words, but, in the silence of the car, they were loud.

"In love?" It's my mother's turn to speak.

"Yes, in love."

The silence stretched with no one talking all the way to Keith's house. Maybe my parents were trying not to dictate, anymore, so that I wouldn't feel even more inclined to go against them.

As soon as the house came into view, I took in a deep breath. It hadn't even been a month since I'd been here, but my feelings were overwhelming. I missed this place so much that now, being there, I feared this was really the last time I would step through that door.

My father paused outside the car. "We'll leave you here to discuss whatever you need with Keith. We'll stay in a hotel in town. Call us if you need me to pick you up." He paused, and then continued, "You're right: you are old enough to make your own choices. We'll just be here when you need us to pick up the pieces. That's what parents are for." He got in the car without any more words or even a hug. My mother was just looking at my father, confused, but she got in the car with a weak smile as a goodbye.

Matilda jumped forward, hugging me by the neck and avoiding the stomach. "It will be okay, you'll see. He loves you back." Without waiting for my response, she got into the car, and I went inside.

The smell, this time, just brought back memories. I closed my eyes and tried to picture the boys sitting on the couch, laughing and throwing curses at the TV. As soon as I opened my eyes, the silence and darkness enveloped me. Would this place see such happiness again?

I sat on the couch with my feet under my legs and a blanket over my shoulders, and I waited. Keith arrived two hours later. He came to a stop as soon as he got inside, turning the light on, and turning to me.

"I thought you'd left. You should've left." His first words were harsh, but I had been preparing myself for this fight.

"No, and I'm not leaving again," I said, thrusting my chin upward.

His face fell, as he shook his head. He came to sit on the couch, as far away from me as possible. "I don't want you here."

"Too freaking bad, Keith, because I'm not leaving. You feel guilty over what your father did. Did you pull the trigger? Weren't you shot, too? I know you almost broke your wrist and finger trying to get free to help me. I know how long you waited for me to be okay before you took care of your own wounds. I saw the art show. I know you love me, too." I took a deep breath, waiting for the kick to the stomach.

"I—" he started, but the front door crashed open and a fuming Ryan came barreling through the living room.

"You—you, I told you to stay away from her," he yelled, jumping over the couch.

I got up and put myself between them. As soon as I was within grabbing distance, Ryan seized my wrist, pulling me against him with such force that pain shot though my not-so-healed stomach. Keith saw me wince and jumped to us, removing Ryan's hand from my wrist with ease, to avoid hurting me more.

"Don't you dare do that. She's my sister and she's coming with me. Don't pretend you want to protect her," Ryan spit, while Keith pulled me behind him and stepped back to keep me away from my lunatic brother.

All of a sudden, I was pushed against the wall, just trying to stop the world from spinning around me, and Ryan was punching Keith in the face. The sound of flesh hitting flesh made me wake up from the daze I was in, and I stepped forward, wondering what I could do to stop my brother without getting hurt. Ryan punched Keith again in the face, and then in his stomach, and the stupid boy just stood there, taking a beating without even putting his arms in front of him for protection.

Keith was trying to punish himself for what had happened to me. When he couldn't beat himself up—at least, physically—he took advantage of my brother's rage. I was done watching them ruin their friendship and watching our families fall apart.

"Stop," I yelled, standing in front of Keith. For a moment, I thought Ryan's arm was coming my way, but Keith put his arms around me and moved me to the side. "You're not going to hurt him, anymore. I'm done with all of you dictating what I should or shouldn't feel, and what I can and can't do. I'm my own person, Ryan. Dad understood it. Why can't you?"

His humorless laugh made me pause. "Understood?" he screeched. "He was the one who asked me to come get you."

I stood, frozen to the ground. I thought my father had given me space to sort my thoughts out. Maybe he'd just played dirty. I wasn't going to forgive him any time soon.

"Leave," I whispered, not meeting his eyes. After not hearing any movement, I yelled, "Leave! You're his best friend! You are supposed to protect him and be there for him! What kind of person does this?" I gestured to Keith, who was leaning over and wincing in pain, with blood pouring from his nose and lip. "You're a judgmental ass, just like Dad. You're not going to play me around, anymore. Just leave."

My brother looked defeated, and, for a second, I felt guilty for lashing out. It just took another glace at Keith to push the guilt away, though.

People-pleaser Jane was dead. She had died in that warehouse.

"Be like that. When he fucks with you, don't say I didn't warn you—that we all didn't warn you." He left, slamming the door and making me flinch. I remembered Keith was in need of assistance, and I rushed to his side.

"Come on, let's get you upstairs." My own stomach was throbbing, but I needed to take care of Keith, first. As soon as we got to his room, he fell to the bed, gasping, and hugging his torso.

"Do you think you broke a rib?" I asked, fearful.

He shook his head and fell back. "I'm going to get something to clean your cut." Before he could protest, I went into his bathroom to get the first aid kit he'd used months before to patch my forehead.

While I tended to his wounds, we kept silent, just staring into each other's eyes. I had no idea what he was going to say, but tell me to leave wouldn't be part of it, from the vibe pouring from him.

His fingers traced my skin from my elbows, up, and then down the sides of my body. The cotton in my hand was soon forgotten. I placed the first aid kit on the floor, next to the bed, and unbuttoned his shirt, which he shrugged from his shoulders. My eyes went to his shoulder, first. The skin was red and a bit swollen. I didn't think he was taking care of it properly. I had gotten my stitches removed a couple of days ago, but the aftercare was still important.

I gave him a weak smile. "It destroyed the dragon's eye." The skin had been pulled, so the tattoo was slightly deformed.

"I'll beg Fred to fix it when the skin's healed." He rubbed my chin. I quickly grabbed his hand in mine, turning his finger to me.

He had an anchor exactly like mine. My eyes shot up to meet his. I then looked to his finger and back up again.

"How? Why?"

He didn't need to answer me. It was there, in his eyes: he loved me. I'd seen it in the art gallery, in every painting and every stroke. Every time his gaze fell upon me, I felt it.

I jumped forward and met his bruised lips carelessly, but he didn't seem bothered by it, because he pulled me closer and tugged my jacket from my shoulders. The house was cold and a shiver ran up my spine, but it was soon forgotten, thanks to Keith's warm hands. He ran them up and down my bare shoulders, and unzipped my dress.

We had come so far and my life had changed irreversibly. I didn't regret one thing—well, except for the part when I'd almost died. I would get past that, though, if Keith stayed by my side and fought my nightmares with me.

We made love, gazing into each other's eyes. I still felt like he was saying goodbye and I wanted to stay cradled in his arms for the rest of my life.

"Don't leave me," I whispered to the quiet room as I sunk my fingers into his flesh.

We intertwined our hands, and both of our tattoos came together. He began, "I tried. I can't. You came into my life when you were just a child, and I fell in love with you at that moment, as sick as that sounds. I knew then that you were it for me. I was older than you, though, and my childhood was long gone. When you befriended Cody and started spending all of your time with him, I knew I couldn't compete." Keith paused, just to breathe into my hair and pull me closer.

"You started dating him and I couldn't get away from you. When my pops needed me here, I saw that as an opportunity to stay away. I didn't expect to lose him like I did, and to feel so crushed by that loss."

I lifted myself on my elbow, careful to not push my body any further than I already had. I kissed him softly, wincing at the bruise forming on his eye.

"You're my world. You take away the pain and darkness he inflicted all those years ago and replace them with hope and light. I don't want to taint you." I started shaking my head, but he placed his finger over my lips. "But I can't stay away from you. I can't breathe without you here, in my arms, knowing if you're smiling, or if someone is hurting you. You heal all my scars. You are the reason I stayed sane—it wasn't just Ryan." Keith pulled himself up, grimacing at the pain he must have been feeling in his torso and shoulder. "You are my Sky."

Tears welled up in my eyes. What could I say that compared to that? "And you are my ground. You made me realize I have a place in the world, and that I'm not just an embellishment for everyone to toss around and show of. You made me realize I have flaws and other qualities beyond the good girl—the people-pleaser. You see me."

"I've wanted to break your walls down for a long time, and feel ashamed I didn't realize how lost you were growing up—how much we needed each other. I can't breathe without you, either. Let me stay." I whispered the last sentence, touching his forehead with mine.

"I couldn't let you go, even if I tried. It will be hell making our families understand us. Are you up for the challenge?" Keith asked.

"With you by my side? Of course." A sad smile played on my lips, thinking about the hatred my brother showed today.

Keith sensed my apprehension. "Ryan likes to pretend he's the king of the world but he'll come around, you'll see, let him fall in love and he'll understand how much I love you."

"Say that again," I asked, already beaming.

"I love you." He smirked at me and leaned in for a deeper kiss.

"I love you," I replied between kisses.

THE END

www.ingramcontent.com/pod-product-compliance
Lightning Source LLC
Chambersburg PA
CBHW032138190626
46814CB00005BA/1746